HOUSEHOLD GHOSTS
A JAMES KENNAWAY OMNIBUS

James Kennaway (1928–68), was born in Auchterarder, Perthshire, where he came from a quiet, middle-class background and went to public school at Trinity College, Glenalmond. When he was called to National Service in 1946 he joined the Queen's Own Cameron Highlanders and served with the Gordon Highlanders on the Rhine. Two years later he went to Trinity College, Oxford, where he took a degree in economics and politics before renewing his ambitions as a writer and working for a publisher in London. Kennaway married his wife Susan in 1951, and something of their turbulent relationship and his own wild, charming, hard drinking and intense personality can be found in *The Kennaway Papers* (1981), a book put together by Susan after his death.

Tunes of Glory (1956) was Kennaway's first novel. It remains his best-known work, and the author himself wrote the screenplay for what was to become a hugely successful film in 1960. His next book, *Household Ghosts* (1961), was equally powerful. Set in Scotland as a tale of family tension and emotional strife, it was adapted for the stage and then filmed – again to the author's own screenplay – as *Country Dance* (1969). *The Bells of Shoreditch* and *The Mind Benders* (also filmed), followed in 1963, while *Some Gorgeous Accident* (1967), and *The Cost of Living Like This* (1969), develop Kennaway's restless involvement with unhappy personal relationships and love triangles.

At the age of only forty, James Kennaway suffered a massive heart attack and died in a car crash just before Christmas in 1968. His last work, the novella *Silence*, was published posthumously in 1972.

JAMES KENNAWAY

Household Ghosts

A James Kennaway Omnibus

Introduced by Gavin Wallace

★

TUNES OF GLORY

HOUSEHOLD GHOSTS

SILENCE

★

CANONGATE

CLASSICS

99

This edition first published as a Canongate Classic in 2001 by Canongate Books Ltd, 14 High Street, Edinburgh EHI ITE. *Tunes of Glory* first published in Great Britain in 1956 by Putnam & Co Ltd. First published as a Canongate Classic in 1988 by Canongate Publishing Limited. Copyright © M. St. J.H. Kennaway, 1956. *Household Ghosts* first published in 1961. Copyright © M. St. J.H. Kennaway, 1981. *Silence* first published by Jonathan Cape Ltd in 1972. Copyright © M. St. J.H. Kennaway, 1972. Introduction copyright © Gavin Wallace, 2001.

2 4 6 8 10 9 7 5 3 1

The publishers gratefully acknowledge general subsidy from the Scottish Arts Council towards the Canongate Classics series and a specific grant towards the publication of this volume.

CANONGATE CLASSICS
Series Editor: Roderick Watson
Editorial Board: J.B. Pick, Cairns Craig, Dorothy McMillan

British Library Cataloguing-in-Publication Data
A catalogue record for this book is available on request from the British Library

ISBN 1 84195 125 0

Set in 10pt Plantin by Hewertext Ltd, Edinburgh. Printed and bound in Great Britain by Omnia Books Ltd, Glasgow.

www.canongate.net

Contents

Introduction

Of that familiar litany of Scottish literary talent cruelly cut down at the age of greatest promise, the case of James Kennaway is stranger than most. When he was killed in a motorway collision in 1968 at the age of only forty, he had already achieved that distinction rare in Scottish literature: an *oeuvre* which can truly be termed 'complete', even though fate decreed that two of his novels were destined for posthumous publication. It was a remarkable legacy for this most anguished of twentieth-century Scottish novelists, and yet a satisfactory sense of aesthetic completion eluded him right up until the tragic, and seemingly predestined, end.

Kennaway's striving for a perfection of fictional form and style was as worthy of any modernist icon for whom pursuit of the 'pure' novel was a quasi-religious vocation. Each of his six novels took a progressively more indirect and sophisticated approach to narrative technique, culminating in the almost shocking minimalism of the posthumous *Silence* (1972). For all the novels' formal variations, however, the constants are clear: intensely vivid characterisation, a powerfully visual quality of narrative, and a consummate control of highly sophisticated dialogue. Thematically, their common ground is that of power relationships in the institutional contexts of family, class and nation. Kennaway's characters are riven by divisions, inflicted and self-imposed and the theme of entrapment, both literal and metaphorical, weaves a bright strand throughout his fiction. His fascination with individuals who are torn between the imperatives of idealistic yearning and social and moral restraints locates his fiction firmly within a Scottish tradition, though only two of his novels were ever set in the land of his birth.

After the remarkable success of his debut *Tunes of Glory* in 1956, Kennaway asserted, somewhat testily, that he was 'a novelist from Scotland, and not a Scottish novelist'.[1] Like his contemporary and fellow creative exile Muriel Spark, Kennaway's tangential relationship with 'a Scottish formation' is a continuing enigma, and his own distinction – shared by many Anglo-Scottish writers – is a salutary one for a country which must be ever more mindful of the dangers of herding its creative pedigree into cosy ethnic enclosures. *Tunes of Glory* and *Household Ghosts* are haunted by a gallery of horribly familiar native spectres – division, defeat, and denial to name but three – but it is also important to be aware of forces within these novels which struggle towards absolution from a nation's cultural pieties.

Modelled closely on the author's own bittersweet experiences of army life (he served as an officer in the Cameron Highlanders), *Tunes of Glory* was an extraordinarily accomplished fictional debut, and remains the finest literary exploration of Scottish militarism – a subject which has received surprisingly scant artistic attention, given its hardly insignificant impact on the nation's historical trajectory and self-image. The novel remains Kennaway's most accessible, and its popular reputation was consolidated by the film version of 1960, directed by Ronald Neame. Kennaway's own flawless screenplay for the film is testimony to the luminous characterisation and visual power of the original text.

The implications of the novel surpass the starkly simple dynamics of the conflict that forms the centre of its drama. Not for the first time, Kennaway takes unprepossessing, if not banal, material and mines from it undetected depths. The barrack-room-boy *braggadocio* of the swaggering and aggressive Jock Sinclair – a soldier's soldier fuelled on whisky and a fading reputation for wartime heroics – is brought into self-destructive confrontation with the introverted and ineffectual, but seemingly privileged, Eton and Sandhurst officer Basil Barrow, who arrives to depose the working-class, ex-ranker Jock as the new Colonel. The ensuing psychological conflict engineered by the resentful Jock is a sublimated war between two cultures fuelled by class prejudice. This is not just a rehearsal of stale Scottish grievance *versus* complacent English insensitivity, however, for the novel's deceptively straightforward narrative subverts the anticipated tragic outcome.

When Jock plays into Barrow's hands by striking a corporal piper he finds with his daughter, it appears that the former will capitulate first. But it is Jock who finds the endurance to sustain himself long enough to undermine, cynically, Barrow's inability to take decisive action against him through fear and repressed admiration. Incapable of bearing the psychological strain, Barrow shoots himself. Jock, in turn, finds that the pity and shame suppressed in Barrow have now been awakened in himself. In the closing chapter, in twenty pages of great brilliance, Jock's hyperbolic funeral orders for the dead colonel are both a moving threnody for the sacrifice of all soldiers, and a mock-heroic deconstruction of the militarist ideology which drags Jock into his final and inexorable mental collapse.

The tragic irony of the novel is that the two protagonists are each destroyed by their inability to comprehend the one virtue they might be said to possess: fear. Within Barrow's brittle inability to destroy the fellow soldier whose heroism he admires there resides an incipient humanity, which the military code cannot sanction. Conversely, it is Jock's dawning fear that his very identity as a wartime hero and leader of men is incompatible with the constraints of postwar society, which finally consumes him.

It is no coincidence that *Tunes of Glory* was published in the year of the Suez Crisis, the humiliation of which effectively symbolised the end of Britain's aspirations as a post-imperial world power. As an anatomy of the dichotomies and hypocrisies festering within Scottish society – telescoped within the claustrophobia of barrack life – Kennaway's ruthless grasp of moral irony closely resembles that of his other great contemporary, Robin Jenkins. But Kennaway goes further. In a post-feminist context, it becomes possible to re-read *Tunes of Glory* as a disturbing study of masculinity itself in crisis. The novel has been faulted for giving its women characters scant treatment, but this is missing the point: the role of women as an 'absent presence' throughout the text acts as a metaphorical symptom of the very condition the novel seeks to anatomise.

In Jock's aggressiveness and Barrow's passivity we find two irreconcilable forces akin to the 'masculine' and 'feminine' principles at war in the male psyche. Absent women figures play a key role in both Jock's and Barrow's respective dysfunctions. The reason for Jock's status as a single parent is left tantalisingly unexplained, whereas Barrow's recent divorce is clearly implied as a major factor in his instability. Jock's relationships with the novel's two women characters – his daughter Morag and his mistress, the failed actress Mary Titterington – both founder on the rocks of male sexual jealousy, and their breakdown ultimately precipitates the events of the tragedy.

Less straightforward are the not infrequent hints of homoeroticism which ripple through the text. It is present in Barrow's repressed 'love' for Jock's heroic past and Jock's ritualised and theatrical final tribute to Barrow; it is present as farce in the parodic spectacle of the soldiers dancing with each other in the opening chapter, and it will re-surface as tragedy in a crucial episode in the novel, when Jock and Mary arrive at a moment of short-lived mutual understanding and redemption in the symbolic confines of her dilapidated theatre dressing-room. Mary's agonised confession of her love for Jock contains the novel's most candid allusion to the repressed sexual ambiguity which Jock is unequipped to acknowledge:

> He held her stiffly, and with hard lips he kissed her brow, by the border of her hair. He asked innocently, 'Are you saying that you love me, Mary?'
>
> It was agony for her. 'Jock, of course I am. Of course I am. Like any other woman that's ever known you,' she said and she looked up at him for a second. 'And I'm no sure it isn't every man, too.'
>
> He laughed at that. He tried to make it all a joke. 'Here, here, now. That's a very sophisticated sort of notion. That's too complex for me.'

Earlier, she has told him: '. . . it's you that doesn't see the half of your men', in an exchange where she cannot decide whether Jock is 'a child', 'a lovely man', or 'a bloody king'. Jock cannot see the other potential 'half' of himself, only the reflection of the 'sad soldier' reflected in the mirror in the couple's final embrace. The sad soldier is conditioned through the military code to suppress the 'lovely man' through a 'childish' reflex to order and control the world as the ruler with blood on his hands. It is as much Barrow's predicament – the other missing 'half' in the mirror in this psychologically and symbolically dense scene – as Jock's.

The subtextual gestures towards issues of gender and sexuality in *Tunes of Glory* suggest a prelude to Kennaway's more direct approach in the subsequent novels, where decisive, and assertive, women characters suddenly occupy centre stage. Mary Ferguson's tortured quest for fulfilment is at the centre of the classic Kennaway love-triangle in *Household Ghosts* (1961), the novel that reveals most about the author's ambivalent perspective on his Scottish background and shows an increasing attraction to allegorical frameworks. The household in question is that of a decaying aristocratic Perthshire family whose fortune rests pre-

cariously upon the 'ghosts' of past disgrace and degrada-
tion: the shadow of widowed Colonel Ferguson's past
indiscretions, and his late wife's lurid working-class past
and alcoholic self-destruction.

The combined legacies of myth-making and dysfunction
haunt and control the destinies, and relationship, of son
and daughter – Charles Henry Arbuthnot Ferguson,
known, unforgettably, as 'Pink', and Mary, whose turbulent relationships with her impotent husband Stephen and
her lover David Dow drive a spare and brittle narrative
which contains some of Kennaway's most taut writing,
much of it in anguished and nervous dialogue. Once again,
the plot centres on rivalry and self-deception. The central
struggle is between the ruthless and self-confessed Calvinist scientist David, whose accusatory and amorous letters
to Mary form a subsidiary narrative, and the strangely allied
Pink and Stephen, for the love of Mary. 'They christened
her Mary. I cast myself, perversely, as Knox': David attempts to drive a fissure between Mary and her complex
loyalties to the nursery world of parody, mimicry and
private language to which she and Pink escape in denial
of their destructive behaviour, and their probable incest
(implied with extreme subtlety), and to her collapsing
marriage.

The effect on the self-effacing Stephen is abrupt: he
attempts suicide. It is in the sophisticated portrayal of
Pink's gradual disintegration into dipsomania and drying
out in 'a baronial nut-house', however, which is the novel's
triumph. As his emotional hold on Mary weakens following
their father's death and the fabric sustaining Pink's depen-
dency collapses, the writing fluctuates between increasing
extremes of tortured parody and barely repressed mania,
culminating in Pink's final bathetic invocation of Rous-
seau's last words as he is driven off to the nursing home: '*T-
tirez la* whatsit, Belle,' he said. '*La farce est jouée.*' Pink is a
brilliantly original creation, and he is also the author's most

consummate fictionalist in a novel whose principal concern, paradoxically, is the deadly power of invention itself.

While *Household Ghosts* wears its archetypal trappings of Anglo-Scottish tensions lightly, it amounts to a disturbing vision of a Scotland so inimical to transcendence that imaginative escape is both inevitable, yet inevitably thwarted. Pink's, but also Scotland's, 'predestinate tragedy', the novel finally warns, is to be doomed to the plight of 'the permanently immature'. Only in Mary's final ability to settle for compromise does this bitter novel offer a glimmer of light.

In a wilfully accelerated and frenetic career, the next seven years saw Kennaway produce a further six novels, a play, and numerous notable film screenplays. He had completed a fourth draft of the novella *Silence* just days before his death. It is a shocking and startling coda, and so compressed and pure a narrative that one wonders how the author could possibly have followed it. The scale of the work belies the enormity of the subject it tackles: racial violence in urban America. Kennaway's bittersweet years in the USA as a scriptwriter were to find an extraordinarily potent artistic distillation.

Silence represents the ultimate refinement of the author's fascination with the dynamics of power. Larry Ewing, a mild-mannered white doctor, finds himself ineluctably drawn into a mission of self-appointed revenge following the ostensible assault of his daughter Lillian by a black youth. The deputation into the ghettoes of Harlem by Ewing, his son, son-in-law and professional associates goes disastrously wrong as a race riot erupts, in which his son, it is subsequently learned, is lynched. Suffering from a stab wound, Ewing flees and takes shelter in a dilapidated room, only to discover that he is not alone. It is inhabited by the near mythical, Amazonian figure of a dumb black woman – named 'Silence' – who first abuses, but then protects, contrary to her own prejudices, her traumatised captive.

Kennaway's fixation with entrapment reaches its peak. The confined couple develop an intense relationship by turns tender, violent and childlike, playing out a sequence of allegorical pairings as Madonna and child, Adam and Eve, Christ and crucifier. In the revelation of their shared humanity, Ewing's fundamental beliefs and his very identity are challenged, to the point that when he discovers that Silence is implicated in his son's murder, his love for her supplants grief and hatred. When their retreat is discovered, Silence assists Ewing to escape, but recognising the enormity of her sacrifice, he returns to attempt to save her from her martyrdom to the black extremists who attempt to crucify her. The couple are eventually discovered by the police, who ironically laud Ewing as the avenging white hero. It is when Ewing realises that the authorities intend to torture Silence into 'talking' that he commits the final existential act of grace: a symbol of the revelation that 'it is only in our impossible love for each other that we can defeat the carelessness of God.'

Few fictional attempts to come to terms with the enormity of racism can boast such a simple but apposite fusion of content and form as *Silence*. Marking the culmination of his increasingly woman-centred narratives, in Silence and her ambiguous inability, or refusal, to 'utter' her identity, Kennaway creates the perfect structural reflex for this 'savage allegory'[2] of the oppression which renders the powerless speechless or invisible. 'There is a staggering strength in your silence. Believe me, the most magnificent pathetic protest of them all,' Ewing concludes.

In a fashion which is strangely reminiscent of *Tunes of Glory*, the novella makes sophisticated use of symbolic polarities which might, in less artful hands, appear groaningly ponderous – in this case, the narrative's shifting patterns of allusions to the colours black, white and red, whether it is Ewing's blood on the snow, or his first glimpse of Silence's otherworldly eyes. In this unrelentingly visual text, the elliptical Kennaway narrator seems to have finally vanished into 'silence' to be replaced with a rapid and laser-sharp lens. It is the organ of perception which is central not only to the action, but to the novella's insistence – encapsulated in Ewing's final devastating seven words – that at the core of racist ideology is how we choose to *see*.

Seldom can a posthumous work have been so poignantly named, nor its re-publication more justified. The novels gathered here, and the last in particular, will confirm the efforts of critics in the 1980s to afford this mercurial literary talent his due place in the tradition of twentieth-century Scottish fiction as one of its most surprising innovators. That he would have found his assured place within the Scottish literary canon a source of amusement (at best) or irritation (at worst) is all the more reason why we should continue to read him. As the parameters of that canon continue to be debated, Kennaway, it is hoped, will be reassessed not just within the context of his contemporaries, but as a precursor: a novelist whose obsession with form and language, intensely stylised and cinematic narratives, and sharp epiphanies of the Anglo-Scottish turns of mind anticipate contemporary fictional talents as different as A.L. Kennedy, Alan Warner, and Candia McWilliam.

Gavin Wallace

NOTES

1. Trevor Royle, *James & Jim: A Biography of James Kennaway* (Edinburgh: Mainstream Publishing Ltd, 1983), p. 121.
2. Alan Bold, *Modern Scottish Literature* (London: Longman, 1983), p. 256.

Tunes of Glory

for
G. St. Q.

BOOK ONE

The Complexion of the Colonel

THERE IS A high wall that surrounds Campbell Barracks, and in the winter there is often a layer of crusted snow on top of it. No civilian rightly knows what happens behind that grey wall but everybody is always curious, and people were more than ever curious one January a year or two ago.

The north wind had blown most of the snow to the side of the barrack square, and not a soul walked there; not a canteen cat. In the guardroom the corporal commanding the picket was warming his fingers on a mug of hot tea, and the metalwork on the sentry's rifle was sticky with frost. In the bathhouse the Battalion plumber was using a blow-lamp on the pipes, and he had reached the stage of swearing with enjoyment. The sergeants were in their Mess, singing to keep themselves warm, and drinking to keep themselves singing. National Servicemen wished they were home in their villas, and horn-nailed Regulars talked of Suez; even the bandboys wished they were back at borstal. In the Married Quarters, the Regimental Sergeant-Major, Mr Riddick, was sandwiched between his fire and his television set.

But it was warm in the Officers' Mess. Dinner was over, and the Queen had had her due. The long dining-room with the low ceiling was thick with tobacco smoke. The regimental silver cups, bowls and goblets shone in the blaze of the lights above the table, and from the shadows past colonels, portrayed in black and white, looked down at the table with glassy eyes. Two pipers, splendid in their scarlet, marched round and round the table playing the tunes of glory. The noise of the music was deafening, but on a dinner night this was to be expected.

The officers who owned 'Number Ones' were in their blue tunics and tartan trews. Sitting back from the table they crossed their legs and admired their thighs and calves. They moved their feet and felt the comfort of the leather Wellingtons that fitted closely to the ankle. Only one or two of the subalterns who could not rise to Number Ones were wearing khaki tunics and kilts. But, drunk to the stage of excited physical consciousness, they too crossed their legs and glanced with anxious pride at their knees. They had folded their stockings to make the most of the muscles of their legs, and they wore nothing under their kilts. Some were anxious that the dinner should finish early giving them time to visit their women. Others of a more philosophic turn of mind had resigned themselves by now. They had ruled out the idea of visiting a woman and they were now falling into a slow stupor. Both sets of officers would in the end return to their bunks, thoroughly dispirited, and breathless with the cold of three o'clock in the morning. The lover as likely as not, if he were still a subaltern, would be disappointed to the point of pain, and the philosopher, bowing patiently and bowing low to the inevitable, would be sick. And both would live to fight another day.

But it was at this point in the evening, when the pipers played, that the officers could see most clearly how the night would end. Their fate lay in the hands of the man sitting half way up the table, and in spite of the Mess President at the head, nobody could deny that the table was commanded by the unforgettable figure of Acting Lieutenant-Colonel Jock Sinclair, D.S.O. (and bar).

The Colonel's face was big and smooth and red and thick. He had blue eyes – they were a little bloodshot now – and his voice was a sergeant's. His hair, which was thin, was brushed straight back with brilliantine. It was not a bit grey. The Colonel did not look broad because he was also deep, and had the buttons on his tunic been fastened there would have been little creases running across his chest and stomach. But at times such as this he was inclined to unfasten his buttons. He had even unfastened the top two buttons of his trews this evening and his striped shirt protruded through the gap in the tartan. His trews were skin tight and it looked as if he need only brace his muscles to tear the seams apart. In his lap he nursed a very large tumbler of whisky, and he tapped his foot on the ground as the pipers played. He did not seem to find the music too loud.

From time to time he glanced round the table, and other officers when they caught his eye quickly turned away while he continued to stare. The look in his eye was as flat as the sole of his polished boot.

He had already made the pipers play three extra tunes that night, and as they played *The Green Hills* for the second time he hummed, and the music comforted him. He put his glass on the table when the room was silent again.

'Get away with you,' he said, surprisingly kindly, to the Corporal-Piper and as the pipers marched out of the room the officers applauded in their usual way: they banged their fists on the table and stamped their feet on the floor-boards. Jock sent orders that the pipers should be given double whiskies, then he leant back in his chair and groaned, while his officers talked. It was some minutes later when one of the younger subalterns at the far end of the table caught his attention. Jock tipped forward in his seat and put his clenched fists on the table. The flat eye grew narrow; the meat on his face quivered, and along the table conversation died on the lips. He made a suppressed sound which was still something of a shout:

'MacKinnon, boy!' Then he lowered his voice to a hiss. 'For Christ's sake smoke your cigarette like a man. Stop puffing at it like a bloody debutante.' He moved his hand as though he were chucking away a pebble, and he spoke loudly again. 'Get on with you; smoke, laddie, smoke . . .'

There was silence in the room as the young subaltern put his cigarette to his lips. He held it rather stiffly between two fingers and he half closed his eyes as he drew in the tobacco smoke. There was still a hush. He looked nervously at his Colonel as he took the cigarette from his lips. Even the movement of his wrist as he brought the cigarette down to the plate had something inescapably feminine about it, and this made Jock shake his fist. The boy's mouth was now full of smoke and he sat very still, with his eyes wide open.

'Go on then, laddie; draw it in, draw it in.'

MacKinnon took a deep breath which made him feel a little dizzy and he was glad that the Colonel could not resist a joke at this point. The sound of his little cough was drowned by the laughter that greeted his Colonel's witticism. Jock looked from side to side.

'We've got laddies that've never put it in, I know,' he said with both a wink and a nod. 'What I didn't know is how we've one who can't even draw it in, eh?' When he laughed the veins on his temple stood out. Then the laugh, as usual, deteriorated into a thick cough, and he shook backwards and forwards in an attempt to control it.

The officers were a mixed collection. One or two of them, such as Major Macmillan, who was perpetually sunburnt, seemed very much gentlemen, although they too laughed at Jock's jokes. The others, if not gentlemen, were Scotsmen. The younger they were the larger were their jaws, the older they were the fatter were their necks, except of course for the Quartermaster, Dusty Millar, who had no neck at all.

At last Jock recovered himself. 'Aye,' he said, with a final cough, 'aye . . . Well gentlemen, I have news for you.'

Someone at the far end of the table was still talking.

'All of you, you ignorant men.' Jock raised his voice. 'News that'll affect you all.' He paused. 'Tomorrow there's a new colonel coming, and he'll be taking over the Battalion. D'you hear? D'you hear me now?'

All the officers hesitated. Their jaws dropped and they leant forward to look at Jock, who was looking at his tumbler.

Macmillan had a light-comedy voice. He touched his fair hair with his hand and he said, 'Come, Jock, you're pulling our legs.'

'Aye,' someone said uncertainly, disbelievingly. 'That's it, isn't it?'

'What I'm telling you is true.' Jock took a sip of his drink. 'Ask Jimmy Cairns. Jimmy knows right enough.'

Cairns, who was his Adjutant, did not know what to say but felt it was a time when something should be said. He moved his hands, and he frowned.

'That's the way of it,' he said.

'Och . . .' The Quartermaster moaned, and others echoed him.

'That's not right,' one said; and another, 'It can't be true.' The Battalion without Jock as c.o. seemed then an impossibility.

Jock raised his hand in the smoky air.

'We didn't ask for comments,' he said. Then, glancing at the younger officers at the far end of the table, some of whom did not seem so dismayed by the news, he added, 'One way or the other,' and he showed his teeth when he grinned. He grew solemn again and drew his hand down his face and wagged his head, as if to clear his vision. 'It's just a fact,' he said slowly, 'it's just a fact,' and he leant back in his chair again.

Major Charlie Scott, who sat next to Jock, had an after-dinner habit of stroking his large red moustache, but he dropped his hand to ask, 'What's his name, eh?'

'Basil Barrow.'

'Major Barrow?' a clear-voiced subaltern said at once. 'He lectured at Sandhurst. He's an expert on Special . . .' Suddenly aware that he had sounded a little too enthusiastic, his voice trailed away. He looked around, brushed some ash from his trews, and continued in a nonchalant tone, 'Oh, he's really quite all right; they say he's frightfully bright upstairs.' The officers looked towards the Colonel again. They were gradually recovering.

'Aye,' Jock said. 'He went to Oxford, if that means anything. They say he was a great success as a lecturer or whatever he was. Quite a turn with the cadets.' He gave a malicious grin and another big wink. Then he belched and made a sour face. He took another drink of whisky.

'Colonel Barrow's a man about forty-four. Eton – aye, it's right, what I'm telling you – Eton and Oxford. He joined the Regiment in 1935 and he was only with it a year or two before being posted on special duties. He has some languages, so it seems. It's as young Simpson says. He's bright upstairs. He got the M.C. and he was taken prisoner pretty early on.' Jock swung his eyes around the table. 'I know all about him; you see that?'

'There was a fellow we used to call Barrow Boy. D'you remember him? A lightweight chap; good at fencing, if I recall.'

'I remember. Good Lord, yes.'

Jock spoke again. 'That's the same chum. That's him. He was well placed in the Pentathlon sometime just before the war.' He grew suddenly tired of the subject. 'Well, he's to command the Battalion and I'll have another tumbler of whisky.'

A Mess steward dashed forward and replaced the empty glass with a full one. On nights like this Jock's drinks were lined up on a shelf just inside the pantry door; lined up in close formation.

'And what about you, Jock?' Cairns asked.

'Aye. And what about me, china?'

'You staying on?'

'Unless you're going to get rid of me, Jimmy.'

Cairns knew just how far he could go with Jock.

'I thought there might be a chance of it.'

Jock was about to smile when the same subaltern who had known Barrow interrupted. 'Staying on as second-in-command, you mean?' and he was too young and a little too well spoken to get away with it. His seniors glanced immediately at the Colonel. Jock eyed the boy with real hatred, and there was a very long pause.

One of the stewards by the pantry door all but dropped his salver; his eyes grew wide, and he felt the hair rising at the back of his neck. Goblets and glasses poised in the air, whisky stayed in the mouth, unswallowed, and the swirly cloud of smoke above Jock's head for one instant seemed perfectly still.

Jock spoke very sourly, and quietly. 'So may it please you, Mr Simpson,' was what he said, looking back to his tumbler.

'Oh, I'm glad you're not leaving us, sir.' But the answer came too glibly. Jock shrugged and gave a little snigger. He spoke as if he did not care whether he was heard. 'You're away off net, laddie . . . and, Mr Simpson?'

It was fairly easy to see that Mr Simpson had been a prefect at school. He looked the Colonel straight in the eye and he never quite closed his mouth.

'Yes, sir?'

'No "Sirs" in the Mess. Christian names in the Mess except for me and I'm "Colonel". I call you just what I feel like. O.K.?'

'Yes, Colonel.'

'Yes, Colonel . . . Now, gentlemen; now then. This is Jock's last supper and there'll be a round of drinks on me. Even one for Mr Simpson. Corporal!'

'Sir.'

'Whisky. For the gentlemen that like it and for the gentlemen who don't like it, whisky.'

He turned apologetically to Charlie Scott, who was still stroking his moustache.

'I'm no good at talking at the best of times, Charlie, and

tonight I'm no coping at all. Will we have the pipers back? It
fills the gaps.'

'Whatever you say, Jock; it's your night.'

'Aye.' Jock opened his eyes very wide: this was one of his
mannerisms. 'Aye,' he used to say, then with his eyes wide
open he would add a little affirmative noise. It was an open-
mouthed 'mm'. Aye, and a-huh. 'Well I say we'll have the
pipers.' He leant back in his chair and addressed one of the
stewards who was hurrying by with a bottle. 'Laddie, call
the pipers.'

'This minute, sir.'

'Just "Sir".' He made a gesture with his flat hand: a little
steadying gesture. It was the same gesture that had steadied
men in the desert, in Italy, France, Germany and Palestine.
'Just "Sir". That's all you need say.' Then he sighed, and
he said, 'Aye, Charlie.' He dug the point of his knife into
the table-cloth again and again as he talked. He first made a
hole with the knife and gradually he widened it.

'. . . And you'll have a tune, and I'll have a tune, and
Macmillan here'll have a tune, and I'll have another tune.
Charlie, why the hell d'you grow that moustache so big?'

Major Charlie Scott continued to stroke it with his
fingers. His great green eyes grew wide, under the shep-
herd's eyebrows. He could think of no explanation.

'Dunno; I'm sure. Just grew.'

Jock leant his chair back on two legs again and his arms
fell down by his sides. 'And you're not the great talker
yourself.'

''Fraid not.'

'No . . . Well, let's have the music. *Ho-ro, my Nut Brown
Maiden* for me, and for you, Charlie?'

'*The Cock o' the North*.' Jock tipped forward at that. The
legs of the chair creaked as they pitched on the floor again.

'Yon's the Gordons' tune!'

'I still like it.'

Jock screwed up his face: he was genuinely worried.

'But yon's a cheesy tune, Charlie.'

Charlie Scott shrugged.

Jock leant forward to persuade him. 'Laddie, I was with them for a wee while. They didn't like me, you know; no. And Jock didn't care much for them, neither.'

'Really?'

'Can you no think of a better tune?'

'Myself, I like *The Cock o' the North*.' Charlie Scott put another cigarette in his holder.

Jock laughed and the veins stood out again. He slapped his thigh and that made a big noise.

'And I love you, Charlie; you're a lovely man. You're no a great talker, right enough. But you've a mind of your own . . . Aye, pipers, and where have you been?'

'Pantry, sir.'

'Are you sober?'

'Sir.'

'You'd bloody well better be, and that's a fact. You're no here to get sick drunk the same as the rest of us are.'

The drones began as the bladders filled with air. The pipers marched round and round again. The room grew smokier, and the officers sat close into their chairs as the drink began to flow. The stewards never rested.

TWO

THE PIPERS WERE in the pantry, recovering themselves. They were drinking beer, and the sweat poured down their faces. Their heavy kilts and tunics were hot and scratchy, and all the paraphernalia of their dirks and plaids was a nuisance to them.

The younger piper had yellow eyes and he spoke in a high-pitched voice.

'He's a bloody terror, and that's what he is.'

'Aye,' said the Corporal, 'and he's a great man.'

'He's a bloody terror, and that's what he is; I'm telling you, Corporal.'

'You can close your mouth. You'll need all your spittle the night.'

Mess stewards in their white bum-freezers hurried by in search of liquor.

'Is it right he was a piper; is that right, Corporal Fraser?'

'Aye. And he could be Pipe-Major if he felt like it, man. You should hear him on the pibrochs. There's nobody to touch him. He's played on the wireless, you know.'

'I'm no a corporal; I never get the chance of listening to the bloody wireless.'

'You'll watch your language in the Officers' Mess, Piper Adam.'

'This is no the Officers' Mess. This is the pantry.' All around them were dirty plates and cutlery. 'Look at the shambles, eh?'

'Just the same.'

'Och, away you go, Corporal . . . He's a bloody terror;
I'm telling you.'

'Aye, aye. You're telling me.'

The Corporal-Piper was a patient young man with the
mild blue eyes of the far north. He came from that queer
strip of flat land called the Lairg. It stretches for thirty or
forty miles along the south side of the Moray Firth, and at
no point is it more than a few miles wide. The road from
Inverness to Fochabers is as straight as the pine trees there,
and nowhere in Scotland is there so much sky. It is like a
foreign land, and the people speak their English slowly, and
with a mild intonation, as if they were translating from a
foreign tongue. So it was with Corporal Fraser.

'Aye,' he said softly; and he finished his pint of beer.

Then they were called into the ante-room to play some
reels. Jock had decided that they all ought to take some
exercise before the next round of drinks and as it was too
slippery for a race round the barrack square he ordered that
there should be dancing. With Charlie Scott as his partner
he led away with the 'Duke of Perth' while the others,
standing in their lines, clapped their hands to the music.

Jock danced with energy and with precision. He leapt
high in the air and landed miraculously softly on the toes of
his small feet. That was how he had been taught to dance
and the others had to try and dance like him. They put their
hands above their heads; they swung; they yelled; they
hooched. Then they had a drink and they began all over
again with a new dance. By this time they were very warm
and many of them had removed their tunics. Every officer
in the Mess was dancing amongst the pillars in the long
ante-room when the door opened and the new Colonel
walked in.

For a moment, nobody observed him, and the dance
continued. He was wearing a tweed suit and his jacket hung
open. He had a moustache and his hair was growing grey,
not at the temples where men like their hair to grow grey,

but all over. Round his large eyes there was a yellowish shadow of tiredness, and his brow was lined. If you saw this man on a platform at a railway station you would at once be certain that there was a gun-case with his luggage; and you would be right. There must be fifty colonels who look very much like this one. He now stood quite still, as only an actor or a soldier can. His hands rested by his sides.

Mr Simpson followed Piper Adam's eye, and he was the first to recognise the stranger. He immediately moved up the line to talk to Jock, who was absorbed with the dancing. He tugged at his elbow. His voice had the delighted urgency of the first man with bad news.

'Colonel!'

'What is it, laddie? Get down to your proper place.'

'The Colonel's here.'

'You're drunk, laddie.'

'Colonel Barrow. He's at the door.'

Jock looked round and stared, first at Simpson and then at the newcomer. Only a moment before he had been beaming with joy. He had joked with Charlie Scott as they gradually worked their way up the set to start their second turn. He had given a little imitation of some of Major Macmillan's worse affectations on the dance-floor. Macmillan was a very smooth performer, and had Jock not been there he would hardly have bothered to move his feet at all. Jock meant no harm by his little demonstration. He was in good spirits. He had forgotten everything but the dancing and the drinking, and the music tingled in his veins. He liked to feel the floor bouncing. But suddenly the dancers and the pipers seemed to fade away from him, and he forgot them. He stopped clapping his hands and they hung in mid-air. A look of real pain crossed his face and he said in a whisper, 'But dammit, he's no due till the morn!'

Then his hands fell to his tunic and he began to button it up. He pulled in his stomach and bit his lip. He shouted at the top of his voice for the dancing to stop. The dancers heard but the pipers continued to play. When he shouted again they too understood and with a drone they ceased. Everybody now turned towards the figure at the door. Colonel Barrow did not sound nervous, but a little tired.

'Good evening, gentlemen.' His voice was very light. 'My name is Barrow.'

Nobody replied. They looked at him, stunned. Then Jock strode down the middle of the room, his heels clicking on the boards. The two sets of dancers at each side of the room still stood in loose formation and they watched him come to a formal halt two paces away from the Colonel.

'Jock Sinclair. Acting Colonel.'

'I've heard a great deal about you.' The Colonel spoke in the same light voice; he spoke pleasantly but seriously and as the two shook hands the officers readjusted their dress. They shifted about, and looked nervously at each other. Somehow, they felt guilty. Major Scott and the company commanders were duly introduced but Jock said there were too many bloody subalterns – all subalterns were bloody, all subalterns were damned – to attempt an introduction there and then. Jock behaved as if it were a parade. He was like one of those commanders you see photographed looking down and talking earnestly to his Queen.

'And now, Colonel,' his voice was very serious. 'May we have permission to resume the dance that was interrupted?'

The Colonel looked surprised. 'For heaven's sake . . . I'm not here officially until tomorrow. You're in command.'

'Very well.' Jock instructed Corporal Fraser and the others to carry on. 'Charlie, we best break off.' He turned to the Colonel again. 'You'll join us in a drink?'

'Thank you. Brandy and soda.'

Jock blinked, and he looked down at his successor. 'Not a whisky?'

'Not a whisky.'

'We all drink whisky in this Battalion,' Jock said, heavily.

'Oh, yes,' Barrow smiled pleasantly. 'I remember that. Whisky doesn't really agree with me. D'you think we could adjourn to the far end of the room? I find it rather noisy here.'

Jock looked over his shoulder at the pipers playing behind them.

'Whatever you like,' he said and he never smiled once. As they walked the length of the room he glanced slantwise at the Colonel, but the Colonel was intent on the dancing.

Barrow put his hands in his coat pockets as he walked up the room, and once or twice he moved them with a nervous little jerk. He twitched his moustache. The officers stared at him and they noticed the rather sprightly step. He sprang on the balls of his feet, again with a sort of nervousness. His tread was as light as his voice.

'This is my farewell party, you understand,' Jock said when they sat down. 'There's not a carry-on like this every night. Four and a half years is a long time to command a battalion, and then . . .' He did not finish the sentence, and Barrow did not finish it for him. He waited, and Jock felt clumsy. His hands clasped and unclasped: they lost their way.

'Where the hell's that bloody steward got to?' he asked, and Charlie Scott, for something to do, went to find him.

Jock tried to settle in his seat and he undid the buttons of his tunic and trews.

'Charlie's a good lad . . . Aye. They're all good men, except for some of the babies, and they'll be good men in their time; some of them, anyway.'

Again Barrow kept silent.

'Ah, well; you found your way here all right?'

'I have actually been here before.'

Jock raised his eyebrows; he was heavily polite.

'Aye? When was that?'

'I came as a subaltern.'

'From Sandhurst?' The question was asked with an air of innocent curiosity.

'From Oxford, as a matter of fact.'

Charlie had now rejoined them and the steward brought the tray of drinks.

'From Oxford? Fancy that . . . Aye. And where were you before that?'

'I was at school.'

Jock nodded. They were sitting on the leather settee by the dining-room door, and the dancing seemed far away.

'Harrow, was it?'

'No.'

'Oh . . . I see, I see.' Charlie Scott did not approve of Jock's questions but every time he tried to interrupt Jock just raised his voice. Otherwise his voice was pitched at an unnatural low.

'A-huh . . . You came in that way; with an Oxford degree.'

The Colonel smiled. He was leaning right back in the seat, with his head tipped back.

'For what it was worth.'

Jock eyed him for a moment and he ran his tongue along his lower lip. Then he gave a little flick of his head: 'Well I came in the other way. By way of Sauchiehall Street, Barlinnie gaol, and the band. I was a boy piper.'

'It sounds a much better training,' the Colonel answered pleasantly, and Jock breathed heavily. Charlie took his first opportunity.

'You'll have another drink, Colonel?'

'Forgive me. I'm rather tired. I think I'll turn in after this one.'

'Are you no going to have a dance?' The flat eyes rested on him.

'If you'll forgive me,' the Colonel said again. 'I've had a long day.'

'You drove up?' Charlie asked.

'Hell of a journey.'

Charlie was sympathetic. 'Family and all?'

The Colonel looked down at his brandy. 'I have no family. I'm by myself.'

Charlie smiled. He felt required to say something. 'Then we won't have to cope with the Colonel's wife.'

But the Colonel did not smile. He paused and sipped his drink. He replied suddenly, 'I suppose there's that to it.'

Then, the dance over, Macmillan came to pay his respects. Macmillan very quickly pitched the conversation on to a higher social level: the shooting and the shooting set. He mentioned some names; some names of titled people; but he did not, of course, mention the title. The Colonel was very pleasant. He did not seem to remember any of these people very clearly. He did not have any names to give in exchange.

Jock's head was cocked on one side. He had had enough whisky to make him persistent. 'It'll be some time since you were with the Battalion, I'm thinking.'

'Yes, I feel quite a new boy. It's some time since I've been with any battalion. I've been sitting behind a desk for a year.'

Charlie screwed up his face with horror. 'Ghastly . . .'

Macmillan said, 'Too boring.' Then he went on: 'One of the boys said you were at Sandhurst.'

The Colonel looked him in the eye.

'That would be Simpson,' he said, and Jock was surprised.

'Aye. You're right, now. He's over there. And what was it you said you did before Sandhurst?'

'I don't think I did say.' The Colonel was still very patient.

'You didn't?'

Charlie Scott and Sandy Macmillan glanced at each other. The Colonel ran the tip of his finger round the rim of his glass.

'Like you, Sinclair, I was in gaol.'

'A P.O.W.?' Jock gave a little snigger. 'That's not quite the same thing.'

'I think I would have preferred Barlinnie gaol.'

BUT IT WAS after Barrow had left them that the drinking really began. All the tunics were loose again. Jock sat on the leather guard in front of the log fire and the smoke from his cigarette crawled up his cheek, over his flat blue eyes. The junior subaltern caught his attention again.

'Mackinnon? D'you know the words of the Lord's Prayer?'

'Yes, Colonel.'

'You do?' Jock's eyes were very bloodshot now. It showed when he rolled them. 'Then you're not so bloody ignorant as I thought you were.' He stared at the boy, who looked very pale and nervous. It was no secret that he had already retired once that evening to be sick.

'Poor wee laddie. Can you smoke yet?'

'I think so.'

'Poor laddie . . . Och.' Jock was restless. He moved now to an armchair and he dropped into it. 'Och, to hell with all this,' he said impatiently. 'Och, to hell with all this.' Major Charlie Scott was lying full length on the settee beside Jock's chair and Jock now leaned over towards him.

'Charlie boy, are you dead yet?'

'Cold. As cold as Flora Macdonald.'

'I can tell you, chum, there's some is colder than her.'

Charlie made no reply further than to let his heavy eyelids drop again and Jock turned to the group still hanging around the ante-room. His voice was a sergeant's again.

'Get away with you, you bairns and cheeldron; away to your holes and your chariots. You've drunk more than you or I can afford and you're the worst lot of bastards I've ever known. And Jimmy Cairns is the worst of the lot of you.'

'I'm too tired,' Cairns said. 'I'm too tired even to insult you.'

'Just try and I'll have you drummed out of the Battalion.' Jock's energy was unlimited.

'I'm whacked.'

'Good night, Jimmy lad.'

'Aye, Jock.'

The Corporal brought a full bottle and the others went to bed, leaving Charlie Scott on the couch, stretched out like a walrus on his back, and Jock sitting in his chair with his knees apart and his hands clasping the arms. They sat there, quiet for a long time. It was Charlie who spoke at last.

'You know, Jock; I once had a woman under water.'

Jock hardly seemed to be listening. 'Aye, man? Was it salt or fresh?'

Charlie sat up. He looked rather dazed.

'Flesh,' he said. 'All flesh.' But Jock did not smile.

'Charlie, have I been such a bad colonel; have I, man?'

Charlie took a long time to reply. He seemed to have difficulty in finding the right words.

'Never known a better,' he said with a sharp shake of his head.

'Och, man. Stop your fibbing. I asked a civil question.'

'Honest to God, old boy. In the war . . .'

Jock shook his head and he said, ' "Old boy, old boy, old boy." '

'You asked me and I tell you. For God's sake, chum . . .'

'D'you really think that, Charlie?'

Charlie seemed a little irritated by his questions. He touched his moustache. 'Sure, sure.' He gave an apostrophied nod and a little belch. Then he lay down again and there was another pause. Jock drew a circle on the leather arm of the chair with his forefinger and he traced it again and again. Then he said in a whisper:

'It's no fair, Charlie. It's no right after four years and
another six months on top o' that. It isn't . . . Och, but he's
here now and what a spry wee gent he is. I fancy the wee
man's got tabs in place of tits.'

'Beyond me, Jock. Give us the bottle will you? There's a
good chum.'

'Aye, and you look as though you need a drink. That bloody
growth must take it out of you. You look pale. But you're a
terror with the women, Charlie; there's no denying it. You're
a great big bloody white-faced stoat with bushy eyebrows.'

Charlie did not hear him. He was having difficulty with
his drink.

'I say, old man. D'you think we could dispense with the
glasses. Is that on?'

'Aye. Never mind the glasses. If anyone has a right to get
fu' the night it's big Jock Sinclair and his friend Charlie
Scott. Did you hear him say that about the whisky? He
doesn't drink it, you know.'

'Poor chap.'

'Aye. That's so; the poor wee laddie.' Jock ran that one
round his tongue with a mouthful of whisky. Then he
chuckled. 'The poor wee laddie . . . the new boy, he called
himself; all in his mufti . . .'

Jock sat musing and sniggering for a moment or two,
then his resolution seemed to strengthen and he picked
himself to his feet.

'He'd no bloody right blowing in here like that without
warning me or Jimmy first. That wasn't right at all. It was
bad form. That's what that was.' Then he clenched his fists.
'Whatever way you look at it,' he said, 'they've no right to
put him in above me. And it makes me angry, Charlie. It
makes me bloody angry.' Charlie did not reply and Jock
continued to walk up and down. Then at last he returned to
his chair and he tapped the arm of it with his finger. His
eyes were narrowed, and perfectly still. He did not even
remember to smoke.

After a while, Charlie sat up and handed him the bottle. Then he rubbed his eyes with his long freckled fingers.

'We're not great talkers, Jock.' Jock was tipping back the bottle, and more out of politeness than anything else Charlie went on, 'Not great talkers at all.'

'We'll have the Corporal-Piper,' Jock said.

'That's it, my boy.'

'That's just what we'll do. And we'll listen to the music.'

He rose clumsily to his feet and he shouted from the door leading into the dining-room. In a moment Corporal Fraser was with them, and Jock had to begin all over again.

'Have you been asleep, Corporal Fraser?'

'No, sir. I have not been asleep. I have been waiting, sir,' the Corporal replied slowly.

'And cursing and binding and swearing . . . Och, man, I've been a piper mysel'.'

'Aye, sir.'

Jock looked up. 'And I was a bloody sight better than you.'

'Yes, sir.'

Jock paused; then he cocked his eyebrow and put his head on one side. 'Have you got a bint down town, Corporal? Have we kept you away from her, eh?'

The Corporal stood to attention. His cheeks had coloured a little.

'You've got a lassie, have you, eh? Well, Corporal, have you got a tongue in your head?'

'Aye, sir.'

'You've got a lassie?'

'Aye, sir.'

The Corporal looked more than uneasy; but Jock persisted.

'What d'you think of that, Charlie? The Corporal's got a lassie.'

'Good for the Corporal.'

'No, no, Major Scott, that's no the thing to say at all.' Jock looked at him very disapprovingly.

'No?'

'No. You should say "Good for the lassie!" Aye, and good for the lassie. It's not every lassie that catches a Corporal-Piper. No it's not. Is she bonny, Corporal?'

'I think so, sir.'

'"I think so," he says; d'you hear that? And, tell me Corporal,' Jock's voice was scarcely more than a whisper, 'Are your intentions strictly honourable?'

'Aye indeed, sir,' the Corporal said stoutly.

Now Jock raised his voice: 'Then you're a bloody foo', Corporal; that's what you are. You're far too young for that. A soldier shouldn't marry young. You leave honourable intentions to fathers like me. It's a father's worry, anyway. I always say if I catch my lassie at it, I'll welt the laddie, but I'll probably never catch her, anyway. So there we are. He's too young for honourable intentions, is he no, Charlie?'

Charlie nodded vigorously. 'I'm too young,' he said.

'You're a bloody rogue, Major Scott; that's what you are. No mistake.'

'Has the Corporal had a drink, Colonel?'

But the Corporal interrupted: 'No, thank you, sir. Not if I'm going to play, sir.'

'We didn't bring you here to look at your dial, however bonny the lassie may think it is. I can tell you that, Corporal . . . We'll have a tune now. We'll have *Morag's Lament* again.' Jock looked solemnly at the Corporal. 'Morag was the name of my lassie, once upon a time, and Morag's the name of my wee girl.'

'Sir.'

'And then we'll have *The Big Spree*. After that we'll think and you'll have something to wet your lips. Come away with you then. Come away with you.'

To the unpractised ear a pibroch has no form and no melody, and to the accustomed ear it has little more. But it is a mood and a pibroch was something Jock felt almost physically; damp, penetrating and sad like a mist. It enveloped him and pulled at his heart. He was far too much the professional to be moved to tears, but the Corporal played well and it took a moment before Jock fully recovered himself. The pibroch very often comes to a sudden end; it is a finish that makes it a fragment, and the more sad for that. Jock nodded his head slowly, three times.

'Corporal Fraser, you'll make a piper yet.'

The Corporal gave a sunny smile.

'Aye, you're better at the pibroch than I'd known. Your grace-notes are slurred but otherwise it was good. Now give me the pipes, lad; we'll have a turn ourself.'

In his trews, with his fat bottom waggling as he marched up and down the room, Jock looked comic. To begin with, he looked comic. But soon he was in the full rhythm of the tune, and he was absurd no longer. A good piper is like a rider who is one with his horse, and Jock was soon part of the music. He played some marches, with a fault or two; then a slow march; then a faultless pibroch. That is something that a man does only a few times in his life; and the Corporal was dumb with admiration.

As he slowly laid the pipes down, Jock himself was aglow with pride. He was sweating with the exertion, but his eyes too were glistening. He was like a schoolboy who has won his race.

'That's how to play the movement, laddie. It's no just a question of wobbling your fingers on grace-notes.'

The Corporal at last found his voice.

'I've never heard the pibroch better; never better.'

Jock nodded shyly.

'I don't think I've ever played it better. So there you are. You have to be in the mood for the pibroch; it is a lament. It is a lament.' He mopped his brow. 'But it is something else as well. That's the catch. It's no just a grieving. There's something angry about it too.' Charlie Scott was sure it was all beyond him and in a moment Jock said, 'Och, well, Corporal, you'll be wanting away to your lassie. You'll have to jump the wall.'

'It's too late for that now, sir.'

'D'you hear that, Charlie? The lassie'll have gone home to bed. Now see what you've done.'

'Wise woman.'

'Then away you go, Corporal. Away to your own bed.' The Corporal put on his bonnet and came sharply to attention.

'Permission to dismiss, sir.'

Jock looked up at him. He liked the formality. Suddenly he approved of the Corporal.

'D'you want me to help you with that pibroch, Corporal?'

'Very much, sir.'

Jock nodded. 'A-huh,' he said, and he clasped his hands and bent forward in his chair. 'Tomorrow morning?'

Charlie said, 'You'll be in no sort of shape tomorrow morning.' But Jock ignored him.

'Half-past twelve?'

'I'll be in the gym then, sir.'

'What are you up to in the gym?'

'Boxing, sir.'

'You're a boxer? Light-heavy, is it?'

'That's it, sir.'

'Then we'll meet some other time. You're a man after my heart, Corporal. We'll make a piper of you yet.'

'Thank you, sir.'

Jock nodded again. He made a little gesture. 'Dismiss.'

Through the biting cold, the Corporal made his way back to his bunk in the band's quarters. He was shivering in spite of the whisky inside him, when, half undressed, he slipped between the rough blankets and drew his greatcoat over the bed. He had put newspapers between the blankets earlier in the evening, and now he was glad of them. As he lay there he could see the cloud of his breath in the pale light of the barrack lamp which shone through the narrow window by his head, and he felt a soldier's loneliness. He thought for a moment of the grace-notes, and the pibroch; then he thought of his girl; just thought of what she looked like. He wished he could keep her more constantly in his mind but she kept slipping away from him, and away again as he slowly fell asleep. But in his dreams her face was transformed, for the Corporal dreamt of his Colonel.

The bottle was three-quarters empty.

'You're a miserable man,' Charlie said. 'It's not three-quarters empty. It's a quarter full.'

'It's your turn.'

'I had some when you were blowing your guts out.'

'You have no music in you. No music in you at all.'

Jock put the bottle to his lips again, then he held it in his lap. The chairs all round faced one way and another. It was as if a storm had abandoned them there.

'I was thinking as I played, Charlie. I should have been the Pipe-Major; that's what I should have been. But that was not the way of it. And I've acted Colonel, and I bloody well should have been Colonel, and by this hand boy, I bloody well will be Colonel. I will.'

But Charlie was snoring. For an instant Jock looked as if he were going to kick him, then he seemed to see the joke.

'Oh, you bastard,' he said slowly and gently. He pronounced the word with a short *a*. 'Oh, you bastard! You're no a good listener, either.' And alone he finished the bottle.

Like a bath of water, the room grew slowly colder and Jock sat dazed. He could not bring himself to move, though the hand which clasped the empty bottle grew icy cold. At last he bit his lip and, stiffly, rose to his feet. Then gently – and it took great strength – he lifted Charlie in his arms, and a little unsteadily, carried him upstairs. He placed him on his bed, and threw a couple of blankets over him. Charlie was still sound asleep. And Jock smiled on him, as if he were a child.

He brushed his hair in front of the mirror, and once more he buttoned his tunic and his trews. He lit a cigarette, and with great concentration he found his way to the cloakroom where he remembered to collect his bonnet and coat. The air outside made him gasp. The wind had dropped but the sky was starless; there would certainly be more snow before morning. He dug his heels into the ground in the approved fashion, but this did not prevent him slipping on the icy patches. Precariously, he picked his way round the barrack square. As he marched up to the gate he walked more confidently and he swung his arms. Then suddenly he felt an urge to call out the guard and he instructed the sentry to shout the necessary alarm. The guardroom came to life with the sound of swearing and of soldiers clambering off their steel bunks. Rifles were dropped and somebody kicked over a tin mug; knife, fork and spoon were scattered over the concrete floor. But by the time they had formed in their correct rank outside Jock seemed to have lost interest in the proceedings. He could see a fault in the dress of every man there but he did not bother to inspect the guard. He just returned the Corporal's salute, and without a word went on his way. He left the guard bewildered and the Corporal apprehensive.

FOUR

ON SUCH A night and at such a time he tended to call on Mary Titterington, but it was six weeks now since he had seen her and he had decided on the last occasion that he would not call again. She worked with a local repertory company and his association with her was one of the many things that the town and county objected to. Not that that made any difference to him.

Anyway, when he left the barracks he thought about calling on her and instead of returning home over the old footbridge he wandered into the town. She had a flat in one of the big houses by the park. He turned his collar up, and he dug his hands into his greatcoat pockets. He passed nobody and the only sound was the echo of his own footsteps. All cities are lonely at night, but the old Scottish ones are lonelier than all. The ghosts wander through the narrow wynds and every human is a stranger surrounded, followed, and still alone. The ghosts always unnerved Jock. He was suddenly chilled and very lonely, so he turned back and went straight home.

Safe inside, he was glad to find his daughter had waited up for him; he let his shoulders drop, and he smiled kindly at her when he said, 'Lassie, you should be tucked up in your bed.'

'Och, I couldn't sleep.'

'It's late. It's awful late.'

'I know it is. It's two o'clock.'

'You should be getting your beauty sleep.'

'It'll take more than sleep to make me a thing of beauty,' she said with efficient presbyterian modesty. She was really quite pretty, with pink cheeks, even at two in the morning; but Morag never gracefully accepted a compliment.

Their home was one of those little villas with bow windows and a staircase that runs straight down to the front door. There was an ugly overhead light in the cramped hall and there was no carpet, but brown linoleum on the floor. Morag was in a sensible woollen dressing-gown and fluffy bedroom slippers. She came downstairs to help him with his coat.

'You look all in,' she said.

'Aye, I'm tired.'

'Did you come straight home?'

Jock glanced at her. They never mentioned Mary Titter-ington and he was not even sure that Morag knew of her, or knew about her.

'Of course I came straight back. Where the hell d'you think I'd go?'

'I don't know, father, I'm sure. But you look tired.'

'A-huh.'

'Come on into the kitchen. There's a kettle on. I guessed you'd be all in.'

Jock touched her shoulder with his hand. 'You're a good lassie, Morag. That's what you are. I shouldn't leave you alone like this, so often.' He wanted to say more, but he paused and she spoke first.

'Heavens, Father! What's got into you? D'you think the bogey-men'll get me?' She moved away and his hand dropped to his side. She never allowed him to be demon-strative. She was far too sensible for scenes. Her mouth gave her character away. It was a very pretty mouth, neither too small nor too large. But it was firm, and her lips were always closed tightly together. She had a neat firm chin, a short nose, light brown eyes and dark hair which fell in an orderly little roll round her neck. She walked quickly into the kitchen and Jock followed slowly. He laid his coat on a chair, and later Morag would tidy it away.

'I passed a tinker woman in the street. That mad woman. She was wheeling her barrow. And at this time of night. It's a wonder they don't burn her. They burnt her mother for a witch.'

Morag tutted. 'You don't believe all that nonsense, do you? Her mother was never a witch.'

'She was the last witch. That's a fact.'

Morag smiled. 'Och, away you go, Father. You'd believe anything.'

Jock was a little nettled.

'She's a terrible-looking woman anyway, with all her scarves and rags. What d'you suppose she keeps in the barrow?'

'Just what she pinches off honest folk.'

Jock sat down by the kitchen table and he played with the spoon in the sugar-bowl.

'She's eerie. D'you suppose she's anywhere to sleep? Walking along, talking to herself. She gives me the creeps. Aye, she does. I passed her on the cobbled wynd.'

Morag filled the teapot. She smiled at her father again. 'Were you feared?'

Jock cocked his head. 'Of course I wasn't feared.'

'I believe you were: same as all the rest of the kiddies. Did she tell you your fortune?'

'Aye and maybe. I didn't rightly hear what she was saying. And I'm bloody glad I didn't.'

'I thought you were keeping your swear words for the barracks,' Morag said primly, and Jock sighed and apologised. She handed him his cup of tea and he thanked her again. She sat down by the table. She pulled her chair in, and her back was upright.

'Well,' she said at last. 'And what's he like?'

'Who?'

'Your new Colonel, of course.'

'How the hell did you know he was here?'

'A wee birdie told me.'

'Aye, someone told you. Who's been here, eh?' He sounded annoyed.

'Nobody's been here. It's written plain across your face. I thought the new Colonel might come in tonight.'

Jock was not altogether satisfied with the explanation. He never allowed her to ring the Mess and ask after him, when he was late. He said this was because he did not want any officer rung by his womenfolk, but there were other more practical reasons. If he went round to Mary's flat he usually said he was going to the Mess. The Mess after all was his club; and a club should be a refuge. But Morag could read him like a book.

'I didn't ring the Mess,' she said truthfully. 'You can check up yourself.'

'I never said you did.'

'Maybe. Well, tell us. What's he like?'

'He's a wee man,' Jock said and he started to sip his tea. He sipped it like a farmer in from the fields, with both hands on the cup and his eyes straight in front of him. He did not want to talk about Barrow. Morag softened a little, and she said in a low voice:

'Father, it had to be.'

'I just said he was a wee man.'

'It had to be.'

Jock put down his cup and he lit a cigarette, knowing as he did so that he had smoked too many that day.

'As a matter of fact, I'm no with you. It need never have been. But that's neither here nor there. It's my belief that he'll no be C.O. for very long.'

'Father, you'll not do any stupid thing.' It was not a question, but an instruction. She took the sugar-spoon away from him. 'If he's any sense at all he'll no give you a second chance. You must promise me you'll not do any stupid thing.'

'Are you feared, Morag?'

'Och, I know you. I know you fine, Father. What's his name?'

'Barrow. Poor wee man.'

'You're bitter.'

'Och, for Pete's sake Morag: d'you expect me to give a cheer? Ach . . .' He returned to his tea-cup and they spoke no more on the subject.

Morag listened, when she got back to bed, and it was a long time before Jock threw off one shoe, then the other. He gave a great groan, and she heard the springs of the mattress creak. Only then did she herself relax, but before she fell asleep she heard Jock give an unusual sigh that was long and trembling. After a moment's hesitation she knocked on the wall.

'Are you warm enough? Have you got enough blankets?'

'You go to sleep or I'll skelp your bottom.'

And she tutted at his vulgarity.

FIVE

IN THE TOWN, a week later, everybody was telling everybody how much milder it was. They were congratulating themselves on it, as if to say Scotland wasn't such a cold place as people made it out to be. They were delighted to hear that it had been bad weather in the South. They had letters from their sons and relations confirming it.

Behind the wall the detention squad was clearing away the last of the snow and the ice, and it was almost uncomfortably warm in the Officers' Mess after lunch. The stewards had cleared the last of the coffee-cups from the ante-room but the officers still did not move.

Superficially there was an air of extreme boredom. The company looked as sophisticated as a cavalry Mess. There was a whisper of glossy pages turning over and a flap as one magazine was exchanged for another. The officers were apparently sitting about wishing they had not tackled the treacle pudding, or promising themselves that they would stop drinking pinks before lunch. There was a smell of cigarette smoke and newsprint, and the sounds of a billiards game being played in the adjoining room. The Mess was a club.

But the officers at Campbell Barracks were deceptive. They were no longer a set of indolent gentlemen with courageous instincts. It is doubtful whether some were gentlemen at all – but then a Mess is renowned for taking on the complexion of its Colonel, and Jock had held command for some years now: this at least was the explanation the county favoured. Had they known better, they would have realised that Campbell Barracks was only one of the many that had suffered the same change. Whether or not it was a matter for regret, it was now an error to believe that the Regiment was commanded by asses. The billiards game next door was not being played for a guinea or two. The officers were not familiar with all the faces they saw in these magazines. Nor were they bored. They were a set of anxious and ambitious men, and some were extremely shrewd. Indeed, the only thing they shared with their fairy-tale forefathers on the walls was their vanity, and even this took different forms. Sandy Macmillan was one of the few whose vanity resembled the old set's. He wore his hair a trifle longer than the regulations formally demanded, he was a scratch golfer, he was never seen out of barracks in a uniform and he wore dark glasses when he drove his sports car. He was lying in one of the deepest chairs that afternoon and his battledress was unbuttoned at the cuff. His stockings were nearly white to make his brown knees look browner and he hoped soon to be posted to Fontainebleau on some United Nations lark. His vanities were not complicated, and his income was largely private. He talked to Simpson, the prefect, who had been attracted to him on arriving at the barracks, and to young MacKinnon, the junior subaltern, who had a face like a faun, and the manner of a gentleman.

The group in the next corner was not so obvious. The redhaired Rattray, who was also christened Alexander, but who styled himself Alec, had been educated at one of the Glasgow day-schools, and he was a real pillar-box Scotsman. He was aggressive in his masculinity and his nationality, and he was busy growing a red moustache to be the more patriotic with. He was violently ambitious and as near to stupid as any of the subalterns reached; he insisted on seeing his face in the toe of the boot of every man in his platoon. His only rival in strict treatment of the men was his friend, Lieutenant Douglas Jackson, who had a head like a

German, a pasty complexion like a German, a fist like a German, and not unnaturally an almost pathological hatred for Germans. Nothing nettled him more than to be reminded that he had never actually fought the Germans but had merely occupied their country and seduced their young women.

There were as many other vanities as there were officers in the room. Dusty Millar, the fat Quartermaster, had long service and a couple of tricks with a matchbox for a shield; Charlie Scott had his reputation; and the doctor had his intellect. Perhaps the least vain of all was the Adjutant, Jimmy Cairns, a mature farmer's boy in uniform, completely and unaffectedly effective. Jimmy had a face to match his character. His expression was fresh and his hair was fair. He was growing, each year, more solid. But a second glance at him would have confirmed that the air of boredom was no more than superficial. He did not look happy now. He looked more worried than anyone, and he kept glancing at his watch.

Everybody looked up when Jock came in, and three or four dashed forward to tell him the bad news. He soothed them like children, like dogs. He put his palms out in front of him and waved them up and down in the air.

'For Jesus' sake,' he said, and apologised to the Padre who pretended he needed no apology. Then he got Cairns to tell him the story.

It had happened only half an hour before. After a week of tactful quiet, of asking questions and making no comments on the answers, of pointing here and nodding there, of listening and of inspection – after all this, the Colonel had made his first move, and he had made it when Jock was out of the Mess.

But telling the story, Cairns fell over himself to be fair.

The Colonel had ordered that the officers should forgather in the ante-room that afternoon at 1430 hours. He had put a notice on the board to that effect, just an hour before lunch. As they sat round disconsolately sipping their coffee, he blew into the ante-room, looking as light as thistledown. He was wearing his bonnet; and in the Mess. He asked them to sit in one corner of the room and as they assembled he stared out of the window at the low grey clouds. He seemed to be deep in thought, and far away from them. There was a minute before he recovered himself, and moving his walking-stick with his wrist he tapped the crook of it against his lips. Then he dropped it to the floor and addressed them in his sharp light voice.

'When I first came to this barracks the social responsi-bilities of an officer – and particularly of a subaltern – very greatly outweighed his military duties.' He glanced at Macmillan and Macmillan smiled, with a flash of white teeth, but the smile was not returned. The Colonel had not wasted his questions or his week. He knew their vanities too. 'This was quite common before the war. The last thing I want to do is re-establish that order.' The Quartermaster nodded 'hear, hear,' to that. He sank his chins into his chest and Barrow continued: 'We are first and foremost soldiers and the greater part of our energies must be devoted to training. On the range; drilling; marching; P.T. and so forth.'

They sat like a dull class. He cleared his throat and struck his stick against his thigh.

'On the other hand, gentlemen, it is necessary that we should play our full part in the social life of the locality. Very necessary. And for this reason it is important that we should maintain certain standards; standards which have been maintained for close on two hundred years. It is part of our responsibility.'

Nobody could guess what he was driving at, but nobody liked it. Some stared unblinkingly at the Colonel's face. Others shifted in their seats, raised their eyebrows and shrugged. The Colonel talked swiftly and without a trace of Scottish accent.

'Each Tuesday, Thursday and Saturday morning at 0715 hours all officers will report in this ante-room.' There was a mumble at that. '0715?' 'Saturday?' But Barrow did not seem to hear, and if he did hear, he did not heed. 'When the weather improves we may parade outside. For three-quarters of an hour there will be dancing, gentlemen. You will report dressed as you are now, but with plimsolls on, and the Adjutant will instruct the Pipe-Major to come and see me to make arrangements for a piper. All right?'

'Sir.' Jimmy sat up straight.

'The following dances will be mastered: the eightsome and foursome reels, the Duke of Perth, the Hamilton House, Duke and Duchess of Edinburgh, Petronella, the Cumberland Reel.'

'But, Colonel, the officers know these dances.' It was Rattray who spoke. It was a stupid thing to do, to interrupt at such a time, but his national dancing was a point of pride. The Colonel's face remained blank, and the silence which followed made even Rattray blush a little.

'No one,' the Colonel went on firmly, 'no one will raise his hands above his head, except in the foursome reel. No shouting, no swinging on one arm. We will go into these details later. You will not be being trained for a professional performance. You will be being – being reminded of the manner of dancing traditionally adopted by an officer of this Regiment.'

Cairns had intended to leave the story there, but everybody was keen to tell what had happened next. Douglas Jackson was something of a hero for what he had said next. At the end of a long, hostile silence he had spoken clearly. Dusty Millar was anxious that Jock should not miss this.

'Come on, Douglas, what did you say?'

Lieutenant Jackson had a deep voice to match his Prussian head. 'I can't remember my words. I said I understood his visit to the Mess that first night was quite unofficial. That's the only time he's seen us dance.'

'Aye, that was it, that was it,' Dusty said, enjoying the moment again.

Jock nodded. 'A-huh. And what did he say to that?'

'It *was* unofficial. That was all he said. But he was pretty angry.'

The doctor grinned and sidled. 'Douglas is a marked man now.'

Jock raised his eyebrows and he walked about, while they waited. 'Well, well. I've always said some of the children could do with a dancing class.'

'Och, heck,' Rattray said, flaming up. 'It's no dancing like that we should be taught. We're not a lot of playboys.'

Jock opened his eyes wide. 'No.' He ran his tongue round his cheek. 'No, we're not that.' Charlie knew the mood well: he knew how much Jock was enjoying himself. He knew the technique, and Charlie knew even before Jock turned that he would walk away and touch one of the chairs with the tips of his fingers.

'You notice he did it when you were out,' someone said.

'Maybe that was tact.' He spread out his hands. 'Gents, we're no wanting any mutinies in this Battalion. We'll leave that to the Navy.' Jock wagged his head. 'I think he's been very reasonable.'

Jimmy nodded. 'Of course he has.'

'Hell, this is the first thing he's done,' somebody said.

Jimmy smiled and tried again. 'There's bound to be some changes.'

'No one's denying that, Jimmy,' Alec Rattray said. 'But this is something different. The way we dance is our own business, isn't it? I'm no sure he's a Scotsman at all.'

'Aye,' they agreed.

'Dancing's off parade; and off parade's off parade.'

Macmillan suggested lightly, 'We do get a little rowdy.'

'Rowdy?' Jock turned on him. 'A-huh. You agree with the Colonel?'

'I'm not sure it was his business to . . .'

'You agree though: you agree?'

'By and large.'

'Aye,' Jock nodded. 'By and large. There you are then. It's what the doctor would call a difference of opinion, or emphasis or whatever the word is, down in Oxford. That's the way of it: so we best say no more about it. We don't want to be rent with schisms asunder. Do we?'

Jimmy had to leave then, and the others shifted places. They were not altogether satisfied, but had they known Jock as well as Charlie did, they would have realised that he had not finished. He was talking in his softest voice.

'It's always difficult, a change-over. It's as Jimmy says. Mind you, it seems a pity that he should choose the dancing. What time was this parade to be?'

Five or six voices replied: '0715.'

'Aye; and for the subalterns?'

A shout of 'No.'

'Oh, captains as well? . . . All officers? It's all officers, is it?'

'Aye, it is. That's what he said. Have you ever heard such bloody nonsense? Some of us have been dancing thirty years,' Dusty said hotly.

'Jock, we know you're in a difficult position . . .'

'I am: I am.' He shook his head seriously at that, but they gathered closer.

Rattray warmed to the subject: 'But this is different. It is. It's a blow at our independence. The likes of this has never been before.'

'Never.'

'And anyway he's wrong about the hands in the eightsome. Of course he is. I question if he knows . . .'

Jock grew reticent, and modest. He scratched his head and blew out his cheeks. He was in a tricky position. But no one would say that Jock let them down. He would see to that. They spoke more freely. They repeated some of the Colonel's more irrelevant questions, and it was the first

time that Jock had allowed himself the luxury of listening.
Every criticism of Barrow was for him another flattery. But
he did not seem to lead them on: indeed, he protested that
they should not make it difficult for him. Even the doctor
was bewildered by his display, and it was generally supposed in the Mess that a knowledge of physiology gave the
doctor an insight into human motive and character beyond
his fellow officers.

'Aye,' Jock said thoughtfully. 'Off parade's off parade,
right enough.'

Many of the officers had to leave before the end, but the
cronies stayed and half an hour later they were winking at
each other. Jock had been like a lamb since the first night
the Colonel arrived. He had done just what Morag had
advised him, and he had kept clear of the Mess. But now he
kept tapping his fingers on a knee that was scarred with
battle wounds.

SIX

JIMMY CAIRNS SAID nothing to the Colonel as they made
their way over to the Naafi canteen to inspect it. The
Colonel was investigating some rumours about pilfering.
He was his usual cool and efficient self, and he treated his
Adjutant almost as if he were a private secretary. He turned
to him constantly asking him to make a note of some detail.
But on their way back to H.Q. block, Jimmy lifted his eyes
from the ground and looked the Colonel in the face for the
first time that afternoon. He was much too honest a man to
harbour something in his heart for long. He liked to get
things into the open.

'Colonel?'

'Jimmy?'

'I'm afraid they won't like it, sir.'

'Who? The Naafi people? They're not meant to.'

'No, sir; you know fine who I mean.' The low afternoon
sun, shimmering red through the cloud, dazzled him as he
spoke.

The Colonel stopped and put his hands on his hips. He
frowned, and moved his moustache.

'You mean the officers?'

'Yes, sir.'

'I wouldn't do it unless I thought it were necessary.'

'But, Colonel, it's almost an insult. Some of them have
been dancing for thirty years or more.'

'I'm afraid it's an order.' The Colonel started forward
again, but Jimmy persevered.

'Surely the officers above field rank might be . . .'

'I said it was an order.' The Colonel's voice was low and icy. Then he stretched his neck and went on in his usual tone. 'There; the windows in that block could do with a wash. I suppose it's all this snow. What's the building used for?'

'Band Block, sir,' Jimmy answered absently.

'I see.'

The Regimental Sergeant-Major was standing just inside the door to H.Q. and he came noisily to a salute, bringing all the corporals and orderlies in the vicinity to attention.

'Party–party 'shun!'

'Mr Riddick?'

'Sir.' The voice was thick and immensely loud.

'Please ask the Pipe-Major to come and see me.'

The R.S.M. despatched an orderly to fetch Mr McLean straight away. He then retired to his office and removing his bonnet called for his cup of tea. Nothing delighted him more than that the Pipe-Major should be on the carpet. It seemed to him that during Jock's term of office the pipes and drums had been granted too many privileges. But then Mr Riddick had no more music in him than Major Charlie Scott.

When the Adjutant and the Colonel walked into the Colonel's office they were surprised to find Jock there. The Colonel was more than surprised; he was irritated. Nobody had any right to enter his office in his absence. Jock turned and nodded: he was still flushed from his conversation in the Mess and he was spoiling for a battle, but the Colonel still managed to keep his patience. He held his stick in both hands and glanced down at it.

'Hullo, Jock,' he said with a stiff informality.

Jock rolled his eyes. 'Do I intrude?'

The Colonel said, 'Don't go, Jimmy,' and Cairns closed the door behind him. He would have much preferred to leave, and although he was not a man to look at the ceiling or at the floor, he could not make up his mind whether he

would be right to meet Barrow's eye, or Jock's. He glanced
from one to the other, and fidgeted. Barrow laid his stick on
his desk and walked briskly round to his chair.

'What can we do for you?'

Jock turned, almost pirouetted:

'I was wondering if you wanted me this afternoon.'

'Oh, thank you very much.' The Colonel was both
serious and polite. 'I don't think there are any more queries
just at present. I'm afraid it must all be a terrible bore for
you, just now.'

'Bore?' Jock was at his most infuriating. 'Bore? A-huh.
What have you been up to, the day?'

The Colonel unlocked the drawer of his desk and
brought out his leather blotter and some papers. It was
the sort of blotter a boy is given by a grandparent who shops
at Fortnum's. He had kept it for many years. He turned
over some papers, pretending to concentrate on them, and
took his reading glasses from his tunic pocket. He buttoned
the pocket carefully before laying the case down just
beyond the blotter, on the desk. He did not feel like telling
Jock the exact purpose of his inspection.

'Jimmy and I have been running through some of that
fire drill. I noticed on the map that there aren't any
extinguishers in the body of the Naafi.'

Jock replied indignantly. 'There are three or four there. I
mind them fine.'

'Really? They're not on the chart.'

He looked at Jimmy, who nodded in agreement and who
was about to say something when Jock interrupted.

'I was never good at the paper work, Colonel. But you'll
find them there right enough. Is that not right, Jimmy?'

Jimmy nodded. He was again about to speak when the
Colonel cut in. 'Oh, quite right. We've just been over and
checked.' He smiled. 'I don't enjoy the paper work either.'

'I would have thought that Whitehall gave a man a taste
for it.'

'Curzon Street, as a matter of fact. Well, Jock, thanks for calling in. I mustn't keep you.' The Colonel would not have put it as clumsily as that had he not intended the hint to be translated as an order. But Jock paused, his weight thrown on one foot. His words did not come as he had intended them to. They came in an almost apologetic rush.

'This . . . eh . . . This dancing caper. You don't expect me to turn up, do you?'

Jimmy felt suddenly cold. He glanced at the Colonel who had removed his glasses.

'All officers.'

Jock hesitated, smiled sourly.

'It's not on, boy.'

The Colonel replaced his glasses and fingered his papers again. But he did not use his artillery. He spoke lightly like a nanny.

'I'm not much looking forward to 7.15 myself. But I think we'd best all turn up.'

Jock's smile had changed to something nearer a sneer. He spoke more rudely than he had dared before. 'Is that an order, when you say you think we'd best all turn up?'

'If you like to put it that way.'

Jimmy moved the handle of the door, but Jock still hesitated. He walked back a step or two towards the desk and he spoke in quite a different tone of voice. He was pleading.

'Look here, boy, if . . .'

'Colonel. I prefer to be addressed as Colonel.' His voice was raised and now Jock, too, grew angry. 'Very well then, Colonel. If I and some . . .'

'If I may suggest; some other time.' The Colonel did not look up, and Jock was badly stung. He clenched his fists. His colour rose. Then he straightened up.

'O.K., Colonel,' he said through his teeth. 'O.K.'

He made a great business of the final salute, smashing his heels together, and Barrow nodded. As he had no hat on, he was not called to return the salute. Jock did not look at Cairns as he marched out. He did not look at anybody: he did not even remember to return Mr Riddick's salute as he passed through the lobby. He looked neither to left or right. He marched.

Much to the R.S.M.'s disappointment, Mr McLean was faultlessly dressed; and he did not look perturbed. Then he never did. Mr Riddick gave a phlegmy cough, about turned, and knocked on the Colonel's door.

'March in, Mr McLean.' He tried to make it sound as near to an order as possible. 'March in.'

The Pipe-Major walked into the room and he came to a halt without making much noise about it. He did not bang his feet on the ground.

Mr Riddick was listening at the door, but his face soon wore a disappointed expression. The Colonel was explaining to the Pipe-Major just how he wanted the officers to dance and he was speaking in a friendly way.

'Oh yes, sir.' Mr McLean sounded like a friendly game-keeper. 'Oh yes; we'll manage that, sir.'

'Have you a piper competent to do the job?'

'All the pipers are good, sir. They're a good band. But I think I had better go along myself. It will make it easier, I'm thinking.' There was just a wash of the Atlantic in his voice.

'You needn't if there's somebody else.'

'Well, if I can't some morning, then we'll send along Corporal Fraser. He's tactful, you know.'

'Very good, Pipe-Major.'

'Thank you, sir.' The Pipe-Major seemed to want to go on talking. 'It is a while since we have had a subalterns' parade of this sort, though Colonel Sinclair once suggested it would be a good idea.'

'It isn't only the subalterns, you understand.'

'Oh? But surely the senior officers . . .'

The Colonel looked annoyed. He touched his moustache.

'The order affects all officers.'

'All the officers. I see, sir.' The Pipe-Major sighed. It was time he left. But as he turned the Colonel said:

'I'm not a great one for spit and polish, Pipe-Major, but the windows of your Band Block could do with a wash.' He said this quite pleasantly, and Mr McLean looked concerned.

'Oh, aye, sir. We'll get that seen to straight away, sir; straight away.' Then he smiled uncertainly, and the Colonel smiled back.

'Straight away.'

'Right this minute, sir. Thank you very much, sir.'

'That will be all.'

The Pipe-Major nearly knocked over Mr Riddick when he opened the door. The eavesdropper moved his feet sharply, and coughed. 'Cup-a-tea for you, Mr McLean?'

'Thank you, Mr Riddick. That would be fine,' the Pipe-Major replied in his comfortable way and they went into the little office. But as they closed the door behind them, orderlies in the next room raised their eyebrows and shrugged. It was never a good idea for these two to get together. Even in the Mess the sergeants did not trust them in the same game of *Housey-housey*. It always ended in the same way.

When they took off their bonnets it could be seen that both men were a little bald, but while Mr Riddick's hair was quite grey Mr McLean's was sandy in colour. They sat silently for a while; then the R.S.M. launched straight into the meat of the matter.

'Captain Cairns was in here this afternoon talkin' about this dancing class. Said he had half a mind to chuck up the adjutancy.'

'Aye?' Mr McLean took five lumps.

'Told him not to be daft. I've seen a change of colonel before today and there's always trouble.'

'A change is usually for the better. That's true in life.' Mr McLean enjoyed universals, but they were not for the R.S.M.

'Don't know anything about that. But I do know it would be damned disloyal to march off now. As Adjutant he has responsibilities, same as the rest of us.'

'Aye. But it's a big change for him. He's known Jock all the way from El Alamein.'

'That's not the point. I can tell you, Mr McLean – I wouldn't express an opinion to anyone else, mind you – but I can tell you, this one'll be the better Colonel. Better by far. Shall I tell you why, eh?'

It was the beginning. The expression on the Pipe-Major's face did not change, but he said gently, 'I don't think I'll be agreeing with you here.' He nodded his head. Mr McLean was anxious that it should be a pleasant chat.

'Right,' the R.S.M. said. 'I'll tell you why he's the better Colonel. Because he's a gentleman.'

Mr McLean smiled a wise smile and the R.S.M. repeated himself more emphatically, with just a flicker of malice in his boss eye.

'Because he's a gentleman.'

Slowly came the reply. 'You're the terrible snob, Mr Riddick. It is always the same with you people who start in the Brigade of Guards. You're such terrible snobs; it is wicked.' As he grew angry, he spoke more quickly.

'Mr McLean. I know what I'm saying.' The R.S.M. poured out another cup of tea and passed his hand over his short thin hair. He made a sour face. 'Rankers may make Quarter-masters. But believe you me, sir, they don't make battalion commanders.' 'Sir,' from one Warrant Officer to another is a gauntlet.

'That's lies. Jock was the most successful Battalion Commander in the war.'

'The war was a different sort of thing. You're arguing off the point, again, Mr McLean. Of course he's a good soldier, no one denies it; but the point is that he should be in my job or yours. And I'm not the sort of man who ought to command the Battalion.'

Mr McLean controlled himself.

'Ah well,' he said, 'we shall see what we shall see.' Then he added, in spite of himself, 'But I think it is Jock who should have been appointed.'

Mr Riddick was in a keen mood. He wagged his nobbly finger.

'The very fact that we call him Jock . . . Och, you must see it.'

Suddenly Mr McLean was unleashed. He spoke quickly. 'You're a diehard Tory; yes, and it's you that stirs up class hatreds.'

Mr Riddick pushed back his shoulders. 'That's a damned impudent thing to say, Mr McLean.'

'It is true. Yes it is.'

'I never knew we had a bloody Communist as Pipe-Major.'

The R.S.M. now stood up and towered above the round figure of Mr McLean, who half closed his eyes, and half whispered, half shouted his reply. 'I have told you before, I am a Liberal, Mr Riddick. A Whig, a Whig, a Whig!'

Rather patchily the R.S.M.'s complexion was changing from blue to vermilion.

'It's an unwritten rule in this Battalion, Mr McLean, that politics will not be discussed. I'd bring that to your attention.'

'Och, you and your rules. It's playing at soldiers that you are.'

'Pipe-Major; I'm reminding you of my rank.' Mr Riddick put on his bonnet. He was shouting now.

'And a man of your rank should know better than to accuse one of his colleagues of being a Communist, when he's a Whig. You had best go back to your Grenadiers or whatever it was.'

'Are you attemptin' to insult my late regiment? Tell me that, Mr McLean.' Mr Riddick's voice was low and menacing but the Pipe-Major, after several years of practice, knew just how far he could go. He put on his bonnet and prepared to leave.

'No,' he said.

'If you want to insult my late regiment then I think we'd better meet in the gymnasium.'

The Pipe-Major smiled and shook his head.

'Peter Pan; that's what we should call you, Mr Riddick. Man, we're far too old to be meeting in the gymnasium. You'd better go home now. Muffin the Mule's on in a few moments.'

'By God, you're a bloody impudent man. I've a mind to put you under close arrest. D'you hear me? March you right inside.'

'Then it's high time I was leaving. Mr Riddick, I am thanking you for my cup of tea. It has been invigorating.'

But the R.S.M. did not return his smile.

'Pipe-Major, I observed when marching by today that the windows of the Band Block are in a dirty condition.'

'Did you, now?' The Pipe-Major's eyebrows nearly touched the fringe of his hair. 'Well, I'll tell you what, Mr Riddick, I'll go right back there now and see that they are cleaned, just for your sake. That's what I'll be doing.'

Shortly after the Pipe-Major left, the R.S.M. spotted a soldier with the lace of his boot undone. He was put on a charge for being improperly dressed, straight away. He was lucky not to be put in gaol.

SEVEN

NOW THE TOWN was small, but the county was smaller. The news of the dancing class soon circulated and seasoned officers blushed like cadets when they were asked if they had learnt their *Pas-de-Basques* yet. Underneath the layer of sunburn even Sandy Macmillan grew a little warm, but if the officers were teased, the county notwithstanding was thoroughly glad. It was a sign for the better. The officers from Campbell Barracks had not made themselves popular over the preceding year or two, with their drinking and their springy dancing. Even those people in the county who did not consider themselves to be purists were a little sick of them. At the Hunt Ball, not that there is much of a Hunt, people had grown accustomed, in an angry sort of way, to seeing the officers form up in front of the band so that the rest of the dancers were edged down to the bottom of the set. They clapped their hands and joked with the drummer, and they hooched and swung their women.

Everybody knew that Jock Sinclair encouraged them: as acting Colonel he was at the root of the trouble, for this is an old axiom: that a Mess takes on the complexion of its Colonel. It was therefore with warm hearts that the county welcomed a man who was instantly recognisable as a gentleman – Barrow Boy.

At first people were curious to meet him; then they were anxious; then, after a month, they were desperate. The county began to talk of nothing else and everybody wished they could peep over the sixteen-foot wall. Rumours abounded. All sorts of innocent tweed-coated men were recognised as the mysterious Colonel. Jimmy Cairns's aunt in Crieff set the Victorian terraces alight with her news items straight from the Adjutant's mother's mouth. A young farmer who had something to do with one of the Territorial outfits in the neighbourhood swore that Barrow was the White Rabbit himself. Barrow had blown up the heavy water plant in wherever-it-was; he had been one of Winston's special boys. Barrow had made the officers run round the barracks before breakfast. Barrow had been doing far rougher things to the idle than any young Alexander. Barrow had been in Colditz. Barrow had said that if any officer held his knife like a pen he would be posted to another regiment. Barrow was the talk of both town and county.

'He's a small man. You never see him in uniform this side of the wall. My dear, he has a look of Lawrence of Arabia.'

'Lawrence of where?'

'Nonsense . . . his eyes are much larger.'

'He's coming to dinner on Thursday,' proudly: that was said with pride.

'Really?' and that said with chagrin.

'Well probably. You must recall him. Tom knew him before the war. You must remember him.'

'My dear, I was a child then.'

In the county the talk is well up to standard. And the county often meets, even when the roads are bad. There were cocktail parties in houses which once had known stronger drinks and fuller servants' quarters, but here as ever gossip, like a leaf, whirled round and round, then with a spiral movement and on the hot breath of a matron, it was lifted upwards to unlikely heights.

'Oh, for Christ's sake,' Jock said, when he heard or overheard such a conversation, and he clenched his fists and screwed up his face. But he never got further than that: instead he cracked that joke of his about red tabs and tits, which usually went down very well. He did not like to hear much talk of the Colonel; he said all the talk at the parties was childish; people going on as if the boy were Monty himself. 'Oh, for Christ's sake,' he said.

'He's English, you know.'

'Nonsense. He's a connection of the jute Maclarens.'

'Dundee?'

'Originally.'

'Really? He has money?'

'I don't know how much now.'

The ladies talked about him most at the cocktail parties, but in the swells' club in the town and after dinner in some of the houses that still ran to dinner parties (proper style) his name came up again. The men treated it with a little more reserve.

'Was he with the First Battalion?'

'Can't have been. Billy would have met him.'

'He was S.A.S., wasn't he?'

Then the older voice. 'Only thing I know about him is he's got a pair of Purdeys, and they say he can shoot with them: that's more than that tyke Sinclair can do, at all events.'

A 'hear, hear,' a finishing of the glass, a moment or two spent in clearing away the dishes for the foreign girl, and it is time to join the ladies.

But the Colonel did not go to the dinner on the Thursday or on the Friday or to supper on the Sunday. He had to stack his invitations horizontally on his shelf, but he still replied to them all in his own neat hand. Each time he refused, and he gave as his reason pressure of work.

When at last, a month later, he invited the whole neighbourhood to a regimental cocktail party it was no surprise to anyone that there was hardly a refusal. The county had decided to come to the Colonel. And the drink had better be good.

And the drink was good. Whatever may be said about

that Battalion's fighting record or social performance no one but a Plymouth Sister could deny the quality of the drinks at one of the regimental parties. There were all sorts of drinks, and there were a great many of them. The officers saw that the stewards circulated amongst the guests swiftly and for a long time. It was impossible to hold an empty glass, and, perhaps consequently, it was impossible to believe that the party was not a howling success. Simpson and some of the other better-known young men were like perfect ushers at a wedding. They welcomed people as soon as they arrived in the ante-room, and they offered plates of savouries and silver boxes of cigarettes to two hundred guests. At the beginning – he'd had one for the road – Jock was pink in the eyes with social affability and he was holding guests male or female by the elbow, pretending to be listening to what they had to say. But often he glanced through the door to the hall where Barrow was greeting the guests.

Barrow made a point of shaking everybody's hand. He had the dazed and silvery look of the bride's father, and as he shook hands he said a word or two; then, as the guest replied, his eyes wandered to the next guest in the long queue. Everybody looked at him as if he were a waxwork that could talk, and although some of the sharper females dared a personal question, nobody was any the wiser at the completion of the ceremony.

The ante-room itself was very pleasant. Some of the worst armchairs and wicker tables had been moved out for the occasion. The tartan and the tweeds toned with the panelling of the walls and the wood toned well with the whisky. The chandeliers and the tumblers sparkled and the Mess servants made friends with some of the grand ladies which, after all, is always a sign of a good party.

The same grand ladies, when they were not making friends with the Mess servants or keeping Sandy Macmillan at a safe distance, concentrated on the Colonel. Some waited in their corners until he came to them while others, a little older and a little keener, moved through the throng to meet him. They all had a shot at penetrating his defences. Only one person had anything like a success, and she wished she had not spoken.

'You ought to have had a girl friend to keep you company when you greeted us in the hall.'

A slight smile: 'Yes? My Adjutant offered to help.'

'We've got lots of presentable girls you know: you'd be surprised.'

'Really?'

'We'll get you a wife.'

'As a matter of fact I have had one of those.'

'Oh. Oh, really?' The girl put her weight back on one heel.

But it only added to the mystery of the man.

Even Morag had a try at opening the oyster. She was in her smartest cherry hat – one with a snout to it – and she wore a black tailored coat and court shoes. The Colonel found her alone, and he recognised her again, immediately. She refused a cigarette from his little silver case; it was one of those old-fashioned cases with a curve in it to fit closely to chest or hip. Morag was standing alone, not because she did not know anybody there, but because she liked to stand alone when she was not enjoying herself. Several officers had come to make conversation to her, but she frightened them away. Simpson tried valiantly.

'What a smart hat!'

'This thing?'

'It's awfully smart.'

'Och, I picked it up in the sales for one-and-nine.' Morag did not smile. Her common sense was almost militant.

'How clever of you,' Simpson replied pleasantly, but the answer was as sharp as before.

'Not very. It's just common sense. If you get up early enough you get the bargains.'

'I think I'd be frightened to death. All those women fighting for the best bargain.'

'Oh yes.' She looked at him as if she thought him stupid, and he offered her some snacks, but she had no time for them.

'Too fattening?' Simpson suggested with a smile, and she replied, 'I wouldn't know about that.'

After that he was stuck with her for a little time and they talked about some of the other people near them. Then she said, 'You'd better go and give them their sardines,' and not with grace, but with relief, he took his opportunity.

But she was more forthcoming with the Colonel, who did not make the mistake of flattering her.

'D'you enjoy things like this?' she asked him, and before he had time to reply she said, 'Neither do I,' and he smiled.

'They serve a purpose, I suppose.'

'Colonel Barrow, I don't fancy it's the time or place . . .' she said, and she hesitated. Barrow's mouth tightened a little, and he looked at her severely. But nothing could stop Morag when she wanted to say something. She was as firm as the regimental Douglas Jackson.

'Whatever Father's said, don't think I don't see how difficult it must be for you . . .' But there was no getting closer to the Colonel. He leant back on his heel, and looked round the room. She only saw the side of his face when he replied, 'How kind of you to say so. You mustn't worry.'

'I wanted to say that.'

'I'm grateful to you. Now, have you met . . .' But as the Colonel looked round for a spare subaltern, Jock shouldered his way closer. He flicked his head at Barrow.

'Aye. You've met Morag?'

The Colonel looked nervous. 'Oh yes. Delighted.' He waved his glass and nodded. 'If you'll excuse me.' He picked his way through the crowd rather as if he were frightened of it. Two or three groups opened like a flower to let the queen bee land, but he hovered and moved on again,

farther round the room. His face was the face of anxiety.
But that again only endeared him to the ladies.

Sometimes, and all of a sudden, they felt that it was only
right that he should be called Boy. In spite of the grey hair,
he looked like a child at a party; looked as if he had lost his
way. And that, to regimental women, is something very
attractive: their own husbands are always so vehement in
protesting that they know where they are going. When Jock
saw one of these take him by the hand and draw him into a
group, it sickened him.

'Well, Father?' He had said nothing to Morag.

'A-huh. Well, you seemed to be talking with him very
seriously.'

'I was just warning him what a bear you are.'

'Aye. What did you say?'

'Nothing.'

'Well you looked bloody pleased about it. He's no the
Brigadier you know; he's just another colonel.'

Morag looked angry. The muscle in her cheek moved
and she looked down at her feet.

'I meant no harm,' she said. 'For goodness sake.'

'Look at them now: look at them. You know these are the
same women that made such a bloody fuss over me in forty-
five. But I couldn't cope with them. You wouldn't remember. I was bloody rude to them.'

'I'm sure,' she replied, tightly.

Because some of the best-behaved subalterns and their
blonde partners asked him politely, if persistently like little
children, the Colonel allowed them to dance in the main
hall, and the pipers were duly organised. Most of the
grown-ups left about then which, as things turned out,
was a blessing for Barrow; but the rest of them really settled
down to enjoy themselves. In the billiards room, one or two
of the wives were all blouse and colour by now, and Dusty
Millar was very drunk, but Jock and some of the others
came through in a group, abreast, towards the dancing.

Morag stayed until the pipers arrived. They both knew her
and smiled politely, but in spite of Douglas Jackson's grip
on her arm, she stayed no longer.

The Colonel disappeared into the ante-room once again,
when the dancing began. But later, as the noise in the hall
increased, he grew more and more nervy and two or three
times he ignored altogether remarks put to him by his
guests. The noise from the hall grew in gusts and it was
soon clear that the style of dancing was diverging very far
from the lines laid down by the Pipe-Major at the early
morning classes. Seeing the Colonel's face, nobody in the
ante-room could think of anything else and the whole Mess
seemed to be shaking.

Suddenly Barrow could stand it no longer. It was as if he
had known all along that the party was building up to this.
He detached himself from the group by the fire and walked
out of the room: then he checked himself. When he saw the
scene in the hall he grew pale with anger, and the liquor
circled even faster in his glass. There were two sets dancing
the eightsome. The first was lively, but their behaviour was
excusable at the end of such a party. That could not be said
for the second. Jock, Douglas Jackson, Rattray, and a
fourth who was a local farmer, were the men in the set,
and they were hoping that the Colonel would come to
watch. Three or four times Jimmy Cairns, dancing in the
other set, had implored them to dance less noisily. But he
had done so in vain.

Barrow's lip twitched and he rubbed his thumb against
the tips of his fingers. The whole floor was shaking, and the
glass in the front door was rattling as the dancers leapt
about the room swinging, swaying and shouting. When
they saw the Colonel the noise increased, and a moment
later Rattray inadvertently let go of the partner he was
swinging vigorously so that she spun like a top across the
floor, lost her balance, and fell. She fell at Barrow's feet.

Corporal Fraser and the other piper stopped playing and

the dance came suddenly to an end. The Colonel reached
forward to help the girl and she shook her hair from her
face. She was too uncertain of the look in Barrow's eyes to
say anything at all and Jock was the first to speak.

'Are you all right, lassie?'

But it was Barrow who spoke next. His voice was low and
clear.

'Mr Rattray. I believe you owe this young lady an
apology.'

'Oh hell . . .' she began. She was a student from St
Andrews, this girl, and she knew all the words, but when
she looked at the Colonel again her vocabulary failed her,
and her voice died away. The Colonel stood very tensely.
The gin in his glass was shaking so violently now that it
splashed, and when Jock observed that a little of it had spilt
he looked at the Colonel's face, and he smiled a half-
triumphant smile.

'Have a drink, boy, have a drink,' he said cordially; then
he half turned towards the others. 'Unless you'd like to join
us. I'm sure Douglas here'll stand out.'

Barrow's voice was a pitch or two higher than usual.

'Piper: this will be the last reel.'

'Sir.'

The Colonel stood and watched as the pipers played
again. He took a gulp of his drink to empty the shaking
glass. The dance began quietly, to Jimmy Cairns's great
relief, and the girls soon adapted themselves to the style of
it. They held their heads high and their backs arched: they
placed their hands firmly with the palms downwards before
them when it came to a swing. Barrow's shoulders dropped
an inch with relief.

But when it was Jock's turn in the centre he let his
bloodshot eyes rest on the Colonel by the door. For the
first circle he behaved himself: he set to his partner and to
the third lady, and he completed the figure of eight with
reserved precision coming near to perfection. Then when

they circled again he sprang off the ground, flung his hands high in the air and let out a scream to crack rock. The others followed his lead. The noise rose, the floor started to shake again, and the glass in the door rattled louder than before.

The Colonel's voice rose above it all; and he was collected no longer.

'Sinclair! Sinclair! Stop the dancing. D'you hear me, Piper? Stop at once!'

He looked sick. Hearing the commotion people emerged from the cloakrooms and the ante-room to witness a scene such as the Mess had not known in forty years. But Jock had never looked so foursquare. He stood in the middle of the dancers and there was still the suspicion of a smile lurking behind the bland expression of his face. Embarrassed by the silence, one or two people in a mumbling sort of way endeavoured to interrupt, but the Colonel snapped at them to keep silent. One of the girls who had spoken blushed with indignation.

Jock's voice was low when he spoke.

'You called me, Colonel?'

'I did. I'll see you tomorrow. Tomorrow. I'll . . . Pipers, we've had enough of this. Quite enough.' Barrow fidgeted as he spoke, and although Jock was just a few yards in front of him, he was shouting. Then there was quiet. The dancers moved, and the pipers marched smartly out of the frozen world. Corporal Fraser looked upset, almost guilty, as if he had seen those things which a good piper should not see.

Now, for the first time the Colonel looked around him and he looked afraid and bewildered as if he had awoken from a dream and found himself at his own trial. He sighed heavily, and stretched his fingers.

Jock stared at him quite steadily, with victorious calm. He did not quite have the audacity to say, 'Are you going to rap me over the knuckles, Colonel?' but he thought of doing so. Instead, he grinned openly at the dancers around him.

Barrow now turned to the guests. 'The party's over. It's late. It's very late. I'm sorry it should end like this.'

Jimmy came to the rescue. 'It's time we all had something to eat . . .' he said with a friendly smile, but Douglas Jackson was not smiling. He had not moved, and he stood on the floor with one foot planted before the other, and his hands on his hips, in a Highlander's pose.

'We were just beginning to enjoy ourselves, Colonel.' It might have been a reasonable enough thing to have said, but Jackson had once before spoken out too boldly.

The Colonel checked himself, and everybody waited again. Jock was now grinning openly. Slowly the Colonel turned his head.

'Who said that?' And he knew perfectly well.

'I did.'

'Adjutant!'

Jimmy was trying to steady everybody. He nodded and moved up to the Colonel.

'Not now,' he whispered, but the Colonel braced his head back.

'Do as you're told. Take his name. Take that officer's name.'

'Yes, sir,' Jimmy said. Of course he knew the name, so he did not move and two or three people in the room began to giggle. Jackson, for all his impudence, was looking very white himself now and he stared at the Colonel unblinkingly. The onlookers were fascinated by the scene, and apart from the two women who giggled, they were petrified by it. In the hall, they stood quite still. But in the doorway through to the ante-room people were shoving and craning their necks to see better. Just in the same way that speeches are passed back in a crowd too large, a commentary of the scene was passed as far as the billiards room and the dining-room where some of the servants stood, their heads on one side, to hear more clearly.

But it was all over. The Colonel turned quickly away and

walked towards the cloakroom, while some of the others went up to talk to Jock and Jackson. Jock laughed and shook his head, but Jackson was still very white. As some of his cronies congratulated him he stuck out his chin a little further.

'I was in my rights,' he said, then he swore a little, but he did not relax enough to smile. In a moment when they were still standing about the hall the Colonel reappeared again, with his coat and bonnet on. He stopped by the front door, and putting on his gloves, he lifted his head and said:

'Good-night, all.'

One or two replied 'good-night', but the door had not closed behind him when the laughter began to ring round the room. Jimmy was sweating now: he was suddenly angry, and he tried to shout them down, but Jock was leading the laughter, and they paid no attention to him. They laughed all the louder when Jimmy grabbed his bonnet and ran out after the Colonel.

EIGHT

HE JUMPED INTO the jeep beside the Colonel just before he drove off, and the Colonel said nothing to him. Instead, he let in the clutch and accelerated fast. He changed his gears swiftly, like an expert, and he took the corners round the square as if he were racing. He braked hard at the gate and Jimmy shouted 'Colonel' to the sentry, who stood aside. By the time he had presented arms, the jeep was clear of the barracks.

In the Mess, the remainder – to use Mr Riddick's term for any party which had lost some of its members, the remainder moved to the billiards room where the drink was handy on the table, and as they drank, each one of them grew more like himself. Jock began to sweat. Douglas Jackson grew harsher until he had no time for any man or any idea except stern discipline. Rattray grew more vehement about Barrow's English accent, and the need for a Gaelic revival. Dusty Millar told story after story. The doctor was sitting on the step by the leather bench, like a mouse with a lot of hair. He said, 'It's surely significant that the quarrel should have revolved round such a primitive thing as folk dancing.'

This united them.

'Och, chuck it, Doc,' Jock said irritably.

'You and your Freud and all that Sassenach cock,' Rattray said, and Dusty Millar echoed Jock.

'Aye, chuck it, Doc. For chuck's sake chuck it.'

'What'll I say the morn, eh?' Jock said. 'What'll I tell him?' and they began to make suggestions.

*   *   *

The Colonel drove for several miles and the cold night air rushing into the jeep did not leave Jimmy breath for any words of comfort. They drove fast out on the south road, which is wide and straight. But in the dips there were patches of fog, and two or three times Jimmy was sure they were bound for the ditch. A wisp appeared in the yellow light of the headlamp, another, then they were driving through a yellow wall. In a second they were clear again and Jimmy sighed and folded his arms to try and protect himself from the bitter cold. At last, quite suddenly, Barrow took his foot off the accelerator and the jeep slowed down; then, out of gear, it glided to rest at the side of the road. Barrow eased himself back in the seat.

'What a childish thing to do,' he said and he closed his eyes.

His eyelashes were long and they came to rest on his cheek with a peculiar softness.

Jimmy said, 'Och, I don't blame you. It's one way of getting something out of your system. Though if I'd known the speed you were going to travel I'm not so sure I'd have come for the joy-ride.'

The Colonel smiled faintly. 'Childish.'

'That fog's nasty. But you can certainly drive a jeep.' The compliment did not encourage the Colonel. He sat still, with his eyes shut, and Jimmy went on. 'And it's bloody cold too. You've got a coat on but I'm frozen stiff. With this kilt blowing about I'm not sure I'm all here, any more.' He went on talking for a moment or two, saying nothing, but speaking in a voice of persuasive comfort and complete normality. At last the Colonel opened his eyes, and he began to move out of the jeep.

'You drive,' he said. 'I'm in no state to drive.'

'Have you had a couple?' Jimmy said, moving into the driver's seat as Barrow walked round to the other door.

'It takes more than a couple to make a man of my age make a fool of himself.'

'Och, people always do bloody silly things at Mess parties. It's part of the tradition. I know somebody who once had . . .'

'Not a Colonel.'

'A colonel's human, isn't he? He has a heart?'

'He shouldn't have: only a complexion.' Then he seemed to withdraw into his own world.

'Drive on,' he said at last. 'Drive on.' And taking it quite gently, Jimmy drove back to the cobbled streets. The street lamps had haloes round them like moons and there was no traffic on the road. But Jimmy never went in for dramatic gear-changing or fast cornering. He obeyed the law, and in the town they drove at under thirty miles an hour. He glanced at the Colonel who was staring straight in front of him. His expression was the expression of a boy being driven back to a boarding school he hates.

'I think we'd best drop into the Station and get a bite to eat.'

Barrow nodded, and bit his moustache. Jimmy had run out of conversation now. He drew up in the big yard outside the hotel and switched off the engine. Then he saw that Barrow had pitched forward and he was holding his head in his hand.

'Ridicule's always the finish. You know that?'

'Who said anything about ridicule?'

Barrow wagged his head irritably, and Jimmy found more words.

'For God's sake, Colonel. They behaved bloody badly and you'd the sense to get out. What's wrong in that?'

Barrow seemed to like that idea. He clung to it, again childlike.

'Is that how it looked?'

'That's how it was.'

They climbed out and Barrow breathed in deeply as they walked to the hotel door. 'I say, thanks awfully,' he said.

'For what?'

'For coming along like this. You know . . .'

'It's part of the service, Colonel; part of the service.'

As the Colonel ate his meal Jimmy was keen to find excuses for him. They sat in the far corner of the large dining-room, on opposite sides of a small table. Jimmy rested his arms on the table leaning forward to listen to Barrow, and to talk to him in a low voice.

'What was your job down in Whitehall? I never found that out.'

The Colonel smiled his former weary but collected smile.

'I gathered Jock had found out everything about me.'

'Oh no. Eton and Oxford was as far as he got.'

'That's not strictly true, either.'

'So?' Jimmy leant farther forward.

'I was only at school for a term or two. I had a private tutor most of the time.'

Jimmy nodded. He said with sympathy, 'Aye. Were you sick?'

'No.' The Colonel ate another mouthful before replying. 'My people thought it was a better idea.' The Colonel busied himself with the wine list. He felt uncomfortable. 'Sounds strange, I know.'

'Not all that.' Jimmy shook his head. 'Hell, I might as well not have gone to school at all. I spent half my time playing games in class and all that. I never listened to the teacher.' There was a likeness between Jimmy and Jock which people often noticed. They were both heavy men, although Jimmy was only in his middle thirties, and they had the same forthright manner. But Jimmy smiled much more. As Adjutant he behaved to the subalterns much as a friendly sales manager behaves towards his representatives. He joked them into doing things. But he was not capable of the same sort of banter this evening. When he remembered his academy days he smiled, but he soon grew serious again. It was like him, just as it would have been unlike

Jock, to fall in with the Colonel's suggestion that they drink a bottle of claret. He certainly would not have noticed had he been served with a glass of burgundy instead, but it was quite obvious that Barrow was something of an expert, and Jimmy drew him on the subject. Then at last he returned to the subject of the Colonel's previous employment. Barrow shrugged.

'Most of my time was spent with M.I.5.'

'That must have been a terrible strain.'

The Colonel nodded. He did not seem to want to discuss his work. 'It was quite enjoyable: I suppose it took a lot out of one.' But it had not been as adventurous as it sounded.

'I'm sure it did. Whatever they say it's that nervous work, and brain work too, that tires a man out. Did you have much leave before you came up here?'

'Ten days.'

Jimmy smiled. 'And you wonder why you were a bit ratty tonight? Ten days is not enough. It seems to me you've been very patient.'

'There were actually other things . . .' The Colonel looked up doubtfully, and Jimmy was staring at him with solemn sympathy. 'I had a marriage you know. I had a wife.'

'I'm sorry.'

'Oh, it's all over now really. But that was one of the reasons I accepted this job, you know: a change. I'd been rather lonely, I suppose.' He paused, and started again. 'I think perhaps all of us who were prisoners in the East are a little cranky now. D'you think that?'

'Och no,' Jimmy said, into his glass.

'No? I do. All of us who were in Jap hands. That's what my wife believed, anyway. She was quite sure of it. She had a friend too, whose husband . . . well, there are hundreds of examples. I suppose we got a touch of the sun. Or . . .' Quite suddenly he decided not to go on. He just stopped.

Jimmy moved his glass in a little circle, on the tablecloth, and some cigarette ash piled up beside it.

'Och,' he said, 'a change of colonel always takes time. When the next man comes along it'll be just the same.' And the Colonel leant back. He finished his claret and collected himself.

'Oh, good heavens, yes,' he said. 'You mustn't pay too much attention to me. These damned social things always unnerve me. But I knew before I came here what it would be like. They told me about Jock.'

'Jock's the hell of a man.'

'A great soldier.'

Jimmy said, 'You're not a dog in the manger, Colonel,' and Barrow shrugged.

'Strange,' he said. 'One man's goal can mean . . . well, quite honestly, not very much to another. I mean, I'm only here really for battalion experience. I expect in a year or two I'll . . .'

'Brigade level?'

'Well, if not, some special thing. A battalion would bore me, you know, after a while.' He seemed suddenly more confident and Jimmy was astonished at the change. It was only when they were leaving the dining-room that the buoyancy failed.

'Of course, all that's between you and me, Jimmy. You understand nothing's certain. I mean, it may turn out I never go farther at all, I . . .'

'I understand.'

'How late it is. Not a bad dinner, really.'

'Damned good, thank you.'

'No thanks, please.'

THERE WAS A smile on the face of both tigers. But then there was nearly always a smile on Mary Titterington's face. Anyhow, it was for her a little triumph that Jock should decide to call again after all that time. She bowed her head low, she swept back the door, and she followed him into the living-room. Then she went to the cupboard and brought out the bottle of whisky. It was cold after lunch; the sun had gone in and the clouds were gathering for snow again. Mary had only just been out to get some shillings for the meter, and the room was not yet warm. Jock looked at her closely, and reckoned she was looking well. It was Jock who first said that rude thing about her which best described the expression on her face: that curious smile. He said that she always looked as though she'd just had it. And Charlie said he was probably right.

Mary must have been over thirty. She came from Belfast, and she had failed to make a success of the London stage. In spite of the chiselled face, and the rather alluring expression, she had only been in one film. She had a figure that could be photographed from every angle, and had been from most, but − after all that − she came north to a repertory company. On the occasions when she had had a good night's sleep she was still capable of a first-class performance. But her soul was not so much in her face, any more: there was only this smile. And with the soul from her face, the Irish had gone from her voice. Once in a bottle, maybe, and usually near the end of it, both would suddenly return. But it was a good thing they reappeared so seldom, because Jock had little time for them: time neither for the soul, nor the Irish.

She lived in flat number 3 in a big house overlooking the park, and Jock had taken the stairs a little too quickly. He was very red, and out of breath.

'Hullo,' he said, with a roving eye, and she looked at him closely.

'Have you been drinking for long?'

'No, lass. I've not been drinking for long.'

After a struggle Jock was free of his greatcoat and he threw it over a chair in the corner. The room had been severely modernised. The tiled fireplace had been boarded in; there was wallpaper on the ceiling and on two of the walls. It was all very surprising, for the North.

'You've just been drinking all today.'

'I have not.'

'You've had a few.'

'How can you tell?'

'Your eyes.'

'That's very romantic,' Jock said, sitting down on the sofa. 'And what the hell's wrong with my eyes?'

'They're pink.'

'You're bloody rude.'

When she had poured out their drinks she put the cork back in the bottle and tucked her feet up on the sofa. She was small enough to fold into a neat parcel and she had very good legs. Jock was sitting as if he had had a very large lunch, and his stomach was full.

He said, 'You're rude. That's what you are.'

She brushed some ash from her pleated skirt and the bracelets on her arms clinked together as she tipped back her glass. Jock continued.

'Are you surprised to see me?'

She did not look in the least surprised, but she said, 'Mm.'

Jock said, 'You're looking very well.'

'I just got up.'

'You're bloody idle.'

She did not think so. 'I did two shows yesterday.'

Jock stared at her. 'What show's this?'

'*My Sister Eileen.*'

'You've done that before, haven't you?'

'Mm. It's a repertory company.'

'So they say. And you're Eileen?'

'No. I'm the other one. Ruth.'

Jock took a gulp of whisky. He watched her face closely all the time he talked, and he was rather enjoying himself. He was surprising himself, and it seemed a very long time since he had seen her.

'Are you not sore you're not Eileen?'

'I'm too old for Eileen.'

'How old is Eileen?'

'She's twenty: or something like that.'

Jock gave a grin: then he chuckled and she looked quite angry.

'I said I was too old for Eileen.'

'But you said you weren't sore.'

'I'm not, for heaven's sake. Jock Sinclair, you haven't changed much . . . Ruth's a better part. If you'd seen the play you'd understand. You ought to come and see it.'

'Aye, maybe.' Jock poured himself out another drink, and he sniffed, because he had forgotten his handkerchief. 'Tell me, Mary. In Belfast, on a Sunday afternoon, do ladies often sit drinking whisky?'

'What the hell are you up to?'

'I asked you a civil question. Do they, now?'

'Sometimes, if it's cold and wet, I suppose.'

'It's always wet in Belfast, lassie.'

'This is just as bad. This is the end of the world.'

'It's not that. It's a very fine city.'

'Och, but the people . . .'

Jock watched her lips when she replied. Now he jerked his head to one side.

'Mary; I'll go next door and sleep if you come too. It'll save you whisky. Eh?'

She stabbed her cigarette out firmly.

'I don't do it that way. I'm not something in a fair.'

'You're just contrary. You know fine you'd . . .'

'Take a whisky with you instead.'

'Just for old times' sake.'

'To hell with old times' sake. I don't mind you calling, Jock Sinclair. But you're going to behave yourself, or it's home you go. For heaven's sake, Jock.' She looked at him kindly.

'Aye,' Jock said, leaning back again, with a sigh. 'Maybe.' He pushed his tumbler forward again and she poured more whisky into it, and lit another cigarette. When she inhaled the first breath of a cigarette she would tip her head back and exhale it out of nose and mouth together. Jock liked the way she smoked.

'I hear you've got a new colonel up the road,' she said.

'Yes, yes.'

She smiled again. 'Are you sore about it?' and he looked at her, then he smiled too. 'I'll put you over my knee, and not just to spank you.'

Mary was always telling Jock he was coarse. She clicked her teeth and put her shoe back on her foot. Jock looked at the foot and the stocking, then he turned his eyes to hers again.

'Who's been giving you your news?'

She stood up and walked across the room to fetch an ashtray.

'Och, it's common knowledge. They say you had your knuckles rapped last night.'

Jock's colour rose at that. 'Aye, well they're bloody wrong. That's what they are.'

'Whatever you say.'

'I don't know who the hell's been telling you this but you've got the wrong end of the stick. It was me that said that, about rapping over the knuckles, or near enough. Who's been speaking to you, eh?'

'A friend.'

'Aye, well he's a liar too. The wee man got badly fussed and I said it; I said it kind of ironic-like – och, you wouldn't understand it.'

'Why shouldn't I understand?'

'Because you're bloody ignorant.'

'Listen to you.'

'Well what does ironic mean then, eh? D'you know?'

She did not reply to him, and after a moment he went on in a quieter voice.

'He lost his head altogether. That's what he did. He gets in an awful rage, you know; Barrow does. Aye, and he's to see me in the morning.' Jock paused again, but it was obvious that he wanted to say more on the subject. Mary could tell that from the way he washed the whisky round and round his tumbler, and watched it as it whirled. Mary had listened to a good many men's stories before this: and for a while Jock had been in the habit of telling her everything, when he went round for his evening chat.

He ran his tongue over his lips, which were cracked by the weather and all the cigarettes he had been smoking lately.

'He was cool enough this morning. I went to see him this morning. He's usually very cool you see. He's springy enough, aye, but he keeps well away from you. Nobody gets very near the Barrow Boy. That's one of the rules.'

Mary nodded sympathetically and she pulled her feet up on the sofa again so her shoe just hung on her toe. She smoked cigarettes all the time.

'On parade's on parade. But the way I dance is nothing to do with him.'

'I've never seen him.'

'Och, he's – he's a spry wee man. In the usual run I mean, but he's got a temper. He's always been famous for that. His wife couldn't cope with it, no. And it's worse 'an it used to be. But I tell you this; it'll no be of any use to him by the time I've finished tomorrow . . . I've got friends in the War Office, just the same as him; aye, but that's not the point.'

Jock was speaking very fast now, and he spoke right into Mary's face. He nodded and tossed his head to emphasise his independence. 'I'll tell you. I've fallen over myself to be fair. I don't know who's been speaking to you, but they'll tell you: everybody'll tell you I've been very reasonable. I've no questioned his command.' He gave a violent shake of his head. 'I haven't. But I could have, Mary. I'm no bragging when I say that. Anyone'll tell you who'd be in command of the Battalion if we went into battle tomorrow. Aye. And he knows that bloody well. "Oh yes, Sinclair," he said, "tomorrow, I think. *Not* a good idea today: not on a Sunday," and away he blew. He's in a funk, Mary. He's windy. He is. And, by God, I'll let him know that the morn. He's bloody good reason to be in a funk. I'm telling you.'

Jock was sweating now and he wiped his brow with his sleeve. He gave a sigh and asked politely:

'Have you got a hanky?'

'Only a small one.'

'That'll give me a thrill.'

She clicked her teeth again, and he smiled.

'No. No. Honestly, Mary. It will. I'm a very simple man.'

She dug into her handbag, holding it in the softness of her lap and Jock forgot about the Colonel's interview. He was still not satisfied that he had said all that was to be said, but he was a little happier. She gave him a handkerchief and he mopped his neck with it.

'I guess he's in a wee bit of a panic. But he's asked for it,' he said. She nodded, and he came back to her. Then he leant forward to fill his glass.

'I'll pay you for this whisky.'

'Of course you won't.'

'Aye, I will.'

'I wouldn't let you.'

'You used to let me.'

'That seems a long time ago.' She turned to put a record on the gramophone on the table by the side of the sofa.

'Och, we don't want that thing.'

'I've got some new records,' she replied, 'if you're wanting to be amused.' She placed the needle on the record and as she did this he leant forward and put a hand on her knee, just under her skirt. She did not turn round to push him away. She was trying to close the lid of the machine and she just said, 'Definitely no.'

'Och, Mary.'

'No.'

'You didn't used to say no. D'you remember that? Or have you conveniently' – Jock took long words very slowly – 'have you conveniently forgotten?'

'You didn't used to be a stranger.'

'Mary, I'm back.'

'And stinking,' she said patiently. 'You left stinking and you've come back stinking. You can't turn the clock back, Jock.'

'You can begin again. Come on.'

'If you're not going to sleep I think you'd better take yourself a walk round the town.'

Jock smiled suddenly.

'I could make you if I wanted to,' he said gently. And she was immediately angry.

'Jock Sinclair, you're the most conceited man I've ever met. You're not all that great shakes. And there's lots that know that, I can assure you.' She added the last sentence quietly, and the noise of the record drowned it.

'What d'you say?' Jock asked and he shook his fingers at the gramophone. 'For Christ's sake put that thing off.'

'No.'

'You put it off, you besom.' He leant across her and tried to open the lid of the gramophone.

'No!' she said again and she tried to push him back but he was already drunk enough to be determined and he lunged forward. Clumsily he pushed the machine and it slipped off the coffee-table on which it rested, and fell to the floor. The needle made a loud noise as it scored the record. Then there was silence. Mary said nothing. She brought her lips closely together and leant back as he sat up again. He left one hand on her thigh and he gave an uncertain half smile.

'That's mucked it.'

She took him by the wrist, and pushed his hand away, then stood up to try and repair the damage.

'I don't know what the hell's the matter with you,' she said as they put the gramophone back on the table.

'What d'you mean?'

'This Colonel's really touched you.'

'What you say? Eh? That's a bloody lie. I've never felt better.'

'All right, all right,' she said, patient again, but Jock was not so easily appeased. He was standing up and he pulled his stomach up into his chest. He braced his shoulders.

'I've had a drink maybe. But there's nothing the matter. I've never been better. Christ, but you're a bloody woman.' He was inarticulate with irritation. He fidgeted, and clenched his fists. Then he drank half a tumbler of whisky in a gulp and he walked about the room. It was a moment or two before he spoke again, in a pleading tone.

'Och, Mary, I didn't come round to have a row. You know bloody well what the matter with us is . . . Why don't we get on with it?'

'Jock, you couldn't even manage now.'

'I could.'

She sighed, and shook her head.

'Och, anyway we could just sleep and that would be something,' he said.

'Oh dear, oh dear.'

'And I'll tell you what.' As the plan formed in his mind he took another gulp of his whisky. More in self-defence than anything else, she pushed the bottle towards him and he sat down again. 'We'll away out tonight, just like the old days. We'll be the *bona fide* travellers. That's how it'll be. It'll be the Highlander and the Red Lion, the Glasgow Bar and the Station.'

Mary was not the one to see a bottle of whisky go down someone else's throat, but she looked none the worse for wear herself. As she put the bottle down she said, 'It would be cheaper at your house.'

Jock turned away. 'I don't drink there.'

'Why ever not?'

'Morag, of course. You know fine. Stop getting at me. I'm no the man to drink in front of my daughter.' He waved his hand. 'We'll go round the publics . . . Look, you'll let me pay for this bottle?' He reached in his wallet.

'You can put your money away.'

'No.'

'I'm all right for money.'

Jock hesitated. 'You're sure, lassie?'

'Sure and I'm sure.'

'And that dress suits you too.'

But soon after that Jock put his finger in his ear and shook his head. He was tiring a little.

'I'm sorry you weren't there this morning. You should have seen his face. And the other night. You know he was near greetin'.'

Not very long after, she saw that it would be impossible for him to leave. The excitement had worn off his cheeks and he grew drowsier and more apologetic.

At last she told him, when he seemed determined to go, that he should stay.

'You can't go. Not in your uniform: for heaven's sake. Away you go next door and sleep it off.'

Jock smiled meekly. 'You'll come too.'

'I'll pull the quilt over you.'

'You're a good girl.'

'There's no use fumbling, Jock,' she said patiently. 'Please.'

'Oh, Christ! Och Mary, I shouldn't have come. That's the truth of it. I thought you'd be pleased to see me. I shouldn't have come.'

'It's no matter. Come on now laddie, and we'll cover you up.'

'You're my bloody cherry-cake,' he said.

'Come away now: come on.'

WHEN SHE HEARD him shouting, Mary ran through to the bedroom. Jock was shouting her name out loud. There was no overhead light in the room and she had to stumble as far as the bedside light while he still shouted. He was sitting bolt upright in the bed and he seemed to be in the throes of a fever: in spite of the chill of the room, his face and neck were covered with sweat, and his shirt was wet. Even when the light was switched on he kept shouting.

She stood back and said, 'Was it me you were calling?' She was groomed all ready to leave for some party, and she looked neat and efficient.

He mopped his brow and his cheek with the hard palm of his hand.

'Aye. It was either you or the Mother of God.'

'You nearly shouted the walls down. Are you sober, now?' Jock opened and closed his mouth once or twice.

'I've got a mouth like a parrot's cage.'

'That doesn't surprise me. It's time you gave up whisky, and that's a fact.'

Jock had grown used to the light now and he swung his legs over the side of the low bed. At some stage he had taken off his kilt and his stockings had dropped to his ankles; the red garters trailed loose round his feet. As he pulled up his stockings Mary noticed that he had climbed between the sheets.

'You'd no need to get between the sheets,' she said a little sourly, but Jock did not listen to her. He still looked half stunned, as if he were trying to remember something.

'What's the time?'

'It's twenty-five to eight. I'm off to supper in another five minutes.'

'Aye. Good for you.' He walked over to the radiator by the curtained window, and picking up the towel there he wiped his neck with it. Then he shivered. The room was very cold and untidy, and nobody likes waking when it is dark.

'That's bloody strange, Mary. I was having some sort of dream.'

'It sounded more like a nightmare.'

'A-huh,' he said gently: he wanted to talk. 'That's what's so strange. Christ, I've been sweating.' He chucked the towel over the back of a chair and ran his fingers through his hair. His eyes were much brighter than usual: they did not look flat any more. 'I'm thinking it wasn't so bad. The dream wasn't so bad. No.'

'Well, you were fairly yelling for me. Here's your kilt. I was thinking of waking you up, anyway, when you started to cry.'

'I wasn't crying.'

'Then it was something very near it.'

'I'd no call to cry, lass. The whole Battalion was on the move.'

But Mary was too busy to listen to dreams.

'Here; take your kilt. I'll be through next door.'

She turned away, but as Jock sat down on the bed again he wanted her to stay.

'Mary, Mary, bide,' he said and she hesitated. 'It was a good dream. I was telling you.'

'Och, for heaven's sake, Jock.'

He gave a little smile. 'I was only wanting to tell you.'

'All right; all right. I'm glad it was a good dream. But it's time you were awake, and out of here.'

'That's the way of it?'

'Och.'

'Hi, Mary. What's the time?'

'I told you.'

'Did you?'

'It's after half-past seven.'

'Ach, to hell. I'm too late for the Mess.'

'Then you'd better go home.' She was standing holding on to the door, half in the room and half out. Jock was as anxious as a child that she should stay.

'I told Morag I'd be out.'

'She'll give you a boiled egg, I'm sure.'

'A-huh.' He smiled and bent down stiffly to collect his shoes. 'I'm no much good at amusing us, so it seems.'

'So it seems.'

Then Jock returned to the dream. 'I can't just mind what the hell it was all about. But it wasn't a nightmare: not really. It's cold, Mary. Is it snowing?'

She knocked her knuckles against the door with impatience.

'How should I know? I haven't left the flat.'

'You would have been as well in bed beside me then.'

Again she was about to leave.

'Mary?'

'I've got company,' she said and Jock looked up from his laces.

'Who the hell?'

'It's all right: it's a friend of yours. Never mind about the bed: I'll make it later.'

Jock was not very grateful. 'If you make it at all,' he said.

Charlie Scott was lying on the sofa with his head tipped back on the arm, and he did not move when Jock came into the room. When Charlie sensed danger all that happened was that his movements were a little slower, and his speeches even shorter. He was known for that. There was a live newsreel taken of his company going into an attack during the Italian campaign and Charlie had been something of a star in it. As the smoke thickened and his men deployed along the line of tanks, a runner came up with some message. There is a wonderful picture of Charlie taken on the spot, and you see it repeated from time to time when they show old shots of battle. The runner has a long message which you do not hear, and Charlie listens to him. He nods, and brushes his big moustache: he does not look flurried or afraid. You hear his voice, with the tanks behind.

'Tell Mr McLaren from me,' he says, 'that he must bloody well bide his time.' The message, though never understood or explained, served as a catch phrase in the Battalion for some time after that. And it was the same calm, dumb expression that confronted Jock when he came into the room.

But Jock could not disguise his astonishment.

'Charlie Scott. What the hell are you doing here?'

Then he looked at Mary's back. She was bending over a table at the far end of the room, pouring out some drinks, and it was all suddenly plain.

'Bit worried about you. Thought you might have tottered along here, old boy.'

Jock looked at him hard, looked at Mary, and looked back at him again. He blinked; then he smiled.

'Aye. Old boy, old boy. And you're a bloody liar, Charlie Scott. But you're a bloody bad liar. I'll give you that.'

'No, Jock lad, I . . .'

'Och, it's no business of mine,' Jock said irritably, turning away, and now Mary put a tumbler in his hand. 'I was just surprised.'

As casually as she could, Mary said, 'Don't worry, Charlie; Jock always judges others by himself.' But Jock shook his head. She was as unconvincing as Charlie. He chuckled as he said, 'And I'm always right.'

'Here's to us,' Mary said; then she put her glass down on the bookshelf and disappeared into the bedroom.

Charlie sat up and he raised his glass with a flippant little jerk.

'Astonishing good luck.'

'Aye,' Jock said, and he took a gulp. When he noticed it was brandy he was drinking he made a sour face. 'I suppose the whisky's done. Was it your bottle, Charlie?'

'Lord, no.'

'I'll repay you, sometime.'

Charlie sat silently and Jock walked up and down the room for a moment or two, touching things. Then he glanced at the door, and stepped back to Charlie. He bent forward and spoke in a low voice.

'Charlie; you're a bloody idiot, man. It's time you got out and got yourself married. You can't go on like this all your life.'

It was just like that newsreel. Charlie's face was without expression. At last he said slowly, 'You must have had the hell of a dream,' and he took a sip of brandy, but he did not much like the taste of brandy, either.

Jock looked at him earnestly then he straightened his back again, and he said, 'Aye; the hell of a dream.' He walked over to the chair in the corner and picked up his bonnet.

Charlie said, 'Sorry about all this.'

'A-huh.' Jock had not meant to say any more on the subject, but now he nodded to the bedroom door. 'Anyway the bed's warm for you.'

'Nothing's warm these days, Jock: nothing except the bathwater.'

'Aye, aye.'

It was only after he had closed the flat door behind him that Jock remembered Charlie's confession on the night the Colonel had arrived. He had said it was fresh water. But Jock did not feel very much like smiling. He was worried: worried first because it had been the sort of dream that leaves a man worried: worried because he should never have gone round to see her; worried because he had said what he had said to Charlie; and finally, but most immediately of all, worried because he should have said a lot more to Charlie. When Charlie had said that about the bathwater he should have had an answer, or thrown a drink in his face. The thought of the bath and the bathroom annoyed him particularly. It was not that he was particularly in need of Mary, or any other woman. He supposed it was just something he had missed. Presumably, amusing men did it in the bath.

He was just about to wander down the stairs when Mary appeared on the landing beside him.

'Jock.'

He was surprised to see her, and she smiled kindly. She quickly closed the door behind her and she touched his wrist.

'Jock, you're all right?'

He stared at her slowly: at her eyes, and the set of the eyes, and at her hair. She smiled anxiously.

'I shouldn't have been cross like that.'

He cocked his head on one side.

'I'm all right, lassie. Dinny fash yourself.'

'I'm glad.' She was almost like a mother, saying goodbye to a schoolboy son. She did not seem to know quite what to say, but she was anxious to say something. 'It's fine seeing you again.'

Jock smiled now and shook his head. 'Will I call back?'

'Of course. I'm always pleased to see you,' she said looking away, and Jock began to chuckle.

'Away you go back to Charlie. Charlie's a bloody stoat.'

'Och, Jock . . .' There was his coarseness again.

'Aye, aye.' He touched her hand and started to walk downstairs.

Charlie did not move from his place on the sofa when she returned to the room, and poured herself a drink. At last he said with a silly smile, 'Touching farewell?' and she gave him a look.

'I don't know what's the matter with you all. It used to be amusing, in the old days.' She shrugged. 'Och to hell.'

'Jock's certainly changed,' he said at last, and she stopped and tapped her nails against the empty glass in her hand. She opened her eyes very wide, as if she were daydreaming.

'And what's that supposed to mean?'

Charlie swung his legs off the sofa, put his glass on the floor.

'I reckon he's heading for some sort of crack-up.'

'Is he drinking an awful lot?'

'That's nothing new.'

She was dreaming again.

'He was in a funny state today, no mistake. He came in here like an eighteen-year-old. Then he just faded away.'

'Oh yep?'

She smiled warmly, and moved. 'Jock's a great man.'

Charlie twitched his moustache.

'Let's not go on about it,' he said rather quietly, 'old girl.'

She looked at him and she knew what she should say. She could have touched him, or joked him. She could have said, 'He hasn't your moustache' or 'I didn't know you cared.' She could have said, 'For heaven's sake.' There were lots of formulae which would have fitted, but she somehow did not feel inclined to apply them. So they just left it at that.

ELEVEN

THE WEATHER HAD changed for the worst. The snow lay two or three inches deep on the causeways and in the wynds, and it was still falling. But there was nothing sleety about it now: each flake was a feather and the flakes fell thickly, with a silent perseverance. Above the yellow street lamps it was pitch dark, and people abroad that night wondered what would happen were it never to cease to snow. No footsteps rang on the pavements, and even voices were muffled and lost in a white felt world that was lonely and eerie. Echoes were suffocated by the same snow that falls each year and that fell so long ago, when the first Jacobites, routed, savage and afraid, retreated, burning the villages as they came. The women then – their lips moving and their voices lost – the women and the children escaped from their houses into this same white winter, and waited, moaning. Snow in those parts is altogether different from the Christmas-card showers in the South. It is more serious and more sinister. Snow once meant suffering and poverty, and even starvation: it brought sorrow, not Christmas. The conditions have changed, the storm is no longer a danger; but the memory of something that was experienced generations before lingers like a superstition. Snow comes not as a friend.

And of all men Jock was the most superstitious. A flake or two fell on his eyebrows so that he pulled his bonnet over his eyes and turned up the collar of his coat. He did not wear one of the short greatcoats that fashionable field officers wear: he wore the regulation officer's greatcoat.

It was long and the two rows of heavy brass buttons ran parallel up to the waist, then flung apart from each other, wider and wider, so that the top buttons were shoulder breadth and the lapels folded across the chest.

He walked down Seaton Street, across the corner of the park to the footbridge. Its surface is cobbled and as it is steeply humped he found it difficult to walk there without slipping. But at the crest he stopped in one of the bays in the stone walls and leant over to look at the black water swirling beneath. By the light of a single lamp he could see where the snow was lying on a foot or two of ice that curved in from the bank of the stream. And although there was nothing heroic about Jock's face, the figure standing there in the long greatcoat had a splendour. The same figure had moved from platoon to platoon when the snow was falling on a flatter, duller land: in every war, back and back, in every siege and trouble that same figure existed and exists: the anonymous commander in the long coat moving through the night, alone. He is the guard.

Anxious, because it was a time for anxiety, he walked on towards his home, to see Morag. He always felt a little guilty when he returned from visiting Mary, but when he found the house empty, he stopped still in the hall, suddenly convinced that something was wrong. He reached out a hand and touched the coat-stand, then took a pace forward to switch on the lights.

'Morag! Morag! Morag!'

He glanced behind him, as always when afraid, and seeing the door ajar, closed it with a brave bang. Then he went swiftly to the kitchen, and finding it neat and orderly, tidy and cleaned, with a little note propped up on a cup on the bare table, his shoulders dropped with relief, and he opened his coat with a smile of shame. The note read:

Father,
   Gone out with Jenny. Back by eleven.

                                                      Morag.

It was written in a sane and slanting script, and was firmly underlined. Jenny was a neighbour, and a friend of Morag's. Nothing could be more secure. Jock looked about the kitchen, and the larder. He looked in a tin and ate a biscuit, then he knew he could not bring himself to make some supper, so he buttoned his coat again, shoved his hands deep into his pockets and retraced his steps down the wynd over the bridge and back into the town. He decided to call into a small hotel which had long ago been one of his haunts but which he had not visited for a full year. In the hall he was about to sign the book on the table as a *bona fide* traveller – between London and Thurso – when the proprietor appeared, ferret-like and inquisitive.

'Eh, Colonel Sinclair?'

Jock had never liked the man.

'Eh, you're travelling are you, Colonel?'

'I am.'

The proprietor pushed his face into the book. 'Eh, is this right?'

'Aye, it's right.'

'You've come fr' London?'

'No,' Jock said solemnly. 'From Thurso.'

'Dear me, Colonel . . . ,' the proprietor began.

'It says so there doesn't it, for Christ's sake?'

'I'm only doing my duty, Colonel Sinclair.'

The man fidgeted defensively. He was nervous of Jock. 'It's no right you should come in if you're no a *bona fide.*'

Jock spluttered. He had always thought it a stupid law and he had no intention of taking it seriously.

'For Christ's sake, all the law says is that we've got to sign the book. That's all you've got to carp about. All right?'

'Colonel, it's important that . . .'

'Well I've signed the bloody thing. O.K. ?'

'There's still a question.'

'There's no question. I've signed it, haven't I?'

'Aye, you have that, Colonel.'

'Well for Christ's sake get out of my way.'

Jock clenched and unclenched his fists as he pushed open the inner door, with his shoulder.

The pub was patronised almost exclusively by the more senior members of the band. No piper would dare to go to the private bar until he was invited there, and after that first invitation he would hardly ever go to any other pub. Not that there was anything special in the way of entertainment. An upright piano was as much as it boasted. But business had been good and since Jock had last called the room had been redecorated, in brown and cream, and it had been filled with new furniture in the shape of pink and green wickerwork chairs and round glass-covered tables. The proprietor had bought these at the sale of a seaside hotel the other side of Portobello. But the bar itself had not changed: it still had the coloured glass screen protecting it from the open part of the house – the public bar, and the saloon. A sergeant was stooping to order two beers and whisky chasers and he grinned, rather embarrassed, in reply to Jock's nod.

Jock himself ordered a whisky from the waiter, and not just a wee one; but it was a whisky that was never to be drunk. As he started to unbutton his coat again he glanced round the room and observed that there were five or six pipers there, mostly non-commissioned officers, in their kilts and spats, their sporrans swung round on their hips, all prepared and all dressed up to get drunk. From the corner of his eye he was surprised to see that there was a dark girl with a pale face in the lounge: there were not often ladies present. Then perhaps almost instantaneously – but this realisation was characteristic of the movements that followed, in that it seemed to him a long time before he understood – he saw that the piper with the girl was Corporal Fraser. He also looked pale and he was rising to his feet, seemingly disturbed. A second glance lasted for a split second, but the picture was so firmly impressed on Jock's mind that it seemed ever afterwards to have lasted for minutes. Morag was sitting with her hands on the table: she was very tense, and pale and her fingertips were pressing on the glass. She put her hand out to hold Corporal Fraser back for she must have known then what was going to happen. Jock advanced on them. With anger, with that blind rage that is always born of fear, he drew back his right hand, and his fist was only half closed as if he were holding a big stick. Then with a back-handed downward blow he struck the Corporal, just as he was finding his voice to give an explanation. Morag's fingers went up to her lips, and she gave a whimper rather than a cry. The Corporal knocked against the table and upset the glasses. Everybody in the room stood up, uncertain whether to interfere or to hold back, and Jock's voice came clear: 'You bastard' – with the same short *a*, but no joke for Charlie this time, 'You bastard . . .'

He would have struck the Corporal again, this time with a closed fist, and Morag had already given out a warning cry, when a voice behind him called out sharply:

'Colonel Sinclair.'

It was Mr McLean, standing absolutely still, just inside the door. Jock turned and saw him, and came to his senses. With a sinking agony he saw what he had done and his jaw dropped, his face blank like a man awakened to the sound of guns. Suddenly all was noise around him. Chairs and tables were pushed about, the proprietor was there, somebody was looking at the Corporal's eye and Morag was in front of him whiter still, crying, 'I'm ashamed, I'm ashamed.'

He must have said something, protested, demanded; but it was the Pipe-Major who was in command and Morag went home to his house. When an officer strikes a ranker it is time for someone else to take command. The others paid up, moved out, gathered coats and chattels like citizens alarmed by war, and Jock found himself sitting in a chair with a stern-faced proprietor telling him to pull himself together and away out of here. The proprietor's face had a lot of lines on it and he looked like a lawyer's senior clerk; like that, or like a wolf.

'Away out o' here: I'm no having carryings on in this house. You must be out o' your senses. And still with your bonnet on.'

Jock nodded, and nodded, and the proprietor disappeared. He sat motionless for a few minutes, stunned by it all, appalled by what he had done, by what one blow had cost him, alone in a nightmare silence that was like the long high notes of a lament.

BOOK TWO

The Beating of Retreat

THE DAWN WAS like an afternoon; the day seemed to break with an immense regret. There were no bright streaks dramatic enough for an execution; but it was a prisoner's day, dull and without birds.

It was just freezing outside and the barracks was at its worst. The high wall closed out the real world like a frame surrounding an etching. A tint of brown in the sandstone was the only colour within the perimeter, apart from the white of the snow, and the grey: the grey of the slates where the snow had thawed a little and shifted in an untidy avalanche; the grey shoulders of the Officers' Mess at the end of the square; the grey figures scuttling about from block to block, the orderly corporals, the pickets dismissing, the bugler in search of breakfast, and the detention squads sweeping away the first paths through the sticky snow.

And in the middle of it all was another grey form, apparently in no hurry, walking clumsily, his head and shoulders wagging from side to side, like a great bear in a ring. Jock had not been to bed at all, and now he felt cold and sick. His feet were wet, every limb was dead-weight, every joint stiff, and his chin rested on his chest. Only once or twice did he look up. He stared blankly at the buildings and the figures moving about as the day began, he observed the lights going on in the barrack rooms, heard the echoes of the first complaints. He turned all the way round to look at every building, at the chimneys, and at the arc of sky. Two or three times he had hesitated and slightly changed his direction; he left a track of his indecision behind him in the snow. Then he lifted his head and marched towards the stucco villas of the Married Quarters (Warrant Officers and non-commissioned ranks). These were hidden behind the Officers' Mess in the northernmost part of the area, and every house was dismally identical.

Jock expected Morag to come into the cramped little room. He was sitting like a bundle in a greatcoat, heaped into a modern armchair. Mrs McLean's parlour was very spick-and-span with its tiled fireplace, piano, antimacassars, calendars, and obstacles galore. If the furniture was displaced by six inches in any direction, there was no thoroughfare from the window to the fire or to the door. Jock stood up awkwardly when he heard the approaching footsteps, and the Pipe-Major nodded to him.

'I'd thought she would come down, but she's very determined.'

'Did you tell her it was me?'

'Yes, sir.'

'Did you tell her the rest? What I said you'd to say?'

'Aye. Mrs McLean and I have both had a word with her.'

'And what did she say?'

'She said she was tired.' He gave a gesture of sympathy. 'The lassie's worn out: that's all it is.'

Slowly, slowly Jock picked his way through the furniture to the little space in the bow of the window. He was careful that the borders of his coat should not sweep away any ashtray or ornaments and he still had hold of the cloth when he replied cautiously, 'But I said I apologised.' His hands came away from his coat. The light shone on the upturned palms. 'I said I was sorry. Does the lassie think it was easy for me? Does she suppose it doesn't cost me anything to say that? What more could I say?'

Mr McLean shook his head. He was at a loss, and he was afraid of Jock; afraid that Jock might fail.

Outside it had already begun to thaw. Some snow had slipped off the roof and there were a few drops of water falling from the rone pipe outside the window. There was some moisture on the window itself: just enough to tempt Jock to draw a double cross with his finger and rub it out again with the side of his fist. He left his fist resting on the pane and stared and stared at the greyness outside.

Mr McLean shifted uneasily and ran his fingers up and down the leather strap of his sporran. He smiled.

'Och, Colonel Sinclair, you know what the young girls are. You know what the daughters are like: she'll come away. She's upset. It's her dignity that's suffered. It is her pride.'

Jock moved at 'pride'.

'A-huh. It's her pride.' He seemed too tired to go further than that and he dug his hands in his coat pockets. Then he smiled, moving his hands in the pockets with a sort of shrug.

'It's like having your own words flung back in your face. I taught her to be proud, Pipe-Major. I taught her independence. Christ, I don't know why I bothered sending her to school. I taught her everything she knows.'

'She's a fine girl. But she's like yourself. That is all that is the matter. She will come away. She is still upset: and the lassie is tired.' His voice fell softly, like truth. But Jock's was grating:

'Ach, I should have known she would not come downstairs. She's ashamed of me. I shouldn't have come – and that's a fact.' He nodded and recovered himself. 'It's good of you to look after her.'

Again he stood still, and there was another silence. Then at last Mr McLean frowned and he said, 'I cannot understand it. I cannot follow.' He put his hand out in front of him as if he were groping for a solution. 'A man of your experience; to do such a thing. Such a stupid thing. You can't have considered.'

Jock stared at him, but did not reply.

'It was a terrible thing,' the Pipe-Major said and he sat down on the arm of the chair. Jock pulled a cigarette packet from his pocket. It was squashed, and there was only one cigarette in it. He rolled the cigarette round his fingers, reshaping it, and tapped the tobacco in at the ends. He lit it with a match from the other pocket, and he smoked, and sniffed. He seemed unwilling to go on or to go back; just as if he were idling; a soldier on a field, waiting to be taken away.

'What d'you think made me do it?'

The Pipe-Major hesitated, nodding here and there with his head.

'Man to man, Mr McLean. Forget the badge of rank. It can be forgotten now.'

The other protested. 'Oh no, sir, it's no as bad . . .'

Jock raised his hand.

'Man to man.' He sat back on the window seat, his coat ruffled about him, his knees apart. 'What are you thinking?'

'You didn't know about the young man?'

'No.'

The Pipe-Major raised his head again. 'She didn't tell you?'

'No.'

'Maybe it was a shock. Just that.'

'A-huh.' Jock looked out of the window, idle again.

And at last the Pipe-Major spoke out: 'I know he's a corporal, sir: but he's a good lad. He's no a fly-by-night, Ian Fraser. His father's a farmer up by Forres there.'

Jock moaned and he pushed his legs out in front of him. His heels clicked on the floor, and he shook his head backwards and forwards as he tried to find words.

'Did you think that? Och, man . . . For Christ's sake. I expected Mr Simpson to say that – not you. I expected every old school tie from here to St James's Palace to say that . . .' He shook his head again, clicked his fingers to correct himself. 'That's not right either. I expected half of them to say just "You know Jock – a ranker born, a ranker aye"; and the others I expected to say what you're saying. I mean the complex boys. The doctor with his fingers tangled in his hair. "Jock's self-made," he'll say, only he'll say it with a lot of whys and wherefores, and "should have thoughts" and "in effects" and all that caper.'

The Pipe-Major was a little mystified. He frowned as he tried to follow and Jock rambled on.

' "It's no wonder Jock was so upset when he saw his lassie with a corporal." Ach. To hell. I've never had time, Mr McLean, I've never had time to get as complicated as that. I leave all that to the county.' For the first time that morning a twinkle of humour lit his eyes. 'I've been most things, Mr McLean, but I've never been a Regimental Sergeant-Major.'

The Pipe-Major understood and smiled, then Jock went on.

'Nach, nach. To hell with that. Whatever they may like to believe I've never had any worries about class. Aye, and I'm sorry. It hurts me that you should think that of me.' Then he added, 'And me a piper, too.'

Jock's intelligence was never to be underestimated. Whether he thought out the moves, and played the game accordingly, or whether the outburst was spontaneous, the Pipe-Major did not stop to think. But his words could not have fallen on more sympathetic ears. Mr McLean, even so early in the morning, began to glow, and to nod. His eyes glistened with favour.

'Aye, sir, and I hold the same views as you do, though they being so near the politics it's no my job to express them. I'm glad of what you've said to me. If it had been the other way I couldn't have felt the same at all. We have no place for class here in a Highland Regiment. No place at all. But we're as well disciplined as the next, are we not?'

The Pipe-Major was throbbing with enthusiasm, and

Jock glanced at him slantwise. His eyes were moving quicker now. He was on his feet again, twisting and gesturing.

'Mr McLean, you've been with the Battalion a while.'

'Seventeen years, sir.'

'Aye. All through the war.'

'I didn't miss any of it.'

'You were hurt, once?'

'Aye. On the great day. I was playing then. I was piping when you took over command.' He allowed himself a moment of pride. 'And I still played when they took me back and bound up my leg.'

'Aye, I remember.' Jock paused and they both remembered the day. Then Jock spoke again. 'They were the days of my glory, Mr McLean. Nobody can deny me that. They were the days of my glory,' he said with wily tragedy.

'Nobody would ever want to deny you those days.' Mr McLean clenched his jaw with the sort of vigour that usually takes whisky. He was not usually boisterous in his loyalty, but this was an exceptional moment. 'Not any piper anyway. I'll see to that.'

'Even if I strike him?' Jock looked up suddenly, his eyes pale.

Mr McLean was about to answer warmly again. But he hesitated when he saw where the conversation had led him, and he was ashamed that he could not answer straight. He let his head drop and put two fists on his knees.

'Colonel Sinclair. Colonel Sinclair.'

Jock gave a weary smile. 'Och, never mind.' He rose to his feet, preparing to leave, and Mr McLean talked fast and anxiously.

'It's not an important thing. It will come out that it's not an important thing. It is a pity; no more. Sir, if it were only Corporal Fraser and myself there'd be no need . . . but you must see. There were others there. There was the landlord and the other pipers. It is not possible to ignore it. It would not be right for me. I cannot forget it. But it will soon blow away.'

Jock shook his head.

'It'll go to court martial.'

'The Colonel could deal with it.'

'The Colonel will put it to Brigade. It will go to court martial.'

The Pipe-Major sighed. He knew very well that was the truth. He smiled sadly.

'I wish I had a television set. I've never wished it before. But if I had a television set perhaps I would not have gone out at all.' He grew serious again. 'At the court martial they will see that it is not important. Then it will be forgotten.'

Jock shook his head again.

'You know very well that if it goes as far as court martial, whatever the result, it is the end for me.'

'No, no. It'll be forgotten. They wouldn't demote you on that.'

Jock looked at him steadily.

'H.Q. Company Commander until they axe me. For Christ's sake.'

Mr McLean fidgeted, and Jock went on, heatedly this time. 'Man, the Battalion belongs to me; without it, there's nothing else for me. D'you know that?'

'I know that.'

'If it goes to court martial, it will be the finish.'

The Pipe-Major grew agitated: 'Colonel Sinclair. You are making it hard for me. It is my duty. No one could be more sorry than myself. Colonel Sinclair, I tell you, I'd walk the plank for you.'

'Would you?' He paused, then he moved away and he said, 'Ach!'

He was suddenly unreasonably angry with the man. Mr McLean seemed to him too resilient to be human, a man sitting on his haunches, riding every punch. His eyes blazed up, he moved, suddenly, pushing his way through the furniture.

'And tell me this; if there's war tomorrow, who's leading the Battalion? Eh?'

The Pipe-Major was hurt. He remained silent, and Jock passed him, saying, 'Och, to hell with this.'

But in the hall as he reached for his bonnet, he practically stumbled into Morag, who had come downstairs, thinking he was gone. She drew back and she saw his hair tousled, the creases in his coat, the soaking wet shoes and stockings. These were things Morag had grown used to observing. Even though she was afraid to meet him, and determined to draw stiffly away from him, she could not hold back.

'Father, for heaven's sake . . .'

There was a note of sympathy in the voice, and such a note, however slight, is impossible to miss. Jock could not have failed to hear it. But he looked at her with pale, flat eyes as if he were defending himself: as if she had spoken in another tongue.

'Ach!' It was a noise, not a word, and Morag drew her elbows into her sides.

'Father, you're soaked through.'

He shook and turned away. In a rough voice, with a drunkard's brutality, he said, 'Och, you can keep all that stuff. You wrote me a lie and you're too bloody late now,' and before she moved, he hurled himself out of the front door, slamming it hard behind him. He walked heels down, determinedly through the snow, with obstinacy in every stride. After only a moment he was miserable but he knew he could not return to the house; his obstinacy prevented that.

TWO

AN HOUR LATER Jimmy Cairns saw Jock, and by then a great deal had happened.

When Jimmy arrived at Battalion H.Q. that Monday morning there was already a buzz in the air. A filing clerk was leaving the Colonel's room, and Mr Simpson had just re-entered. The Colonel himself was in a fever of excitement. His hands were on his hips, his eyes were bright and he was lighter than ever, lighter than thistledown, perpetually on tiptoe. He was like a politician flitting house, sending people here and there, talking on the telephone, jotting down notes on a pad. Nobody knew exactly what was happening. Everybody made a guess. All this Jimmy saw from his own office as his assistant dashed in and out, but it was a little while before he picked up the first scents of the story. The key seemed to lie in the doctor's visit. Barrow and he had spent half an hour closeted together and it was known now that the doctor had been called across to the Band Block because a piper had been hurt. From one of the sergeants in the office, from a brief talk with Mr Riddick, and from the hush-hush expression on Simpson's face, Jimmy managed to piece the story together. Then he was called in himself. Barrow made an effort to look grave, but he could not stand still. He bounced about the room as he said how serious and awkward was the situation.

'I have reason to believe – no evidence, you understand, Jimmy, but reason to believe that a corporal was struck by an officer in a bar last night.'

Jimmy nodded, and Barrow continued.

'Well, well,' he clipped his words, in this mood. 'Of course we must take steps.'

'Sir. Have you rung the proprietor?'

Barrow smiled. 'No evidence there. The men shouldn't have been given drinks anyway. He won't make any statement. If the newspapers got hold of the story he'd lose his seven-day licence. He might lose his licence altogether. No . . . no. The evidence lies within the barracks. There were other people there. We could get some sort of a story but it's a question of whether we want to go so far.'

Barrow bounced over the other side of the room and flapped a piece of paper that was pinned on a board there.

'Whether we want to go on,' he said again, with a little drama. 'It would probably be a court martial, you know.' He shook his head. 'That sort of thing doesn't do the Battalion's name any good.'

'It does its name more harm if the story leaks out and we do nothing about it.'

'You think so?' Barrow opened his eyes wide: he looked curiously innocent. But Jimmy did not have a doubt.

'Of course.'

Barrow nodded, and he steadied a little.

'It's very difficult.'

'So,' Jimmy often said when he did not quite understand.

'The personalities in the case complicate things. I've called for Charlie Scott. We'll talk it over, the three of us.'

'So.'

Almost in passing Barrow said, 'Jock's involved,' and at last it all made sense to Jimmy. He understood the buzz now, and the Colonel's fidgeting. The game had fallen into his hands. As the situation dawned on Jimmy he began to look sad. He did not enjoy the look in Barrow's eye: he did not quite believe in the anxious expression. He almost felt that Barrow was cheating. But Jimmy could not have explained these things even to himself. He just had a feeling that way, but his distaste showed clearly in his expression. Meantime Barrow rested on his heels.

'A very unpleasant business. And, as you can appreciate, awkward. My motives are bound to be suspected. Then that's neither here nor there.' He was anxious to talk: the words came fast. 'Clearly I can't be expected to take a purely objective view of the thing. That's why I've asked Scott to come along. It's all a great pity.'

'Jock never struck a corporal,' Jimmy said slowly.

'Well, yes . . . I'm afraid he did. There's really not much question about it.' He went into a few details. The doctor had picked up a great deal of information. He knew Morag was staying over in the Married Quarters.

'All that proves nothing. It's no business of the doctor's either,' Jimmy said. 'He's always talking.'

'Jimmy, five minutes ago I received a request from Mr McLean that I should see him as soon as possible.' He handed over a piece of paper on which the formal request was made. *I remain, Sir, your obedient servant.*

'So,' Jimmy said again, and he was prepared to wait until Charlie came round. But he did not get the chance of seeing Charlie before they saw the Colonel. Barrow was too good a tactician. He kept Jimmy with him until Charlie arrived. He invented one reason after another to keep him in the office. Barrow's mind seemed to be working five times faster than ever before. He was planning fast: interviews ahead.

And when Charlie came things did not go at all as Jimmy had expected. There was no long discussion. All the pros and the cons were not trundled out. Indeed the preliminaries to the interview were as long as the main discussion itself. Barrow was at his most tortuous. He had a habit of discussing general political news, perhaps because he always knew more of current affairs than any of his colleagues. For the most part the officers lived body and soul within the limits of the high wall; Macmillan could gossip a little on social items, but even he was inclined to concentrate on county news. Some of the other more earnest officers knew something of the disturbances in other parts of the globe, Malaya, Kenya or Korea, because they had friends there, but by and large they were innocent of world, and even of national, affairs. Something had evidently been happening in the United States: it had to do with Communism. There was some scandal about a trial on television. Barrow made reference to it, described it, and condemned it. That took a moment or two and gave time for Charlie to sit back in his chair and stretch out his long legs. He laid his crook beside them. Charlie always carried his crook, rather than the regulation ash walking-stick.

Jimmy sat on the edge of his chair, impatient of the preliminaries, and he looked hard at Charlie while Barrow outlined the reason for their meeting. To give him his due he put the matter very fairly. He did not ask for a decision until he had mentioned Jock's name. He could almost certainly have won a tactical point by asking for Charlie's decision on the basis of the accused being an anonymous officer. But he did not try any tricks, and he added, too, that all he wanted now was Charlie's opinion. The decision must rest with him, and the only question at this stage was whether a formal enquiry should be conducted. Depending on the results of this independent enquiry a report would or would not go up to Brigade, putting the question of court martial. It was a very fair statement, and Barrow was at his best, a barrister in command of his brief. He seemed much concerned: seemed very sincere. He did not add an unnecessary word.

Charlie stroked his moustache, then he pouted.

'Well there's no doubt about it, is there?'

'Please?' The lines about Barrow's eyes grew deeper in his anxiety.

Charlie gave a shrug. 'Well, of course you've got to make an enquiry. We can't have chaps poking corporals in the eye, after all.'

Jimmy's fingers came together: he pitched forward in the low chair. He was so upset by Charlie's reaction that it took him a moment or two to find words to express himself, even inadequately. He stuttered and made a false start. Then he came back again.

'Charlie . . . of course we know that, but Jock . . . hell, it's different. Jock's always had his own methods.' He stopped, and twisted. 'Och. He must have had reason. If the Corporal was to put in a complaint it might be different, but you know what they are with regard to Jock up at Brigade. A thing like this would kill him. It's dynamite. Surely the way to do it is for the Colonel here to have a word with him . . .' Jimmy looked from one to the other. Barrow's face was a blank. He stared hard at Charlie who was staring at his toes. Barrow said nothing; he just stared at Charlie with a strange amazement. At last Charlie lifted heavy eyelids and rested his baleful eyes on Jimmy.

' 'Fraid I can't agree, old man,' he said, and Jimmy felt cold.

'But, Charlie . . .'

He was interrupted there. Charlie clambered to his feet, addressing Barrow. ' 'Course, it's your decision.'

'Of course,' Barrow nodded, recovering himself.

'It won't make you very popular, I'm afraid.'

Barrow gave a stiff nod.

'That's the fate of a c.o.,' he said bravely, and Charlie nodded. Jimmy was still groping about him, hopelessly, but the interview was already over.

'Not nice at all,' Charlie said, as he knocked along. He explained to Jimmy, at the door, that he had to trundle: there was some sort of kit inspection on that morning. But Jimmy would not let him go. He spoke almost in a whisper, and he made sure the door was closed behind him.

'Charlie, we can't let it go like this.'

Charlie shrugged.

'Charlie, we can't.'

'Old chum: we've been boiling up to this for some time. It isn't nice, but it's one of those things. Old Jock's on the rocky side. I wouldn't have been surprised if he'd brained the chap.'

'But it'll finish Jock: it'll fix him once and for all.'

'That is a pity.' Charlie drew himself up, and Jimmy looked down at his desk. Just before he went, Charlie said, 'Don't take it too hard, chum. I mean we've got to think of the Battalion sometimes. Have you ever seen such a shambles? That cocktail party, eh?'

'That was half Barrow's fault.'

Charlie smiled.

'That's quite another problem. But it's Jock who led us into this state when all's said and done. Did you see how he behaved over that dancing class? What? The old boy's a warrior and all that but, old chum, it's about time we had a colonel again, isn't it? And just a fragment of discipline. How can you look after the Rattrays when you've Jock at the top?'

'D'you think that? D'you really think that?'

'Yep. 'Fraid I do.'

Jimmy tapped his fingers on the desk. 'I've sometimes thought it,' he admitted, unwillingly.

'There you are. It's rough I suppose. And really I don't want to be involved. Couldn't want to less. But maybe some day someone'll put his nose over the barrack wall and really see what goes on. Then what? Eh? It's not going to be nice at all.'

Jimmy wavered. 'Maybe you're right there. But Jock – well he's different.'

'Don't let it give you ulcers, Jimmy. They'll do the same to you and me one day. I must be rolling. Bloody kit inspection. 'Bye.'

Simpson, now one move behind events, was anxious to talk things over with Jimmy but he got no further information, and at last he went on his way, leaving Jimmy pacing up and down his little office, biting his lip and scratching his hair.

A few moments later his train of thought was disturbed by noises in the lobby outside, and he recognised Jock's voice among them. He went out to discover Jock talking to Simpson and Mr Riddick.

Jock was still looking very crumpled, and if he had not been certain before, Jimmy was then certain of the truth of the story. It was written in every crease in Jock's clothes, in the hang of his coat: it was written straight across his face. Jimmy was shocked by the sight of him.

Jock nodded good-morning to him.

'Jimmy, what the hell's going on here?'

But Jimmy had still not had time to recover himself. Mr Riddick in twenty years of loud shouting had never lost his voice, and always with his seniors he had a glibness.

'Colonel Sinclair, sir, suggests the Commanding Officer ordered him here for interview this morning.'

Jock would never ordinarily have let Mr Riddick speak for him. He was the one man in the Battalion who could send him chasing: but he now made no complaint. He merely nodded and said, 'The other night after the cock-tails.'

Mr Simpson, in his fortnight as Assistant Adjutant, had developed the manner of an aide-de-camp. Everything was difficult if it concerned Barrow. Barrow was always busy.

'The Colonel didn't mention it this morning. Perhaps he intended to see Colonel Sinclair later.'

Jimmy looked at him as if he were very far away, then he looked hard at Mr Riddick.

'I'll cope with this.' They moved, to go their separate ways. Jimmy looked at Jock and looked away again. 'There must have been some muck-up. Hang on a minute, Jock, if you will. I'll go and see him.' He touched Jock on the elbow as he passed him. Jock nodded gratefully, like a patient at a clinic, and he wandered into Jimmy's office and played with the inkpot on his desk while the other went next door to tackle Barrow. The sight of Jock fumbling with the inkpot touched Jimmy. He stared back at him through the doorway and he was suddenly ashamed and angry, both at once.

When Jimmy reminded him of the interview, Barrow rose from his seat and he said secretively:

'Close the door Jimmy; close the door.' And Jimmy wearily obeyed. 'Look, I'd forgotten this one. It's rather awkward. I don't want to see him now. D'you think he knows?'

Jimmy did not help. He looked hostile, and Barrow continued, 'D'you suppose he's gathered we're on to something?'

'I haven't the foggiest idea.'

Barrow nodded. He was upset by the idea of the interview, and he was fidgeting again, but this time not with impatience. He did not know which way to turn. He snatched at the air.

'I say, perhaps it might be an idea if you were to tell him that this business had come out, and it's clearly better that we didn't have a talk now. It wouldn't help. You needn't tell him I consulted Charlie and you. But put him in the picture.'

Jimmy was amazed. He took a step forward, and his head was held slightly to one side.

'Me, tell him, Colonel? *Me?*'

Barrow panicked a little. He fluttered. He looked back at Jimmy with eyes that had grown darker as his face grew pale. He gave a nervous little smile.

'I thought it might be more tactful.'

'Tactful!'

Another horrid little smile: Barrow cleared his throat.

'You don't think that's a good idea?'

'Colonel, for God's sake.'

'No. No, perhaps you're right. Yes, of course. It was only a passing idea. Stupid of me. It would place you in an awkward position. I tell you what. Later. Tell him I'll see him later.'

'What time?'

'Well, this afternoon.'

'He'll want a time.'

'Five-thirty? Rather late perhaps, but . . .'

'Five-thirty.' Jimmy turned, but Barrow spoke again before he opened the door.

'Jimmy, I say. I was rather surprised by Scott's reaction. What?'

'Yes, sir.'

'He's right, of course. Hadn't expected him to take such an objective view. Jimmy, we must take an objective view. That's essential. We can't take any side other than the Battalion's side. You see that?'

'I understand that.'

'I can assure you that's what guides me. That's true. The Battalion's side.'

'Yes, sir.'

Barrow's shoulders dropped. 'I say, I was thinking of nipping down to the Mess in ten minutes: get a cup of coffee. It's been quite a morning.'

Jimmy looked him straight in the eye, and without mercy. Barrow went on:

'Care to come?'

'I've a lot on hand, sir.'

'Oh.' Barrow moved nervously back to his desk. 'Of course. Righto. I'll only be gone fifteen minutes.'

'Colonel.'

A SOLDIER DOES not most need a brain to think with, nor yet an arm to strike with; he needs teeth to hang on with, and Jock had those teeth. He went all the way back home, that same Monday morning, and he washed and shaved. He brushed his hair, he put on his best tunic, pulling it tight under his belt so it had no creases, he stared at himself in his mirror, saw to it that his teeth were clean and he said 'Resilience, boys, resilience.' He put clean stockings on, and adjusted the bright red flashes on his garters. He dusted his brogues and polished the badge in his bonnet and said, 'Aye, and we're dead but we won't lie down, come away then, come away.' He polished the buttons on his coat and turned the collar neatly down, he pulled his bonnet over his eye, then with a swagger and a bright dash he swung down to the bridge, across the park, back to barracks.

He must have understood that they all knew as soon as he put his big nose through the door of the ante-room soon after one o'clock. He twitched his nostrils and his eye roved round the room. Officers were huddled over beers and pink gins. They glanced up at him and mumbled 'good-morning' or nodded with studied normality. Barrow had gone into lunch, but most of them were there talking and smoking. Jock gave a little smile as he strode up the middle of the room to the big log fire. Turning his back to it, he lifted up the pleats of his kilt, to warm his bare bottom.

'A-huh,' he said, 'Dusty would you be so kind as to push that tit in the wall there, and we'll see if I can get myself a drink.'

When the waiter appeared with a tray in his hand, Jock shouted at him across the room.

'Good-morning, Corporal.'

'Morning, sir.'

Jock eyed him. 'You're feeling the heat, Corporal?'

The Corporal smiled uncertainly: the other officers were all watching now.

'It's cold, sir.'

'No wonder it's cold, lad. You're nude. Do up your collar button.'

'Sir.' The Corporal obeyed very quickly and Jock said:

'And you can bring me one hell of a whisky.'

'Sir.'

'Steady, steady; wait there, laddie. What are you drinking, Charlie?'

Charlie hesitated, 'Actually, thinking of lunch . . . you know . . .' he mumbled on.

'What are you drinking, eh? I'm asking something that's a question of fact.' Jock gave a little grin, and looked all round the room. 'Not just a rumour,' he said, and there was a little stir. 'What's in your hand?'

'Pink.'

'And one hell of a pink,' Jock gave the order.

'You, Jimmy?'

'Bottle of beer.'

Jock turned to the waiter again: 'And two bottles of beer in one can. C'mon, c'mon gents, make your orders. It's too cold a morning not to have something to drink . . . Well, well; and what's news today? Eh, is there no news?' His head on one side. 'Surely we've some bit of gossip, eh, MacKinnon?'

'It snowed,' MacKinnon said, rather frightened, and then he blushed. Jock gave a roar of laughter.

'Plus ten for observation, lad,' he said, but with a broad grin that would have made anything he said sound pleasant. It was as if the officers sitting there were tired members of some orchestra, and in the hands of the cleverest conductor. Slowly, with something less immediate than magnetism, more like a sort of suction, he was drawing life out of them. They all began to look up, and take notice. They stared at him as if it were the first time they had seen him; and perhaps more – as if it were the last time.

Jock had never looked so gallant since the days before the peace. He found his charm again that morning: his eyes twinkled, and his hands moved with an eloquence. Soon after, he was recalling the days when the Battalion had been taken back for rest, shortly before the end of the war. The officers had stayed for a while in a ridiculous Belgian country house which still had great oil paintings on the wall, but which was equipped with Naafi furniture. There they had stayed until they dispersed for leave. Most of them had gone as far as Brussels. Some had gone home. But Jock had stayed there all the time, and when they had returned in ones and twos, lonely and dejected, Jock had been there in front of the fire, warming his celebrated bottom. The memory was only vivid for one or two of them now: others were of an age to have known it but they had been with some other Battalion at the time, with the Second in the Far East, or on special duties, or they had been prisoners. But they were all interested to hear Jock speak of it, because he never spoke much of the days of his glory. It would have been impossible for him to recall truthfully one week of the campaign without sounding now as if he were bragging, and something made him brag about other things. They had all heard about his piping and his boxing days, the days he had told the Sergeant-Major off, and so on and on. But this was the very first time some of them had heard him speak of the war, and he suddenly engulfed them with the same charm that buoyed them all up in the bad old days. Those that had been there remembered only too vividly, and Jimmy looked quite upset. He had been a platoon commander then, dressed up to be shot, and he came back from his aunt in Crieff, taking two nights on the journey. At three o'clock, burdened with kit and straps, he had shoved his way into the hall of this house in Belgium. There, on a red trolley with chrome wheels, two other subalterns were tobogganing down the corridor. They greeted him with the kind of sickeningly hearty welcome that athletes give you when you are wrapped up in your overcoat, and Jimmy did no more than nod and say as enthusiastically as he could that he had enjoyed his leave. He wandered over to the table in a spin of loneliness and there he found a letter from his sister which had been written to him before he went on leave. He knew about it; he knew what it said; he had seen her since: but the pitch of his loneliness was such that he put it in his pocket and gripped it hard as he went into the room which they called the ante-room, just for old times' sake. It was really the drawing-room.

Jock was sitting by the fire, eating a huge jam sandwich. He was alone in the room and he just gave a little flick of his head. He spoke quietly.

'Come away in, Jimmy lad, and I'll give you a jammy piece.' And he gave a great wide smile.

Jimmy suddenly could not stand it any more, as Jock recalled those days.

'Jock man, I've got to speak to you,' he interrupted, and the others looked round at him. Jock was in the middle of a description of one of the female cooks. His hands paused, and he looked up.

'What's that?'

Charlie frowned, but nothing could stop Jimmy now.

'Look, Jock . . . I've got to have a word with you.'

'A-huh. Well, what is it?'

'Not here,' Jimmy looked embarrassed.

'Is it shop?'

'Sort of. It's dead important, Jock.'

Jock looked slowly round the group; then he nodded

towards Charlie, and stroking his upper lip as if he wore a moustache, just as Charlie had done in that ridiculous news film, he said, ' "Then tell Mr McLaren from me, that he'll have to bide his time." '

Jock always laughed at his own jokes; but a catch phrase is irresistible. Jimmy was the only one who did not laugh. Even Charlie gave a funny, vain little twitch of his moustache.

'It's dead important, Jock,' Jimmy said again, but Jock shook his head: more than his head, his whole shoulders moved from side to side as if he had to roll to articulate.

'Jimmy, Jimmy lad: nothing's that important, nothing at all.'

Jimmy looked at the others. Charlie was leaning back, looking at his tumbler. Macmillan with a gesture of the long brown fingers said, 'It might be important; really quite.' Macmillan's nails were perfect.

'Christ knows what you boys think I am,' Jock said, smiling again; twinkling as he raised his glass to his lips. He held his glass between finger and thumb with the other fingers out in the air. 'Christ, you must think I'm deaf, dumb and blind.' He grinned. 'You're all bloody cheeldron. Now I was telling you about Lily . . .'

'Who's Lily?'

'Christ man, this cook I was going on about.'

'She was called Bella.'

'Dusty boy, you're losing grip of yourself. It was Lily.' Dusty shrugged. Jock very nearly insisted, then he too shrugged and he said, 'Well whatever she was called, she . . .' And away he went. There were more drinks, and everybody started talking louder. After a while even Jimmy seemed to have forgotten his frown in the flood of pleasant recollections. They were talking about the regimental orders then: the kit they used to walk about in – the jerkins, corduroys, peak caps, striped scarves. It would not have suited Douglas Jackson, so they had a laugh at his expense.

Jock was speaking louder, but he still seemed mellow. But when the swing door squeaked and Barrow walked in from the dining room, the conversation died away. Barrow looked up nervously and he seemed to be about to make one of his famous 'Good-night all' remarks but Jock saved him. His voice had none of the usual challenge. It was perfectly sincere.

'Come and join us, Colonel.'

'Thank you.' But the Colonel was not flexible enough, nor his ear true enough; so he mistook the tone. 'Thank you; I've had lunch.'

'Well, have a cognac.'

He looked at Jock, then from one face to another. He seemed to want to join them but suddenly he decided to leave. 'I've got to shoot this afternoon. I won't, if you don't mind.'

'A-huh,' Jock said, disappointed, and he turned back to the others. Barrow paused, his weight on one foot. Again he looked as if he were going to say something: then very suddenly he turned away and left the room. In the hall, just outside the door, he paused, trying to listen. Then with a frown of self-condemnation he moved away. He was not going shooting. That was another unnecessary lie. He seemed incapable of speaking the truth to Jock. He was almost like a son with a father too fierce: in order not to offend he told a half-truth, until the time came when he found it more natural to lie. It was perfectly obvious to him why he did this. Everything about Jock frightened him. His authority, his unpredictability, his bluntness. It was more than that. The very depth of his voice and the thickness of his forearm made Barrow afraid.

Jock never got into lunch at all, and that was a mistake. The others ate in ones and twos and returned to the anteroom to take their coffee with him, and he must have had more than half a bottle by then. But even Jock knew very well that he had drunk the charm away. He was much louder now, and bantering, and sarcastic. Every time he made a sarcastic remark he tried to withdraw it, laughing, shrugging, throwing his arms about and roaring, 'And away we go.'

When the telephone rang, MacKinnon, as Orderly Officer, went to the hall to answer it, and he returned to say that it was the exchange asking for the c.o. who was being called by Command at Edinburgh.

Jock insisted that he should answer it.

'Away we go then. Big Jock Sinclair'll have a word with the gentlemen in Edinburgh. For Christ's sake tuck your feet in or I'll fall on my neb.'

He pushed his way through chairs and tables, like a tank, and he opened the swing door by striking it with the palms of both hands at a level above his head.

His mood when he returned was one they all knew. As he addressed them, and they all kept very quiet, he fumbled with the coffee urn, the milk and the sugar. He rattled about the tray, looking for a spoon. He said nothing about the call for a moment, then he began:

'A-huh, Charlie. You're the lad for a crisis,' and Charlie's cheek muscle moved. He pushed his legs stiffly in front of him. Jock's head was turning and his eyes rolling as he brought them all into the act. 'Aye, aye. And you're the hell of a one for the women. Bloody good! Aye. I've always said it. The rest of us is just envious.'

'Jock, Jock, Jock.'

'Who's there? Eh?' Jock laughed at that. Silly little musical puns always amused him. 'You'll have a coffee, Major Scott, Scott, Scott.' He rushed forward. 'No, no, no, no: don't move. I'll get it for you. Aye. Sugar, is it? And a dash of angostura? D'you take cream in your coffee? Do you not? Yon's very sophisticated. Isn't it, Major Macmillan?'

'I'm sure I wouldn't know.'

Jock reproved him. 'Oh don't say that: if you don't know

then there's nobody as does know and we must have one or two to keep the tone up.'

It was all an agony to Jimmy Cairns. Meantime the subalterns were trying to hide themselves in their chairs, dreading the moment when their name should be called.

'Mr Simpson?'

'Yep?'

'Yep. Is it not sophisticated to take your coffee black?'

'Not specially, I shouldn't have thought.'

'Not specially he shouldn't have thought. Which means no, I think: but he's not just sure.' He ran on with hardly a pause. 'Yon was Command at Edinburgh on the 'phone. The c.o., I says, is away out flying a kite, but I'll take a message. The mannie was very anxious. A lot of look heres, and shouldn't-have-thoughts and all that caper. D'you think he takes his coffee black?'

Jock turned. He paused, and saw them all about him.

'Oh, my babies!' he said with a sudden indulgent smile. Then sadly he repeated it, 'Oh, my babies!'

They all sat quiet.

'It seems there's got to be a contingent from Campbell Barracks at this tattoo they have for the Festival, and they're having a meeting about it. When d'you think? Was it sugar you said, Major Scott?'

'Three lumps.'

'Oh, that's not sophisticated at all.'

Jimmy tried to interrupt here. 'It's time we got on with the work,' he said, moving; but Jock kept him in his place with a flat movement of his hand.

'Tonight. All the councillors and patrons and so forth are busy civilians you see: they can only manage tonight: they're sorry and that, so the mannie said. The mannie was a brigadier, so he said. And with the voice of a captain! Well, well, Charlie here's your coffee. Here it is. And now I'll cater for myself.'

'Has someone to go across to Edinburgh now?'

'A-huh. That's the way of it. An officer. Have we any volunteers?' Nobody moved. 'Good for you laddies: I've never liked volunteers . . . This coffee's awful unwilling. It comes in wee drips.' He looked tired again.

'Not just any officer. Field rank. And away out of here at four o'clock. Well I'd go myself but . . . well it mightn't be the best thing, if Jimmy's got to have a serious word with me, whatever that might be about. Two of you have got your wives to go home to, and Macmillan's got his Bentley motor car to keep him warm. It's an independent sort of person . . . mind you he'll probably get a good dinner.'

Charlie crashed his coffee on the table.

'All right, all right, all right. I take it this is an order.'

Jock feigned surprise. His eyebrows shot up. He dropped a teaspoon.

'That's very good of you, Major Scott.'

'Righto, let's get it straight. Four o'clock train. Will I be met?'

'In a bloody Daimler I'd say. I wouldn't be surprised if they had the red carpets down. Now, Charlie, you're sure you had no plans for this evening? I mean if there's anything . . .'

'Oh, for crying out loud.' Charlie looked extremely angry. Glancing at his watch, he stood up and adjusted the belt of his battledress so his kilt lay smoothly. Then he looked at Jock.

'You ought to go to bed.'

'Oh, I'm studying hard just now for this Staff College. Didn't you hear? I'm keen to be a brigadier. And with the manners of a corporal. Aye.'

'You can have my room. I'll be clear in five minutes.'

'You've plenty of time . . .'

Charlie paid no attention to him now and Jock just sat grinning and stirring his coffee. Charlie turned to the Orderly Officer, the only one wearing tunic and Sam Browne, and a very new Sam Browne at that.

'MacKinnon. Fix a jeep would you? Ten minutes.'

'Righto, sir.'

In spite of all the rules nobody had ever got used to calling MacKinnon by his Christian name.

When the others, except for Dusty Millar, who was sound asleep in the corner, had drifted away, Jimmy came across to Jock who was still stirring his cold coffee. He hesitated, and leaving the spoon in the cup, Jock looked up, and he laid a hand on Jimmy's arm.

'Dinny fash yoursel', laddie. I don't want to talk about it.'

'But, Jock, I ought to tell you the whole thing.'

'No, no. Let's leave it, laddie.' A look of real pain crossed his face and made him blink his eyes. 'There's nothing we can do. Away you go.'

A moment later, Jock laid down the coffee, undrunk, and he wandered out of the room, touching things as he went, with a sort of idleness.

He met Charlie on the upstairs landing. The wood in the corridor had newly been scrubbed and it smelt like a schoolroom at the beginning of term, part clean, part damp, part musty. Charlie was carrying a little canvas case, and he looked up at Jock. His eyes were large and resentful.

'Mm?'

'Look, laddie, I was joking really. If you've fixed to see Mary, I'll go mysel' or I'll get one of the others.'

'For Christ's sake.'

'Charlie, are you mad at me? Are you?' Jock was very serious and he was speaking quickly now.

'All's fair in love and war,' Charlie said with a crooked smile.

Jock's hands reached out. 'Man, there's no question of love. I don't care about Mary . . . It was a joke. You were mad at me.'

Charlie shrugged. 'You took such a bloody long time about it.'

'Aye, I was a bore. I was trying to be funny, mind. But it seems I'm no so amusing any more. Not any more. Just a wee bit boring.' He gave a little smile.

'It's not important,' Charlie said.

'Aye and it is. Mary was saying that the other day: saying I was a bore.'

'Chum, you're shagged out. Go sleep. You look all in.'

'No hard feelings, Charlie?'

Charlie was just about to go downstairs and he turned.

'Old boy, you're going to need that sleep.'

Jock understood. 'It's like that, is it?'

Charlie opened his mouth, then closed it again. ' 'Fraid so.'

'Och, it'll be all right in the end.'

'Good boy.' And as if he were frightened to say more he ran downstairs, like a much younger man. Jock watched him go, and he was thoughtful and he was sad. Then he snapped his fingers and marched along to the bedroom, where he lay down, covering himself with rough blankets. He gave a long sigh, with a waist to it, and clasping his hands behind his head, he closed his eyes.

FOUR

BARROW WENT TO Charlie's room obliquely. He was
determined to collect himself. First, when he heard voices
in the bathroom he walked as far as that door and paused,
listening. Then he opened it softly, and entered, sideways.
Simpson and Douglas Jackson were in there and Barrow
nodded, shyly. Jackson was in the shower, proudly watching the water trickle down his white body. Simpson, looking rather pink and exhausted was sitting across the bath,
watching the brown water swirl in. The room was warm
with steam. Simpson jumped up and said 'Hello, sir!' with a
friendly nod, which Barrow returned, then he continued to
mix the water in his bath. Jackson, unaware of the Colonel's
arrival was singing a marching song, loudly and flatly.

Barrow smiled uncertainly and walked a few steps into
the narrow room, his shoulder brushing the wall. He was
still wearing his kilt, but he had taken off his battledress top,
and put on a cardigan. He was wearing bedroom slippers,
and he pretended he had been asleep.

He smiled a little more firmly, as Simpson stood up and
pushed back the hair on his forehead.

'You chaps been playing squash or something?'

'Wish we had, sir. 'Fraid there's no squash court in
barracks.'

'No?' The Colonel looked concerned. 'I'd forgotten.
None nearby?'

Simpson shook his head. 'I haven't found one.'

'Pity. You're a bit of a hand at squash, aren't you,
Simpson? I seem to remember you won some cup.'

'Oh, I don't know.'

'Don't be modest. Never be too modest. If you're good at something, say so.'

Simpson looked at him curiously and Barrow halted. Jackson stopped singing and then suddenly Barrow started talking again. He had to talk loudly against the noise of the running water.

'Never any good at any ball game myself really, except golf. I used to play a round occasionally. I suppose it's a question of what you're brought up to. I never played much when I was young.'

Simpson said, 'I had two brothers. They were always playing games. Then I can't shoot for toffee.'

'Oh, that's only practice.'

'Really?'

'Of course it is. You must come out with me one of these days. We'll soon teach you to hit. You just follow round till the barrel covers the bird, then swing through. It's not very difficult, but one needs practice. I used to be all right. I find it amusing, you know.'

Simpson turned off the taps, and now that he had finished his shower, Jackson walked forward drying his muscles and puffing out his chest. He greeted Barrow solemnly, and Barrow raised his eyebrows, as if he were surprised by the meeting.

'Hullo! Just enquiring what you two have been up to.'

Jackson looked at Simpson, and answered as if he were in a witness box.

'Eric and I have been for a run, Colonel. I hope there's nothing wrong in that.'

'Hard going in the snow?'

Jackson grunted. He would never have gone had the conditions been good. Jackson was always proving himself, lifting chairs with outstretched arms, approaching women direct in hotel lounges, climbing every mountain that presented itself.

'You been out yourself, Colonel?'

'Not yet.'

'Light's failing.'

'Mm. I thought I might take a shot at a duck. Drive out
you know. Fields are flooded by the river. Duck are best at
this time.'

'Mm,' Jackson said, studying the few hairs on his chest
and Simpson said secretively and importantly, 'You're
remembering sir? You have something on at five-thirty.'
He gave a knowing nod, keeping Jackson out of the secret,
and the latter turned away as if he were not interested.

'I hadn't forgotten, Simpson.'

Simpson climbed into his bath. But when he had im-
mersed himself in the water, and twisted round to pursue
the conversation, Barrow had vanished. He went as quickly
as he had appeared. Simpson was a little bewildered, then
he lay back and soaped his arms. Now that Jackson and he
had gone a couple of runs together, discussing hard training and the need for firmer discipline in the Battalion, they
were on much more friendly terms.

'He's a bit eccentric.' Jackson nodded and Simpson went
on, 'But he's a damned good man, you know. Really he is.'
Jackson did not seem to have the same interest in the
Colonel's sudden call. He was bending and stretching
his knees.

'If I were c.o.,' he said, 'I'd make the whole Mess go for
a run. Think what good it would do that fat bastard Millar.'

When the knock came the second time, Jock gave an
unwilling little grunt. Barrow was pale, but he walked into
the room quite swiftly, closing the door quietly but firmly
behind him. Jock moved a little so that the mattress
squeaked, but he did not move far enough to observe
his visitor. With his eyes closed, and his face against the
wall he said that Charlie was in Edinburgh.

'He's away. He'll be back the morn.'

Barrow was firm and collected. But his neck seemed to have grown longer and he stretched it frequently. He clipped his words short. He said quietly, 'Yes, I gathered that. I came to see you, actually. Did I wake you?'

Jock rolled over and looked at him with a bland eye.

'A-huh.'

'I'm so sorry. It is rather important, Jock.'

Jock seemed exhausted. He hauled himself up on one elbow and nodded his head. His hair was tousled and spiky. He reached out for a cigarette, but the packet on the bedside table was empty. Barrow watched him and he felt in his cardigan pockets.

'I'm afraid I haven't brought my case.'

Jock nodded towards his battledress, flung untidily over the chair. 'There's another packet in my pouch there. My lighter should be in there too.'

The Colonel started to burrow for them and Jock said:

'What's the time, Colonel? I thought it was five-thirty, our date?'

'That,' he touched his moustache, 'that was the plan. I wanted to change it. I'm sorry to have woken you.'

He gave Jock the cigarettes, and they each took one. Barrow tried valiantly with the lighter, taking it in both hands at last, striking it clumsily with his forefinger. But his hands were not steady and the gadget refused to work and Jock grew impatient.

'Here; give.'

Barrow smiled as he handed it over.

'My hands are useless.'

'A-huh,' Jock replied, still bored, and with one sharp movement of his big thumb he turned the steel, and the flame appeared. Barrow gave a funny little shrug but Jock did not smile.

'I thought you were out shooting.'

'No. I . . .' He paused. 'I decided not to go till later.'

Jock adjusted his pillow, and taking a breath of his

cigarette he lay back, and stared at the ceiling, prepared to say nothing. Barrow looked at him for a moment, then he twisted, and moved to the far corner of the room. He stood beside the basin, and as he talked he leant back on the window-sill behind him.

'Jock, this is quite unofficial, you understand. I don't know how much the others have told you. I don't know how much you've heard.' Jock ran his tongue round his lip, and spat away a little flick of tobacco.

'Well, actually the cat's out of the bag,' Barrow went on hurriedly. 'I like to have things out in the open, you understand. I know all about it.'

Jock looked at him slowly.

'If you're trying to bewilder me, Colonel, you're doing fine,' he said at last, and Barrow leant forward and started to play with the tap on the basin. He turned it off and on once or twice before he composed himself.

'I'll be quite frank, Jock. I've nothing to hide. I haven't come here to bewilder you, as you say. I've come for quite another reason.'

'A-huh.'

The tap was turned on again.

'I think you know quite well what I mean when I say the cat's out of the bag. Come, Sinclair, as I say, this is quite an unofficial visit. I know very well you struck Fraser last night.'

'You've got the evidence?'

He replied quietly, 'I said I know very well.'

'Who told you?'

'More than one person.'

'McLean?' Jock sat up and looked at him suspiciously. 'Did you say you'd seen McLean?'

'I didn't say so, but I have. Jock, this isn't the point.'

'It is for me, Colonel. Who else have you seen?'

Barrow moved impatiently.

'Please. Let me say what I have to say. I like to have

things in the open. I don't like deception. But this isn't easy for me.'

Jock gave a little chuckle. 'For Christ's sake. What d'you think it is for me? A bloody picnic?'

'No.' Barrow looked at him steadily. 'No, I don't think that. I think it's very serious for you. And I'm sorry. Really sorry. I mean that.' Jock still did not reply so Barrow turned the tap on again. 'I must add . . .'

Jock couldn't hear for the splash of the water in the basin.

'For Christ's sake turn that thing off. Come again. What d'you say?'

Barrow turned off the tap, pointed his fingertips together and stretched his neck.

'I must add that I haven't come here to say that I am sorry for what I have done. No. Rather am I sorry for what I have had to do.' It was a prepared speech. The mirror rehearsal was reflected in every sentence. 'I am sorry for what has had to be done.'

'Och, to hell with all that.'

'I'm sorry.'

'A-huh. All right. Good for you. I don't know what the hell you've done, anyway.'

The Colonel did not seem to hear him. He was saying the things he had prepared himself to say, like an unpopular candidate at a political meeting, reciting his manifesto to an inattentive crowd.

'In spite of the interpretation some people may like to give to my actions I can say honestly, Sinclair, I can say truthfully, that it has not been pleasant for me. On the contrary.' He began again, 'Although our relationship has not been an easy one I myself believe this to have been entirely dictated by the circumstances in which we found ourselves. Given another set of circumstances I think I can say that we could have taken a very different view of each other. Perhaps we have in common more than is supposed . . .' He paused there. He had flung out a rope, and he waited but Jock never moved, so he was forced to go on. 'It is a pity . . . But whatever the circumstances no reasonable man can be expected to enjoy the business of hurting a brother officer . . .'

'Och, for Christ's sake.'

'Believe me Sinclair, circumstances allowed me no choice.'

'Man, you're not making sense to me at all. Just what have you done?'

Barrow shrugged. 'I have done what I considered it my duty to do. That's all. I have started formal enquiries . . . Of course, it will be a matter for Brigade.'

Jock blinked. Barrow went on, as if the details bored him. They ran out one after another.

'Oh, I checked that the stories tallied, then I had Simpson in, and then,' he shrugged. 'Then I set the ball rolling. Mr Riddick's busy now collecting formal evidence with a view to court martial.'

'Mr Riddick would be pleased,' Jock said with a snort. 'He's not a friend of yours?'

'It's a surprise to me how much you've learnt so quickly, and how much you've missed.'

Barrow smiled warily. 'That's always the way in a foreign country.'

'A-huh.' Jock was alive enough, once again, to give himself time to regain some sense of tactics. 'So you're sorry.'

'Yes. Yes I am. I don't say I shouldn't have done it. Mind you, Sinclair, I'm not here to justify myself. The decisions I took were not, I believe, the wrong ones.' He paused and looked out the window. 'But when I saw you this afternoon by the fire downstairs, I suppose I knew just how sorry I was. I genuinely hope Brigade decides to dismiss the thing. I can assure you I would support any such recommendation.'

The Colonel seemed to want to say something quite different and quite plain but his words, like his feelings, were half strangled. He turned, expecting some encouragement: some reward for his gesture. He wanted more than anything in the world the relief of a handshake. 'Well,' Jock might have said, 'There it is. Just one of those things.' Or even, 'Good of you to say so.' That was part of the equation. That would have been enough. But Jock never fought to finish with a handshake. He fought to kill.

'A-huh. Well, if you're all that sorry, do I take it you're withdrawing the enquiries, eh? Do I take this as the rap over the knuckles. Is that it?'

Barrow was stiff and collected again. 'I wish you could. I'm afraid that's out of the question.'

'What d'you mean? Has the report gone off?'

'No . . . No, I haven't even seen it. The charges haven't been formulated. But it must be common news by now. Mr Riddick's started.'

'You could still refuse to pass the case up farther. Say you're dealing with it yourself . . . Well, couldn't you?'

'You know I couldn't. It's a court-martial offence.'

'You're still the Colonel.'

The Colonel swallowed: 'That's exactly what I mean.'

'Och, to hell with you, Barrow. Are you a man or a book? You said yourself, you said to Jimmy, you're only here a year or two. You'll be away up to Brigade. You said yourself you didn't care about this lark. Didn't you?'

The Colonel shrugged. He nearly laughed.

'News gets around,' he said faintly. 'How news gets round!' Then he turned away. He got nearer to the truth than was comfortable for him.

'God in heaven, nothing's ever mattered to me more. You said a minute ago that I wasn't observant. I'm surprised at you.'

'You do care?'

'Of course I care,' he said softly. 'Isn't it everybody's dream to have his Battalion?' He was hurting himself purposely, with a sort of joy.

'Then what was all that you said to Jimmy t'other night? What was all that in aid of, eh?'

Barrow now sighed, softly.

'I suppose it was the same as the shooting this afternoon. Call it a fib.'

Jock shook his head. 'You're a bloody queer one,' he said, and leant back on his pillows. Barrow smiled rather hopelessly and he agreed.

'Yes, I suppose I am.'

'Oh, for crying out loud,' Jock said scornfully. 'You're too yellow to see me this morning, then off you go and you start all these enquiries to axe me down. Then you're in a funk again so you come and say sorry, but you're still too bloody funk to go back on yourself.'

'Yes.' Barrow's face fell. He nodded slowly. 'I suppose that's one way of looking at it. It's not actually the way I see it.'

'Och. For Christ's sake. What the hell are you?'

'I'm sorry, Jock. It would do the Battalion great harm, you know, to let a thing like this ride. It is my business to think of the Battalion. I can assure you it was that which guided me. I'm most awfully sorry.'

Jock's fists grew tight with anger. He spat as he talked, and his face grew very red.

'To hell with you, Barrow Boy. You haven't heard half of it. I've given you your chance but you wouldn't bloody take it.' He made a wide sweeping gesture. 'It's your own bloody funeral. D'you think I've no friends, eh? When it comes to it, they'll matter, and they saw you at the cocktail party, Barrow. For Christ's sake, they've come all the way with me. What about Charlie, eh? If it comes to court d'you no think he'll have something to say? Aye, and what about my Adjutant? What about Jimmy? Eh? What's he going to say? He was a boy, Jimmy was. I taught him to be a soldier, d'you follow? D'you think he's going to say anything except what a bloody piece of check it is you taking it as far as a court?'

Barrow looked at him sadly, and let him run on. Jock shook his head like a turkey.

'Bachch . . . it's you that'll be looking silly, I'm telling you.'

Barrow put his hands in his cardigan pockets.

'I blame myself most for not having come and spoken to you earlier on. We could have avoided all this.'

'Ach,' Jock said, and he leant back on his pillows again and closed his eyes. He pretended Barrow wasn't there. But Barrow, almost to spite himself or purge himself, seemed determined to go on. He went on and on, although Jock never spoke: not a muscle of his face moved. Barrow might have been talking to a stone and he knew this very well. Indeed he spoke as if he were addressing trees. He spoke at length, but apparently without feeling. His voice was as resigned as a ghost's. The pitch of it never rose or fell. And Jock never replied. They might have been ignorant of each other's presence.

'. . . That's why, I suppose, it meant so much to me. As a matter of fact I've always wanted to be with the Battalion, and somehow I've always been moved on elsewhere. But I know a great deal about it, you know. Perhaps you'd be surprised to hear I'm writing a history of it now. That's why I've such an admiration for you. I have. I . . . I know that desert campaign as if I'd been there myself. The night you took over, in the light of the flares. Five hundred were killed and wounded that night. Five hundred and forty-two officers and men, to be precise. Quite a battle. The wounded put their rifles, bayonet in the ground, to mark where they were. And you brought in the carriers, wasn't that it? Somebody had a phrase for you – I think it was the Pipe-Major – "Like a Bobby at a tattoo",' he said.

His words fell on the air. The only other noise was the faint scraping of the shovels as the detention squad continued to scrape clear the square outside.

'I was in gaol, as you put it: I was cooped up then with

some very unpleasant Japs. But I said I'd get back to the Battalion: back to Scotland. I loved it here, you know, as a subaltern. Even the weather had a sort of thrill for me. I used to look out at this barrack square and dream that one day I . . . I knew a lot of people who have gone away.'

'For Christ's sake.' Jock still kept his eyes closed.

'Of all people, I'm sorry I should have had to do this to you. Then perhaps that's fate. D'you ever feel that you're just playing out some move that's already been arranged for you? D'you feel that?'

'Never.'

'Oh. That's how I've felt. I . . .'

'Look, I'm tired. I'm played out.'

'Yes, I'm sorry. You look tired. Well at least I've said something of what I'd meant to say. I can't expect you to forgive me now, but I do hope, in the future, sometime, you'll . . .' His voice trailed away, and there was a pause.

Then suddenly Barrow sounded angry; angry with Jock for his rudeness, but more angry with himself. He began to sweat a little.

'No man is bigger than the Battalion, Jock. That's what I've had to remember. So don't misinterpret me. I didn't come here to apologise for my actions. Oh no. I came here to say I was sorry that it had to be you. Sorry you'd made such a damned ass of yourself. There it is then; there it is.'

Jock lay absolutely still, waiting for him to leave. Then at last, very suddenly, Barrow said, 'Of course you're tired,' and with that same little stretch of his neck, he left the room, as if he'd just called to borrow a cigarette.

'Yes? What is it, Sergeant-Major?'

Mr Riddick never enjoyed being called Sergeant-Major but this was a mistake Barrow often made when he was in an impatient mood.

Mr Riddick had caught him just outside the Battalion

H.Q. offices. He had a board with several important papers attached to it tucked smartly underneath his arm, as if it were a drill stick.

Barrow looked hopelessly round the square as he waited for Mr Riddick to speak. He looked at the barracks as if it were a prison from which there was no escape. The sky itself was like a low roof.

Mr Riddick took some time to compose himself. Barrow pitched his weight back on one heel and knocked a little bit of hard snow to the side of the path with the toe of his other foot.

'Well, what is it?'

'Sir. Been talking with the Pipe-Major, sir. I believe he's had a word with the Adjutant.'

Barrow stared into his face, half savage and half bored.

'Go on, go on.'

When he was uncertain of himself Mr Riddick talked louder than ever.

'Perhaps we're being a little hasty with this enquiry, sir.'

'What did you say?'

'Sir. Wouldn't express an opinion of this sort unless I felt it was the over-all opinion of the non-commissioned ranks, sir. It does seem as how they feel such an enquiry would do more harm . . .'

'Mr Riddick, you astonish me.'

'Sir.'

'I thought I gave an order that the evidence should be collected.'

'Sir. I understood the order, sir.'

'Well, dammit, obey me.'

'Sir.'

Barrow relaxed a little.

'Of course, this can't be a popular order. But it is an order. It's the good of the Battalion we must think of.'

'Begging your pardon, sir, it was the good of the Battalion we were considering. Feel the Battalion might be best served if you were to deal with this little matter yourself, sir. Battalion would support you, sir.'

'There's no question of that, d'you hear me?' Barrow could have been heard a hunded yards off. 'No question of it. Dammit, the Sergeants' Mess isn't a senate.'

'Sir.'

Barrow lowered his voice.

'For God's sake, Mr Riddick, if an officer strikes another rank he has to pay for it, hasn't he? Well, hasn't he?'

'Sir.'

'Well, get cracking with it.'

'Sir. Considered it my duty to raise it, sir.'

'Very well. You raised it. Now get on with it.'

'Sir.'

A tremendous salute followed and the R.S.M. about-turned and marched off. Barrow watched him, and he fidgeted. Mr Riddick would not have raised the question unless the pressure had been very strong: he loathed Jock.

This would be a perfect opportunity to redress some of the damage. As he thought of that, Barrow heard his own light voice echo in his ears. The banalities were like a chorus. The good of the Battalion. Duty. Honesty. There was something false about the very sound of the name Sinclair, as it fell from his lips.

'Mr Riddick?'

Had Mr Riddick come back to him it might have been different but he did not. He halted some twenty paces away and he shouted from there. His voice echoed giddily round and round the cold square.

'Sir!'

'Mr Riddick, I . . .' Barrow's hands fell limp. He twitched his moustache. 'I want that report tonight,' he said flatly. The echo of his voice was tired and high and it was smothered by Mr Riddick's final '*Sir!*'

Still Barrow did not move. Then at last a little orderly from the office came out of the block and approached him.

The Orderly gave an affected salute. His battledress was creased smartly in every direction and his bonnet had been clipped and shaped. The Orderly spent his evenings reshaping the clothes with which he was issued. Barrow stared at him with undisguised hatred.

'Please, sir, d'you wish a doughnut with your tea, sir?'

Barrow screwed up his face.

'A *what*?'

'Sir, some of the lads have doughnuts with their tea on Mondays, Wednesdays and Fridays. We get them across at the Naafi. They're fourpence each, sir, but they're very good. I strongly recommend them, I do.' The Orderly smiled his mother's smile. 'I could arrange it, sir.'

'Not for me.'

'Colonel Sinclair always used to like one.'

'I don't care what Colonel Sinclair liked for his tea.'

The reproof did not seem to upset the Orderly. 'No, sir; I thought I'd just ask you.'

'O God,' Barrow said suddenly, 'O God.'

THAT AFTERNOON AT five o'clock the flag had been lowered and Retreat had been played. But sundown was a technical point. The sun had been hidden behind a bank of cloud all day. Corporal Fraser took the pipes and drums back to the Band Block and it was his last duty of the day to see that the piping room was cleaned up and tidy.

'Corporal, there's a friend of yours out there, his bottom out behind him,' Piper Adam said.

Fraser was waiting patiently for all the kit to be cleaned and cleared away. He turned round slowly, and he looked down to the square to see Jock marching slowly across. It was just light enough for him to be recognisable, a black figure against the snow.

'Is he no a friend of yours, Corporal, eh? Is he no a friend any longer?'

'D'you see that broom over there, Adam?'

'No, Corporal. I don't see it.'

'Get over to it and start away.'

'It's no my turn for the sweeping.'

One of the other pipers, a serious boy with steel-rimmed glasses, now said, 'What's that he's marching at, Corporal?'

The Corporal turned back again. He said slowly:

'Jock always marches at 120 to the minute.'

'It's no as fast as that. Not nearly as fast as that,' Adam said. 'Maybe it's the weight on his mind that slows him down.'

'You talk too much.'

'That's a terrible black eye you've got, Corporal. It looks terrible sore.'

'Get on.'

'Corporal, I'm sympathising with you. That's what I'm doing.'

The other piper said wistfully, 'Whatever it is he never changes his pace. Look at his footsteps, too. If the steps were there in front of him he'd put his foot right in them.'

'It's no where he put his feet that worries the Corporal. It's where he puts his fist.'

'Your mouth's too big, Piper Adam.'

'That's a personal remark, Corporal.'

'If you don't get on you'll no get out the night.'

'I've no money to go out the night.'

'Then you'll go on a charge.'

'That's bloody victimisation, Corporal. That's what that is.'

'You'll be telling that to the Pipe-Major, d'you hear me?'

'Och.'

'D'ye hear me?'

Piper Adam at last obeyed but as he moved across the room he continued to mumble.

'. . . and it's the bloody fiddle I should a' taken up. No these pipes at all. I'm telling yous. There's no all this bull in the Hallé. Aye, I'm telling you.'

The Corporal turned to the square, but it was empty now. Jock was on his way. It was as bare as oblivion.

Jock went down the dark alley to the stage-door, and without a word of explanation he passed a ten-shilling note to the porter behind the window. The porter winked and welcomed him back, but Jock only nodded. He threw the note to the man as if he were throwing it overboard, and then he walked up the stone steps. Turning to his left he climbed the narrow staircase to the second floor where Mary had her dressing-room. She was not there, but the unshaded overhead light had been left on, and the room had hardly changed since he had known it. Over the light-switch was a notice scrawled in lipstick on the lid of a shoe-box: *Please turn me off.* It was balanced on the top of the switch. The walls were badly in need of redecoration; the dressing-table, which had been bought at some sale years before, was as untidy as ever, and the big mirror still had a postcard slipped into the corner and one or two official notes pinned on to the frame. All around the room budding actors and actresses had scrawled their names on the walls, but none of the names meant anything now. The sash of the window was broken and Jock walked across to try and force the top shut, but he had struggled with it before, in vain. At the top right-hand corner there was a gap of two or three inches. The window seemed to be set in a wall which was only one brick deep. Jock felt that if he shoved with his shoulder then the side of the room might collapse with a rumble into the alley below. He grasped hold of the shutters and pulled them together. The bar to lock them had broken off its coupling and the draught through the window pushed them open again. But the room was cold. Methodically he carried a chair across and placed it against the shutters to hold them close. There was a gas fire burning low in one corner and he turned it up.

Finding the kettle half filled he lit the gas ring too, and put the kettle on. He had to kneel down to adjust it. Then with his knuckles he pushed his weight back and he squatted in front of the fire, warming his hands. At last he stepped back and sat on a little chair with a plywood seat which creaked as it took his weight. The legs were loose and he rocked gently, in a little circle, holding on to the seat at his sides. He was sick with tiredness now, and the gas fire made him nod. His eyes were smarting, and he was too exhausted to find himself a cigarette. He did not get up when he heard her coming: his chair creaked as the door opened and she entered, but he still could not be bothered to climb to his feet. He looked over his shoulder and said just, 'Mary.'

'Laddie, they never told me you were here.'

'I thought I'd find you. I know my way. I mind it fine.'

She moved with a rustle. She was wearing a long grey dress that did not bear close inspection. It had been mended and remended and the hem was very dirty. The lace at the sleeve was pink-brown with grease paint and the apron was marked with dust. They were performing an adaptation of *The Heart of Midlothian*, and Jeanie Deans was one of Mary's star parts. Almost like a professional, because Jock never thought of her as a professional, she took some cotton wool and began to clean some of the make-up from round her eyes.

'I'll get the sack if they find you here. How did you get in?'

'I tipped Mac.'

'Och,' she said. 'There was no need to have done that. What did you give him?'

'Ten bob.'

'Ten bob!' She was astonished. 'Laddie, that's far too much.'

He shrugged, and climbed wearily to his feet. She was watching him in the mirror and now she turned. That smile of hers was not there any longer.

'Ten bob's about as much as I make for each performance.'

'I didn't think.' All the time he stared at her, with a sadness, and because she found his stare unnerving she turned away. But she was courteous, and she was kind. She was even tender.

'Let me help you with your coat. You'll just catch a cold when you get out again. Did you close the shutters?'

'A-huh.'

'That's nice of you.' She took the coat from him and she hung it on one of the pegs which was already laden with clothes and hangers.

'Untidy as ever,' Jock said and he attempted a smile.

'In this room it's not worth being anything else; well, is it?' She went on; 'Now why did you tip Mac like that? You're a terrible man.'

'I thought maybe Charlie was here before me. I thought then that Mac would need some persuading.'

'Charlie's in Edinburgh.'

'I know. I sent him. He was sore about that.'

'You're right there.'

'Did he have a date with you? I told him if he had, I'd get someone else. It was a joke. It was a joke that went wrong.'

'It'll do him no harm,' she said, 'no harm at all. Charlie's a cool one.' She brought her lips tightly together when she had said that. Then she looked at him again. She looked hard at his face, and about his eyes. She said with a sudden surge of pity:

'I'm glad you came, Jock. I'm glad. Laddie, you're worn out. I can see it in your face.'

'I've got reason to be.'

The kettle was beginning to boil and she knelt down to attend to it. She was reaching for the teapot, not looking at Jock at all when she said, 'I know you have. I know fine, Jock. Charlie was here.'

'Ach, well.'

'But he wasn't here long after he'd told me, Jock,' she said suddenly, looking up at him. 'I got it all out of him, and I'm glad you sent him off. You were right to. When he told me it all, I sent him away myself, and if you'd not come here I was going to try and find you. It's a shame, Jock.'

'It's just a fact.' His palms turned outwards. 'That's all it is. It must have been written down somewhere. I never thought at all. I might have been one of your actors. I just played out the lines, and I struck the laddie and ever since then, Mary, I've been following my own footsteps. They lead me hither and thither.'

'Is it real serious?'

He touched the dust on the narrow mantelpiece. 'Sometimes I tell myself it isn't. There's lots of ifs and buts to it. But just as I see the way out, just as I see the light and I see the chance, I know fine at the same time just how bloody serious it is. Maybe the same devils as saved me before have turned the thing against me now.'

'Och, away you go. The devil takes care of his ain.'

'Oh, dearie me,' he said suddenly and with a sigh he sat down on the little chair again so she was by his feet where she sat. She had found cups and she poured out the tea. Then she said:

'I told Charlie I'd never see him again.'

'You what?'

'You heard. He'd no right to do that.'

'It's none of Charlie's fault.'

'Barrow would have never dared to move without him.'

'But Barrow has moved. I've just seen him. He came to say he's sorry.' He laughed. 'That was comic.'

Then he waved his hand in the air wiping out all they had said.

'Och, Charlie didn't come into it lassie.'

She handed him up the cup. 'Did they not tell you, then? Did you not hear what happened?'

Jock looked at her suspiciously. He felt a little frightened of what she was about to say. She must have had a right row with Charlie. But he had not come to discuss all this. He had come to see her and to forget it. She looked at him cautiously as he replied very slowly:

'I know fine what happened. Barrow's just told me. It was the doctor who gave the show away, then Mr McLean had to see him too. It had nothing to do with Charlie.'

She shook her head. 'Are you blind, Jock? I saw it coming last night; for heaven's sake. He didn't like it when you called. Did you not see that?'

Jock blinked. He had long been trained in the school which teaches that women are the trouble-makers, and it was not the first time that he and Charlie had had the same girl. But it had never destroyed their friendship, and it never would.

'You're away off net.'

'That I'm not. D'you fancy I'd just say a thing like that?'

'No.'

'Charlie told me, Jock. He told me himself. Barrow had him in. He asked him what he thought. He asked him if he ought to chase the rumour up.'

Jock sat very stiffly, with his knees together, and he looked down at her, awkwardly, with his chin in his collar.

'You've had words with Charlie.'

'When he said that I had words with him, I . . .'

'Before that you'd had a tussle with him.'

'No.'

He looked at her solemnly. 'You're no in love with him any more?'

'With Charlie?' She shook her head and gave a weak little laugh. 'Of course I'm not in love with him. For heaven's sake, I never have been.'

'You were carrying on with him,' he said hotly, and she put a hand on his knee.

'Och, Jock Sinclair. You're a child. You're a child.'

He looked angry now; hurt that she should make a fool of him. He moved a little in his chair and he looked away from her as he said:

'Did Charlie say he'd seen Barrow?'

'Yes.'

'He never told me.'

'Maybe he wasn't going to.'

He flared up at that. He rose to his feet and his cup rattled in the saucer.

'That's an awful thing to say. Charlie'd tell me. Charlie's no a sneak. It's just that he hasn't had time. Did he tell you what he said to Barrow? Did he?'

She shrugged. 'The enquiry's gone forward, hasn't it?'

Jock looked back at her, over his shoulder.

'Charlie'd never have done that out of spite, if he did it at all.' He seemed to be angry with her, not anybody else. When he started his voice was low, but it grew louder all the time. 'Women like you don't understand. You see us when we're drunk and playing the fool. You never know the real men. You don't see the other side. Aye, maybe Charlie was called in.' He walked as far as the wall at the other side of the room and he pushed his fist against it, softly, once or twice. She sat very still, with her cup in her lap. Everything looked bare and yellow in that light.

'Aye, and maybe when he was told the facts he saw his duty. He's a good officer, Charlie. When it comes to it he knows what's right and what's wrong. If you sent him away with a flea in his ear, you did wrong. If he had to do that to me, then he had to do that to me, and maybe he was right to. But he'd never want to. Not Charlie.'

She watched him solemnly, and his eyes were brimming and burning with a sort of hot pride. Then she looked down at her cup, and she moved it to her side.

'You know I've never tried to make trouble.'

'I know nothing about you. Nothing at all.'

She was hurt, and he saw that he had hurt her. His own face screwed up with the same pain that he had inflicted. She had turned her face to the wall.

'Mary, I'm sorry, I shouldn't have said that. I'm sorry I said it. Really I am.'

She still kept her head turned away, and he moved forward clumsily. He did not know what to do so he bent down, and with the flat of his palm he stroked the top of her hair, stiffly but softly, as he would stroke the head of a dog.

'It's no business of mine,' she said at last, her voice a pitch higher, but she was not crying.

'Aye, it is. I came along to you. I'm sorry, Mary, I'm clack-handed. I didn't mean to be angry with you. I know you did me fine, and I'm glad of that. But you're wrong about Charlie. He wouldn't do what you think he's done. Och, lassie, in a battalion, it's difficult you see: whoever it is, whatever the circumstances – Christ, you can't have officers bashing corporals. That's just the way of it. I know that fine. I'd have said the same thing myself. I'd have done the same.'

She looked up at him and she just said, 'Never in a hundred years, Jock.' He opened his eyes wide: he hesitated, and he nearly lost his way. Then he turned round, and the fist banged back into the palm of the hand again and again. She went on talking in a low voice, but with such conviction.

'Never in a hundred years. And you know that, fine, don't you? Oh, Jock, you're always talking about your soldiers, and your Battalion, but it's you that doesn't see the half of your men. And for all your mucking and binding, and all your nonsense, laddie, you're . . . you're a child, Jock.'

'Och, for Christ's sake,' he said. She had often said this to him and it always irritated him.

'You expect too much of them. You expect them all to be the same as yourself, and you're twice the man of any of them. I mean that. You're too good for them. I've never said it before because your head would grow too big. But it's true. It's true.'

He said sadly, 'No, lassie. It *was* true. It *was* true. But it isn't true any more.'

'Well, tell me a better man, eh? Is Macmillan better? Who are all the others? What about Barrow?'

He shook his head and he dropped his weight on to the chair again.

'Och, to hell with all that,' he said. 'I'm about awa' with it now. I don't know which'll bust first, my head or my heart. So to hell with all that. C'mon out with me.'

She looked up at the round clock face above the door. 'Laddie, I can't. I've another show in half an hour.'

'What is it tonight?'

'Jeanie Deans.'

'Aye,' he said and slowly he smiled. 'I saw the bill. That's what it is. And Mary Titterington in the big letters.'

'Don't bully me. Don't bully me now.'

'No.' He put his head on one side. 'But it must give you a wee thrill. Just a wee one.'

She closed her eyes for a second.

'Let's not have all this again, Jock.'

'But I'm not mocking.'

'Oh, for heaven's sake.' She rose to her feet. 'Look I'll tell you. You see that wall. Twelve years ago, Jock, twelve years ago, before you ever had your war I was here, in this dressing-room. I was playing Effie Deans then, and I was good, though I say it myself. And I wrote my name up there with the rest of them. Oh, for heaven's sake.'

'Did you? Maybe I saw you then. Where's your name? Where is it?'

She turned away. 'When I came back I rubbed it out.'

'Och.' He looked genuinely sad. He gave a kind smile. 'Och, you shouldn't have done that. Lassie, when I was your age I was a Corporal-Piper; you've plenty time. C'mon, we'll make you write it again. C'mon.' He touched her tenderly.'

'Not for anything.'

'Och, well,' he said with a little kick of his head. 'I'll sign it for you. And shall I put mine by it?' He got out a pencil. 'Eh? Maybe I'll play Hamlet yet. Hamlet it is; is it not? That's for me, eh?'

'No,' she tried to stop him but he was determined and he reached high above her. She took it all seriously.

'What'll I put, eh?'

'I'll never talk to you again,' she said angrily as he paid no attention to her.

'What about this, eh?' He wrote down something and then he stood back with a great grin. Pretending to be very angry she looked gloweringly at what was written. '*Rex Harrison and Mary Titterington.*'

'Is that not good eh?' He said, 'Sexy Rexy: does that not fit the bill? Is that not me, eh?' He waited.

She clenched her fists, and she was shaking.

'Oh, Jock,' she said and she was suddenly in tears. 'Christ alive, you're a lovely man.' She shouted out loud, 'Oh, Jock. Jock, man, you're a bloody king.'

'Mary, Mary.' He opened his arms and comforted her. 'Come away with you. You mustn't cry.' He spoke tenderly and he held her close to him. 'You'll have me greeting too, and that'll never do. That'll never do, lassie.'

'It's not Charlie that I love,' she said hopelessly. 'Not Charlie at all.'

'But you turned me away.'

'I never, I never. I'd never turn you away. You're too good for them all.'

Suddenly it all seemed to frighten Jock. She was hugging closely to him and he pushed her back gently, to look at her, but she kept her face downcast.

'I'm a mess,' she said. 'Don't look at me, Jock. I don't want you to look at me now.'

He held her stiffly, and with hard lips he kissed her brow, by the border of her hair. He asked innocently, 'Are you saying that you love me, Mary?'

It was agony for her. 'Jock, of course I am. Of course I am. Like any other woman that's ever known you,' she said and she looked up at him for a second. 'And I'm no sure it isn't every man, too.'

He laughed at that. He tried to make it all a joke. 'Here, here, now. That's a very sophisticated sort of notion. That's too complex for me.'

'I used to be a very sophisticated girl.' She dried her eyes. 'In London.'

'And Edinburgh. And here. Until I knew you.'

'Did I drag you down?'

'You could drag me anywhere. I'd burn at the stake – so there; that's love for you.' Jock let her burrow her head in his shoulder, pushing at him so his weight fell back on his heels. She clasped him tightly.

'I love you, Jock; I love you: I've said it.'

'No, no,' he said upset, but still holding her. 'No you mustn't say that, lassie.'

'But I do.'

'You don't really. You're just upset.'

'I do, I do.' Her hands were clasped tightly on his arms.

He soothed her again, with hands and arms, looking anxiously over her shoulder.

'I tell you what, Mary. We'll have supper tonight, eh? Morag's left me now. Morag's gone away. So we'll have supper just for old times' sake. I'll pick you up here and we'll go across to the Welcome. That's what we'll do. I'll choose a good menu, and we'll have a wine too, the whole thing. Just you and me, late on.'

'Not just for old times' sake.'

He nodded, 'No, not just for old times' sake.'

'Jock, whatever they do to you . . .' but he wouldn't let her go on. He patted her back.

'I know, I know. I know you'd be good to me . . . Will you have supper, eh?'

'Mm.'

'And the wine?'

She nodded vigorously, swallowing to control herself again.

'Mm.'

'Smoked salmon and the whole lot, eh?'

'And coffee.'

'Aye, and Drambuie too.'

She said, 'Then will you come back?'

He looked at her solemnly and cautiously as she dabbed her eyes.

'Mary, I've done you enough harm as it is. I've done

enough damage. I'm down on my luck, but there's no need
for you . . .' He couldn't go on. He just shook his head.

'I want you to come home with me.' Her face hid nothing
now. She stared at him with a sort of blank passion.

'Oh, lassie, you're kind . . .' he said and he took hold of
her again and hugged her tight. He closed his eyes for a
moment. 'Aye well, to hell with them all,' he said with a
great sigh, and he whispered to her, 'and all their bloody
enquiries, we'll forget all them. We'll make love, like the
old times. Maybe again and again, after our supper. We'll
make love, lassie, we'll make love.'

But even as he spoke, and patted her, his mind wandered
away. She seemed to sense this and she pushed closer and
closer to him in despair while he looked over her shoulder
into the long mirror at the sad soldier there.

SIX

WHEN HE REACHED the hotel he nearly turned back again. There was a giggling girl wheeling the revolving door, and her partner was chasing after her, rocking forward on his toes as he walked, with the sort of totter that irritated Jock. The girl was in a long tulle dress of grey and pink, and she had a travelling rug wrapped round her. That was the joke: she'd forgotten her coat, or thrown it out of the car window. When she arrived in the hall people turned to her. She said she was so poor she had to use Johnny's car rug to cover her now. She thought she was rather fetching as a peasant.

'Excuse me,' Jock said. 'If I can get past.'

They were holding some sort of dance and the hall and lounges were crowded with people talking at a high pitch. The older men looked well polished, the younger men looked arrogant, and the middle men seemed to be searching for their parties. There was a sound of a band coming from the ballroom at the back, and people were preparing to waltz. The ladies were dragged away to the dance floor, still looking back and talking, while they searched for somewhere to leave their handbags. All the available sills and shelves were already covered with handbags of sequins and brocade.

Amongst the white shirts and the black coats, squeezing between the bare shoulders of the women, Jock felt self-conscious in his khaki and he did not enjoy the sensation. Two or three people he knew nodded as he went through, and others a little farther away talked in urgent whispers: 'My *dear*, look. There's Jock Sinclair. What *do* you suppose?'

'A-huh,' Jock said, and 'A-huh,' as he passed.

He got as far as the cocktail bar, but it was full of dancers. Macmillan was there, draped against the bar, talking to a lady torpedo with eyes like a fish. The dress she had chosen was salmon-pink, but she flushed a deeper colour than that when she recognised Jock.

'Sandy, *tell* me. How absolutely *awful*. D'you suppose he heard? D'you suppose?' She straightened. 'My dear boy, I don't care a rap if he did. Not I. But do tell me.'

Sandy shook his head and took a sip of his drink. He nodded politely to Jock.

'Not dancing?'

Jock shouted across two heads and a torpedo's back.

'Not me. What's the caper?'

'Spinsters of the district. Spinsters' ball.'

Jock did not find a reply. He turned away, and the effect was of rudeness.

'What was I saying?' the torpedo said, pleased that her description of Jock's manners should have been demonstrated so accurately. 'Sandy, what did I say? What did I? No manners at all!'

'Yes, quite,' Sandy said, nodding, glancing sideways in search of relief.

'Of course. But of course. *Just* what I was saying. Now Barrow Boy's *very* different, but well, I always say if a man . . .'

'He was sorry he couldn't come tonight.'

'Nonsense. He refuses everything.'

'He's awfully busy.'

'Pooh, to that! My dear, let me tell you that before the war officers at the Mess – officers and gentlemen, isn't that what they say?'

'That's right.'

'Sandy, of course, you're a gentleman. You're always the same. Now what was I saying?'

'I beg your pardon?'

'Sandy, I do believe you're not attending to me.'

'Isn't the band noisy?'

'Yes. Look at that awful man now.'

'Who's this?'

'That's Sinclair, leaning over whispering to the barman like that. What a big sit-upon he has, Sandy. Not a well-bred sit-upon at all, no. I suppose the barman's his best friend. I suppose that's it.'

When she looked round, Sandy had turned away.

'Carol,' he was saying. 'How glorious to see you.'

The torpedo just pounced on the nearest person. 'I do think that Sinclair man is frightful, don't you?'

'Too awful.' So the music went around and around.

Jock went upstairs to find the manager, but he was to be disappointed. The head waiter was the only person he could find, and he quickly confirmed that there was no possibility of supper after ten-thirty. It would have to be a very special arrangement in the ordinary way, but with the dance on, it was out of the question.

'Ah well,' Jock said, apparently resigned and the head waiter was all napkin and coat-tails as he bowed good-evening. As he turned away Jock heard his name called, and there beside him was the red-haired Rattray, dressed in a kilt and tweed jacket.

'Jock, it's fine to see you,' he said and he had had one or two. Rattray only needed one or two to set him off. Jock screwed up his eyes and nodded.

'A-huh,' he mumbled.

'I'm bloody chocka with all this carry-on down the stairs. Have you ever seen the likes? I saw Simpson there, and some o' the others. What are you up to, Jock? Eh, man?'

Jock seemed to be far away.

'Just a minute,' he said, and he went back to the head waiter. Rattray saw him take out a pound and offer it to him but the head waiter shook his head and refused it. He looked like a professional football player: he had blue, outdoor eyes. He smiled and said 'no' again while Jock talked harder and harder. It might have been a matter of life and death, but the waiter shook his head. Jock was disappointed. Looking rather dazed by his failure he wandered back to the top of the staircase, where Rattray awaited him.

Rattray started asking questions, and when Jock didn't answer, he just asked them again. Jock shook his head.

'Och, it was just about supper.'

'Have you not had your supper? Man, you didn't have lunch, I saw that. You need food. You looked washed out. Aye, you do.'

When they came to the bottom of the stairs something else caught Rattray's attention and he said, 'Oh for pity's sake look at the way that puppy's wearing the kilt. It's a bloody crime.'

They had to pass this boy as they walked to the door and Jock wandered round him without difficulty, but Rattray pretended he could not get past. He braced his shoulders and he said, 'If you'll excuse me.'

The young man looked round surprised.

'I said if you'll excuse me.'

'I'm so sorry.' He stepped to one side, and Rattray flicked his head like a Nazi, and marched squarely to the door. Jock was already outside and had nearly escaped him, but Rattray was soon at his side. When he was in this mood he talked right into people's faces and now he suggested a plan of campaign to Jock. They would get a sandwich at the Palace Bar, where men were men. Jock looked wearily at the freckled face, green in the street light, the crinkly hair and the uneven teeth, and eventually he allowed himself to be taken along. He was only vaguely conscious of Rattray's hand on his elbow and he hardly listened to his talk at all. This was probably a good thing, as Rattray was the world's worst comforter. He kept saying how he would never have ruined Jock in the way the others were doing. He said what he would do if he were Brigade.

'But we've got to face the facts. Brigade's not like that. And Brigade's no friend of yours, I'm sure: and more's the credit to you, Jock. But we've got to face the facts.'

Jock nodded and Rattray said, 'Believe me, Jock lad, if Barrow'd called me in and not Charlie and Jimmy I'd have given him a funny answer.'

For the first time since they had met, Jock was interested. He stopped and he said quietly:

'Who did you say Barrow saw?'

'Christ, did you not know?'

'Who?'

'Jock, I thought you knew, man.' Rattray looked alarmed. 'I'm no the lad to tell tales. I thought it was common knowledge.'

'Who did you say?'

'You'll no tell them I told you, Jock?'

'I'm not interested in telling anybody anything.'

'Charlie Scott.'

'Aye, I heard that.'

'And Jimmy Cairns.'

'Not Jimmy. You made that up. You made that up, eh?'

'Jock lad, I swear . . .'

'You can't be right.'

'Jock, I'm right enough.'

'For Christ's sake. Oh, for Christ's sake,' Jock said, then very suddenly he walked on. Tears were running down his cheeks. But as they walked and as Rattray went on, he recovered. Rattray did not see his tears.

'Aye, Jimmy too. The both of them. They were in together. Douglas Jackson got it out of Simpson who was outside the door and I got it from him.'

Jock said no more, but he looked and felt very cold and weary now, and he wondered if he was maybe going to collapse.

He said once or twice that he ought to go to the theatre to

leave a message but Rattray said they could do that later. Now Rattray was explaining what was wrong with the Regiment.

'It's recruited from all over. That's what's the matter with it. I say we ought to stick to the old way. D'you know that? Look, Jock,' the face loomed in front of Jock again, pink-eyed and fanatic. 'The Regiment was based on the clan system, and Scotsmen have always fought in clans. If we got back to that, then you wouldn't be in the muck you are now. But you mustn't worry, Jock. We'll find a way. Here's the Palace now.'

'I don't want to go in.'

'You'd be better for something to eat.'

'I don't want anything to eat.'

'Och, you will. We'll have a wee dram first. C'mon, Jock, it'll pull you together.'

'You go in. I'm going on.'

Rattray braced his shoulders. 'Alec Rattray's no the lad to desert a comrade. No, no. I'll come in with you.'

'I'll manage on my own.'

'I said I'll come with you, Jock. Did you hear, man? I can see you're in a state, and Alec Rattray's not the lad to leave you. D'you follow?'

Jock followed, and further, Jock followed his own footsteps. He persuaded himself that he was walking home although he knew the house would be dark and cold. He would rest a while, recover, and return to the theatre. And he could get rid of this Rattray. It was a strange night now, half frosty and half damp. There was fog on the river and it crept through the streets. The cold was penetrating and depressing at the same time. When they had walked as far as the same hotel that Jock had visited an age before, just twenty-four hours before, he stopped on the threshold, and looked into the lighted hall.

'Aye, here's a place,' Rattray said. 'C'mon in,' and he led the way through the same little private bar, where the same people were sitting, except for Morag and the Corporal. There was no sign of them.

Conversation died on the lips when Jock appeared, but he seemed quite resigned to that. He made no qualifying gesture. He unbuttoned his coat, like a man shown into a sickroom, slowly, as if the buttons hurt the tips of his fingers. He looked sadly round while Rattray gave a hearty welcome, mentioning a couple of the sergeants by name.

'We'll have two big drams,' Rattray said, poking his head under the glass, where the landlord was crouching, like an anxious ferret.

'No, we won't,' Jock said quietly and flatly. 'I'll just have a round of ham.'

The landlord seemed satisfied by that. He looked relieved and he disappeared, repeating the order again and again to himself, as if it were a word of comfort. 'And a round of ham; aye, and a round of ham.'

The others resumed their conversations with the same air of studied normality that the Mess had assumed that morning, and Jock hung up his heavy coat. When he looked at them, each one looked away, but in spite of that they did not seem unfriendly. Jock smiled when he recognised that there was pity in their eyes, then he moved through the tables, slowly, touching chairs and tables as he went, in a shy and longing sort of way. His hands seemed to linger where they touched: even his eyelids seemed to pause when he blinked and turned his eyes from one group to another. He found a place in a corner and there he watched one of the sergeants who had sat down on the piano-stool and opened the piano lid. But for a while the Sergeant did not begin to play. He stared at the keys as the room grew quiet, and Rattray said, 'Give us a tune.'

Rattray carried the sandwich across and Jock took a bite of it, then he looked at it as if it were made of paper. He put it back on the plate and put the plate on the glass top of the table. He began to chew, and people started to talk again.

The Sergeant at the piano let his fingers run down the scale.

Gently he played *Kelvin Grove*, and then another ballad. Soon they were calling out the names of tunes, and he was playing them. Then a drink or two later, they began to sing. Jock himself did not take a drink all evening and he did not sing, but he began to look quite happy as they went through some of the favourites. To Rattray's chagrin – 'That's a Sassenach tune, for Christ's sake' – the Sergeant played some English tunes too, but they did not sing to those, so he soon returned to the Scottish ones. Like all drunk men, they got round to the sad tunes, and they sang all the Jacobite songs with sweating vigour: *The Skye Boat Song, Will ye no come back again?*, *Charlie is my darling, my darling*. They returned for a second time to *We're no awa' to bide awa'* and *I belong to Glasgow*.

'Aye well,' Jock said, when at last there was a pause. 'I'll be on my way.'

'There's plenty time yet.' Rattray was aflame with patriotism now. 'You can't go yet, Jock.'

'I'm tired now.'

'Och, come off it. We'll no let you go.'

For the first time Jock raised his voice.

'I said I was finished,' he said, and they shuffled away to let him through.

The pianist began again and they turned back to him, and forgot about Jock. But the proprietor was standing in the hall, hanging his head, and Jock stopped beside him.

'Was there any damage last night?'

'Och, no, Colonel Sinclair.'

'I'll pay if there was any damage.'

'I wouldn't think of it, Colonel. Let's just forget the whole incident.'

'Aye,' Jock said. 'Let's forget it,' but Rattray had followed him by then.

'Where are you off to?'

'I'm fair enough.' He started to walk away, then he
turned and he pulled a crumpled pound note from his
coat pocket. It was the same one he had tried to give the
head waiter.

'Would you do me a favour?'

Rattray was enthusiastic. He seemed to have grown taller
as the evening wore on. He was looking down at Jock.

'I'd walk the bloody plank for you.'

Jock blinked. 'That'll not be necessary the night.'

Rattray thought that was funny; he grinned and laughed
and repeated it.

'You're a one,' he said.

'A-huh. Will you go to the theatre and pick up Mary
Titterington, and give her supper?'

'What, Mary Tits?' Rattray opened his eyes wide. Jock
just waited. Rattray said, 'Is she good for it? Eh?' And Jock
closed his eyes. His fists closed tight.

'Will you give her supper?'

'Christ I will.' Rattray gave a vigorous nod that was
almost a bow.

'You'll find somewhere?'

'Christ, I will.'

'Well, here's a pound to you.'

'I'll no' take your money.' His hackles rose.

'You will. And you'll say I'm sorry. Will you mind
that?'

Rattray put his head on one side.

'Here, here. Is she expecting you? Is she? She'll no be
pleased to see me, eh? Why don't you go along yourself,
Jock?'

'I'm asking you.'

'Christ, man!'

'A-huh.' Jock stood still, with the pound in his hand.

'O.K. boy. If that's what you want. Alec Rattray's no the
lad to reason why.'

'Good. And you'll mind to say sorry?'

'I will.'

'And you'll get her a good supper?'

'Nothing but the best, Jock.'

'Then here's your money. Now away you go.'

THE ORDERLY OFFICER was inspecting guard, and Jimmy Cairns was the only one in the Mess when the telephone rang. He was in the billiards room, playing a pointless game of snooker with himself. It was rather cold there, and only the lights over the table were switched on, but once he had begun the game he could not make up his mind to leave it. It was the old story of the bath growing cold. He was too uncomfortable to move. But the Corporal came for him, and he went to the box in the hall to answer.

Two minutes later he was on the telephone to the guard-room, now shivering with an excitement which he was unable to suppress. At last MacKinnon came to the telephone. He knew the voice perfectly well but he double checked.

'MacKinnon?'

'Speaking.'

'This is Jimmy. Look, come back here as quick as you can, laddie. There's been an accident.'

'What's happened?'

Jimmy looked over his shoulder, although there was nobody near. The hall was cold, light and empty.

'Don't let on to anybody. It's serious.'

'Right.'

'I've just had a 'phone call. An officer has been found shot.'

'God. Who?'

'The Colonel,' Jimmy said. 'Now get cracking, laddie.'

*　　*　　*

Not much longer than half an hour after that, MacKinnon, feeling half excited and half frightened, hurried down the cobbled roads, then branched left over the snow-covered grass in the park. The fog was quite thick in patches, but he could just make out the lights by the old footbridge and he could hear the river running by. All the way across the open ground MacKinnon felt afraid and he kept glancing about him. He tried to force himself to march slowly and he put his hand on the firm leather of his belt, because it gave him courage. But belt or no belt, he was cold with fear when he reached the lamp and he started, as we start when we dream that a seat is withdrawn from under us, when he suddenly observed the dark figure on the bridge. The man was standing with his hands in his coat pockets, staring at the water beneath. He wore a long coat, and he seemed to be frozen there, until suddenly he took a step forward to the parapet, and spontaneously MacKinnon called out, 'Guard!'

When the face was turned to the lamp MacKinnon immediately recognised Jock.

'Who's there?' The voice echoed in the fog.

'Colonel, it's me – MacKinnon.'

MacKinnon had never seen Jock look frightened before. Even when he had replied it still seemed to take Jock a moment to recover himself, then he turned as MacKinnon walked forward. As he recovered he grew more angry, and it was an anger born of fear.

'What the hell are you doing out here at this time?'

Almost guiltily and still looking very pale, MacKinnon drew closer.

'Sir, I was coming across to your house.'

'Are you Orderly Officer?' Jock shouted at him, shouted this question and all the others.

'Yes, sir.'

'Then what the bloody hell are you doing out of barracks?'

'Captain Cairns said, sir . . .'

'I don't care a . . . I don't bloody care what anyone said. D'you know your orders, boy? Do you?'

'Yes, sir.' MacKinnon stood rigidly to attention.

'I'll have you on a charge, d'you hear me?'

'Yes, sir.'

Jock moved forward.

'You've no right out of the barracks gate. You've no right at all. Sneaking about the fields at this time. Did you say you were looking for me?'

'Yes, sir.'

Jock looked at him, but he did not speak for a moment. His fingers were moving in his pockets but otherwise he held himself quite still.

'The Adjutant sent me, sir. There's been an accident.'

Jock was quiet again. 'A-huh?'

'Colonel Barrow's been found shot, sir. Adjutant got a 'phone call.'

Jock scowled at him. The news did not seem to surprise him. It seemed to have no significance for him at all. Worried by Jock's stillness, MacKinnon continued:

'It's true, sir. Shot himself dead.'

Jock looked at the boy as he might look at a guard coming to take him away.

'Barrow Boy,' he said at last. 'No. You can't be right.'

'Yes, sir. It's true, sir.'

'Aye, it's true. I can see that. I can see fine it's true.' He moved a few steps and pushed the snow with his toe. It was cold that night and damp. Their very bones were cold.

'I shouldn't have lost my temper with you like that.'

MacKinnon did not move.

'If Captain Cairns sent you, you were in your rights.' Then, 'Christ Almighty,' he said wearily. 'Here's a carry-on. Poor Barrow. Poor wee man. Did you ever hear the like?' He gave a funny little shrug and a noise came from him which MacKinnon supposed to be a laugh.

'I'm sorry I surprised you, sir.'

'You didn't surprise me,' Jock snapped.

'Sir.'

Jock looked down at the water. 'Aye, well, and I suppose it had to be somebody,' he said at last.

'Yes, sir.'

'You look like a ghost, laddie. You've a face like a scone.'

MacKinnon still stood to attention.

'Are you feared?'

'Yes, sir.'

'Of the spooks?'

'No, sir. Of you.'

Jock did not laugh at that. He looked hurt and he put his head on one side. 'Of me? You say you're scared of me?'

'I think I should be getting back, sir.'

'No, no.'

'I am Orderly Officer, sir.'

'Jimmy'll take care of that.' Jock waved the objection aside. 'The great James Cairns'll look after that. Aye. He's a great one for fixing things. Who telephoned him anyway?'

'Some farm, sir.'

'Where? Where did it happen?'

'By the bank of the river, sir. So I understand.'

'Aye, by its bonny banks. And only about an hour ago. Is that it?'

'About that, sir.'

'Did you take geography at the school, MacKinnon?'

MacKinnon nodded, but Jock did not care to cross-examine him further.

'This water,' he said sententiously, 'passed him by. It is the same river flowing under our feet. It is the same water.'

MacKinnon nodded even more vigorously.

'Fancy that!' Jock said lightly, suddenly. 'Och, we'll away out of here. It's a lonely place, the bridge, neither one side of the river, nor the other. Why the hell haven't you got your coat on?'

MacKinnon panicked a little.

'I . . . I . . . Haven't I, sir?'

There was an instant as MacKinnon waited for the shout. When Jock really shouted loud a little foam used to form at the very corner of his lips, and MacKinnon suddenly felt he could not bear it. Then the instant passed away, and Jock was not shouting into his face.

He had stepped back and he was chuckling.

'Christ Almighty. I nearly started at you again. Poor laddie. Oh, laddie, don't look like that. Don't look afraid of me. If you knew me better you would not be afraid. Eh? Tell me, what happened to your coat?' He asked quietly and gently, but MacKinnon still did not relax. He looked wary and bewildered.

'In the excitement I forgot it, sir.'

Jock smiled at him kindly. 'That'll never do. Whatever the excitement you've got to remember to eat and keep warm. That's the sign of a soldier. It's only the neurotics that forget to eat. D'you know what a neurotic is?'

'Yes, sir.'

'Maybe Barrow was a neurotic.'

MacKinnon grew braver. 'Not exactly, sir.'

'No. Not exactly. Just bottled up, I suppose. Never bottle up your feelings, laddie. It's against the Queen's Regulations mind, if you don't bottle yourself up. D'you know that? If you want to be a Colonel, laddie, bottle up. I didn't bottle myself up, then I'm no a Colonel. Not the real MacKay. But I'm no drowned in the deep river.'

'Sir,' MacKinnon said.

'You'll come up to the house. You need a dram.'

MacKinnon hesitated. He looked at Jock anxiously with his big faun's eyes.

'Aye, you will come. And you'll no tell them you found me on the bridge. They'll say I've taken to the poetry if they hear that.' He looked hard at the boy. 'You won't say anything about that, will you?'

'Not if you'd rather I didn't.'

'Then you won't.'

'Righto.'

Jock was still standing half towards him and half away.

'How did he do it?' he asked suddenly. 'Did he do it through the head?'

'Through the mouth.'

'Oh.' It was a cry of genuine pity. Jock screwed up his face. 'Mercy me.'

He gave no explanation for the state of the house. There were no fires lit, but every light was burning and every door, including the front door, was open wide. MacKinnon did not like to ask why, and Jock just said, 'Come on round. We'll switch off the lights.'

He closed the front door behind him and he led the way upstairs, where they started to turn off the lights in the bedrooms, to close the cupboard doors and the drawers. All this MacKinnon took, if not for granted, without comment, but when Jock took off his greatcoat and flung it on the bed in his room he could not conceal his surprise. Jock was in full Mess dress. He was in the bright scarlet tunic with gold braid, his best kilt and dress sporran. He was wearing a stiff white shirt and all his medals lay in a single line across his chest. It was an outfit that MacKinnon had never seen worn, although the officers used to wear it for dances and special dinners before the war. There is perhaps no dress so splendid. Jock looked at him, then looked away again to push in a drawer. He said, by way of apology:

'There's a ball at the Welcome. I was in there earlier. Maybe I'm a bit overdressed.'

'It's terrific, sir,' MacKinnon said with wide eyes, and Jock glanced at him in the wardrobe mirror. He was pleased by the effect and he gave a bashful smile.

'D'you think so?'

'I've never seen anything like it. Honestly, sir.'

'Aye. It's an expensive luxury, mind you. And I never get the chance to wear it. The whole thing cost me a couple of hundred pounds, would you credit it?'

MacKinnon gave an open smile, and Jock liked the flattery. He braced back his shoulders and pulled the tunic down so it lay smoothly.

'D'you think it fits?'

'It's perfect. At least I think so, sir.'

'A-huh. Does it suit me?'

'I've never seen you look better, sir.'

'Aye? Is that a fact?'

'Yes, sir.'

'Och, I'm glad of that. I thought I was never going to get the chance to wear it. But I'm glad it's good.'

MacKinnon swallowed. He said, 'You'll get the chance now, sir. Soon we'll be back to full dress. You're the Colonel again now, sir.'

Jock thought for a moment and then he nodded slowly. 'Aye, so I am.' He said, 'C'mon, let's get the place ship-shape. With my daughter away, it gets a wee bit out of hand.' The room was as untidy as it could be. A bomb might have dropped there. Clothes, dirty and clean, dressing-gown, shirts, half the contents of the drawers, were strewn about.

'I'd better fix a corporal from the Mess to come across and look after you in the morning, sir.'

'Aye, that's a good idea.' Jock was surprised by the suggestion. 'You're getting used to the Mess now, aren't you? You never used to open your mouth.'

MacKinnon blushed. 'I suppose I am.'

'It was your grandfather wasn't it, was Colonel?'

'That's right, sir.'

The boy was a far cry from being Colonel, but the link amused Jock. 'A-huh. Are you used to whisky yet?'

'I'm getting used to it, I think.'

'D'you like it?'

'Yes, sir.'

Jock shook his head and laughed. 'Och, c'mon then. Out with the lights. We'll leave this to the Corporal. We'll away down and have a dram.'

MacKinnon took a single to each of his Colonel's double whiskies and they got on very well. Jock had never talked to him before as if he were a man, and MacKinnon grew in confidence.

'There was one thing, sir.'

'Aye, laddie.'

'The Adjutant said to tell you he was awaiting orders about a file of papers the Assistant Adjutant was holding.'

'What's this?' The very word paper made Jock screw up his eyes.

'About a corporal being struck, sir, in a hotel.' MacKinnon looked at him with his big brown eyes, and slowly Jock caught on. Then he began to chuckle.

'It's an ill wind, laddie, that blows no one good. Aye, and they're quick enough, some of these laddies. Jimmy Cairns'll have more in his skull than most of us'll ever guess. That was quick of him. D'you know what it's all about?'

'We all have some idea, I think.'

'The Colonel struck the Corporal, and the Colonel it was that died . . . You can tell the Adjutant from me that he's to keep these papers in the meantime. He's no to forward them to Brigade.' Jock laughed quite loudly, and MacKinnon, less frightened of him now, began to laugh too. 'I thought they'd gone,' Jock said. 'I thought the report was away. It must have been something that damned fool Rattray said.'

MacKinnon swallowed. He looked hardly more than fifteen, like a midshipman at a pirate's table. He nodded and he said suddenly, 'Yes, Rattray is a damned fool isn't he?'

Jock looked at him astonished. The boy never usually said boo to a goose. Then he smiled at him. He was genuinely surprised and pleased by him.

'Christ, laddie, the whisky suits you. It does,' and he poured him another. MacKinnon gave a little swagger of his head, and he took a large gulp that burnt all the way down.

'All that bloody Scottish Nationalism,' he said strongly. 'Why, that's tripe and onions.'

'Tripe and onions? Is it? Aye, maybe you're right.' Jock shook his head and he began to laugh again. MacKinnon just smiled broadly at him. Then, looking at the tumbler in his hand, Jock suddenly grew more serious.

'Do I look tired?'

'You look all right, sir.'

'I've never been so tired. I'll never be so tired again, until the day I die. You wouldn't understand it, laddie. But when you've a battalion, and when you've a child, and when you've friends you've fought with . . . Och, I've been carrying it, the whole thing, for five years. And I thought I knew about it. Maybe Barrow knew more than me.' Jock saw MacKinnon frown as he tried to follow, and he smiled.

'I understand, sir,' MacKinnon said. 'Really I do.'

'No. But it's good of you to try. Neither you, laddie, nor anyone else knows just what all these things mean to me. And in one day, in one day,' he looked at the back of his hand, 'with one swipe of the hand the whole thing busts.'

'It must have been a shock, sir.'

'When you get to my state nothing's that shocking. You're kind of punch drunk. You just get more and more numb till there's two of you. And there's one Jock Sinclair knocking about the town with his heart breaking and there's me looking down at him . . . Laddie, are you scared of me still?'

'No, sir.'

'By reason of the whisky?'

'Not only that, sir.'

'Good for you. I'm sorry I'm no a more cheerful companion. You'll away back to the Mess and say "Christ, the old boy was weeping in his dram the night" – you will, you will.'

MacKinnon protested that he wouldn't.

'You can trust me *implicitly*,' he said and the expression amused Jock again. He approved of the child.

'I didn't get you right, laddie,' he said suddenly. 'Not right at all.'

MacKinnon did not know what to say. He looked at his cigarette and he said at last:

'I've learnt to smoke properly.'

Jock looked at him, mystified. Then the recollection was clear.

'Christ alive, it was you I shouted at for your smoking, was it?'

'Yes, sir. But you were absolutely right to.'

'Right? To hell with that, laddie. You bloody well smoke as you like. Here, here,' he said and he rummaged in a drawer of the dresser behind him. He fumbled until he found a new packet of cigarettes and he pushed them across the table.

'Here's a packet for you. It's no bloody business of big Jock Sinclair's how you smoke them.'

'Oh no, sir, I couldn't take . . .'

Jock raised his hand. 'You take them. You take them when they're offered.' Then he opened his fingers out and he smiled shyly. 'I want to give them to you, laddie, I want to.'

'Thanks most awfully.'

Jock couldn't get over his expressions.

'"Thanks most awfully." Dammit, dammit,' he said, 'It's a different language altogether.' Then they went on drinking a little longer, and MacKinnon was thrilled by it all. Jock spoke very quietly, and they had talked on many

subjects when MacKinnon at last recalled one of the war
stories they always told about Jock.

'Is that true, sir?'

Jock nodded. 'It's true enough.'

'But it's fabulous.'

'Did you no hear?' he said with a little smile. 'I'm a
fabulous man.' Then when he'd said that the world seemed
to fall away from him again and he looked immensely sad,
as he remembered. He could see the admiration in the
boy's eyes, and for the first time in his life he did not enjoy
it. He moved away from the table and stood up. He was
suddenly ashamed. He brushed some ash off his tunic then
he turned and he said:

'You'll no say anything about this get-up, will you?'

'Not if you don't want me to, sir.'

'You will.'

'No, I won't sir.'

'Good for you.'

But Jock was restive now: he was tired of their chat.

'Would your grandad have let his lassie marry a corporal?'

'No, sir.'

Jock clumped his fist down on the table.

'Aye, well I'm going to. D'you hear?'

'Yes, sir.'

'That's what I'm going to do.'

'I'm sure you're right, sir.'

'Och, things'll be fine. I'll fix that, and Jimmy Cairns'll
help fix Riddick and the others. I'll no lie down yet. You'll
see, we'll fix it. We'll forget all the little things. We'll start
anew. D'you know what? D'you know what the real trouble
is?'

'What's that, sir?'

'The Battalion's been at home too long. That's the
trouble. When it's yours, laddie, remember that. There's
always trouble when a battalion's too long at home. Remember that.'

'I shouldn't think I'll ever be Colonel, sir.'

'Laddie, d'you want to be?'

'Very much.'

'Then you will be. That's the trick about life. If you want something bad enough, you can get it. That's the way of it. Barrow, you know, Barrow wanted to be Colonel. He told me. He told me this afternoon. Oh, for Christ's sake, I should have seen it coming. I should have seen it.'

'Oh no, sir. I don't think anybody could have seen it. How could any one know a thing like that?'

Jock sat down again by the stove and he played with the poker as he talked.

'You can tell,' he said. 'If you take the trouble to.' He sighed. 'Och, what a carry-on. D'you know what I said to him the day when he was trying to speak to me?'

MacKinnon waited.

'I said I wanted to go to sleep. And he just left me. Aye. Och, well. C'mon laddie, it's time you were away back to your chariot.'

But when MacKinnon had gone Jock still walked about the kitchen, smoking cigarettes – 'for Christ's sake, like a bloody neurotic.' He sat down and pushed the bottle away. He felt so much that he couldn't feel at all. He was happy that he had been saved. Happy that he should let Morag go, because he already felt the reflection of her smile. He was angry with Charlie, sad about Mary, amused by Mac-Kinnon, annoyed by Rattray, bitterly disappointed by Jimmy, and afraid of what he had let Barrow do. He was all of these things, and none of these things, because he was tired. Exhaustion swept over him, leaving him ragged and apprehensive, too tired to think and too excited to sleep, even now. Worst of all, he knew, as he had known every night since that night in the desert, that in the morning they would be waiting for him to cope with the thing, and suddenly he did not want to cope any longer.

He wanted nothing. It was as if he had prepared himself to die, and death for a joke had passed him by, so that he was doomed to go on making the same noises and meeting the same people, like a ghost of himself. Suddenly afraid, he started to say the Lord's Prayer out loud. But the echo of the very first phrase killed it and he shrugged. He walked over to the shelf and picked out his favourite book. He had put Morag's note to say that she was out with her friend inside the cover of it, when he had picked it up to read it on the previous evening. But now not even the note, not even the lie, seemed to touch him. The book was not the Bible but a book of nursery rhymes which he had practically learnt by heart when he was teaching them to Morag. On the previous evening when he read the little fairy story he had written for her long before, he had nearly cried, but he read it now as if he were looking at it from another world. Even the self-pity had vanished now. It was about a skylark never dying but soaring straight through the golden gates. His eyes passed over the words again and again, but he did not read them. As with the words, so was the rest of the world, and all its problems. It was like a merciful concussion. The only thing he could think about now was the riddle that had occurred to him and he looked at the back of his hand as he said again and again, 'The Colonel struck the Corporal, and the Battalion it was that died.' He tried it over again until at last he said to himself:

'The Colonel struck the Corporal,
And how come that to pass?

'Aye,' he said out loud. 'And that'll finish as a rude one.' The thought of that gave him just a little relief and he clenched his fists together.

A colonel does not need an arm to strike with; he needs teeth to hang on with.

BOOK THREE

The Funeral Orders

THE ORDER GROUP foregathered in the piping-room, according to instructions. The Regimental Sergeant-Major was there with the Pipe-Major. The Company Commanders were there, and Mr Simpson had unfurled the map over the blackboard. They all stood around, talking nothings, like candidates outside an examination hall. But they stood to attention when Jimmy announced the arrival of the Colonel.

Jock had not looked so smart since the days before the peace. He gave his orders with battle conviction; with complete command; with attack; with effect. They sat in folding cane chairs, silent and attentive as he started according to the book:

'Bonnets off.'

He faced them. He never took his eyes from them. He never referred to a note.

'INFORMATION:

'You see behind me a plan of the streets of the city. Most of the places I mention will be familiar to you but for the benefit of those of you who have confined their outings to a ground sheet on the park there, or a motor run to the nearest country house, I will point out the places to which I refer in the following orders.'

No one laughed at his joke, but nobody was supposed to. He was merely collecting their attention.

He took a deep breath.

'Colonel Barrow was found dead late on the evening of February 20 and on February 23 was adjudged as having committed suicide while the balance of his mind was disturbed. Enquiries were made of his wife, who abides in a London mews . . .'

There was a little stir, and Macmillan nodded as much as to say he had known. Some pouted and Charlie said out loud, 'I'd forgotten that one.'

Jock's eyes flashed.

'I do not expect to be interrupted when I'm giving orders.'

The effect was like a slap in the face. Charlie winced. They all sat up straight in their seats. There was absolute silence in the room and Jock waited a long time, so that the effect would sink in. Then, as they expected him to continue the orders he said sharply again, 'Not now; not in the future; not ever; not by anyone.' And he paused again. Charlie sat like a statue, with his eyes in front of him.

'Mrs Barrow referred us to her husband's lawyers, Holden Good and Co. of Bedford Row, London, who stated that the Commanding Officer had no relations other than his wife. At her request it was decided that the funeral arrangements should be made and executed by the officer now commanding the Battalion.

'The Colonel's remains are at present in the C.R.S. attached to this barracks. A site for the grave has been found in the cemetery which lies some third of a mile east of the main bridge. Here. It lies on the hill.'

Jock pointed on the map with a pointer that had until then lain untouched on the desk.

'And here.'

He laid down the pointer again and let his hands drop to his sides. His audience was completely attentive, and although it was one of those rooms where every scrape of a chair carries and every cough is magnified, there was still no sound, but for the echo of the click as the pointer came to rest on the desk. Jock was breathing faster now. His eyes moved round the company sitting in the two rows in front of him. All the other chairs had been folded against the walls and the floor had been scrubbed for the occasion. Even the boxes on top of the lockers at the back of the room had been dusted, and the high narrow windows washed. Jock took off his bonnet which was tight enough to have marked his brow, and he smoothed down his hair with his hands, so that it lay absolutely flat. He looked at them all, and at each one of them: the Company Commanders in the front and the Adjutant and Warrant Officers behind.

'All companies, full strength, except for various members of H.Q. Company who will remain in barracks together with the guards and pickets of the day – all companies will take their part in the operation. All officers and other ranks on leave for any reason other than compassionate will be recalled today before 1500 hours. Various officers at present attached War Office and at present attached Royal Military College, Sandhurst, who were personally acquainted with Barrow, will also take part. Regardless of rank or seniority for the purposes of this operation these officers will count as part of this Battalion and the contingent will be under my command.

'The pipes and drums will parade.

'The Burgh police will be acquainted with the orders which follow.

'So much for Information.'

They moved in their seats and Macmillan glanced at Jimmy Cairns and made a little face. The Order Group, like a charger, was held hard at the bit and being pushed on by the urgent boot. It had been the same on the Adjutant's Parade earlier that morning.

'INTENTION:

'The Battalion will bury the Colonel.'

Jock blinked and glowered at Macmillan who gave just the shadow of a smile. He was always inclined to mock the army's more ludicrous regulations. The object of the exercise – to kill the enemy, to capture the castle, or to bury the dead – always struck him as vaguely amusing. Charlie moved his moustache, but he looked quite serious. Jimmy was anxious lest he should miss anything and he had his notebook on his knee. The Pipe-Major nodded at the end of each sentence and the Regimental Sergeant-Major stuck his legs out in front of him, with an air of resistance. Mr Simpson endeavoured to look keen and intelligent and he was so self-conscious that he missed a great deal of what was said.

'METHOD: The Colonel will be given the full honours of the martial funeral.'

Charlie cocked an eyebrow and in reply Macmillan gave the slightest shrug. Jock said 'martial funeral' again, as if in reply to them, then he took another deep breath.

'For the purpose of these orders we can divide the operation into three distinct parts. Before the ceremony. The burial itself. The return to barracks.

'Taking two, first. Exact orders concerning the burial will affect only some senior officers and Warrant Officers and the Padre will run through the service with us tonight at 1930 hours. Parade in the reading room in the Mess.'

The officers were glad to have something definite to write down. Some put '1930, Reading room,' others 'Padre 1930 hrs.' Jimmy Cairns noted all three relevant facts: the time, the place, and the purpose. But as soon as they had made their notes they looked up again. Jock waited until the last word was written down. He did not hurry. Jimmy was biting his lip. The orders were all new to him. Three or four times he had asked Jock what the arrangements were to be, but Jock had ignored him. He had looked straight through him. For two days he had hardly said a word to anybody. He had been building up to this. He still looked nervous, his voice was a little too loud, his gestures a little sudden, but it was a Jock they hardly remembered. The victory and the years that followed had made them all forget the days when he had been nervous and electric like this. Simpson, who had not known him then, was bewildered by the change.

But as the orders continued, and the full scale of the operation was made plain Jimmy grew frightened, and he could see that the others were uneasy too.

It was soon clear that the plan anticipated was the sort of funeral usually reserved for heroes who were also generals. The first picture Jock gave them of the long winding column of men, the music and the mourners, opened their eyes to the scale of the thing. There had not been such a funeral from Campbell Barracks in a hundred years, and there had been a score of colonels since then.

'Before the ceremony:

'The R.S.M. will parade the Battalion in line, A Company on the right, the carrying party and the pipes and drums in the rear, and the colour party, under Mr Simpson, ahead of the line. The extra contingent I mentioned will not parade, but will stand ready by the guardroom under the general guidance of the Quartermaster. They will join the marching column separately in the position which I will indicate in due course.'

He gave some details of the personnel forming the colour and carrying parties, and some orders concerning detailed rehearsals to be carried out that afternoon.

'The carrying party itself will be comprised of the eight senior sergeants acting as bearers and a full platoon of men drawn from all companies to pull the gun carriage.' There was a gasp at that. The gun carriage was reserved for marshals. But Jock continued without pause. 'The whole will be under the immediate command of the R.S.M.'

He moved back, and rolled up the map, displaying the blackboard.

'On my command the Battalion will move to the right in column of threes, and slow march out of barracks in the following order.'

He pointed to the blackboard, and as he read out what was written there he indicated each item with the pointer.

'A Company.

Pipes and Drums.

Carrier Party and Gun carriage.

Colour party.

Commanding Officer, Adjutant, and extra contingent of mourners.

H.Q. Company.

Transport Company, on foot.

B,

C,

D Companies.'

Jimmy at last caught Charlie's eye, but Charlie gave nothing away. Macmillan looked round at Simpson, who was behind his right shoulder, and he made a wry face. Simpson made a schoolboy's gesture with his hands: the sort of gesture boys make when a master is talking about something beyond the class's comprehension. Feet moved, and the chairs creaked a little, while Jock ran on. His voice never varied in tone. The words came loudly and quickly:

'As the Battalion moves off there will be ample time for the various detachments to join at the correct juncture while the companies wheel round the three sides of the square. The order of march will be final as we pass the guardroom and the barracks gate.

'The R.S.M. will consider the march-off in detail with the several Company Sergeant-Majors and party commanders. I suggest there is a rehearsal parade tomorrow at 1000 hours.'

Mr Riddick always liked to raise an objection, but after the rebuff Charlie had received he was careful to be correct in his behaviour.

'Permission to interrupt, sir.' He stood up, and Jock eyed him warily. He carried the pointer horizontally in his hands.

'Granted,' he said, using his short *a*.

'1000 hours is Battalion Orders, sir.'

'There will be no Battalion Orders tomorrow.' There had been none since the Colonel's death. Jock had had no time for detail, and no inclination for it.

'Begging your pardon, sir, there are several persons under arrest, sir.'

Jock turned back to him, savagely.

'Don't answer me back, Mr Riddick!' He clasped his fingers tightly round the pointer then he moved to the tall desk and he placed the pointer on it softly.

'Not now,' he said, looking down at the desk. 'Not ever.'

Mr Riddick was red and indignant.

He shouted 'Sir' and Mr McLean tapped him on the knee, suggesting he should sit down again.

'My suggestion, perfectly in order,' he murmured indignantly, and Jock looked up at him with pale blue parrot's eyes.

'Ssh,' Mr McLean said, and he leant back in his chair, so it creaked. Mr Riddick felt foolish.

'Pipe-Major!'

Mr McLean jumped. He was afraid Jock had thought he was whispering to Riddick.

'We'll deal with the music after "Intercommunication." I'll come to that later. Understood?'

'Yes, sir. Yes.' His reply was a little song.

'Very well.'

Jock was more like a preacher now. He hung on to the tall desk as if it were a lectern in a pulpit, leaning over it, swaying about it. The sweat was forming on his brow, although all the others in the room were cold. The hands that held the pencils were blue with cold.

'Is the order of march clear, gentlemen?'

Two or three of the officers nodded, and Jimmy mumbled a general assent.

'Clear, Mr Simpson?'

'Yes sir.'

'Clear, Major Hay?' to one of the Company Commanders.

'Quite clear, Colonel.'

'Mr Riddick?'

'Sah.' Mr Riddick still shouted his assent fiercely.

'Very good then.' He unrolled the map of the town again. He took the pointer and stood to one side. The orders were given according to the book.

'The Battalion will proceed at the slow march down to the cross-roads where they will turn right, off Stuart Road.' Always he pointed to the place which he named. 'At this point the band will stop playing and the Battalion will continue along Bridge Road to the High Street.' He followed the whole route, naming in detail every street and every corner and the pointer followed the procession along the map.

'In Lothian Terrace the Battalion will halt and turn by companies and contingents left into line and order arms. The carrier party, colour party, H.Q. group and extra contingent will detach themselves, and they will follow the Padre to the graveside in the following order. They will follow in slow time.

'Padre.

Band contingent.

Carrier party – that is the eight sergeants and the Regimental Sergeant-Major.

Colour party.

Commanding Officer and H.Q. Group.

Mourning Contingent.

Firing party to be drawn from A Company.

'The band party will consist of the Pipe-Major, Corporal-Drummer, and your picked piper. The band remainder will remain . . .'; the noise of the repetition seemed to please him and he began the sentence again. 'The band remainder will remain in Lothian Terrace under the command of the senior sergeant. Mr McLean!'

'Sir?' Mr McLean always sounded anxious to please. His voice was always the very breath of sanity and civility.

'Have you got your pibroch piper picked?'

'Aye, sir. He's waiting next door.'

'We'd better have him in.'

'I'll just be getting him, sir.'

'Obliged.'

The Pipe-Major pushed back his chair and Mr Simpson stood up to let him by. The break was welcomed by everybody and again they all stirred in their seats. Jock himself was lighting a cigarette and there was a little hum of voices. Mr Simpson leant forward to Major Macmillan and he said, 'I'd no idea it was to be as big as this.'

Macmillan raised his eyebrows high. 'I don't think they'd give you or me a show like this.'

But the R.S.M. was more serious in his complaint. He said out aloud:

'Dammit, Montgomery couldn't expect anything more than this.'

Charlie was the only one who spoke up.

'Pretty elaborate do,' he said, but Jock did not seem to hear him. So Cairns followed up.

'How long was Barrow with us, all told?' and he glanced at Jock, but Jock ignored him too. He was preparing the next details in his mind. If he saw that his officers were uncomfortable about the scale of the operation he gave no sign of it. There might have been a soundproof screen between him and the others and his face was quite expressionless until the Pipe-Major returned with the picked piper.

'Corporal Fraser,' the Pipe-Major said, and the Corporal saluted smartly. His face was pale and he still had a dark blue shadow round his eye. Jock was thrown off balance and his hands fumbled for the pointer on the desk. He looked fiercely at the Pipe-Major.

'You didn't say it was Corporal Fraser.'

'No, sir. He's the only one with the pibroch good enough, sir.'

'Aye.'

Jock looked nervously from one face to another, and he tried to recover himself quickly. He pulled himself up and he said, 'The Padre'll give the officers a talk on the ceremony tonight at . . .' He looked blankly at them as he remembered he had said this before. He paused: he looked lost for a moment.

'1930 hours I think, sir,' Jimmy said.

'1930 hours,' Jock echoed, then his eyes wandered back to the Corporal again. He was standing stiffly to attention just inside the door. The blue ring round his right eye made his face look paler, like a moon in the shadows of the corner. For a moment or two Jock seemed to see nothing other than this face. He gazed at it. It was the first time that he had seen the Corporal since he had struck him. All the business of the cancellation of the enquiry had been done through the Pipe-Major. Mr Riddick had not liked it at all: but when he opened his mouth with a threat, Mr McLean looked at him so hard that the words would not come. Charlie, when he learned, just shrugged his shoulders, and said, 'Luck of the game.' Jock nodded, at last.

'A-huh, Corporal Fraser.'

'Sir.'

'I haven't seen you. Where are you staying?'

'Been on a pass, sir. I am back in barracks again now, sir.'

'When did you come back from leave, eh?'

'This morning, sir.'

A little of the old wiliness returned. 'A-huh. Are you married or single, Corporal?'

'Single, sir.'

Jimmy leant forward anxiously. Jock was standing at the side of the little platform by the blackboard, facing the Corporal.

'Colonel, we're short of time . . .'

'Is Morag with you, Corporal?'

Jimmy had spoken softly and he wondered if he had been heard.

'Colonel . . .'

'Hold your tongue!' Jock glowered down at him. He turned back to the Corporal and spoke softly again.

'Is Morag with you?'

'No, sir.'

'Where is she?'

Charlie shifted in his seat. Major Hay whispered something to his neighbour and the R.S.M. gave a heavy cough.

'One of the officers,' he said, 'should take steps.'

'Wheesht, man,' the Pipe-Major replied.

'Wait, the rest of you,' Jock said without looking at them. 'Answer me, Corporal.'

'She's staying with my people, sir.'

'Where's that?'

'Forres, sir.'

'Christ,' Jock said. 'There's a carry-on. There's a bloody carry-on. At ease, Corporal. Nobody. Nobody told me this. You never told me this, Jimmy.'

'No, sir.' He gave a friendly smile. 'After . . .' he suggested, but Jock waved his hand.

'Och, for Christ's sake: there's no bloody secret now. There have been too many damned secrets and whispers. I like things in the open, and I always have done. That I have. You'll be playing the pipes over the grave, Corporal. Take a seat. We've to deal with the music yet. Sit down like the rest of them and you'll get your orders.'

The Corporal took a chair from the pile at the back, and he brought it up behind the others. He unfolded it and sat down.

'Bonnets off,' Jock said. 'Bonnets off.' And the Corporal put his bonnet on his lap. He had swung his sporran round to his hip.

But Jock could not bring himself back to the orders as

quickly as he had anticipated. He was an actor who had forgotten his words. There was a little silence, then he looked at Jimmy and he said fiercely:

'Where the hell was I?'

Jimmy could not recall fast enough.

'Oh, for Christ's sake, someone. Where did we get to? Were none of you listening, eh, is that the way of it?'

Macmillan of all people answered: perhaps his social experience had taught him to keep his head in moments of embarrassment.

'The actual ceremony, I think, Colonel.'

'I told you the actual ceremony's the Padre's business: he'll speak to you tonight at . . . in the Mess at . . .'

'1930 hours, sir.'

'We've been through all that . . .' As he faltered again, Charlie spoke, very calmly.

'Seeing we've come to an interval, I wonder, Colonel . . . This is a pretty elaborate funeral you're planning for, what?'

'Have you an objection, Major Scott?'

'Well,' Charlie poked the point of his crook into a crack between the damp floor-boards. 'It isn't as if Barrow was with us a long time. I mean he may have been a good man and all that but . . . What does anybody else think?'

Charlie leant back as he threw the question open to the others. Jock was standing crouching over the high desk, staring at them.

'Agreed, sir,' Mr Riddick shouted.

'It does seem quite a do,' Macmillan said. Jock waited patiently with a pained smile on his face, and Jimmy spoke again:

'Of course it's right he should get a proper burial, but the whole Battalion, and the gun carriage. Would that not be overdoing it – or d'you not think so?'

He looked back at Jock who made no movement.

All the other Company Commanders, now the tension had been broken a little, said the same thing in different ways and Simpson, because he'd always been taught to speak up, said, 'I mean, the circumstances of his death alone.' And here Jock cut in. He came down heavily on Simpson in his old bullying way.

'The circumstances of his death, eh? What does that mean, Mr Simpson?'

'Well, sir, there's been talk enough. I know it was of unsound mind, but,' his voice trailed away; then as Jock waited he said, 'I mean, sir, suicide's suicide. I'm not sure the Church . . .'

Jock clenched his fists. 'No, it bloody well isn't. It's bloody murder.' With an effort he controlled himself and he threw the next sentence away, so that some of them did not even hear it. 'But that's neither here nor there. For Christ's sake.' He stepped off the platform and he walked over to the window and looked down at the barrack square. Most of the snow had disappeared now, but there was a little pile round the edge of the square. A squad was doubling along from one end to the other under the direction of a corporal with panic in his voice. Jock watched them as if they were toys.

He said, 'I rang his wife, and she had not seen him for three years. I rang his lawyers and they knew of no brothers and sisters. Mind you, he had his friends in Whitehall and he need never have left. Fifteen years after he left this Battalion he came back to it. Fifteen years after he had left Scotland he came back to it.'

He turned his face to them, and he lifted his arms.

'Can you not see?' he asked. 'Can you not understand? And this is the Battalion that's known as the friendly one: and ours is the Mess where it's Christian names only. You mean bastards; you'd grudge him his burial.'

'Oh, hardly,' Charlie said.

'You do, Charlie Scott.'

'It's only the method, Jock.'

'We'll bury him as he should be buried.'

'It isn't as if he even led us in battle.'

'He could have done.'

Charlie's face hardened. 'I merely said he didn't. Jock, whichever way we look at it, we're only burying a colonel.'

'Oh!' Jock shouted it out. 'Oh! Oh, for Christ's sake! Only a colonel. You don't know, do you? None of you; you don't begin to know. Only a colonel! Aye, and that's what he said himself.' He turned back to the window. He seemed now quite out of touch with the others in the room, and he talked as much to himself as to anybody else. He made a little cross in some dust that had formed on the sill: not a Christian cross, but a double cross for noughts and crosses. 'Only a colonel and a colonel's heart. And I wonder about that, too. I'm no sure it's only the Colonel: I'm no sure it isn't the whole bloody glory.'

The murmurs grew louder in the room, and only Corporal Fraser, sitting by himself at the back, kept quiet. He just stared at Jock unbelievingly. Then at last the big shoulders swivelled round and the conversation dried up.

'We'll bury him the way I say we'll bury him, and that's an order, and that's a fact.' He walked quickly back to the platform and he faced them again.

'METHOD:

'After the ceremony. The return to barracks.' He shouted it out loud.

'I say,' Simpson said. 'He's gone round the bend, hasn't he?'

'For Christ's sake, shut up,' Jimmy replied.

'But it's true.'

'Shut up.'

'The groups taking part in the ceremony will slow march back to the formation in Lothian Terrace and the Battalion on my word of command will march off in column of threes, in the reverse order, D Company in advance of the retreat.'

He pointed at the board again, this time with his finger

and he went through each group, finishing with A Company.

'When the leading company – D Company in this instance – reaches the crossing of the High Street and Stuart Road the Battalion will halt company by company, contingent by contingent. Then under my general command, but company by company, the column will retreat to the barracks at the slow march. The companies will turn into line, and I will dismiss the parade.'

The last set of orders seemed to take a great deal out of Jock and he leant forward on the desk again, and took a sip of water. The rims of his eyes were pink with weariness. All of the officers, save for Charlie, were staring at him. Charlie was looking at the floor. Like a boxer at the start of another round, Jock moved away from the desk again and stretched himself straight. As he opened the next paragraph, what had been a doubt before now became a terrible certainty. There was an audible gasp, and Jimmy covered his face with his hands. Simpson looked round at the others who looked neither to left nor right. There was no pity in Mr Riddick's eye but he was twitching his little moustache with discomfort. Jock, wide-eyed, rolled into the attack. Nothing would have stopped him now. His face was florid and his eyes were bright. Words flowed from his lips.

'ADMINISTRATION:

'The Colonel will be laid in his coffin in the full scarlet of a Lieutenant-Colonel of this Regiment, his headdress beside him.'

Jock glanced along the line.

'The Adjutant acting with the Q.M. and the Medical Staff will see that this order is discharged.'

He paused and looked at Cairns, who had not moved.

'The Adjutant,' he suddenly said with the voice he usually used for sarcasm, 'is hiding his face. Is my order understood?'

Jimmy did not even want to look at him now. He just

glanced up for a second, and he bit his lip. Then he said softly, 'Sir,' And Jock went on, 'The full scarlet. The full dress, even if it has to be tailored tonight. D'you hear me? The full scarlet. Is that understood?'

'Sir.' Jimmy was looking white. He closed his eyes to recover himself.

'The coffin will be carried to the final resting place on the traditional gun carriage which the officer commanding Transport Company will put at the disposal of the Regimental Sergeant-Major commanding the carrying party. Is that understood?'

'Sir.'

'Mr Riddick, is that understood?'

The pantomime continued.

'Understood, sir.'

Soon nobody was looking at Jock; nobody dared, nor did they dare look at each other, any longer. They had turned their eyes away from him much as boys do in a classroom when one of their number begins to cry. Only Mr McLean glanced at him from time to time, and he nodded to show that he was listening. All around him he saw the bowed heads. Not long after Macmillan told some of his friends how ludicrous it had all been: but he was not laughing at the time. He did not feel at all like laughing, at the time. He had the same desire as all the others there, then: he wanted to hide himself.

'The Quartermaster has already been warned about dress. The necessary accoutrements will be drawn from the Battalion stores, company by company, in accordance with the Q.M.'s detail. The aprons and the plaids.

'The full parade rehearsal will be at 1000 hours tomorrow. This afternoon and tomorrow at 0900 hours the separate companies . . .'

There were a score of details, and the orders seemed to go on and on. Jock did not hesitate now. He had remembered the words, but the others still looked away. Jimmy listened and prayed that it would soon come to an end. None of them noted down any of the points: none of them moved. It might have been a stranger standing on the platform, talking so fast. They had a horror of him. Jimmy searched for pity, but could find nothing other than the same horror.

'Mr Riddick will personally supervise the gun carriage drill, and brief the senior sergeants forming the carrying party. Understood?'

'Understood, sir.'

'The Assistant Adjutant will make it his business to report the details of routes and timing to the Chief of Police.'

'Yes sir.'

'INTERCOMMUNICATION:

'The column will be of considerable length and halting by companies or changing time will present difficulty. Warning orders should be passed back from Company Sergeant-Major to Company Sergeant-Major and arrangements for this are again the responsibility of the R.S.M.'

Jock scowled. He seemed to have forgotten something here and he leant forward. The group waited, half expecting him to collapse over the desk, but he pulled himself up again. As the silence continued, the others, one by one, looked up, aware that it was all over. Jock stood perfectly still. He stared down at them until they had all raised their heads, and he completed the formula:

'Any questions?'

Nobody spoke until at last Charlie said, 'Absolutely none.'

Then Jock remembered.

'What about the music?'

'Oh, yes. The music.'

'Aye.' The eyes flared up again. 'There's the question of the music.' They waited with clenched fists.

'Aye, let's see. No music when we parade, but the march off. The slow march. *The Flowers of the Forest.*'

They watched him now. He was talking with feeling again. Every note of the tune seemed to pass through his head when he mentioned the title, and he repeated it. '*The Flowers of the Forest.*' Then he spoke quite plainly as if the recollection just amused him.

'Charlie, you remember that dream I had about Barrow?'

'Sorry?'

'About the Colonel. I had a dream, you mind that day in Mary's house.' The thought of that made him frown. 'In poor Mary's house,' he said, then he brightened up again. 'I said it was a good dream. I told her. And I couldn't mind the dream at all, and you said it must have been a nightmare. I mind it now. The whole Battalion, you see, was lined up on a grey afternoon, lined up ready to move off and at the back there was the gun carriage, with a platoon round it, commanded by a tinker. That's why I'm so sure of the music. We'll have *The Flowers of the Forest* at the ceremony, of course, but we'll have it as we march off too.' He smiled hopelessly and Charlie looked back at him blankly.

'Can't say I remember.'

The smile stayed on Jock's face, but he seemed to have forgotten it. It was a mask.

'In a way, I was right. But I was wrong in thinking it was a good dream. It was a nightmare, after all. You were right about that, Charlie. So you were. Charlie's always right.'

Mr McLean's voice was gentle. 'And after *The Flowers of the Forest*, sir?'

'Aye, we'll have *My Home*, and then it'll be time for the quick ones. The three-fours. What'll be right then?'

'*The Green Hills.*'

'Aye, I like *The Green Hills*. And one or two more but most of the way through the town you'll no play. Play when you turn up the hill there.'

'Sir.'

Jock was warm again:

'The Burial Party. Your one corporal'll lead with the

traditional *Flowers of the Forest* there again, the whole way from the gates to the grave, and take it slow, Pipe-Major, take it slow.'

'Yes, sir.'

'Now what about the pibroch?'

'That's for the Corporal, sir.'

Jock looked over their heads at the Corporal, who nodded. Jock winced when he looked at the bruise on his face and he lifted his own hand to his eye.

'Are you right?' he asked. 'You're all right?'

'I'm all right, sir.'

Jock blinked. 'I'm glad of that. I'm glad of that. So you'll choose your own pibroch.'

'Sir.'

'And what'll it be?'

'*Morag*, sir.'

'*Morag*, aye. Can you manage it?'

'Aye, sir.'

'You're a man after my heart, Corporal. That's the bloody silly thing.' Then he turned back to the Pipe-Major.

'The death they say is a victory. The death they say's the great triumph. We'll march away to the *Black Bear*. The *Black Bear*'s to pull us together.' Jock was lost in the music again. 'Then the regimental march; *Scotland the Brave*; the *Cameron Men*; some others, Pipe-Major?'

'*The Cock o' the North*.'

He was suddenly angry, like a turkey: 'Yon's a cheesy tune. You'll no play that till Charlie Scott here's Colonel. You'll no play that. Some others, aye. *Lawson's Men*'d do.'

He tapped his fingers on the desk and he mentioned several more marches.

'All the tunes of glory!' he suddenly cried. 'We'll have them all, to remember the more clearly. We'll have all the tunes of glory!' He turned towards the window again and he raised his hands with a triumph and excitement: he stared up at the sky and his eyes glistened as he said:

'It'll be a right funeral. I know it will. It's as I said. I've seen it once already. And it'll be the least we can do.' He wheeled round again, and the moon faces watched him.

'And all along Stuart Road, Mr McLean, along Stuart Road until the cross-roads . . .' Suddenly he looked back at the window again and he said very quickly with a sort of clown-like bathos, 'We'll have no music at all: all along the road there, we'll have no music. Just the long column winding through the town, winding all the way. Just the noise of the marching and the straps and bayonets. Just the rattle of the wheels of the empty gun carriage, bumping along the cobbles there. And all the people'll be watching us. Mr Riddick, the marching must be perfect. D'you hear me? Perfect!'

It had gone too far again for anybody to stop him: there was no chance of interruption now, and again the heads began to drop. But this time Jimmy did not lower his eyes. He watched Jock all the time, with awful anguish, as he talked on and on. It was as if he could not leave off: as if he knew that it was his last speech in court, and when that was ended, all was ended. With a fever, with every gesture, his voice growing loud one moment and soft the next, he went on and on.

'. . . And it'll snow again. Those are the snow clouds there. But the snow'll not break until the end of the day. It'll not start snowing until the parade is over. When we're finished it'll snow. But when we march back from the hill it'll be bitter cold, and a wee bit misty maybe, and pink, over the roofs. I see it fine, with the aprons over the kilts and the pink picked out in the stone of the houses: and the daft purple of the drapes over the kettledrums. Now the last bit . . .

'Aye, the last bit. The last bit into the barracks at the slow march. We'll no have the *Flowers* then, nor any other tune.' He suddenly spotted Charlie and he said quickly, 'We'll no have *Charlie is my darling*, either.'

He turned his head in a little circle and he spoke softly, almost secretively as he walked back to look at the barrack square below. 'We'll not have the pipes at all. That's how we'll do it. We'll come the last bit through the gates with the muffled kettledrums alone. No music at all. Just the drums. The whole long column, the whole Battalion of us at the slow march and just the four kettledrums rapping, beating, with a die – with a *die, dittit-die, dittit-die.*'

He waited, and there was no sound. He turned very slowly and his face was frozen with a curiously questioning expression. The tears were pouring down his cheeks. For a terrible moment he must have seen himself reflected in their eyes.

Slowly he put his hand to his face and felt the wetness of the tears. He looked about him, trapped and appalled, then again he was quite lost and he moved like a waif across the room.

There was silence until Mr McLean's voice broke gently, like a soft wave on an Atlantic shore.

'Aye, sir,' he said, 'it will be done exactly as you have said.'

Jock did not turn back to them, so Mr McLean got up without another word, and the others followed. They walked from the room leaving only Charlie and Jimmy behind, and when they were outside they dispersed immediately, going their different ways in silence, like monks.

Inside the room Charlie moved slowly towards his friend as if he were approaching an animal and he said, as he always said:

'Jock, old chum' and Jimmy said, 'Laddie.'

It was then that he broke. It was then with a great groan of relief as much as of sorrow that it came to an end for him. It was the end of what had started in a desert. His shoulders began to shake, his lip quivered and first he gave a whimper. Then with great gulps of air like an inconsolable child, he began to sob while the two officers supported him.

'All right, laddie; all right.'

'We'll tell Mary,' Jimmy suggested kindly but Jock shook his head violently. They got a car and put him into it because he asked, at last, to be taken home.

'Tell Morag, you fools, tell Morag, and take me home.' And there were soldiers passing by, who stared at him. 'For Christ's sake,' he said. 'I'm bashed the now. Oh, my babies, take me home!'

Household Ghosts

for Susan

BOOK ONE

A Country Dance

THE GYMNASIUM AT Dow's Academy that night was a monumental patch-up of ugliness and joy. Fifty tables covered by hand-stitched linen cloths were squeezed into the shadows, at one side, hard against the climbing bars; and at the other side, beyond a huge square mirror (in front of which, in term time, flat-footed grammar school boys performed remedial exercises) all the instruments of torture or of glory – the horse, the horizontal and the parallel bars – were crowded into the corner and inadequately covered with a huge Union Jack, as if for a mass burial at sea. Sad streamers were looped across the hall but all they succeeded in doing was to draw the eye to the two climbing ropes strung up like giant nooses. Amongst the climbing bars by the mirror pale ribbons were interwoven and tied in pussy bows. Framed in the middle of these was a coloured photograph of the Duke of Edinburgh on his wedding day, provided by the local confectioner whose best pre-war line had been boxes of George V chocolates. Above the platform, at the end of the hall, set against blue sackcloth curtains was a big banner which shouted VOTE UNIONIST and carried, one each side, prints of Sir Winston Churchill and Sir Anthony Eden, both wearing confident smiles.

Around the tables sat a hundred Auntie Belles ('Gin and ginger, thanks, pet') and Mary, brilliant, red-haired Mary moved amongst them, expecting the answer yes. Hardly had an Uncle Harry or a Douglas time to reply – to say 'Hello there, Mary', with joy, because no man was anything but pleased when Mary touched their sleeve or laid the flat of her hand on their lapel – before she moved on again. Mary bending forward, listening keenly; Mary leaning right back and laughing; nodding worriedly to one or sympathising with the next; she talked to practically all of them.

And there was a phalanx of square-shouldered fur-capes to talk to; a great aroma of bath salts and moth balls and a loud tinkle-crash of jewellery.

At the top of the hall, beside the platform but not directly below the band, a table for some guests and parents of the Committee or Landed added the Kitzbuhl and Consolidated Steel touch. Below the band, some perched on the stage, others standing biting their nails or holding each other's hips, were many girls in pretty cotton frocks with full skirts; pinks and greens and whites. These girls were anything from fifteen to a rather raddled, on-the-make elder sister of twenty-eight, and they darted glances at the unaccompanied young men who were standing by the main entrance flattering each other with obscenities and loud, long laughs. Most of these seemed, at least at first, reluctant to dance. Two of them were dressed more or less as Teddy boys but they were unteddied by their own pink cheeks. In the end, the younger of the two forgot his grimace and assumed a leery grin confirming that he would have come in a cow-boy's get-up, if only he had had the nerve. The other boys were all in blue or brown suits and they looked as if they had shaved in a circular movement along the chin and around the back of the neck. They were sharply critical of the girls in their pretty frocks, of the bar prices, of the band and of the old bags sitting at the tables; but polite, abashed and confused as soon as Mary said:

'You must be the crook who sold us short on coke—'

And she talked to the important townsfolk too. Each one jumped to his feet, from the provost to the clerk's assistant. But they did so not only for Mary. It was as if they were desperately canvassing votes not for any political cause but for some imaginary, competitive election to be decided on the basis of obituaries in the local Press and on the market-day epitaphs collected on the week they should die.

A few gaps at the tables where men should be looking after their wives betrayed the group who moved between the bar and Classroom III. These were the Boys from the Queen's private bar; the vet, half a dozen farmers, the potato merchant, the town's second solicitor and estate agent, the golfing pro, the undertaker and building contractor, and a couple of others. But somehow the women who had been abandoned looked happier than those who had managed to hang on to their husbands, diverting their appetites from whiskies and Exports to soft biscuits, sweet tea and creamy meringues. ('Will you not have another, pet?')

Mary, jokingly, held her hands against her ears to dull the blasts of laughter and the noise of the smart-Alec concertina and fiddle band with Flying-Officer Kite type on the Kettle Drums, then slipping past a couple of young girls who were dancing together at the corner of the floor she went to the table where an absurdly good-looking little man with white hair was staring into the middle distance. She approached and spoke in his ear and he was obviously very fond of her. He put a hand on her shoulder. She said quickly and seriously:

'Daddy, darling, you don't blame me, do you?' He leant back and against the noise of the band he mouthed a long 'No'. She began again:

'For God's sake, darling, what does it matter? It's too idiotic. It's a silly joke, even if he has fallen for me which I don't suppose he has. I can tell you he's never really said a friendly word. And if they think I've fallen for him they're absolutely batty. He never smiles at me. He never says a kind thing. Not to me or anyone else, I bet, except when he's laying on the charm. But don't blame me. I just met him at this bloody silly cocktail party, only down in London

it seems to be after supper when they throw about the gin.'
She sighed and shrugged. Again her father reassured her
with a shake of his head. She persisted:

'I've told them about a hundred times – So he glared at
me? I didn't hide my wedding ring or anything like that. We
danced to some ghastly Rock and Roll, and that wasn't
much of a pleasure I can tell you. He's the world's worst
dancer. He rang and rang, and all right, so I did have lunch
with him. After all, I was there for a holiday.'

She flung out her hands.

'Well, since then he's followed me about, even to the
extent of turning up here.' She referred to a man called
David Dow, a physiologist approaching middle age who
was the son of the first headmaster of the Academy, and
that is why she added, 'After all, I can't stop him. This place
is more home to him than me.' Her father was a little deaf.
He cupped his hand round his ear. She finished, 'You
know? Let's not make a situation. That would be too boring
for words.' Then quickly she kissed him on the cheek, said
'Big official stuff' and hurried away. At the bar she touched
her husband and her brother, and as she led the way
through the swing doors to the quiet of a corridor lined
with classroom doors she said:

'Come on, you slobs.'

The two men she touched were of very different kinds.
Stephen, her husband, correctly, almost fastidiously
dressed in kilt and black Highland jacket, had the look
of a man who expects the answer no. He was very pale and
thin to be a farmer, with dark wavy hair, blue eyes and a
long thin red line for a mouth. He was somehow like one's
mother's idea of how a young barrister (not a farmer)
should look. But closer examination made one less confident of his success. His eyelashes, almost girlishly long,
fell on his cheek with the softness of failure. There was
intelligence but also resignation in his expression; it was as
if he were mocking himself very gently all the time. He did

not seem to dwell on his success, which was considerable. He had managed Mary's father's farm for four years – married for two of them – with pessimism, but had achieved superb results. He was known all over the county as the most effective of the young farmers, and of this reputation he once said, lugubriously, 'Even cheated of failure by limited success, that's me.'

Brother Pink – Charles Henry Arbuthnot Ferguson – needs altogether less description. He was balder and fatter than a man should be at thirty. He wore a single-breasted pin-stripe suit, that he had long outgrown. It pinched his shoulders and was tight at the cuffs. He took extraordinarily short steps for such a big man, and his feet were almost ludicrously small.

He answered his sister's call, 'Come on, you slobs,' with a vague, 'Oyez, oyez, tea-break: a bracing cup of chah,' not because it was tea-time or even because he intended then to drink tea, but because it was one of his formulae, and Pink and Mary had talked in a private and complicated language made up of just such phrases since their night-nursery days.

He paused and looked back at the hall. He closed out the talk from the bar, refusing to listen to the heifer prices or the advantages of Wolseley cars and heeded only the voices of the wives and Auntie Belles. They spoke of common sense and cookies, and Pink could imitate them all.

('I don't fancy the South, dear, you can have your San Tropez or Brighton. My skin's too delicate. I fancy Troon myself.')

They lived on the land which the first farmers in Scotland had defended again and again from Highland thieves and clans. But Rob Roy and Montrose and the anti-Jacobites are well buried now.

('She was three up and two to go, pet, but I beat her on the bye. And that's not counting her lost pill. I beat her on the bye; so I did.')

Voices of tidy angels fading into tidy graves; the names

do not matter. They were part of Pink's myth, and therefore of Mary's too.

Then, at last, Pink pulled himself away, saying 'Oyez, oyez, there's a great-time coming. You can ring those bloody bells.' He trundled after his sister, checking his fly buttons as he went.

TWO

EVEN OUT OF term-time a junior classroom smells of something other than chalk dust and scrubbed wood. There was an inseparable but unmistakable ingredient which both Mary and her brother Pink seemed to recognise as soon as they came into Classroom IV, even if they could not define it. They had overtaken Stephen in the corridor.

Mary smoothed the skirt of her party frock and taking short steps crossed swiftly to the table on which rested sandwiches, glasses, soft drinks and a bottle of Gloag's Old Grouse Malt Whisky. She said, very quickly:

'It's rather smelly, but never mind. They seem to have organised the eats.'

Vaguely, Pink looked round at the pine panelling, the scrubbed floorboards, the glassy blackboard and the narrow Gothic windows set safely above boys' eye-level. He tried to define the missing ingredient.

'Sex?' he suggested, sniffing once or twice and looking up at the dark space between the overhead lights and the high vaulted roof. Mary, grabbing a sandwich, shook her head, then spoke with her mouth full.

'We're jolly lucky to have it.'

Pink put his thumbs in his pockets. He was still sniffing the air. He made a further suggestion.

'Sex cruelly denied?'

Mary said, 'You eat this one, it's horrible,' and placed the bitten sandwich on the white linen cloth. As Pink obliged, her husband, Stephen, followed into the room. Apparently she did not think he was so close behind because she blushed a second after she had said:

'We've got David to thank for that. He went and talked nicely to that horrid headmaster who could hardly refuse old Dow's flesh – not in Dow's Academy.' She started thumbing through the sandwiches, announcing the choice. Only she did not do so accurately. Instead, in broad Yorkshire, just for the hell of it, she quoted from a Priestley play. She was almost like a child whistling to cover her guilt.

'Salmon, salad, trifle, two kinds of tarts, lemon cheese tart, jam tarts, two kinds of jelly . . .'

But her husband did not listen. He ignored or pretended to ignore her. He too seemed to be affected by the room which contrived to be both damp and dusty at once. His smell-suggestions were more abstract.

'Of nervous anxiety?' he asked, looking over the desks that had been shoved up the far end of the room. 'D'you think?'

The grandeur of this comment drove Mary back to the sandwiches. She tucked her head down and the light shone on her thick red hair.

Her husband continued, solemnly, 'Perhaps the smell of being laughed at?' and brother Pink nodded enthusiastically at that.

'Absolutely, old man,' he said firmly. 'Of the extraction of urine. You bet. That's the stink-a-bomb.'

'Ugh,' Stephen said, then smiled faintly. He raised his eyebrows and protested gently, 'Honestly, I'm not a fastidious man. Really I'm not.' But this denial did not ring true. His hair was carefully brushed, his nails were perfectly clean.

Mary walked over to the desks and began to play with a china ink-well, pushing it up and down in its socket. Pink, meantime, examined the bottle of Gloag's as if he had never seen whisky before. He went through a dumb show of discovery. In the gymnasium they were now dancing a reel, but the gym doors muffled the sound of the fiddles. The only noise that reached Classroom IV was the thumping of feet on the floor. It sounded like distant gunfire.

'Of cut-throat competition for brainy, swatty boys like me,' Stephen said with a quick, shy glance at Mary, and then he stepped up to the master's dais. He strolled as far as the blackboard where he picked up a copy of Kennedy's *Revised Latin Primer* and he drew an isosceles triangle on it with his finger then blew the chalk dust away. Mary said:

'Oh, come on, boys and girls, everything's going swimmingly. You are a couple of damp cloths. Do open up that bottle, Pink, I swear the others won't mind. Anyway they won't have to. They always do as I say – or does that sound rather horrid and bossy?'

'A bit on the boss-eyed side, old flesh,' Pink replied after he had assumed an intensely thoughtful expression. It seemed that he felt bound to mime every thought that passed through his head. He therefore squinted.

Stephen ignored this. Just before he opened the primer he said, with his eyes closed:

'A right-hand page, about the middle, *Mensa, mensa, mensam, mensae, mensae, mensa.*'

Duly finding page seventeen he smoothed it with long fingers and said:

'I'm right.'

'I'm so glad, old man,' Pink replied affably and reached out for a couple of the cheap, fluted tumblers, mumbling, 'Gloagers.'

It was cold in Classroom IV, even in September. Gusts of wind occasionally rattled against the narrow windows, but Mary still looked warm. She put the back of her hand against her cheek which was glowing pink. Hers was a very small hand with freckles of which she was ashamed. Every gesture seemed to be calculated to imply that this was just another Young Conservative dance; nothing out of the usual.

Stephen, still turning over the pages, said:

'It's just the same. I confess I find that reassuring. *Tristis, tristem, tristis, tristi.*' Then he turned over some more pages and smiled again. He said, 'Here's one for Pink. *Vomo, vomere, vomui, vomitum.*'

'Oh, do shut up spouting Latin and enjoy yourself, darling,' Mary said, a little edgily.

Stephen looked up innocently.

'But I haven't enjoyed anything so much for years. Perhaps I'm not the scholar your friend David is, but I'm strictly the serious type.'

Mary let the ink-well drop into its socket. As if she meant something quite different, in the same firm tone in which one might dismiss a servant forever, she said:

'If you lean back on the board like that you'll get your jacket covered with chalk.'

Stephen looked back at her, his eyes wide open.

'Does that matter?'

And when she shrugged, he asked:

'Do you mind?'

This was Pink's cue, as fool. He at once grasped the phrase, repeating it cockney style as if he were a typist finding a hand above his knee.

'Do you mind?' And as Stephen did not react he turned back to his sister and spread his arms wide.

'For God's sake,' he pleaded. 'The boy's doing his best.'

She said suddenly, to Pink, in one breath, 'Don't worry, it's only Steve. I'm laughing like anything.'

Pink's method of blowing her a kiss was to stick his finger in his mouth and make the noise of a cork being extracted from a bottle. The imitation was loud and successful.

'Right up,' he said, and his sister replied:

'I'm so glad I only understand half the things you say. They get fouler every day.'

Stephen closed the book. Looking round again, he said 'Of guilt,' and sniffed.

'Oh God,' Mary said, dropping her head and gripping the edge of the desk.

'Of ambition,' Stephen went on, quietly, with a nod, as if he still had a list of alternatives.

'He only does it to annoy,' Pink said, and added, instructing himself, 'Do stop fumbling with that bottle, old chum.'

But Stephen continued:

'I think it really makes rather an appropriate sitting-out room . . . Odd to think it used to be your friend David's home.'

'Oh, come on,' Pink said quietly, warningly.

'But correct me if I'm wrong—'

'Stephen!' Mary pleaded.

Pink drank his whisky, then spoke again to Stephen.

'My chum and I,' he said, with a gesture towards Mary, 'are rooting for you. What Moo has joined together let no black-eyed intellectual expatriate Dow put asunder – it's in the Book. All right?'

'Please,' Stephen insisted. 'I just said it was his old home. And he was at school here. You've told me so yourself. D'you suppose his initials are carved on one of the desks?'

'I haven't looked,' Mary replied, staring him straight in the eye, and there was a moment's silence, broken only by that noise like distant gunfire. The top half of Mary's face was in the deep shadow cast by the bakelite shades, like Chinese hats, above the bright bulbs, but her eyes shone.

She then persisted, 'D'you want me to make a search?'

'Why should I do that?' Stephen replied, turning his head to one side, almost as if he were showing his neck.

Mary shrugged and said, 'You raised it,' and another sticky silence was only broken by the noise of the ink-well dropping in the socket again. Mary spilt some ink on her fingers. 'Bugger the thing!'

Pink said, 'The world's your oyster, Lilian.'

'Can I borrow your hanky?' she asked, and Pink pretended to be shy. He blushed and gave a very dirty laugh.

'Well actually, old girl,' he began. 'Farmers' hop and all that—'

'Oh, do stop being foul and give me the thing. I'm covered in ink.' Then, still furiously trying to rub the ink off her fingers, she rushed across to her husband, saying:

'Poor, poor Stiffy,' and she put her arms round his neck. 'But we do root for you, honestly we do.'

She leant back a little and smiled, then adjusted his jaw so that he grinned more broadly, saying:

'Light up the lantern.'

For a second she looked seriously, almost sadly, at his white face. Just before she turned to Pink she said:

'Old chum?'

'Old chum,' Pink replied.

'A tiny triple old chum.' She stepped away from her husband.

'For Madame.'

'Absolutely, old chum,' she said, still seriously.

'No sooner said than done.'

He poured her an enormous whisky, and sliding some sandwiches on to a Dundee cake that looked like a fighter, he put the tumbler on the plate and carried it across to her, speaking once again in their curious code, a language drawn from anecdote and limerick; from family jokes and nursery rhyme; from a lifetime spent together; from a myth they had had to weave for themselves.

'At the Savoy,' he said, 'we do it with a warm spooner-ooni,' and at once understanding, she hauled up her dress, which since she raised her arms to hug Stephen had begun slipping down her breasts.

For the first time she smiled warmly.

'I love Pink,' she said, 'L.U.V. Mary loves Charles Henry Arbuthnot Chuff-chuff Ferguson,' for Pink had been 'Chuff-chuff' before he was old enough for gin.

The only bright things shining in the two brutal arcs of light were Stephen's silver buttons and the table-cloth.

Then, as Pink moved, there was a third reflection which Mary increased by poking her brother in the middle. His remarkably white shirt which did not quite button up at the neck had escaped between waistcoat and pin-stripe trousers. Mary pulled the shirt out further.

'You haven't even buttoned it,' she complained.

'Dress optional, old Dutch,' Pink said, tucking it in again.

In a loud and false voice, Stephen answered a remark which Mary had made only with a doubtful look. 'My darling, I promise I'm being perfectly reasonable.'

'Then why did you mention his name?'

Stephen shrugged.

'I thought this was a great family for jokes . . .'

Mary blinked and Pink, his chins folding into each other as he gave a little burp, recommended his sister to lift her elbow. He did this, of course, by signal; a signal which he could not resist developing into an imitation of a big dog lifting his leg. He was answered more or less, in code. This time Mary spoke in a strongly respectable Kelvinside accent.

'The elbow?' she asked. 'D'you think that's wise, Bun?'

And they went into one of their acts.

Pink was convincing as a respectable spinster. He blinked as he plunged into the imitation.

'A little of what you fancy, Belle – it'll do you the world of good.'

'Is that a fact, Bun?'

'That's a fact.'

Stephen's dislike of the Kelvinside 'respectable' game seemed to be out of all proportion. He groaned, said 'No' and screwed up his face as if he were experiencing physical pain. His fists were squeezed tight. It seemed possible that it was not the act itself that annoyed him. The act merely provided him with an excuse to express some of the feelings of nervousness and irritation which until then had only just been kept under control. Laughing quietly, as if it hurt him, and as if he were about to break into tears, he said:

'No, please. I don't think I can bear it if you go on like that. I know what it's like once you've started. We won't hear a sensible word all night.'

'Oh dear,' Mary said, taking a big drink. 'It's ages since we've done Bun and Belle. We used to do it for hours on end.'

'I know,' Stephen said; and Pink said, very sentimentally:

'Always on a rainy day.' Catching his mood, Mary answered:

'And it always rained.' She gave him a very sweet smile, then they all drank again, quickly. A second later Mary was frowning, and Pink picked up her hand and kissed the back of it before he returned to the table for a sandwich. They could still hear the thump of the floorboards.

Stephen sat down on the bench along the wall and pushed his legs out in front of him. He said:

'We're very nostalgic, suddenly. The story changes, as you grow up. I thought you used to spend your time smoking cigarettes or lying in the loft, watching the bull at work. That was much more convincing as a picture of country childhood.'

Mary was still sitting dreaming and she did not listen to Pink as he said:

'You wait till we write our book. We will write one, won't we?' Then, polishing the imaginary screen in front of Mary's eyes, he said much more loudly:

'Won't we?'

'That's it,' she replied, swinging her feet on to the floor. 'Children of the Caledonian Forest.' Suddenly she started laughing, and dropping her head to her hands on the desk she said, 'Dear me!'

'What?' Pink was half smiling. It was as if he did not know what exactly she was laughing at, but knew at once the nature of it.

Stephen had moved towards the classroom door. Down the corridor he could see the reel being danced in the gym. He pretended not to hear Mary, as she began to giggle, hopelessly. It always irritated him. In the pitch of her laughter he recognised an oblique attack.

Her eyes were sparkling. She put her fingers over her face as she began to blush as well as giggle. She managed to blurt out:

'Those competitions in the bunkers— No, they were too bad.'

Pink imitated her frown.

'Too bad,' he agreed. 'Strictly Wolfenden stuff. I've always said it. Children ought not to be brought up in the country. It's altogether too near to Nature. The things we did on that golf course would turn Bank Lizzy green.'

'With horror!'

'With envy,' Pink said.

Stephen still did not turn round and it was perhaps the sight of his thin neck (14½-inch collar) with his dark hair cut just so, neither too short nor too long, that drove her to continue the conversation.

'And in the loft,' she said. 'In the spare room, on the bridge, in the rhododendrons and the attic and the black shed—'

'Even in the garage,' Pink agreed.

'Dear!' She was again horrified by some memory, but still could not stop herself laughing. 'I swear to you, Steve, one time we—'

She ignored Pink's long face of warning.

'Steve?'

For a second it was doubtful how she would cope with him. Then she put the point of her little finger, her pinkie, into the ink-well and said:

'Steve's huffing.'

When he turned, pretending that his thoughts had been miles away, she said, warningly:

'Darling—'

'Me?' Stephen said. 'I'm not huffing.' He walked over to the table and said, 'I'm pouring myself another drink.' Mary was once again furiously trying to remove the ink stain from her skin, with Pink's handkerchief.

She said, 'You won't huff, will you? After all you started it.'

'I?' Stephen said. Pink's eyebrows jumped up.

'I, Mother?' Mary asked very grandly. It must have been another of their library of private jokes. If it was not marked under 'huffy' it could be found under 'stuffy'.

'I'm sorry, darling,' she said, seeing the tiny muscle in his jaw, which always worked when he was angry. 'But you did start it, you know. About the loft and the bull. Oh dear, how awful. Now you're really huffy.'

Stephen said, 'I don't know why you choose to use these childish expressions whenever—'

'Blame it on old Pink,' Pink said, trundling back to the table, since the cork was out of the bottle again.

'That's it,' Mary said, swinging her legs again. 'He's the eldest.'

Pink turned to his brother-in-law who had wandered as far as the corridor again, and said, 'Tell us, old fruit, was childhood in the Doctor's house just about the same?'

'I can't say I found it so.' Stephen, by a turn of his head, implied that he was still listening to the music. He had spent most of his childhood south of the border, and it made him very sensitive to things Highland and regimental. At last he said, rather stiffly:

'I do wish they wouldn't play Cannon Woods. They don't seem to know it's originally a German tune. It was never played here before the war.' Mary glanced at Pink as if to say, 'Don't tell me he's pompous.' But Pink knew how far to go. He did not embarrass her. Instead he turned back to Stephen, saying, as affably as ever:

'Oh, come clean, Stiffy. We're all chums, we're all girls

together.' When he toasted his drinking companions he raised his glass to eye level rather formally. He held the tumbler between finger and thumb and his other fingers splayed out in mid-air. Then, literally, he lifted his elbow.

'Astonishing good luck,' he said.

Stephen said, 'I'm sorry to disappoint you, but I really have nothing to hide. Perhaps it was the English influence, or living in a town. Even when we were in the country, hay-making meant a ride in the buggy, not a day in the loft.'

'Really?' Pink sounded serious and amazed, but it was doubtful if he was thinking what he was saying. He seemed to be more worried by the tumbler in his hand, which he emptied in one gulp.

'Perhaps it was just me,' Stephen went on pleasantly, then suddenly, coldly, with one remark, he killed the conversation. It was at an end, as soon as he said, 'Sex was never my strong subject. It isn't now, as we know.'

Mary moved across the room. She spoke seriously, as if someone had suddenly, unnecessarily displayed an ugly open wound.

'Darling, why must you be so silly?'

Stephen seemed perfectly cheerful. His voice and his manner were bolder again.

'My dear, it isn't I who needs sympathy. It's you. There.' He smiled, put an arm round her shoulder, and kissed her cheek. She dropped her eyes. Pink's stomach seemed to grow bigger. He almost stood on tiptoe, and he stammered slightly as he said:

'Come on, my loves. Blame it on Pink. Old Pink started it.'

'Not true,' Stephen said, depressed again, and Pink was irritated. He took it out on the plates and glasses which he clattered about as he said:

'Damn it all, chum.'

'Pink,' Mary said softly, and Stephen's voice rode over hers as it so often did.

'I'm afraid I am a bit of a cold sponge at—'

'Darling!'

But Stephen went on. 'A fact's a fact, for heaven's sake.'

Pink said, as nicely as he could, 'Okay, chumbo, but don't let's go on about it at a farmers' hop.'

'True.'

Mary had sat down on a bench at the side of the room. She looked straight in front of her, over the desks, towards the panels covered with carved initials, and the long cords falling down from the small, high windows. She said to Stephen:

'Nobody is as ruthless with himself as you are. I don't know whether to admire it or—'

'Shudder,' he said, in the icy tone of someone who not only has the courage to admit to others that he is no good in bed, but braver still, to confess it to himself.

'No.' She was angry for a second, as she looked up at him. 'Not shudder – I never felt that.'

Pink took a couple of steps backwards. Stephen ran his finger round the rim of his glass. He said very calmly:

'Tell me, does your friend David know the situation?'

'No,' she answered sharply. 'Of course he doesn't. You know he doesn't. Unless you've unburdened yourself to him.' She drank a little of her whisky.

'That's hardly likely,' he said and at once, in a low voice, she replied:

'I'm not so bloody sure.'

'Bab – Ba – Bambinos!' Pink moved softly forward, but Mary kept her head away from him. She was looking firmly at the glass in her hand.

'He's not my friend, anyway, I told you.'

'Darling,' Stephen said, 'I trust you implicitly.'

Mary looked at Pink, not Stephen, but Pink also turned away.

Stephen swallowed and still talking of marriage and of bed, he went on:

'Whatever happened, I could hardly blame you when the fault is so patently mine.'

But Mary, perhaps to his surprise, did not rush to deny this. She remained perfectly still, and silent. Pink, putting one foot in front of the other, walked carefully up the line of one of the floor-boards, and then the gym doors opened, and Young Conservatives came flooding in saying, 'Really, Charles? But I thought there was a pile to be made in broilers' and other more ornate and surprising Young Conservative things, like 'I said, "Jack, I careth not for thee."'

WITH AN ASTONISHING lack of hard evidence, the mind-benders insist that the dreams we forget are the important ones. But at least we can each prove to ourselves that the letters which we never send are the revealing ones. And for months, in a corner of a bench in David Dow's laboratory in the Medical Research Council building in Mill Hill there lay scores of these; letters which went back over all the scenes with Mary; letters of love, of protest, of explanation and angry letters too. Some spread themselves so far as to become something beyond a letter, striking out from specific apology to woolly confession. Some were addressed privately and passionately to Mary, others seemed to be directed to nobody, prepared carefully and laboriously for the waste-paper basket.

The first letters, some no more than torn scraps of paper, are written in a spidery hand, corrected and recorrected, advancing painfully, inch by inch, as if reluctant to reach the kernel of their relationship. At the end, the handwriting grows bolder and grammar itself seems to oblige and bend to the material. These last pages will be quoted, but the first ones, laboriously pursuing minute events in Classroom IV and the gym, matter too.

The first does not directly concern Mary and David, but David's observation of Mary at work that night; Mary as she was then but is no longer; Mary, oblique and hysterical. She played for David that evening, involving herself at first neither with poor Pink nor with Stephen but with the steadiest member of the Ferguson family, Flora Macdonald, the huge Nanny, housekeeper, nurse and rock.

Mary, Mary, cousin as you are now, you've told me [David writes] that I looked that night, in my white tie and tails, like a mixture between a second-class pugilist and Deacon Brodie on the prowl, just because I watched silently the performance that you put on for me and forgot to speak to your friends who *you*, remember, called harmless and I called kind. And though I write always, other, countless, unpostable and unposted letters only to be forgiven, in this one scene at least, it was you who behaved badly. Promise.

Just reconsider it. Forget all the talk *to* your Conservative friends, *at* me; forget the loudness of your voice. Forget the brassy laugh, and that comment, advertising yourself, as you filled your glass, about yourself but put, horribly, in the third person, 'Well, her father was a card-cheat and her mother was a drunk . . . Ha-ha-ha!' – Suggestions, incidentally, which you had denied with such a show of passion in London only a week previously that you successfully reduced a cocktail party to embarrassed silence.

Remember only poor Macdonald coming in – poor, huge, gloomy, loving Macdonald who you had told me not once but many times was (your phrase) 'a guardian angel in your life, not a Nanny but a foster-mother'. I always remember her, perhaps the one person who comes out of the story with credit, as she looked that night, in a dress that was more like a toga. I imagine her now as six foot four but perhaps she was shorter than that. It was as if all the expression in her features had been swept back with the gold-grey hair to that big bun at the back of her neck. She had huge, chicken-killing hands and feet made for plough. Yet she was gentle.

If I had not known by then the extraordinary amount of alcohol you were capable of holding I would have sworn that you must be drunk to be so cruel. I may not have all poor Macdonald's lines right, but it was the look on her face that mattered. On the other hand I have, as you can judge for yourself, an unerring memory for Mary lines. Proof? You greeted her, as she loomed through the door, mauve dress and square fur cape, by turning more than half away from her, addressing one of your girl-friends who was (please note) on my side of the room, 'Lerwick's answer to Cassandra. Whistler's maiden aunt.' This announcement, needless to say, was made in a voice loud enough not only for me to hear but for poor Macdonald to hear, as well.

'Can I speak to you, Mary?' I think she said, at the door, and with a whirling turn and a kind of enthusiastic rush of innocence, you grasped both of her hands and said:

'Yes, *darling* Macdonald,' and I saw the 'darling' make its mark on wary Macdonald's face. What invited 'darling' now, after twenty years without?

I could have told her. I was flattered, I confess.

'Darling Macdonald, do come and have a proper drink – you've been doing marvels through there, I know.'

'Heavens,' one of your dairy-minded friends gave you away, 'from all the darlings and that I thought it must be a man coming through the door.'

'Goodness, don't look so grim,' you were now saying irritably to Macdonald, as if suddenly you had changed your mind and never wanted to see her again, then even as I watched, you changed back and stretching out your hands to her again said, 'Dear, lovely Macdonald, Rock of Gibraltar only much prettier and nicer really – you are so M.I.5. It can't be all that bad.'

'A word in your ear, Mary.' One step forward. She approached the erratic animal.

'Oh, don't be so silly,' quietly from you. With your nail you picked at the Cairngorm brooch which she had clasped in her dress, then stopped yourself with a flick of the hand – a hand which you hated, so you told me; but you left it flat on Macdonald's shoulder for everybody to see.

You said to her, 'If it's so embarrassing you can tell me in a whisper,' and encouraged by a titter round about (and not my laughter, I assure you) you said, not exactly to Macdonald, 'Well, it's not a children's party any more. Not Mr Reed's dancing class and bow to your partners. Pink and I have grown up on you.' Then directly to her face, 'I won't be shocked.' And to the brooch, quietly, but oh, so audibly, 'Has your sweetheart jilted you?'

God, she was patient. If I'd been her I would have slapped your face.

She said, wearily, 'Don't get so excited, Mary dear. I know the mood.'

'Well, what on earth have you come to say?'

Macdonald looked round then, nodded good evening to somebody, before she asked, 'D'you not think it's time you went back to your father, next door? You know what he is. He won't move away from the table at all.'

'Haven't you been there, for heaven's sake?' A pause. A sly glance to your yes-friends, with your eyes right round to the sides. Then you add, 'You and your sweetheart, I mean?'

Don't you blush to read this? Wasn't it obvious to you then? Surely everybody in the room must have seen what you were up to, attacking and teasing Macdonald while you kept me within earshot. I see you now, as you were at that moment, circling round like a brightly coloured bird, flapping a wing, fluttering the feathers in your tail.

Poor Macdonald bit her lip. She must have known how dangerous it was to mention her boy-friend's name. But she took the plunge, while you waited, ready to strike. She did not say Captain Gordon, but stuck to his Christian name.

'Jack and I have held the fort for over an hour now.'

Saying Jack she used his short 'a'; what you and Pink used to call his 'immaculate Edinburgh and Bombay'. I wonder if she did so as a sort of dare. But you didn't fail.

You got another titter for your echo. 'Jack? Captain Jack Gordon? M.C., R.A.M.C.?'

Imperviously, Macdonald frankly confessed:

'It's the gay Gordons. That's Jack's favourite,' and you, pure bitch, threw back your head and laughted, then quickly, like a school-girl, clasped a hand over your mouth (fingers long and straight of that hand you hate so much) and said:

'Oh God, I'm sure I shouldn't laugh.'

It is difficult to keep up with you at this point. At once you followed with the short a's again, mimicking (not very well) poor Captain Jack Gordon.

'Tripping the light fantastic?' you asked and then swung round to your brother who, give him his due, was not enjoying this very much.

'Pink, darling, do say "Light fantastic Saturday, Jack." Do it properly. In Jack's voice.'

He was then gasping for air, trying to warn you what you already knew, that Macdonald, with great dignity, was leaving the room.

Then, by golly, you covered. I don't say it was for my sake alone, but certainly for my sake as well.

Sweetly and desperately, 'No, Macdonald, don't be so silly, don't take on so. Macdonald dear.'

Rushed after her. Caught her in the corridor and held her, not in front of *all* the guests but in front of some. In front of me, by the way. Held her again by the arms and looked imploringly at the big solemn face.

'So it was silly, on your part,' Macdonald said. 'I'd say you've got no reason to be unkind about Jack.'

A big shake of your head. A wag from side to side.

'It was just a joke.'

'What's the joke?'

You shrugged at that, but still clung to her arms. The alarmed spoilt child; contrite, insecure, cunning. 'Just ridiculous. I've said I'm sorry.'

'What's ridiculous, Mary? Are we too old, is that it?'

'No.' She had you there. 'Don't look like that, Macdonald. Don't ask questions.'

'Is it that he's small and I'm big?' [In my mind's eye, just as Macdonald has gained stature, I remember Captain Jack Gordon as only two feet tall.]

'No!' You looked a little afraid. 'No honestly, please forget it. You must forgive me. Otherwise it'll ruin my evening. I promise it will.' You were pinching her arms, now.

'Are you coming through then?'

'This minute.'

'Okay, toots,' she said, forgiving. You stood on tiptoe and kissed her. Then dropped on your heels again and leant against the wall pushing both the flat of your hands and that red hair, cousin, against the glossy surface. Frock? Short and pink. Legs? Well set apart. If you doubt me, cousin, it is for a good reason; remembering you are ashamed. But it is true enough. I'll give you another echo to prove it to you. But in proving, I give myself away: my own shame. There's not a moment of Classroom IV which escapes me, I've lived it so often again.

That farmer, of course, is the echo – the one who wandered down the corridor at just that moment. The big round moon-faced one in the brown suit who was so proud of his tenor voice. As you stood and watched Macdonald go, presenting me with the perfect sideface, he came by, insisting to his friends:

'I've got the technique I have . . . Semi-trained.' Something like that. 'When I was just a treble my singing teacher said – she said I'd a most remarkable voice. So she said.'

You looked at your shoes as you came into the classroom again. You were ashamed even then, cousin. If not from your own heart then at least from the look on my face you reckoned you had over-played and you were very quiet as the Young Conservatives drained out. You leant your

backside against one of the desks and stared at your
tumbler, whirling the whisky round and round. I tried very
hard, I confess, but you wouldn't look at me.

You weren't at all happy at being left behind with me,
then. Not after you'd over-played.

Voices and gestures:—

Stephen, in your ear, 'Best if you follow us through,
darling. We'd better not delay.' He had both a dark look
and a bright smile for me.

You were clasping the bridge of your nose as if your head
ached.

'No,' holding your hand out to your husband, and for the
first time, daring a look at me. 'I'll come through now.'

After that it's only voices for me. I turned to the blackboard then. There were only the three voices: yours, Pink's
and Stephen's. The others were mere murmurs of complaint against taxation, echoing down the corridor.

Stephen's voice, without confidence: 'Give David another drink. No please do.'

A shifting of fcct, a glass thumped on a table, then
Stephen's voice again. This time bright and cheerful.

'Please do. One for all the good work he did with you on
the flags and streamers next door. He helped decorate,
didn't he?'

Stephen's voice again. 'You entertain him, darling.'

Then yours, sharp and clipped: 'Very well. We'll follow
you through.'

Last of all, Captain Jack Gordon, R.A.M.C. (Indian
Army), precisely, but it came, I assume, from poor Pink.

'Yes. Yes. "A bit of the light fantastic, Saturday."'

Then Pink in his own voice: 'Oyez, oyez. You can ring
those bloody bells.'

AS MARY REACHED for the bottle of Gloag's she knocked over one of the fluted glasses and she only just saved it from falling to the floor. David watched her with dark and tender eyes as she picked it up and reached for the bottle again. He walked away from the blackboard to the far wall and played with one of the thin cords hanging from the tiny area of window which could be opened. The cord was low enough for the master to adjust, but high enough to prevent boys from hanging themselves without difficulty.

Mary said, 'I was told to give you a drink,' and when she drew in a breath it made a small wavering noise.

'Why did you stay?' he asked.

'Because my husband asked me to.'

She looked up at him. She was pale now, and not at her prettiest. When the colour ran from her cheeks her skin sometimes looked almost green. The effect had something to do with the tiny freckles.

She rested her hands on the table, behind her back. 'David, I do want to speak to you about yesterday.'

'No, that's really a wrong one—' he said, coming round to her, flicking his fingers and thumbs.

'Please, I'd like to explain.'

'Explain nothing. Forget what happened.' But as he laid a hand on her skin just where the neck curves into the shoulder she walked away and she said a little hysterically:

'No, please don't touch me.'

'Oh no,' he said, again snapping his fingers with irritation. 'This is snakes and ladders. Each time one has to begin at base.'

'If you really want to know, I feel I never really want to be touched again. It's all so complicated. But that's what I do feel.'

He had turned right away from her and going back to the window and the cord he said, very quietly:

'Please, miss. Don't tempt me by telling more lies. You're really on form tonight.'

At once she said, 'You mean about Macdonald? You don't know it but I was being kind. He's a dreadful little man. Her boy-friend, I mean. Jack Gordon. He's half her height.'

He simply shook his head, refusing the excuse and at once on a debby note which sounded almost an octave higher she said:

'I absolutely confess it, I was rather tough . . . But Macdonald understands. It's just that I'm fearfully jealous I suppose. I'm that sort of person and I've always been bitchy about Macdonald's friends. It shows how much I love her, don't you see? Poor old cow. Anyway, I didn't tell any lies about her or anybody else . . .'

He quoted her own words, ' "My mother was a drunk." '

'Oh, that was just a joke.'

'It's something you weren't so prepared to joke about in London.'

She answered quietly, 'No, of course not. Here everybody knows. I mean they know it's not true. That's why I can afford to joke.'

David raised an eyebrow. He was prepared to leave the subject as her mother had been dead for ten years anyway. Moreover when she was alive she was rather a pathetic, self-pitying invalid who later took to drink. David even could remember meeting her, once, in Forfar when he was a boy; a fussy, nervous, dumpy little woman wearing a hat and white gloves. His mother had introduced her as Lady Ferguson.

Contrarily, Mary had decided to talk about her mother. 'Anything to do with Mummy's complicated,' she said and drank a gulp of whisky. It was not easy to see what she was up to, but her movement across to the desks, back to little-girl land, seemed to give something away.

She said, 'I don't know why I get so worked up about her, sometimes, but it annoys me. People get such wrong impressions of what she was, and even if you did see her once, she was my mother and I know. It doesn't matter if they get a good impression or a bad impression, it's still the wrong impression and it makes me mad. It's probably very silly.'

'I'll buy it,' David said, a little mystified. 'Go on.'

'I'm not selling anything, David.' She turned back to the ink-well. 'Really I'm not. Absolutely the opposite. But I'd hate you to go away thinking I'm bloody about Mummy because honestly, honestly I'm not. She was awful and mixed-up, but she was a great woman really. Most people up here met her when she was at the end of her tether. Didn't even meet her, just heard about her, lying in her bed, drinking and that. Maybe she did drink, but she was a great woman; a very passionate woman.'

David watched her very carefully as she circled round and returned to the desk. The approach was nothing, if not oblique. He sat down and smoked. Mary, meantime, sat down on the desk and told her story with bright eyes.

'I could tell you things about Mummy almost beyond belief that nobody knows – I mean outside Pink and Co. And it's only lately, really, since I was married that I added it all together. Not just the card cheating, the scandal and their coming back north: not about that at all. Until a year or two ago I just used to frown when people asked me about Mummy. She was just a washed-out woman in bed. We never used to see her get drunk, but we'd hear her some-times at night, shouting and often laughing, saying the most extraordinary things. Pink and I never could make out whether she was talking to Daddy or one of the dogs. Whichever it was they never answered. Then there would be a long silence and Pink and I would hold hands.'

She moved the ink-well again. She did not look at him for a moment as she spoke. Very quickly she went on:

'You've been home, you know where – just by the top of the stairs by the nursery gate, there's a linen cupboard there. We'd hide in it. Then another silence or perhaps a click of a door and we'd dash back to bed, shivering cold. I wonder we weren't more frightened. She came in once and found us in the same bed and I thought there would be an awful rumpus. Macdonald never used to allow us in the same bed. She said that's how keely children slept. But Mummy wasn't really angry at all. She put on all the lights, she blinked, then she moved across to us. I remember it like yesterday. Then she sat down at the end of the bed and pitched forward and her hair was all undone. She kind of pushed us through the bedclothes as if we were the dogs under the blankets. I kept my eyes tight shut until I heard her. I thought she was laughing, but she wasn't. Tears were pouring down her cheeks. I don't think she was drunk at all. We were scared stiff. We didn't move or speak, even after she went out. We stayed like that until it was light outside, and the sun was shining on the floods.'

David sat patiently. Nothing could have stemmed the flow. Mary talked and went on talking for about half an hour, with hardly a pause for breath. Her eyes were here and there and everywhere; for a second staring honestly and emphatically into David's; then looking up at the light; at the ink-well; at her white, pointed shoes. She still talked of her mother.

'Another time once she got out of bed. She took us into Dundee right down by the docks and the tenements there, it's almost as bad as Glasgow. We didn't know then much what it was all about. There were a lot of men standing about at the street corners. There must have been some strike or something like that. They'd got banners, some of them, God knows what they said . . . We'd done something wrong, I think. We'd put our rice pudding under the chest in the dining-room hoping the dogs would find it, and when she discovered it hours later, it was a day later, I think, she bunged us into the back of the car and took us into Dundee. I suppose she was pretty high. She shouted, "Open! P.N.!" That's what the kids cry there at night when they come up the wynds and can't get in the door. The Inas and Sheilas and Elspeths and Jeans. The Cathies and Normas. She threatened to leave us there until Macdonald said, "For heaven's sakes, that's enough." Macdonald never said, "For heaven's sake," it was always, "For heaven's sakes," with the "s" on both.

'We were very frightened then. Pink was a great weeper. I didn't cry out but Pink cried all the way there and all the way back in kind of short bursts. Macdonald told him he was a great bubbly and that just made him worse.'

She walked over to the sandwiches again. She ate a lot. Speaking with her mouth full of smoked salmon, she said:

'But we didn't know, then. We weren't told anything. Daddy never said much to us beyond, "Old boy" or "Old girl", and Macdonald's as secret as the grave. The only time we ever got anything out of her was when she was bathing us. Soap seemed to do something to her discretion. She'd cackle away.

'It's only lately I've kind of discovered, and now I feel awful for all the things I used to say about Mummy. That's why I feel bad now. I confess you've got me on the raw. Even as a joke. I feel bad about saying she was a boozer. I probably was in the wrong. I used to say awful things about her at school. Tell fibs.'

'Even then,' David interrupted quietly, and she looked at him, a little puzzled.

'Yes . . .' Then she checked herself and said, 'What do you mean? You never will say quite what you mean.'

David shook his head. He wondered if there was any truth in her stories.

'Forget it.'

'That's a very womanish thing to say,' she replied, and frowned. She scraped her nail against the wood of the desk and began again, speaking even more quietly than before.

'Anyway. It's as I was saying. People don't really know about Mummy. She was terrific, really. I mean she had an awful time. You see that day in Dundee was awfully significant really. Her taking us back there, because when she was very little, well, about eleven, I suppose, until she was about eleven she lived there. Can you believe it? It explains a lot. I mean, when she was younger, God knows what she didn't go through.'

She moved away a step or two, then she turned round to him and smiled.

'Honestly, David, I do wish we could make it work as sort of friends. Cousin-type. I so adore talking to you.' She put her back to one of the old desks and jumped up and swung her legs again. Pointing her toes, she continued:

'There's a really terrifying background. This one Macdonald knows and nobody else. I don't think Mummy properly knew it herself. You can have a kind of block with these things, can't you? When she was eleven she was living in one of those horrid tenement things. Her father wasn't a labourer, actually. He was an actor or music hall or something, but at one time he'd had to do with the jute business . . . clerk or checker, I think . . . You didn't know who you were cousin to, did you? All your long looks of the poor schoolmaster's son? God knows who my cousins are on Mummy's side, probably all sailors and drunks.

'Anyway, Grandfather doesn't come much into the picture. It was Mummy's mother looked after her and she was supposed to be redheaded but even littler than me. She used to go out and work up the Perth Road or one of those places, sometimes in a private house and sometimes in the

Infirmary. You didn't get much as a cleaner in those days, so she had to kind of work all day and Mummy spent all her time in those gloomy streets, I suppose, skipping and playing peevers and all that with Ina and Sheila, and Elspeth and Jean and Cathie and Norma and all. Mummy never talked of it exactly but little things came out when she was plastered. They lived in two or three rooms up eighty-nine steps, and some people thought they did too well. There were ten people in one room below. And there was an old creepy man opposite, he smelt like a cat, or his room did. I don't know. Anyway he used to give Mummy jube-jubes and watch her until she ate them. He always watched her until she swallowed them right down. Mummy, when she was drunk, you know, whether it was to the dogs or Macdonald or me, she always used to give a great sweep of her hand and say, "You don't know very much."

'It's an awful story really, but it explains so much. I'm sure if things had gone the other way she'd have been so different. She'd got,' she clenched her fists here, 'she'd got a sort of passion. Did you notice that when you met her?'

But David did not reply and Mary went on in a lower, steadier tone.

'Mummy had a brother. My uncle, I suppose, if he'd lived, and that's actually where Pink gets the Arbuthnot. I know it sounds funny but they called him Arbuthnot, and my grandmother absolutely worshipped him. She couldn't see past him and he was delicate. Maybe that's why she was so fond of him. Worse than delicate. He had fits. He was epileptic or whatever they call it. Isn't it awful how life works? Get landed with a no-good husband and no money in a tenement in Dundee and you bet your son's an epileptic. And this wasn't all that long ago. That's what makes it more frightening. They had the whole works in the tenement.

'But it wasn't fits Arbuthnot died of. I don't think you do die that way, do you? Not unless you smother? He was evidently a terribly complicated, tidy sort of boy. It's too awful really, it makes me laugh. Pink does a splendid imitation of the scene. There was a bucket, you see. Uncle Arbuthnot was so tidy . . .'

She broke off and laughed. Then she clenched her fists.

'God please don't let me laugh,' she said. 'Please. I promise I don't really think it's funny. If I'm laughing when the wind changes perhaps I'll die of hiccoughs like that queen.'

She diverged for a few seconds, perhaps to gain control of herself.

She said, 'It's like a woman in the village, Bank Lizzy, in her new car, only last winter, in the snow. She wasn't very good with this car and she ran over the village cripple. That's bad enough, but then the poor dear panicked and instead of putting on the brake and getting out she jammed the thing into reverse and by mistake,' she began to laugh again. 'Bumpety-bump,' she cried and leant back with tears of laughter forming in her eyes '. . . she went straight back over him and finished him off.'

She shook her head. 'When Pink and I are really blue we always think of that.'

She shifted her seat along a desk, toward David and asked for a cigarette. She smoked very ineptly, like a schoolgirl.

Anyway,' she said, as she always did, resuming the tale, 'This poor Arbuthnot boy decided things were a bit much for him. One's been sixteen, but not in a tenement. One hardly blames him. So one afternoon he slits his wrists, only he does it very methodically, getting on to his bed, and holding the wrist over the bucket. Appalling, really. But there it is, and Mummy came up the eighty-nine steps back from school, or Salvation Army or Ina or Sheila or whatever it was she was doing – walks into the house and calls his name. She was about eleven, yes, just eleven. She hears nothing, but a moment later there's a clanking next door, and a groan.'

She had stopped laughing now. She looked quite pale. 'I mustn't go too quickly,' she said. 'I must get it right . . . The first thing is that the boy has changed his mind and he's trying to stop the blood coming. In doing so he's knocked over the bucket which was about half full of blood, and oddly enough what strength he does have seems directed against the fearful mess around the floor and the rug – one of those woollen rugs you make yourself, you know . . . In the space of two seconds Mummy's out the door again and across the gallery to the body 'lives next door. But they're all out working, the women at the Perth Road or Broughty Ferry, and old jube-jube and the rest at the jute or the ships . . . Some of them worked on the railways, there. Well, by the time Mummy's tried some doors, and got no reply – "Open . . . P.N." for another reason, then – she sees she must go back herself. He has righted the bucket which is filling with red again. In doing so everything has got covered with blood. And he's dead.

'Now Mummy's got two hours before her mother's back. And what's so odd about life is that of course because her mother adored Arbuthnot, Mummy worshipped her mother. And she knew it would break her heart if her mother learnt how the boy had died. She's got two hours—

'She starts with the bucket. Then Arbuthnot. She heaves him until he's face downwards on the bed. Then with a big wet clout from the kitchen she starts on the floor, the chest of drawers, the wall, even the window pane. She's not sick – she's sweating. There's less than an hour to go. Downstairs she runs – "I'll play with you later, Sheila, Ina, Elspeth, Jean, Cathie and Norma, I'm in a hurry now!" Up comes the doctor, a funny kind of strip across his jacket at the back – a Norfolk jacket don't they call it? And he's quite good about things. He's worked in the tenements. He knows the family. He says nothing but plays the game, and when my grandmother came home he said it was one of the fits. "The boy's suffocated," he says, "it was a tragic accident . . ."

After that there were screams and yells, I suppose. I don't know. But anyway the whole thing was in vain, as might be expected. Of course she wanted to see her child and she found the open wrist. There are some horrid details there. She was half crazed with distress and she didn't even seem to remember Mummy's existence so the doctor did the right thing. More than that. He took Mummy home and later adopted her and all that, and that's another story, because he wasn't quite the angel he looked either. Not when Mummy grew a little older, anyway—'

David was still watching her very carefully. She suddenly stretched her neck and said:

'Oh God, now I feel awful and guilty and ashamed. I shouldn't have told you that. Mummy didn't remember half of it herself. It's only Macdonald and . . .' She frowned. 'I don't know why I told you. It's silly of me. I can't think what made me do that.'

Slowly David said, 'Are you meaning to sleep with me?'

She looked frightened.

'No. No. I don't understand.'

'Yes, you do.'

'I promise—'

He said, 'You are without exception the worst teaser that I've ever met. The ends you go to – the ornate – the—' He could not find words enough, so he leant back, saying in amazement, 'Lord help us.'

'IT IS TRUE!' she cried. 'I promise it's true. Really, I can't think why I told you a thing like that. I'll never tell you another word of anything that matters to me—'

'I didn't say it wasn't true,' David slowly and quietly replied. 'Even if you expected me to. Your ear has recorded, even if you firmly reject another quite different comment which I made.'

'I heard it,' she said, on the move again, 'and it doesn't make sense. "Ear has recorded" and "rejecting" – God, if you knew how I hated the way you spoke you'd never say another word to me! That's if you loved me, which I don't suppose you do.'

She steadied and looked straight at his face. 'David, I promise it's true. Maybe not all the details. I've thought of it so often; so often I have to laugh about it, don't you see?'

'But you're still at work,' he said. 'It's perfectly amazing.'

She frowned deeply. 'You mean about teasing? I don't think I understand what you said. I never touched you at all – not today, I mean, and I was going to say about yesterday. I'd forgotten that. You must let me explain—'

'You've prepared a statement?'

'Don't look like that. Don't talk sarcastically.' Suddenly she spoke more slowly. 'Nobody likes sarcastic talk, you funny, ugly little man.'

'Help,' he said and shook his head.

'Why d'you say that?'

'I'm exhausted. Exhausted by your dishonesty—'

'But I told you, I swear—'

'Not your lies – if they were lies, I don't know about that. But by your dishonesty.'

She picked up another sandwich and seemed to try to collect her thoughts together, before he spoke again. There were rival noises in the distance now. Against the thumping from the gym there were odd phrases of songs being sung by some of the more cheerful farmers and locals, Pink's chums from the Queen's bar, who had encamped themselves in the classroom next door.

Mary said, 'They sound cheerful enough,' and she looked around the classroom as if she were a little amazed to find herself there. 'God knows what's happened to everybody else. I suppose they're wondering what's happened to us.' Her mind seemed to be flitting along like a fly on the surface of the water, as if she were very tired or had just woken up. She made no effort to leave.

'Some details may not be right,' she said. 'One had to piece the story together from shouts in the night, other things Macdonald has heard. Mind you, nobody else knows this. They don't even know Mummy was adopted. But I only told you because—'

'Because?' he asked. 'I'm very interested in this.'

'Because you said I was being unfair to Mummy.'

'It seems an odd sort of way to answer the charge—'

'No,' she said. 'I just told you. I don't have to pretend she's something she wasn't – not at all, she was pathetic, she drank, she gave up, she wasn't very pretty any more but if we'd had that life we'd be a bit battered too. I mean, after all that, just when she thought she was safe there was the card game too – you know, the scandal.'

'I think I remember this one,' he said.

'Oh, you must. If you lived there you must remember. It's the only thing people know about the Fergusons.'

She turned away from him again and he said:

'Remind me of the details.'

'Oh, they're not known exactly.'

'In outline.'

'Well, I shan't say whether Daddy was the scapegoat or not. Obviously I have an opinion. Let's leave that aside. Either way the result's the same as far as we're concerned. Instead of being in London in some stuffy house in Chester Square or something like that, here we are on our lovely farm. I don't complain about that. But it's true enough.'

'Facts,' David gently suggested.

'Not very original really,' she said, gliding across the room. 'A country house. Ascot I think it was. A lot of smart people. Daddy was in the Guards, you know. Well, there was one person there much smarter than the rest. There was evidently some sort of trouble. Anyway the men played cards half the night and argued what to do about the fact that somebody had cheated, for the rest of the night. Rumour has it that it wasn't Daddy who did cheat, but Daddy certainly took the rap. The very next day, you know, he resigned from his clubs.'

'What a dreadful hardship,' David said.

'Oh I know—' she said quickly. 'We're marvellously lucky really. Nobody cares up here. Nobody at all. Not in our generation anyway.'

'And in mine?'

'Oh, don't be so silly, you're not as old as all that. No, you mustn't get the idea that I'm complaining about things. And of course to us cheating at cards sounds such a little thing. I'd do it like mad, I'm sure—'

'I'm sure,' he agreed.

She went on, 'Resigning from clubs and all that. It's all terribly grand, but in those days, you know—'

He interrupted, 'D'you not think it's perhaps a little too grand?'

'I don't understand you.' She seemed alarmed again.

'I actually do remember this story . . . I mean both the one you're telling and what was told at the time.'

'Oh yes?' very slowly.

'Yes. I can't remember why I learnt. I don't honestly believe that people were sufficiently interested—'

'Everybody knows the Ferguson scandal,' she replied firmly.

'I'm sure you're right. I wonder who could have told them?' He smiled. 'I confess I'd never thought of it in quite the same way as you. I didn't think the operation had quite the scale to merit the word scandal. What we gathered was that your father used to make quite a habit of gambling, even soon after he was married, and your mother put her foot down. It was one of several things of that nature. But she used to ring him at his club. I believe it was one of the St James's Clubs. It was said, jokingly, I believe—'

'I don't think you've got it right.'

He persisted. 'Purely as a local joke, that your mother brought him north because he spent so much time in his club, playing bridge. I don't remember any suggestion of cheating.'

'Of course there was cheating. That was the whole point. And as a matter of fact,' she added, 'Daddy did cheat. He's wonderful, Daddy, really.' She snapped her fingers. 'He doesn't care that for what anybody says. Never did.'

David shrugged. 'I only tell it as I remember it. You may be right.'

'I am.'

'I didn't know your parents, myself. But I remember the farm being pointed out to me. That's when the joke came up. I remember it quite clearly because it was one of the most human jokes my father ever told me. And I remember my mother enjoying it enormously and pretending to be rather shocked.' He added, 'It doesn't really matter, you know.'

'Of course it matters. I know exactly what you're thinking. That I'm untruthful.'

'I think you may get muddled. There was quite a famous case called Tranby Croft, but that was at the turn of the century, I believe—'

'Of course I've heard of that,' she said, her colour rising. 'And I don't muddle it a bit. In fact usually when I'm telling the story I mention Tranby Croft. The circumstances were quite extraordinarily similar – a different guest of honour – you know?' The way she added 'you know' with a childish haughtiness made it clear that he had caught her and he suddenly looked sad, too. He sat down on one of the desks and reached out both hands to her. If one suspects one's best friend of pinching things, there is, after all, no satisfaction in finding out that one's suspicions were well founded. She stood biting her lip, refusing, shaking her head.

'It doesn't matter,' he said very kindly. She came near enough for him to be able to reach forward and touch her only with his fingertips. Rather moodily, still with a deep frown she banged her hip again and again against one of the desks. She looked at him solemnly and bitterly. She was not afraid to meet his eye. He said, again:

'It doesn't matter a bit. And I won't tell anybody.'

She continued to stare at him.

He went on, 'But you ought to know why you did it. Why you exaggerated. Let's put it kindly – the Ferguson scandal and maybe the Dundee—'

'No,' she said. 'Not Dundee. That one's sacred. That's quite a different thing. Really it is. I confess the Ferguson scandal thing – it's a bit of a fib. Not really all fib. One's forgotten just quite what's right and what's wrong about it. Pink and I had lots of versions, once. Some better than others. But it doesn't do any harm. People like a good story. It brightens their lives.'

'Go on.'

'You know too much, don't you?' She looked at him, for a second, as if she had loved him for a thousand years.

'No,' he shook his head. 'I haven't said your story-telling didn't work. On the contrary, you'll remember that the basis of my complaint is that it works too well, if you don't mean to go through with it.'

'Did I tell you these stories just to make myself more attractive? Is that what you think?'

He nodded.

She laughed suddenly, and touched the ink-well again. 'Isn't that clever of me?' she said. 'You may be right. I'm amazed. I must say it would be nice to have you around, as a friend, cousin-style. We could employ you as a kind of fortune teller. Pink would love that too.'

She moved quickly away, laughing rather loudly while he sat still. But as she suggested, 'I think it's high time we went back,' and walked towards the classroom door, he said:

'Stop.'

She turned and actually arched an eyebrow in a little pose of dignified surprise.

He shook his head and rubbed his eyes, saying:

'I shall never learn. It doesn't pay to tell the truth. But I promise I'm not going to tell anybody. You don't need to feel guilt or shame—'

'Over fibbing about something that happened thirty years ago? Don't be so silly, David. I'm hardly likely to feel guilty about that. I am a woman, after all. Anyway, a girl. And they're allowed little lies.'

'Only when they know they're telling them. That's a very important point.' He smiled again as he raised a finger of warning and she returned his smile with real warmth. She came back into the room a few steps.

She said, 'I daren't approach more than this, else you'll go all grim again and call me obscene names and charge up and down, scratching your head to find new ways of making me feel small.'

He shook his head.

'Am I as bad as that?'

She said, 'You do seem to like knocking me about a bit.'

'No.' He shook his head.

She replied, 'Yes, you do. You're a kind of schoolmaster at heart. No, honestly, I'm saying something nice. Will you

go up there and pick up Kennedy's *Latin Primer* and read
me a bit?'

'If you want.'

'No, don't,' she replied quickly. 'That was a silly idea.
David, don't bark at me and don't call me that other hateful
thing even if you think it, because if I am what you said I
am, then I honestly don't think I can help it very much.'

'Who's getting complicated now?'

'It's a plague,' she said. 'You should hear Pink try and
tell someone how he feels. It always comes out backside
foremost. David, I was going to ask. We were having a love
scene, weren't we? Just now, I mean, not just for the last
minute or two. Even when I was telling you about poor
Mummy.' She looked at her watch. 'God, we must go
through.'

'That's what I was trying to tell you,' he said. 'You put it
much more nicely. At least I know that I'm making love.'

'When you're cross-examining me? That's very modern
living. Look, I won't make a speech, David. I'd got a little
speech ready. About yesterday.'

'I could see that.'

'You tell me, then, what I was going to say.'

He thought and smiled slowly, then he spoke on her
behalf.

' "Look, David, about yesterday. I don't want you to
misunderstand. I'm not sorry that I said 'no'. I'm just sorry
that I didn't say 'no' much sooner. I don't mean just
yesterday afternoon. Not just in the car. I mean in London.
From the very start." ' He laughed, pleased with his own
performance, then grew more serious as he saw that there
were tears in her eyes.

She said, 'But it's exactly . . . Darling David, do you
know everything about me, as easily as that?'

'No,' he said thoughtfully, and he did not move towards
her. She stared at him as she spoke.

'Anyway, I've made up my mind – it is "no". Because?

Well, because it is, darling.' He still did not move, and she went on, 'But you've every right to bawl me out. I know that's why I hated the word as much as I did. I did encourage you and then said "no". It was a very bad thing to do. Please forgive me for that.'

He said, 'It happens quite often. I wouldn't feel too badly about it. In fact it always happens. It's just a question of how long you go on doing it. Beyond certain limits it slips from good technique to bad judgment, bad taste and then crime.'

She looked at him solemnly.

'David, am I doing it now?'

'Yes,' he replied.

'Yes, I thought I was,' she said. And turning quickly, she ran out of the room. As she did so, Peebles, the singing farmer, was returning to the gym with his friend. He was saying:

'I've been told on the highest authority that if I'd got the professional attention when I was younger I could have made my living that way. It was a conductor told me that. He said to me, "You have some remarkable pure tenor notes." He said that.'

AS SOON AS Mary re-entered the gymnasium, which, in Pink's words, now smelt strongly of what your best friend won't tell you, she realised that she had stayed in Classroom IV too long. The group round the Ferguson table by the door had that particular look of indecision which follows some minor calamity. Macdonald was standing by the table staring in the direction of the band and alongside, her boy-friend the tiny Captain, Jack Gordon, M.C., R.A.M.C. (Retd.), who looked like a sick Mr. Esquire, was joking as he picked a green pill from his silver snuff-box.

'May I offer any one of you one of these anti-coagulatory pills given to me by the kind services of that bloody awful organisation the National Health Service?' he asked, but Mary, as always, brushed him aside. Stephen was sitting back in the chair drinking some white wine and the blank expression on his face betrayed that he was up to his usual trick of contracting out of a scene. He was looking at Pink, but at the same time ignoring him.

Pink, meantime, was stuttering and sucking in air. Whenever he had words with his father there appeared an impediment less in his speech than in his brain. He was saying:

'Not just sitting in front of the nursery fire! Oh no! Not right! Fact.' He twisted his head in a little circle. 'Not the whole truth. Absolutely not.' He assumed a mysterious smile. 'No question of sitting-sickness these days. I may hang on a bit in the nursery alone, sometimes, you follow, but – but not just sitting. You may be very surprised. Things have changed. Pink's got pink plans. You may be very surprised indeed. I've come to my senses.'

To which Mary said, almost under her breath:

'Oh God. Guv'nor stuff,' and she meant that there must have been a row between Pink and her father. She looked at Macdonald. 'Right?'

Macdonald nodded but Pink interrupted again.

'Nothing to it, Nelly,' he said to Mary. 'Just a little ruffling of the old feathers. I was trying to tell him to cheer up, it wasn't such a bad hop, he seemed to be a bit snobbish about it. You know what he is. He suggested rather snobbishly that it might suit me. Said it suited him too that I should hang on here as it would save me sitting up all night in the nursery drinking his booze.'

'Is that all?' Mary asked.

'More or less, old flesh.' Pink took a little drink. 'When I offered to buy him a bottle he said it was the sitting, not the whisky, that offended him. Then he pushed off.'

Macdonald said, 'It was just this minute,' and Mary ran into the hall. She caught her father on the steps. He wore a perfectly cut, rather gay dog's-tooth check coat over his dinner-jacket. He looked round with his usual blank, blue-eyed, flat-eyed stare when somebody said:

'You're being called, Sir Harry,' but he smiled at once when he saw that it was Mary.

She said, 'Darling, you're not huffing, not on my account? I couldn't bear that.'

He stopped with one foot a step higher than the other. He had a royal knack of pose. He smiled very slowly and kindly and took both her hands.

'I wouldn't dream of it.'

'Then do come back.'

He shook his head. He said, 'I've had the one dance I wanted,' referring, of course, to their dance. 'I'd only look what you call stony.'

'You'd still look the best.'

'Bed-time for old bones,' he said, plonking a tweed hat on his head. He always looked brown.

'Daddy, did you snap at Pink?'

'Snap?' He frowned, seemed puzzled. 'Not that I know.'

'He's a bit hectic.'

The Colonel shrugged. 'Well, then he's being too idiotic.'

He kissed her and moved off, careless of the others' transport problems, intending to take the family car.

The cars were parked in the school's ashcourt or playground, and when he arrived at his he found that it would be awkward if not impossible to reverse out. He stood for a moment, staring at it, and he did not turn round when one of the social secretaries of the Young Conservatives, a boy called Alec, with long fair hair, suede shoes and enthusiastic manners came dashing out.

'This'll never do, Sir Harry. I'll just move Mr Scott's car, here, and that'll let you out.'

The Colonel did not smile. He looked faintly surprised as he said:

'That's extremely kind of you.'

It was somehow never necessary for him to say thank-you.

Much as the business man blames himself unnecessarily for the deal that's fallen through, if he spends an afternoon with a tart, so Mary, tight-lipped and clenched fist, blamed herself as she returned to Pink and Stephen. Macdonald and the Captain were by then having what they called 'a difference' by the bar at the end of the room. ('My dear Flora, my dear girl . . .' the Captain said, again and again.)

Pink was still shaking his head and talking mysteriously and secretively of a public relations firm which he and some connection of a neighbouring family were going to set up in Montreal, or maybe Sydney. He had dark plans, but they rather petered out when Mary returned.

The hiatus that followed was suddenly, swiftly broken by Mary. She pulled in her chair and seeing David over by the bar she turned her back on him, firmly. She talked to Pink with her special kind of excited innocence; as if unbroken conversation would keep the bogey-man away. Stephen examined the label of the hock bottle throughout her next outburst, as if it had as much written on it as the label pasted on those tiny bottles of Angostura bitters.

'There's the most fascinating thing going on in Classroom III.' She drummed her fingers on the table in front of her and then quickly continued:

'It's all your chums, Pink. You're really missing something. They're all in Classroom III sticking pins into the effigy of David's papa. You know they're all his pupils, practically all of them, anyway—'

As she ran on, naming the group, Maclaren, Miller, Peebles, Davidson and all the rest, a sad smile passed across Pink's face.

'I promise. Honestly,' she said, which Pink knew to be the mark of pure fiction, then she went back to her story.

'All of them, about ten or twelve, and I couldn't quite see whether one was pretending to be old Dowie or not – they probably just imagined him.'

The music seemed loud as a new dance began. It was a dance called Hamilton House, which begins with the girl setting to one man, as if to dance with him, then quickly passing to the next and turning him. The girls were all enjoying it and some of the younger ones put great spirit into the rejection of the first man, twisting their heads away or even flicking their fingers in the first man's face before grasping the hands of the next.

Mary still talked.

'I honestly don't think there was anybody up there actually imitating him, but they were all acting as if they were back at school. I was riveted.' The heels of her hands banging against the table seemed to say 'It'll be all right,

Pink, it'll be all right. Forget his bullying.' She ran on, as Pink covered his face with his hands.

'Can you imagine all the lads squeezed into desks, half of them laughing and poor old Bill Davidson [the proprietor of the Queen's], he'd fallen fast asleep at the back. They were shouting at him to wake up at the back and old Baldy Maclaren was standing up in his desk waving his arm about, asking the ghost of Dowie if he might be excused. He was quite funny, I must say, going "Please, please sir", flicking his fingers too.' She spoke more and more swiftly. 'Some of them were imitating Old Dowie too. And wee Peter Forbes was shouting the most of all. All glowing and red, the way he gets, though I must say he's kept his figure better than the others have, and he must be over fifty now. He's shouting at the top of his voice, "Aye, and I still feel the strap across my palm. I do. 'Peter Forbes, you're dunce!' Wham! 'You'll no do any good in this world or the next.' Aye and here's me," Peter shouts, "And the mill's never done better and that's a fact. It's me that's done it! Three thousand a year I make! Three thousand pounds and expenses on top of that! Bloody old Dowie! Bloody old man!" He was shaking his fist quite violently.'

She smiled brightly as she finished her story.

'Aren't men so silly when they get drunk? Especially the little ones. They get so aggressive. You must have heard Peter Forbes. You must have heard him when he's drunk. Pink, darling, you're not sobbing really. And Peebles, too, going on about his tenor voice—'

But Pink had recovered. He dropped his hands and opened his mouth in what almost appeared to be a cartoon of a toothless, noiseless laugh. Then he laid his hand on the top of Mary's head and said cheerfully:

'As a matter of fact, kid, I confirm you as a member of God's Holy Church.'

'I do love Pink.'

Not very long after that, the band leader played the first bars of 'The Dashing White Sergeant'.

Mary said, 'Isn't that perfect? Just right for three sparrows on a wire,' and Stephen put down the bottle.

'Are you dancing, Belle?' Pink asked and Mary gave a skittish little giggle, as Belle.

She said, 'That's a fact. We'd better bring hubby too.'

Mary seemed prepared, as they moved to the floor, to ignore David. But Stephen was polite to him. He said, very pleasantly:

'Sit down at our table. There's lots of room.'

Mary looked at her husband furiously. As they moved into their first circle she said, 'That's a bloody silly thing to do.'

COUSIN, D'YOU remember? All three of us felt badly about it, I'm sure. There were some sticky moments, at that corner table, after your Dashing White Sergeant and before poor Captain Jack Gordon diverted us.

Even the atmosphere had changed. It was vaguely Teutonic, when the squeeze-box man came down from the stand. All your Young Conservative friends tried to yodel. In my mind the scene is marked as a notable chapter in Scotland's war against taste. Burns had given way to Lehár. Somebody lowered the lights to that particular degree of dimness which makes the younger girls (and a few of your Auntie Belles) scream, yet fail to lose their inhibitions.

I remember your face, white, and your eyes looking darker than I'd ever seen them as you hung on to Stephen, pushing your face against his arm. When you did look at me it was with hatred. Or is that quite accurate? With something resembling hatred, something a little sulkier. I can't get nearer it than that. And remembering it now, in a bright neon-lit laboratory, it's like something out of a dream. It was as if we were in a huge, unhaunted night club on the outskirts of Berlin. The wooden beams and the music lead me to Germany. The square mirror, the instruments in the corner and the giant nooses above added a macabre touch to excite the macabre; these take me to Hamburg or Berlin.

How did it start? I can't remember. Perhaps talking about Pink who had gone to join the Queen's bar cronies in that other classroom. Yes. Stephen mystified me, I remember now, with some reference to the antics in that classroom: something about their imitating my father, his former pupils abusing him, now that he was safely dead and buried. But of course, not having heard the story you wove for Pink, I was lost.

I remember your bracelet fell down your wrist as you watched the dancers creeping round, most of them, rolling Hunt Ball-Night Club style. You weren't drinking whisky any more. That added another German touch. Lager, now. You leant your head back until your hair pushed against the climbing bars, and there were dark shadows under your eyes, giving you, rather alarmingly, and suddenly, a great deal more sex. You blew some cigarette smoke that had drifted close to your eyes and then cut into our conversation, saying to Stephen, not to me (nothing was addressed directly to me), 'I made the story up. More or less.' You said it with a sort of shamelessness that added, perhaps you knew, to the sex. Before we said anything you ran on, 'I am rather worried about Daddy. Perhaps he was huffing because I was away so long.'

Then you twisted back to the classroom story. It was typical Mary.

'I just said it to keep old Pink afloat.' You never smiled. Then you said, 'David didn't rape me or anything like that.'

'That wasn't going through my head.' Stephen, on the other hand, smiled kindly at you.

'Prop me,' you said, and leant against him. He put an arm behind you and played with the back of your hair.

Two, three years ago?

I can't have taken my eyes away from you. I can live every second again. But I was already beginning the game I played so mercilessly for six months, pressing you for answers to the unanswerable. Stephen rather took my part, I remember, as we tried to examine what had made you make up the particular story about the Queen's bar gentlemen. You were not to be provoked. You shrugged and answered, looking into the lager glass:

'Even *my* nose is too small to get into this thing. I wonder what proper craggy Scotsmen do.' You looked at Stephen then, at his thin pointed nose and at my pugilist's job. 'You two are no good,' you said.

Gently, I remember coming in. 'Let's take that other story you told me about your mother,' I saw your grip tighten on Stephen's arm.

'He only does it to annoy,' you said lightly, but Stephen, oddly, was solidly on my side then, falling over himself to be generous to me, and friendly and fair.

'Answer the gentleman,' he said. 'Tell him what's true about all the stories you've spun him.'

Silence from you. A little superior laugh from me. I said:

'Come on, it's only a point of interest,' and you lifted your eyes to me then. It was not hatred. That is the wrong word. It was a sort of self-hatred. And yet an invitation of a sluttish kind. Then you sat up and pushing a finger into Stephen's cheek, you said, a fraction louder:

'I didn't tell any more stories. I hepped up the gambling thing a little, but I don't think that was such a bad thing to do.' To Stephen you said with a smile, 'I served him Tranby Croft.'

'Why do you do it?' Stephen asked. The lights grew lighter and then dimmer. I suppose some young farmer had found and could not resist the running control. The brown suits and green frocks were having their own back on the Hunt Ball-Night Club crawl. With Scottish accents they were singing Lili Marlene.

'If David was anything of a friend he'd go and fish out Pink, else he'll get sick drunk.'

Stephen said at once, 'I'll get him, darling.'

A shake of your head. You said:

'No, really,' as he began to move, then 'No' again, much louder.

'But it won't take a minute,' he said.

'No, please,' clenching your fists round his sleeve, 'Stay here.'

We knew by then, all three of us: of course we did. You looked at me once again, I remember, when Stephen described your mother as respectable Dundee jute. Silver teapot, I think he said, and what are those paper serviettes called? Doyles or something like that. It hardly fitted with the buckets of blood in the tenement but I let another lie pass. I was playing the old dog's games now. I did not even have the subtlety to bully you. Just looked at your mouth. All the time Stephen talked coolly and disinterestedly as if he were a little embarrassed that you should hug his arm so tightly and press your head against his chest. You brushed your cheek along the black cloth, from time to time.

Stephen, with prefect's authority now, put us right about the Ferguson scandal. I don't suppose I listened to a word at the time but it must have been a very important scene, this one. I only have to close my eyes, and listen, and I can play him back. He smoked rather elegantly as he talked of your mother.

'Pregnant at the time,' he said, and I remember your blink of distaste at the phrase that followed. 'Carrying Pink.' Once or twice you tried to stop him. I think you were always frightened of Stephen being a bore. You tugged, but it made no difference. He did not talk so quickly or irrationally as you so often did, distant cousin, but he talked for the same reason. Talk takes the edge off a scene. So long as conversation is suspended one can ignore the caveman stuff going on beneath. 'That makes it about 1926—' he went on. 'For whatever reason the Colonel had started going back to some of his bachelor habits and he was in one of the smarter jobs, White's or Buck's or Boodle's or Pratt's, or one of those, when Mona kept ringing him up to get him home; she became tearful and evidently quite obsessional about his club life, nobody can quite explain why. It got to the stage when she rang the club about every five minutes and then she arrived in a taxi. There followed a scene which sounds pretty farcical, whereby she was bundled out of the place, weeping and yelling, but the Colonel evidently didn't think this was such a joke. There's a missing link here, but it seems that his friends and acquaintances behaved rather cruelly. They were all very bright sort of men, most of them fairly idle, and one assumes they must have teased the life out of him. Anyway, rather obstinately, and certainly very stupidly, as he had a huge future in front of him – he was a colonel at thirty-three, after all – he tried to get his own back at cards. He cheated. It was discovered.'

At that, you interrupted sharply. Lifted your head to say, violently, 'He didn't care if he were discovered! That's the whole point. He doesn't care what anybody says. He's marvellous like that!'

Stephen ignored you again. He seemed to consider your outburst understandable but inaccurate. He went on, smoothly, as before:

'I fancy the other men would have done nothing about it but he felt he'd let himself down, he lost confidence, resigned from the club, resigned his commission, sold the Knightsbridge house – the whole lot. To Mona, from Dundee – and she'd done pretty well, for jute from Dundee – all this meant an end to a dream. Anyway, she was a nervous sort of type – rather plump. They came back and bought the farm and the family's been here ever since—'

I couldn't be bothered to tell him the story didn't fit together. Colonels aged thirty-three don't cheat at cards because their wives kick up a row at the club door. It's good for prestige to have a woman howling up and down St James's, crying 'Bring him out'.

But the silence had to be broken. It was you, at last, speaking sleepily.

'Now he knows I'm a bloody liar. But some of the things I said were true. Mummy was adopted, you know. That's the point. Honestly.'

'Oh darling—' Stephen warned you.

'Yes, she bloody well was.' You spoke into his face and he betrayed you with an easy smile, saying:

'Yes, of course she was.' Then he laughed and patted you. 'Pappa understands,' he said, and to me, almost as if he were selling you, 'She's a remarkable little woman, my wife.'

'Christ,' right under your breath.

Even the music had stopped. People were shuffling about. Dishonest you were, cousin, but the least dishonest of the three of us. You sat yourself up to say, 'I'm in a cold sweat. I feel horrid and old.'

Then you took your handbag and said, 'Don't follow me, Steve darling. I'm hopping it to the loo.'

He knew as well as I did that you said that to me. Everybody knew, everybody knew. That's why we all felt sick.

EIGHT

PINK WAS NOT the first to see Captain Gordon lumbered in the Gentlemen's lavatory, but because, in a mild sort of way, he was extremely observant, he took a good look and noticed a detail was wrong. Captain Gordon was sitting in one of the cubicles, with the door wide open. His elbows were on his knees and his head was in his hands.

Pink said, hesitantly and politely, 'Old knob, I'd take your trousers off,' and Captain Gordon swayed unhappily from side to side. He looked up and opened his mouth, once or twice, like a salmon on a rock. His collar was undone.

'Pissed, old chap?' Pink asked kindly, and perhaps because the Captain shook his head Pink said 'Never mind.' He then looked around, and seeing a sort of refuse bin, not quite as big as a dustbin and with a lid that opened by pressing a foot pedal, he dragged that across to the door of the cubicle and there, more or less comfortable, he sat down. 'As a matter of fact,' he said, banging his knuckles against the bin a couple of times, 'I'm fit for the human scrap-heap myself.'

Gusts of noise, of music and of laughter came from the corridors, the classrooms and the gym. They were like two boys in the sickroom, kind of poignantly out of things. It was doubtful if the Captain knew what it was all about. He seemed to have lost his knack for his semaphore of winks, belches and rubber faces, or at least the energy needed for its execution. When at last he did answer Pink he applied one of these Scotticisms, which mean nothing but which have a use. They keep friends along the bar from falling fast asleep, and save grandmother in the parlour, on a Sunday afternoon, from dissolving into tears. The one he used translates approximately as 'life is a labour', but curiously enough is seldom exchanged between men at work.

He said, 'It's an awful trachle.'

Pink, apparently delighted to get a reply, as the Captain's heavy breathing had been beginning to upset him, knew exactly the sort of thing to say to this. A thousand crawling hours at the bar of the Queen's made him answer, without hesitation:

'Absolutely, old man. But then the fun's in the ficht.'

'D'you think my collar was too tight?' the Captain asked. He referred to the pills he had to take, when he added, in a hurt voice, 'I took my coagulation Johnnies. I didn't forget.'

Pink said, 'I hate these bloody collars. You want to wear a soft job like this.'

'Yours looks tight.'

Pink did not like the idea that he was, weekly, growing fatter. 'Not a bit, old man,' he said huffily, 'perfectly all right.' Then added, 'They always shrink things in the laundry. And, by God, the price.'

'It was mixing drinks, I think,' the Captain said, recovering a little. 'Jack Gordon's all right. I hope.'

'Could be,' Pink said, pensively. 'Grain and grape.'

'I'm sure that's what it was,' the Captain replied. And then, *non sequitur*: 'I remember fine, at Territorial camp, it must have been 1913, anno domini, September I think. There was a big camp over Crieff way; I fainted that night. Now I couldn't have been more than seventeen then. I was a sprinter too. I was nimble on my feet. It happens sometimes, with people. In adolescence too. Fainting, like that.' He breathed noisily and shortly, two or three times.

'Good Lord, yes,' Pink said. 'You bet. There's a chum in my house at school, Blinkers somebody. We used to make a book on which Collect it would be. "Lighten our darkness, we beseech Thee, O Lord" used to crack him most times. Real Blinkers' Beechers. "Lord have mercy upon us".'

'Christ have mercy upon us.'

' "Lord have mercy upon us" and bonk, there's old Blinkers hooped over the stall in front, like a rag doll. Out for the count. As much as twenty-five bob would slip through from the first treble to the altos. It whiled away the time,' he said.

'I'm Episcopalian,' the Captain said, swallowing.

'There's more music,' Pink said. 'Am I right, old man?' But the scenes from his schooldays demanded his attention. He said, in the pause that followed, 'Old Blinkers' eyes used to shoot up before he went. I remember the whites of them. We didn't like him for it, you know, poor chum.'

The Captain rested his elbows on his knees again. He dropped his head for a second, then lifting it again, he said, with a curious, uncertain little smile:

'You panic, you know. Anything to do with breath. I was a doctor, I should know. It's not that there's real danger . . . I still go to the kirk.'

'Good for you,' Pink said. 'It's good for the— it keeps the thing together.'

'I haven't the same faith, you know. Not now.'

'Not?'

'No. You'd think someone's been to death's door. I've been to death's door. I do not joke, Charles. You'd think it would go the other way. It's not what's happened to Jack Gordon. My mother was a great believer, a hat on every Sunday morning and down the road – I've always been to the kirk. And now, mind, at the eleventh hour, I don't hear a peep. No angels' trumpets—'

The look in his eye was one of blank fear.

Pink said affably, 'You're still this side of the door, what?'

'I know it—' The Captain spread out his hands. He seemed bewildered in a curiously practical sort of fashion.

It did not look as if he were saying that his most fundamental beliefs had crumbled. He resembled a man who had
been done out of some money. Seeing his face and hands
alone, Pink would have imagined that he were saying, 'I've
known this man Moo for years: I've been in there to put a
bet on every Saturday, regularly. And here, he says to me,
no ticket, Captain Gordon, no divvy.' His smile broadened,
and froze on his face. In a tiny voice, he went on, about
himself:

'It's the other way about with Jack Gordon. There's just
nothing. I can't explain it more than that, Charles. A kind
o' tidal wave of nothing coming hellish fast.' He said 'fast'
with a very short 'a'.

After a pause, Pink said, 'I never was much of a God-
botherer myself, old chum.'

The Captain looked at him again. It was difficult to know
whether he was anxious to find out if he had got his point
across, or whether he wanted Pink to find some sort of
comfort for him.

'Mind,' the Captain said at last, 'it wasn't always like this.
I was at Passchendaele, and—' He looked at Pink uncertainly. 'You've heard of Passchendaele?'

'Absolutely,' Pink answered him. 'It's in the book. Part
of the myth for me. Don't you worry, chum. A kind of
Golgotha for me.'

The Captain frowned. 'I wasn't there,' he admitted,
about Golgotha. 'But Passchendaele—' He managed one
of his gay little whistles. 'Boy, you don't get nearer to death
than that, no – and the mud? The mud! Up to here. I do not
exaggerate. No. I tell my stories, maybe, but I would not
exaggerate about that day. It was a week really. Mud above
the knee. Some places it was higher, but to the knee was far
enough for Captain Gordon, R.A.M.C., Lieutenant, as he
was then.' He frowned. 'I can't remember what I thought.'
He sounded frightened by his own forgetfulness. 'I can't
remember it clearly now. But I'd a Bible in my pocket. I can

tell you that. A photo of my mother and another of a lassie I never saw in my life. She was somebody's sister, I think. I don't remember.' He tried to pull himself together a little, but he did not have the courage to take a drink of whisky from Pink's flask. 'No, no,' he said, and paused for a long minute. 'Up to the knees!' he repeated, and then added vaguely, 'My knees are awful cold now.' More firmly he continued:

'When we got there, Jerry's machine-gun—' He relapsed into semaphore to mark a thousand of his countrymen dead. He put his hand flat on his forehead. 'When we got there the boys had no fight left in them.' His eyes suddenly filled with tears. 'Oh my goodness me,' he said. He brushed his forehead with the sleeve of his black Highland jacket and one of the sharp silver buttons scratched his cheek, but he did not seem to notice it. He put the cloth to his nose again.

He said, 'This thing smells of moth balls. It's most unpleasant. That's my dotter's doing. And I don't think you get moths in a caravan at all.'

He sat back and closed his eyes and then, almost in slow motion he tipped forward, and Pink let him gently down to the floor.

'All right, old man?' Pink asked anxiously, and moved forward to help pick him up again. But he lay where he fell and Pink said to himself, out loud:

'Cheri – cheri – bim, by God. A regular thing.'

Then he went to look for John the policeman. Shouts of laughter still rang through the corridors, coming from the gym.

It was a few moments after this when Macdonald and Mary arrived. Although she had been near to tears herself when she met Macdonald, Mary now played it gay. Her laughter tinkled a little falsely as she came down the corridor, accusing Macdonald of respectability and false modesty for not having ventured into the gentlemen's lavatory and further for having refused to accost any men on their way in or out. But then she did not see herself blush and laugh gaily as she led the way into the same lavatory saying 'Good heavens! Look at those awful stalls!'

But the lavatory was by then as busy as a railway station. People were hauling the poor Captain this way and that. Around the body there were twenty pairs of legs, and six or seven people were talking at once. Somebody other than Macdonald, who came edging through, recognised that perhaps the Captain was something more than drunk, but John, who was a very young policeman, seemed determined that drunk he was, and badly confusing his duties, as he had himself drunk an illicit pint, he seemed further determined to make some moral judgments. He had his cap off and his short hair stuck upwards and outwards. His only concession to civility at this point was to name the person he was talking to as often as a comma turns up in a sentence. Each clause was punctuated by a Mr Miller, a Miss Macdonald, or in the end, a Miss Ferguson, which anyway was incorrect, as Mary's surname was now Cameron.

Somehow or other, action continued in spite of the confusion of argument, medical advice and a general atmosphere of clumsiness and indistinct focus. The groaning Captain was lifted to his feet and Mary, with unthinking annoyance, tore a strip off John the policeman, who could not have had better intentions as he said again and again to one person or the next:

'A good evening's one thing, Mr Hogg, but this is no' right at all, Mr Hogg. This is the sort of thing that spoils a party. This is tantamount to public nuisance, Mr Hogg. So it is. I'm not at all sure that it shouldn't go down in the book.'

'It's in the Book,' Pink sang to himself. 'Oyez, it's in the Book.'

A moment later a flaming argument grew up, the same points being put again and again, as John the policeman refused to let Peebles, the singing farmer, take Macdonald and the Captain home.

By then, half the dance and all the boys from Classroom III were involved, but perhaps for reasons of class as much as personality they inclined to back Mary who dictated the following course of action. If the only car big enough to take the Captain in comfort was Peebles' massive fawn Humber, then that was the car that should be used. Pink would drive it, Macdonald would go with the Captain, and John the policeman, himself, must also go to help carry the Captain from road to caravan, should this be necessary.

The Captain himself had offered only one positive note. He was not going anywhere except back to his burrow, namely the Captain's caravan. John seemed doubtful about this, but as the body of spectators were solidly behind Mary, he at last agreed. There were two amendments, or additions, to the plan. The Captain himself, with a guilty look at Macdonald, asked that Mary should come, too. Somewhat to everybody's surprise, after an important two seconds of thought (or better, forethought) Mary announced, and announced particularly plainly, that she was willing to do this. And as soon as she had said so she looked round the heads at the back of the crowd. There was no sign of David, but Stephen was there. He signalled, at once, that he had heard and understood. The other last-minute addition was that Peebles said he had a sheep-dog, named Flossy, in the back of the Humber. He was careful about the name. He said that as she was nervous he had better come along too. At last, the whole nebula of confusion gradually moved from the lavatory to the hall and then to the ashcourt. The description of the Captain's embussing would be as laborious as the procedure itself. Somehow they squeezed him in (and he was looking very ill, now), then the car drove off. By some disturbing reflex, the crowd gave a little cheer, as if it were the send-off at the end of a wedding.

In the hall, meantime, Stephen told David, who had emerged from the gym, what had happened. He added, turning away, 'Mary's gone along too.' Then at the gym door he paused, and said, 'Want a drink?'

David shook his head. For a moment he seemed about to explain himself, then he decided on a simple 'No, thanks' and with a flick of his fingers about turned and made for the room where all the coats were kept. The crowd of well-wishers sauntered back, knocking their feet against the top step, as if they were used to mud. Most of them then decided that it was long past time to go. Some looked rather angry with themselves. But the hard nucleus of the Queen's bar boys sidled back down the corridor, while the younger couples, shouting nonsenses at each other on a slightly high pitch, went back to the dance floor and tried to recapture the mood of the clinch.

But the country dance was at an end. Patchy music was provided by a rather dreamy young farmer who played the piano as if he had only one hand: the left being an automatic pump. Satisfied by this, several young couples dragged out the proceedings by dancing more or less in the dark, in front of the mirror. They swayed very slowly in their twos, looking only at those strangers, themselves.

Stephen did not stay in the hall to watch David run down the steps to his car. He returned to the gym and sat on the platform where all those girls had sat; those who were now being taken home in little cars or walked through blue, echoing streets. Stephen looked calm enough but he was then obliged to talk to one of the leading Young Conservatives, a nice boy, without looks, without money and without talent for games, dancing or sports, who for some reason spent all his time, outside the estate agent's office in which he worked, doing everything in his power to preserve, or more accurately to recreate a society in which looks, money, field sports, games and dancing would have importance. This young man affected a Highland pose, with arms crossed and one foot splay, and he enjoyed talking to Stephen. He told himself that he found Stephen sympathetic because he was one of the most intelligent young men in the district. Stephen himself thought how awful it was that he should sit discussing politics and crops with the dullest man in the area, and how inevitable. Soon he looked bored stiff.

Five or six minutes after the pianist had packed up, the couples drifted away and Stephen was in the gym alone. He sat a little while longer then, confirming that nobody else was there, he walked as far as the big square mirror. He stood for a few moments seriously considering the nice-looking dark young man in Highland dress who there confronted him, so passively. He seemed bewildered by the image's inaction under provocation; puzzled by the flatness of jealousy. Then he took a step or two forward and looked very carefully at the blue eyes almost as if, having found himself so unconfident of his sex, he felt confused about his identity.

NINE

THE CARAVAN WAS not particularly clean or comfortable, but it was tidy. The books, but for *Treasure Island* and *Journey's End*, which rested on the ledge by the bunk, were neatly clasped between a pair of stirrups which had been made into book ends. The Captain's silver hair-brushes were carefully aligned with his comb and stud box. But the final scenes of his life were played clumsily. His own appearance was pathetically untidy, and even his clipped speech deserted him, because in the end, one half of his face was paralysed.

Pink, as soon as he had helped the Captain as far as the caravan, funked it, and saying something, weakly, about Peebles' dog which had woken another at the cottage nearby, he hastened back to the car where Peebles lay snoring, sprawled half along the back seat.

Mary, when she was still shouting orders, had lost her nerve. At first, as if she were dealing with a drunk, not an invalid, she shouted to the policeman to undress him.

'We'll have him into bed and he'll be right as rain.'

She smiled uncertainly at the Captain, but he could not reply. As he arrived at the caravan he was once again gripped with a pain that went across his chest, to his shoulders, even down his arms: a hollow and burning pain. In the car he had not attempted to speak. It was the policeman who had done most of the talking. He had protested all the way that the Force was the best career, Miss Macdonald, for a man such as himself coming from a big family like he did. He had done well at the Police

College. 'The Force offers the opportunities', he said as the little Captain swayed and fell against his shoulder. Macdonald was in the back of the car and she reached forward and grasped the Captain's shoulders. She spent half of the journey crying and the other half adjusting him in his seat as if he were a ventriloquist's dummy, and for a moment, until he regained balance, holding him firmly there. Rabbits' eyes shone in the headlights when they approached the river. At the sight of them Peebles' dog began to bark, and Peebles, waking from a noisy sleep, hit it on the nose.

In the caravan, Macdonald, as they began to undress the Captain, clicked her teeth at Mary and said, 'There's no need to shout.' They took off his shoes and his stockings, they unbuckled his sporran, then with difficulty undid his kilt. His legs were almost the same thickness all the way up, and white as the sheets. They took off his Highland jacket, and with his handkerchief, Macdonald dabbed the scratch on his cheek, but it was already dry. They removed his collar but they did not manage the shirt. The scene flared up for a moment as they tried. The Captain groaned in protest. He was sitting on his shirt tails and he could not lean forward and stand up. Mary said, 'Well, lift him up then,' her voice again rising to a shout. Macdonald stood back and the policeman could not manage on his own. His whole face was aglow with sweat. Mary's hands moved in sharp nervy circles. 'Go on, go on.' Effortlessly, like a baby after his bottle, the Captain was a little sick and Macdonald took his hand towel and mopped it up. The policeman had stepped back and even Mary grew silent. For a second they did not seem to be friends helping the sick, but accomplices stripping the body.

Mary said suddenly, 'Well, just leave him like that, for God's sake, it doesn't matter if he's got his shirt on.'

'He's real bad,' Macdonald said.

'He's half asleep,' Mary retorted. 'He's tired out. Of course he is.'

They laid him in his bed in his vest and his open, boiled shirt. A meticulous Highland officer to the end, the Captain wore nothing under his kilt. As he rested against the pillows the front of his shirt pushed up against his chin, and curved like a board. Macdonald pulled up the sheet and blankets.

She said, again, 'He's bad,' and Mary bit her nail.

She turned to the policeman who was putting on his cap and said:

'Don't just stand about then. Get over to the farm and use the phone.'

'Who'll I ring?' he asked, and Mary's impatience overwhelmed her. She clenched her fists as if she were going to scream. Macdonald moved back to the door of the caravan and in a low voice, like a voice from another room, she told him the numbers of the doctor and of the Captain's daughter. By the time the policeman had noted them down, the Captain had momentarily recovered enough to indicate to Mary the syringe by his bedside. There was a tiny sealed phial of morphia in the drawer beside it. With a smile, the last smile that was not crooked, he said, 'Jab.'

Mary, with an outward show of courage and appetite for action, removed the syringe from its case and shakily fitted it together. Her hands did not tremble. They were steady for a second, then leapt two or three inches at a time. She fumbled several times before she had the syringe fixed together. When she was trying to break the seal of the minute phial, because she did not understand that it was rubber to be pierced, her hand slipped again. The phial slid along the hard surface of the table and fell with a crash on the floor.

Mary cried out, then she shoved the syringe away from her.

'Oh, damn the thing,' she said, pushing her knuckles into her brow.

Macdonald, picking up the phial, saw that the contents were spilt.

The Captain said, very faintly, 'It'll not matter,' and Mary did not dare look him in the face, lest she saw pain.

Macdonald, suddenly, for personal more than practical reasons, was determined that Mary should leave them. She stood over her and said, 'There's no point in both of us staying now. You've had a day of it. I'll stay with him.'

Mary might have obeyed. She looked up at Macdonald and she did not recognise what was in her mind. She was clearly thinking 'I'm so bloody useless anyway' and that was why she was for once grateful to the Captain who sat up and protested. But again, and for a moment at least, fortunately, because it gave her confidence, she misinterpreted him. She thought he said, 'No, stay, Mary,' meaning 'I find comfort in your presence.' He did in fact say 'No, stay, Mary,' meaning 'I'd find it more difficult if you left me alone with Flora.' Even at this time, when the Captain was certain he was going to die, even in pain, although it was a little less acute now, he dreaded being left alone with the woman whose affection he could not return. He knew there was no chance of their both leaving him, but he was not sorry about this. At the Private bar at the Moray Arms, his local hotel (not pub), he had actually stated that when the time came he would like to be alone. He used to say, 'Like the animals. They know a thing or two. They crawl away on their own to die.' They crawl away on their own because there is no one to console them. And when the Captain had suggested, so gaily, that he would do the same, he was certain, somehow, that there would be another consolation. But he found none, and he therefore did not want them to go. As sensations slipped away, faster and faster, he wanted to hear voices and see people. As they grew dimmer they must sit closer. As their voices grew fainter they must shout louder.

Macdonald now sat close to him and she began to offer the only comfort she could, which was false comfort. She said the doctor would soon be there; she talked of the doctor, of how good he really was. She said his daughter would be back by breakfast time. The only comfort was in the sound of her voice, not in the things she said. He would rather that she spoke of other people and other things now; it did not matter what. Macdonald, more because the manner of the scene disappointed her, than because her friend was dying, began to get tearful. Her mind could not cope with the tragedy and she fixed on the irritation. She turned again to try to make Mary go back to the farm to make sure that John the policeman had made the phone calls, but Mary obstinately refused to budge. With much effort, the Captain touched the copy of *Treasure Island* by his bedside and Macdonald picked it up. She refused to let Mary read and, in a wan voice, she began at the beginning of the book which the Captain almost knew by heart. It was at the end of the part where the pirates come to the inn that the Captain stirred again. He used to say of his mother 'she was an awfully nice wee body' and he meant to say of *Treasure Island*, 'It's an awfully good book.' But his words were blurred and indistinguishable. They both looked up at him and with one eye, he recognised in their faces his own paralysis which had followed the stroke. It was his left side which was affected, and as he reached across with his right hand to feel his lip and chin he overbalanced slightly and fell against Macdonald, who was leaning forward beside him. They stuck for a moment, in a ludicrous position, their foreheads together like a couple of stags with their antlers caught. Then she pushed him back on the pillows. She looked back at Mary who was staring wide-eyed at the figure in the bed. Macdonald slowly turned back to the book.

At that point, without another word, Mary walked out.

Pink had moved the car along a little from the old bridge in order to try to stop Flossy and the dog in the kennel at the cottage from barking so incessantly, but the sun was rising and Mary soon discovered where he was. She walked across the corner of the field where the stooked corn looked damp and black. The clumps of trees by the river leaning gently with the wind were still without colour. The water itself looked like treacle, but the concrete face of the new bridge was light and bare. A couple of fish lorries rolled along the main road, their sidelights on, their tyres whining against the new surface. The sky was a deep duck-egg blue, with one or two streaks of black.

It was her turn to weep. She did so, hanging on to Pink, who looked very big beside her. He patted her back as she buried her nose in his jacket, and he said:

'The world's your oyster, Lilian. You mustn't forget that.' Then, as she did not recover for a moment, he went on, 'Full marks to old Pinky boy. He funked it altogether.'

At last she paused to take a breath, and tipping back her head she asked, 'Oh God, oh God, why was I no good at all?'

'Purely subjective thing. You seemed to be doing wonders. "Rip his clothes off," I heard you shout. "Don't forget the rings, Nelly—" '

'No, Pink—' she said, meaning 'Don't joke,' and Pink said, with a sort of tight jaw, '*De peur d'être obliger d'en pleurer, je me hâ-hâ-hâte de rire de tout*, old mole.' It was something he often quoted.

Mary said, 'Macdonald's not much good either. She would be, mind you, if he wasn't going to die. It's just because he's going to die, I think that's why one's so incredibly bad.'

'Is there something we should do?'

On the main road above they heard a car stop and a door open and close. 'Maybe that's the doctor,' she said after a moment, but when nothing further happened she dropped her head on to his shoulder again.

Pink said, 'Courting couple, you bet. The doc would come right down.'

'Pobbles?' she asked, meaning Peebles.

'Snogging.' He nodded towards the car. 'Really killing them in Covent Garden – "Signori signore", you can't see him for flowers.'

She laughed a little at that. It struck true.

Then she went on, 'I suppose it happens to everybody but I always thought I would cope with death. Should I go back?'

'God, no.'

'He's not dead yet, but he's kind of paralysed.' She gripped him a little harder.

He said, 'Good-oh. No mistake, it's the light fantastic tonight.'

'He was rather brave, I thought. She's reading to him now.'

'What? *Journey's End?*'

'Pink, don't.'

'Well – hell—' he said.

'Actually it's *Treasure Island.*'

Pink's shoulder began to shake. It was difficult at first to know if he was laughing or crying. But in a moment it became quite clear. It was laughter, all right.

'But that's marvellous,' he said. 'What, sitting there?'

'Yes,' she said, 'it's not funny.'

But Pink could not stop laughing.

She started battering at him with her fists.

'Don't, Pink. Don't. We'll both sink into the ground. I'll kill you. Don't.'

But he was out of control now and she too began to laugh, a little hysterically, as her fists began to hurt.

Then, very suddenly, Pink sobered. There was a figure of a man standing on the road above them.

'Oh crikey,' he said. 'Don't look now, old fish, but there's a boy on the Via Flaminia.' He jerked his thumb over his shoulder and she looked up.

'Very strong,' Pink said, as she stared at the figure looking over the low concrete wall of the new bridge. It was David, but for a moment she did not seem to take him in.

'It's nearly light,' she said. 'It must be bloody late.' Then she bit her lip. She looked down at her knuckles and licked a scratch which one of Pink's buttons had made.

'He looks so idiotic there,' she said. 'It makes me rather cross.'

'Are we leaving Macdonald?'

'Yep.' She was still sucking the scratch.

'Shall I go up and tell him the wedding's off?' Pink asked. She did not reply. He raised his eyebrows.

'It is off?'

She said, 'Why doesn't he come down, or shout, or do something?'

'If you like to bundle into my limousine here,' he said, 'you can bed down with a noted tenor and a hysterical Welsh collie.' For once he tried, quite strongly, to lead her. 'Come on.'

She pulled her hand away from her face, irritably, correcting herself—

'Don't! It's worse than biting your nails.' Then she looked up into Pink's face and said very plainly:

'You take Pobbles home. I'm going to walk.'

He looked more hurt than anxious. Rather mechanically he rattled off another of his imitations – this one of the Sunningdale set.

'You take Jack, Babs can ring Daph, I'll get the Bentley and we'll all go up to town.'

'I mean it.'

'You won't drown yourself, Bubbles?'

'I'm not going to do anything silly,' she said, and took a step away. 'But unless I speak to him he'll stand up there looking idiotic for everybody to see.' At once she turned and rather seriously, putting one foot carefully in front of the other, she walked up the narrow track which led diagonally through the long wet grass to the main road, above. Pink turned away long before she reached David, and with a sniff he climbed into the Humber and prepared to take Peebles home.

Not very far away, nearer the source of the stream, the Humber stopped at a disused slate quarry.

Peebles said, 'I don't smoke because I've got an outstanding tenor voice,' as he bundled out of the car.

Flossy, too, leapt out and waited by the narrow entrance as Peebles, quite soberly, walked farther into the quarry. Pink followed. When the dog saw them relieve themselves, she settled down and put her head on her paws, as if she now understood the reason for the stop. But she sat up again and put her head on one side when Peebles suddenly announced loudly, to Pink and the blue sky:

'Ladies and gentlemen, I should like to give you my rendering of an old Scotch ballad.' He coughed and it echoed round the bowl. He took up his stance like a Victorian tenor, with his hand inside his coat. His moustache looked very small, in the middle of his moon for a face.

The dog settled again, with one ear cocked. She and the sheep had seen some odder things than this, up on the hill, when Peebles had had a drink. Pink, meantime, with his hands clasped behind his back, listened attentively. He seemed to be glad of a pause, at dawn, before getting more deeply entangled in what he called the process of predestinate tragedy. He smiled as Peebles sang, rather well:

> Oh my luv's like a red red rose,
> That's newly sprung in June,
> Oh my luv's like the melody,
> That's sweetly played in tune.

BOOK TWO

A Breakfast Cabaret

THE SUN WAS low across the flood water and it hurt Pink's eyes as he sat, an hour or two later, by the kitchen table. So he turned his seat round and stared blankly at the big white refrigerator. He took a sip of tea from a huge cup and swilled it round his mouth.

'My cake-hole', he said, 'is like a parrot's cage.' But there was nobody else in the kitchen. He moved over to the big cupboard where most of the provisions were kept. On top there was a china jar marked 'Spices'. Inside there were a few of Pink's aids. Amongst other things there were two ball-point pens, an amber cigarette holder, a packet of chlorophyll tablets, a machine for cutting off the ends of cigars, a small hand pump for blowing up a Lilo, a screwdriver with fuse-wire fitted in the handle, two golf balls, a gold watch and a pair of dark glasses. It was these last which he now extracted and put on.

'A little windy,' he said, describing his condition, almost as if he meant it literally, then he put his hand on his stomach and belched. He looked out at the bright sun and knew that it was the beauty of the morning that most unnerved him; that, and the drink, and the Captain, and maybe Mary too. He belched again. 'Just a trifle shaky.'

Mary had not yet returned home, and it was a moment or two before Stephen arrived. Pink had time for two more cups of tea.

When Stephen did come in, Pink pushed the dark glasses further up his nose.

'Hullo, old man, long time no see. What happened to Steve?'

But Stephen did not reply. He took off his green hat (a hat which Mary hated) and dumped it on a marble shelf in the corner. He looked pale, tidy and depressed. He began to unbutton his coat.

Pink raised his eyebrows and looked at his watch. He was wearing his best one, as he had, in all, half a dozen, but he had forgotten to wind it up. Before he could think of a suitable formula, an 'On the tiles, old man?' or 'Burning that candle pretty low', Stephen said:

'I decided to walk.'

'Really?' Pink sounded enthusiastically interested. He asked, 'Now tell me, did you see our Macdonald as you came down?' and Stephen shook his head.

Pink said, 'I think she's still out at the caravan. Captain's very bad. They were ringing for his daughter earlier.'

Pink said again, 'His dotter,' rather feebly and Stephen, surprisingly, gave a wan smile. He laid his coat on one side and sat down on a clumsy kitchen chair. He stretched his legs out in front of him and, cupping his hands behind his head, tipped back his neck.

He said with a sigh, 'I can't take it in,' and that was the last he said of the Captain.

'There's a kettle on, if you want it, old man.'

Stephen shook his head. He reached in his pocket for his silver cigarette case. It was only silver gilt. He kept his lighter, always serviced, in his sporran.

Pink, meantime, went to his own coat pocket and brought out a half bottle of whisky, which was almost full.

'Something stronger, old boy?' he suggested.

Again Stephen smiled rather faintly. On one note he quoted one of Pink's own phrases, 'Oblivion, old man, or cigar?'

Pink saw that there were no cigarettes in the silver gilt case.

'Of course,' he said, searching his pockets. 'I've got one somewhere.' Out of his pockets he brought three empty packets, one Capstan, one Passing Cloud, and one Player's Weights. He was a splendidly random buyer.

'I don't think I will after all,' Stephen said. 'Have you ever observed the Colonel? Before dinner he drinks and smokes and even talks. After dinner he doesn't do any of these things. He hardly even listens. I've stopped.'

Pink was wielding the half bottle.

'I think you ought to have something, Stiffy, if you've walked all that way. You couldn't come by the river with these floods, could you?' he asked a little obviously. If Stephen had come by the road he could not have missed David's car. 'Did you come over the top?'

'I tramped down the main road.'

Pink nodded, and said, 'Good Lord.'

Then Stephen added, 'As far as the old bridge, from which I looked up and down the river, and saw what there was to be seen.'

That left no margin for error. Pink circled round once or twice then halted with his feet together. He rocked his head from side to side, and suddenly tried another subject. 'Matter of fact I shan't be hanging around too long, old man,' he said. His face looked pale behind the big dark glasses.

'Oh yes?'

'Oh yes, old man. Today or *domani*. Business, you follow. London first stop but I've got Montreal in mind. Oyez, oyez. Big opportunities there.' Then suddenly he leant forward and spoke in an altogether less portentous way.

'Old Stiffy,' he began. 'Look, you don't want to take this thing too hard. Mary's all right. She wouldn't do anything silly. I mean two and two don't make five. She's probably just trying to make you a bit jealous.'

'Then she is succeeding.'

Pink gave an uncertain smile. His language was more important to him than might have been imagined. Pink's way was to humanise things by referring to them as well-known friends: to reduce their proportion. If somebody went raving mad Pink would say, 'Bit of the old basket work,' and faced with a homicidal maniac carrying an axe he might well manage, 'Spot of the old butcher's itch?' To Stephen he said, 'Touch of the green-eyed, what?' His expression was set half-way to a smile. Stephen, at this point, pushing his feet along the hard stone floor, decided to talk. He used a matter-of-fact sort of voice.

'Not much more green-eyed than usual. I suppose if I work it out I'm jealous all the time of all of you – even the Queen's bar lot—'

'Steady on.'

'I'm quite used to the sensation. It comes down to the size of my shoulder and the span of my hand. I'm so used to jealousy and envy that David doesn't seem to make any particular impact. He numbs me, I suppose.'

After a pause he moved a little and said:

'Perhaps I deceive myself.'

Pink sat down by the window, behind Stephen, where he could not see his face.

Stephen said, quietly, 'It's warm in here,' and Pink put the bottle on the floor beside his chair. The kettle on the slow plate hissed as a drop of water ran down to the range.

Stephen's cheeks were now wet with tears. He said, without a break in his voice:

'The ruling emotion is shame.'

Pink tiptoed to the shelf and found a kitchen glass. He poured some whisky into it and pushed it across the table to him. He said:

'Come on. You'd better have a tot. Doctor's orders, old man. You're tired out. Go on.'

Stephen picked up the glass and drank.

'A dram before seven, dry by eleven,' Pink said and Stephen tried to laugh.

'Good man,' Pink said, as the empty glass was placed back on the scrubbed wood table. Stephen turned his chair round, put his elbows on the table and played with the empty glass. He rolled it along the surface.

He said, 'I love her. That's what's so hopeless. That's what it's so difficult to explain. And useless to try, now. But I've looked at it all ways and I love her. I just don't seem able to express it in words, in bed, and now in simple, definite action.'

Pink said, 'Old cock, if you feel it as badly as that why don't you just say so? Just say what you said to me just now. Say it to her.'

Stephen shook his head.

'You could give it a try, damn it,' Pink said.

'It wouldn't work.'

'Can't do any harm, can it?'

'Pointless,' Stephen replied and Pink rocked his head impatiently.

'Damn it,' he said, hopelessly.

Stephen, sitting up again, said, clearly, 'I just don't bother to fight impossible battles.' The tears had all gone.

Pink shrugged. He said, 'I suppose that's sensible enough, in a way. Best generals do that, so they say.'

'Yep,' Stephen replied. 'And I often wonder if they're cowards too. Unsympathetic creatures that they are.'

Pink would have developed that, if only to keep Stephen's mind off himself, but they were interrupted by a noise in the scullery by the back door. They waited quietly as the footsteps came nearer.

'Hello, Mary-bags,' Pink said.

ELEVEN

PINK SAID, 'Stephen's just got in.'

Mary stood quite still with her hands behind her on the door.

Pink went on, 'Celebrating with me here; celebrating my proposed departure.' Hearing the lie in his voice, Mary hardly bothered to listen, but his opening remark helped her. She swam in, asking Stephen:

'Where on earth did you get to?'

He said, 'I promised to clear up the classroom.'

'Which classroom?'

'The one we used.'

There was no change in her physical appearance. Her cheeks had been pink before, her eyes had looked as bright. Her hair, when it had been washed, was always the same brilliant colour. In the morning sunlight the down on her cheeks and her forearms always looked golden. Her movements were no more energetic than they had ever been. She did not look happier, or wiser, and her voice was neither higher nor lower.

She said: 'It can't have taken you all night to do that.'

'No,' Stephen looked up at her. His eyes were bloodshot. 'I walked home.'

'What a stupid thing to do.' She did not take her eyes off his face as he looked back at the buckles on his shoes. She said, 'You look quite worn out.'

'I'm quite tired,' he replied.

'We're all a bit whacked,' Pink said, but she paid no

attention to him. She was close to Stephen looking down at him, hard, demanding a full answer; almost predatory.

'When did you go back to the classroom?'

'At the end.'

'After I'd gone?'

'Long after; I was the last.'

Stephen was silent.

Pink shuffled forward. 'Look here, old sis, we're all a bit whacked. What say we leave the post-mortems?'

'No,' she said.

Stephen lifted his head and stared at her. Pink shuffled back.

'You saw David go?' she asked.

'Yes,' Stephen said.

'You didn't ask him where he was going?'

'No. I told him where you had gone.'

'God, but I think that's despicable.'

'Steady on,' Pink said. 'You won't do any good this way, old flesh.'

Stephen, forced to it, had found, if not courage, a positive value in his cowardice: a point beyond which he could not retire. Looking at Mary, he said quietly:

'It's all right, Pink. I'll walk away when I want to.'

'But it's horrid,' Mary said.

'I'm not very proud of it.' Stephen answered coldly.

Mary moved and said, 'You knew, didn't you, at that horrid time – when we were all sitting round at the table, before old Fishface, Captain Fish-face – before all that? And after that when I was going off to Peebles' car, you knew. Yes, you knew.'

'Yes.'

'And you followed David?'

'No.' Stephen frowned. 'I had no desire to do that.'

There was a long pause and Pink said:

'D'you want me to go? Old Pinkie boy to knock along?'

But she shook her head. She did not listen to what he said.

She put her fingers on the rail by the cooker and talked to Stephen without looking at him.

'If you weren't here I was going to put it in a letter. If you were here I was going to say it all. Lots of things about you, not nasty at all. I don't want to say these things now.'

Stephen sat stone still and Pink, his weight awkwardly on one foot, did not dare to move as she sailed in, with the breeze firmly behind her, and destroyed.

'You've done me no harm, Stephen, and I've harmed you. I'm sure you've never said anything wrong about me and at the end I despise you.'

There was a click as Pink put the half bottle down on the table. Then he lifted up his head and listened, looking at nothing, much as if he were attending a funeral service in a private parlour or listening to the Queen at Christmas time. Mary continued:

'I don't feel sorry for you, because I see you, Stephen. Really see you. I feel repelled by you and not just in the way that you've evidently found me repellent. I feel it very suddenly, very strongly, yes I do, I do. And you'll say to yourself, it's because I've slept with David, which I have: yes, as you know perfectly well, although you haven't said so. But it's got nothing to do with that. One day you'll realise that you can't blame everything on that. Bed is only the smallest bit of it and if you go on telling yourself that I left you because of bed, you'll be lying to yourself. I'm leaving you for all the other reasons – the ones that made you stay behind: that made you stroke my hair when you knew: for all the cowardice and self-pity – for the whole "no". For the whole bloody great boulder that I've had to try and shove up the hill. And in ten hours altogether I've been alone with him, never mind the new bridge, in ten hours with him, because I've counted, I've felt – I've felt like a girl and it is a strange and wonderful feeling.'

Her eyes were glistening with tears. Pink held his head

low now. Stephen stood up and turned away, at which Mary took a step forward.

For a moment Pink thought she was going to try to undo some of the harm. Her voice had changed. It was pitched a little higher, and the words came even faster. It rose as she spoke, but she was not offering mercy or apology.

She cried, 'I suppose you're going to say nothing? That's it!' as Stephen walked steadily to the door. She shouted after him as he moved away, 'You might say something you'd regret, even something that might hurt me so you won't risk it. You won't. It's just negative.'

Stephen had already disappeared into the house and the door swung closed behind him. She stood shaking, her head very low.

Very quietly, Pink said, 'It's all right, my love, he's gone—'

'No,' she said, quickly turning away from him, walking back to the rail which she held on to, tightly. 'Don't comfort me. I don't need it. But I feel sick. I don't know which makes me sick, him or me.'

'P-p-punishment,' Pink suggested, in one of his enlightened moments. 'It's got its own stink.'

A few moments later she held out one hand and said:

'Pink, darling, may I have a swig?'

'Of course, old girl.'

'Old girl, old girl. I suppose you hate me now.' She took the bottle from him, and he put the glass which Stephen had used back on the table. 'I know you're fond of Stephen.'

'No, no, no,' Pink protested.

She said, 'Even now I lie. Oh Christ, I lie. Even now. Isn't that awful? I had to do something. I had to change. I had to look like a woman has to look – am I woman? Aren't I a girl?'

'Steady – steady, love.'

'I had to do all that. I really did.' She suddenly covered

her face with her hands and laughed. 'Oh Christ, oh Christ, oh Christ. You hate me, don't you?'

'You're certainly slashing about.'

'Oh darling, Pink. I couldn't bear it if you were nasty. What are you thinking?'

Pink steadied considerably. He poured some whisky into the glass.

'Self observation,' he said. 'The curse of the Fergusons. Thinking, "interesting situation, by God, little woman done by dark stranger, now, what next?" That's the sort of thought. But little woman's certainly rather rough on poor old Stiffy.'

'You don't care about Stiffy,' she said, almost casually, suddenly hitting very true. 'Nor anybody else,' and before he had time to answer she went on:

'Of course it's not true, what I said to him. Of course I don't really feel like that. Not really, really. I just rather wish I did, I suppose. I must have a drink, a cigarette or five packets of chewing gum, I don't know – something to put in the mouth . . . Pink cares about Pink. A little about me too. Yes, I know that's true. I bet you've been sulking?'

'No.'

'Oh yes, you have. D'you want me to tell about David? I want to tell.'

'Old corruption,' he said kindly. 'Old, old snake.'

'Well of course I was fibbing really, but I wouldn't fib to you.'

Pink tapped the bottle in the palm of his hand and tried to remember; 'You said to me, "Off you go, and take old Pobbles home. I'll walk myself." '

'No.'

'You said, "I'll see him off." '

Again, she shook her head. 'I never did. Pink, don't be cruel. You know exactly what I said.'

'But Stephen's nice.' Pink stretched out his arms.

'Shsh!' she said, and went right to him and sorted out his tie. 'Pink darling, don't huff on me now.'

'I'm falling over myself—'

She interrupted. 'Yes, I know you are. Tell me, though, tell me what I really said.'

' "You hoof it," you said.'

'Yes.'

' "You hoof it and I'll swear I'll be good." '

'No, I didn't say that.'

'You did.' He frowned and spoke again. 'I'm sure you did.'

'No, I can prove it, I didn't. I promise I can. I didn't say that at all.'

'Stephen's nice. He is,' Pink said, almost sang, again.

'I can prove it if you looked. Did you look when you got into the car?'

'No.'

'Then what did you see?'

'I had the hound and old Pobbles—'

'No,' she said, clenching her fists. 'No, no, no, no! What did you see of me – even if you didn't look?'

Pink tried to remember. 'You walked up the bank.'

'Yes.'

'Up the kind of track – footpath, whatever you call it, through the nettles and the grass and that.'

'Yes—'

Pink shrugged.

He said, 'That must have been out of the very corner of the old peepers.'

'What else?' she asked.

'After that, we'd gone.'

'What did I look like?'

'Lady with a mission. Head down. All that.'

'Good,' she said. 'Go on.'

'No,' he said. 'Can't, old thing. Big blind blank. Big blank blind.'

'Quite unnecessary blind, I promise,' she said, then she held on to his coat. 'Darling, I promise I was only like that with Stephen because – because, because, because. Oh, I don't know, that special thing annoyed me, at the table. You didn't see, you were with old Fish-face in the Gents, but it was all rather foul. Everybody kind of knew, at once; David, Steve and me. Everybody obviously knew and it wasn't for me or David to say. I nearly did say. But honestly if you work it out Steve should have said something. "Veto." "I object." I don't quite know what, but he should have said something. Just as a girl. Just as this shape and no beard and all that; I promise I know. Deep, deep, deep down, I know he should have said something. There was plenty of time.'

'Glands?' Pink asked. 'That's really it.'

She shook her head.

'Not directly – promise,' she replied. 'Maybe connected but not just that. I knew even then, when we all three knew at that miserable table and when nobody was saying anything. That's the one thing I did know: I was going to lam into poor old Stevie. He asks for it, I promise he does. Be me and you'd know. He really does ask for it.'

Pink pouted.

'All this boulder stuff,' he said, raising his eyebrows.

'Well, I have to push a boulder. I honestly have.' She looked up at him and corrected herself. 'You've been all right but the rest of it – honestly, think of it. Pink, you do look huffy and constipated.'

'Old girl. I'm being most awfully good.'

'Are you?' she asked.

'Yep. Really am.'

'Are you angry?'

'Touchy,' Pink said.

'No need. That's what's so silly. You've absolutely no need to be. I didn't lie to you. I wasn't so wrong with the boulder, I promise—'

Pink could read her like a book.

'You thought it out before,' he said.

She stopped for a moment and he moved to the bottle again.

'A welcome pause,' he said, and nodded. A phrase which he always applied, when she was getting over excited, and speaking so quickly that even he could hardly understand. 'Bang, bang, bang on the lug-hole.'

She said, 'I'll be good. I'll be eminently what'sable. Reasonable and calm.' And she swallowed. 'The boulder. Yes. Complete confession. I did rather think that one up. It sounded awfully good outside. Little me hauling you all up the slope.' She laughed, hopelessly, looked at Pink and then turned away again. She went on:

'It's me that's foul, I know. That only makes me hate him more. And I do hate him. I promise you that.'

'It's not awfully fair,' Pink said.

'Yes,' she said, 'I think it is. And I know what you think. I know, because you said so. You said "glands". And that's such a horrible idea. It's all wrong too, I promise. I'll tell you if you want.'

'If you don't rush—'

'I'll take it terribly calmly, I swear.'

'Tell then. Slowly. In words of one syllable. Not in code.'

'All right,' she said. 'Perhaps we don't love each other after all. You're huffing really.'

'I've been surprised.'

'So have I,' she said. 'Thank God.'

'You don't have to tell, actually,' Pink said.

'Oh yes I do – I have to tell somebody. Now I think of it there's nothing in my life that I haven't had to tell—'

'Absolutely,' Pink said. 'Matter of fact there seems to be quite a few things that never happened in your life that you feel you have to tell, too.'

'Not now,' she said. 'I really mean that. I mean I've always known if I really did live I wouldn't have to think up things. Now life's really going to go, I think I shall find I've absolutely no imagination. I won't need it, you see, not any more. It's sort of Lourdes, isn't it? I mean I'm flinging away crutches right and left?'

'You're sure about David?'

'No, not a bit. I'm sure about Steve. That's what's wrong. One can't be sure about David.'

'But you love him?' he asked, again extraordinarily responsibly and seriously.

'I'm not even sure about that.'

'I'd have thought that was rather important.'

'I love Pink as the uncle,' she said. ' "I-should-have-thought" from Uncle Pink! You must be huffing really, because you wouldn't be so sane . . . Mind you, it wasn't awfully true what I said to Steve, about the boulders and that: about the breath of fresh wind or whatever I said. Or did I stop myself before I said that? I confess that's the sort of thing I thought I'd say if ever – well if ever I did find somebody else and yell and scream and that. But it does give rather a false picture.'

'You were a bit careless to leave the car there.'

'Oh no, not careless,' she exclaimed. 'I wouldn't have done it unless I thought I was going to be found out and I'll tell you something very peculiar. Something rather reassuring, maybe, except if you think about it too hard, perhaps it's rather ominous. He didn't mind about that either. He didn't suggest we took the car up on to the Wade road or in the woods or somewhere like that. I thought he'd insist. But not at all. He's terribly open about things in some ways. I mean first ringing me after that party in London. He knew I was staying with terribly respectable people. He knew I was married. He didn't even bother to give a false name. Then following me up here, like that, I mean actually on the same train. He told the sleeping compartment man, you know, he wanted the berth next door. And the sleeping-car man knows perfectly well who I am. It wasn't graft either. Not a very big tip; I saw. He just persists. Then at the academy. All the others were there but that didn't put him off a bit. He was going to do those decorations with me. Then you saw him at the dance. Extraordinary he is, really. I suppose he's just very bright. But he's an awful lot of people, isn't he, all at once? Kind of clumsy turning up like that in a stuffed shirt. But very smooth in not caring a damn. Sometimes he talks in that kind of language these big intellectual wolves do and the next minute I feel after he's paid for a drink I'd better count the change because I'm sure he's incapable really. Anybody who really knew how to cope couldn't be so idiotically scandalous as he really is. But I thought it was rather nice. He didn't even suggest "in the car" which I'd rather dreaded – I don't know if you've tried? He didn't actually suggest anything. We just crossed the road and went down through the long grass the other side.'

'Dialogue?'

She shook her head.

'Not much from him, I mean. Just telling me to shut up, I talked a bit about Captain Gordon and that, you know. I felt it rather a reflection, that; not being able to cope with death. I'm sure that's something to do with not really living. Anyway I was a bit upset and you obviously disapproved so maybe that's what made me go on. We never know quite what does. Anyway I said how foul I'd always been to old Fish-face who was really quite harmless and obviously jolly brave. He just said "Shut up" to all that. Rather rudely, you know, so I followed him down the bank. Then we passed that barking dog and that's when I said everybody would soon be awake and I mentioned about the car being there for everybody to see. He said he didn't care a damn. I thought that was good. But let's not talk about it too hard.'

She frowned.

'He's just a bloke who knows his mind,' Pink said.

'Well, yes,' she replied, but she was still quite clearly troubled. 'That's what it would seem.'

'You're doubtful?'

'I suppose there are people who kind of like people to know they're having a great bomb of an affair. Really the affair's not quite all what it should be for them unless they're certain other people know about it. They drop clues all over the place.'

'Who, for instance?'

'Nobody,' she said, thoughtfully, even gravely. 'But there are people, I know, because I absolutely understand. At least I absolutely don't understand, but I can see myself doing it very well. I can see myself making a lover leave a note at my hairdresser and then when she gives it to me I make her swear, get a Bible, or a Koran or whatever it is hairdressers use and say "Swear you won't tell anybody he left this note. Swear!" Lovely,' she said, with a sudden little smile. 'I should almost like to live in London just for that. But I'm sure he's not really like that. It was just a horrible cloud over the moon. I think he's the opposite, after all he's terribly old. He must have done all this a hundred times before. He'll probably sack me, but it'll be living. In a kind of way I think we'll be all right. I can see myself having a row with him in every capital in Europe. Late at the Uffizi, I shall be, and tactless at the Vatican or somewhere like that. I can see his impatience with me. He can lecture, you know.

'But I wasn't lying about the main thing. No. We went down to the river, actually holding hands, but a little kind of cold. I mean "prose" really. "Prose" is the word. We weren't at all daisy chain and wild duck, you know. None of your Edinburgh Festival films. I mean, actually, I suppose if you look at it with the grass and the brambles and the two bridges, the flooded river and the dawn, we might be expected to have felt a bit that way. Otherwise I suppose it's a wonderful setting for a jolly old murder. Can you see me floating down the river, nymph in thy orisons, or whatever it is? But we were cold and prose.

'Actually, in the end what was rather odd about it, really,

was that it was me that said it. I wasn't very flirtatious or anything like that. I just said, "There's one place, I know", and he nodded. We didn't even hold hands then.'

Pink had sat down at the table again. He was playing with the tea leaves in his cup and now she sat at the table with him. She continued to talk as quickly as ever, regardless of contradictions, constantly almost losing direction yet somehow in the end pulling the story back. After a moment's description of her leading the way along the bank to the cart track and then to the place under the new bridge, she settled for, 'Cattle, really.'

She said, 'That's what we were like. I'm sure it does me good to tell you. It's like an old war song or something. If he was an Aberdeen Angus, then I was a Jersey cow. Oh God, isn't that awful? I only meant that to give you the picture of us walking along, but it really says rather too much.'

She began to giggle. She said, 'Do do that cow look.'

He shook his head firmly.

She ran on, 'You know that awful look, over the shoulder, rather bored and yet decided. A kind of look of distaste. You'd think it would put the poor bull off for life. But it doesn't actually,' she said. She drew breath and continued more steadily:

'Anyway eventually we got ourselves sorted out towards the top of one of the big concrete support things – the widest beam. But there's not an awful lot of room. We were right up at the top of it, hidden from the track by the uprights, the lorries lumbering along the road above us – cars, for all I know – and the river underneath. All the pigeons flapped away, madly, as we settled down. One couldn't really move to right or left very much, but it was all right, you know. Quite quick. I closed my eyes most of the time and I didn't have to pretend I was somebody else. I was somebody else. God knows who. I felt rather like a pink-cheeked, dark-haired dairy maid, rather soft and fat and seventeenish, I suppose. I don't mean I had to think her up. I enjoyed it rather a lot. Or she did. I'm not explaining myself very well. I shouldn't think boys understand. Do you?'

'I think I can guess,' Pink said.

'Yes, I thought you probably could, but when I tried to tell David this, after, I mean – strictly no dialogue at the time, not a word said until I'd hauled on my pants—'

'Mary!'

'Well, I told you it was prose.'

'Yes, but there's a kind of limit.'

'Oh, don't be so stuffy. I wasn't going to leave them there, after all.'

'I mean there's a limit about how much you tell.'

She looked rather hurt.

'But I wanted to tell.'

'I know,' he said.

She frowned deeply. 'Now you've ruined it. You've made me feel bad.'

'Go on,' Pink suggested.

'No,' she said. 'I'm huffing now. Is there something to eat?' She walked over to the cupboard and found a tin of biscuits.

'For you, slob?'

Pink nodded. 'I wouldn't say no.' She extracted four water biscuits then put back the lid and closed the cupboard door. She gave him his ration and with her mouth full, said:

'After all I'm only telling you. I wouldn't shout it all out in the middle of the main street.'

'I'm not so sure,' he said.

'Come to that,' she said with a sudden laugh, 'I'm not so sure either. D'you think anybody would believe me?'

'No.'

'Why?'

'Charity. They like you round these parts.'

She said, 'D'you believe me?'

'In every detail, old thing. That's what's putting me off.'

'It is true, you know.'

'I know damned well it is.'

'How d'you know?' she asked.

'How do we ever know?' he replied.

'Oh my God,' she said, 'I was rather savage at Stephen
. . . Perhaps detail's what makes you so sure.'

'Could be the pants,' he said.

'Oh no,' she replied. 'You're quite wrong there. I could
easily have made up the pants. In fact I think I'd be bound
to hit on the pants. It only takes a mind with a practical
bent. I wonder how?'

'Probably dog's whistle stuff,' he said. 'Unknown accuracy of Pink's ear. I always know when you're lying. And
I'm often in the know.'

'Yes,' she said, very vaguely, suddenly. 'Yes, I suppose
that's true.'

'Let's take the pants as on,' Pink said.

'Well, then things frankly weren't awfully romantic.
Very, very prose indeed. I said about this girl, you know,
how I'd felt.'

'He didn't like that?'

'He cut me short.'

'That doesn't surprise me,' Pink said, wisely.

'Well, it did me. I wasn't insulting him. I mean I didn't
say I was so bored I had to think her up to give myself a lift.
That wasn't true. I just fell into her. It was probably being
so flat on my back like that, and concrete's jolly hard. I
shouldn't be at all surprised if my shoulders looked like a
stucco bungalow; like a bothie wall. Anyway, he wasn't
going to talk about that. We walked away, oddly enough,
holding hands then, though neither of us felt terribly like it
– well, that's not quite true. I did in a sort of a way. I
actually asked him to hold my hand. More from kind of
wrath of God, I think, than love. I'm sure God's moosh is
just like Macdonald's, big, gloomy, hurt, disapproving and

so irritatingly patient. But even she's been angry with us once or twice . . .' She thought for a second, then asked, 'You know that feeling when you keep looking at the sky and feel absolutely certain that your favourite dog's going to die? Like that. So there we were, not going up the bank to his common little car, oddly enough. But along the cart track back towards here, between the red puddles, and the stones those school children fling at each other – he and me, Adam and Eve, picking our solitary way. A likely pair. Only no paradise. Not yet. There will be, though, I think. I'd have the most tremendous row with him, I know, if ever we went to Monte Carlo. Don't scientists have conferences there? I know he'd hate gambling. He's rather puritanical, I'm sure. I'd throw my coins or whatever they're called, all over the board and, goodness I'd boast about Daddy like mad . . .

'Well, when we came to the garden wall I thought it would be rather romantic to walk along the top of it and he could reach up and hold my hand. "After the ball is over" stuff. I felt like it. I really did want him to pick me a flower. But that suggestion seemed to bring him sharply to his senses. He didn't walk about "mm"-ing and shaking his head like he usually did. He just stood there picking his nose or something. Kind of solidly indecisive. Not crying. But not smoking either.' She broke off for a second. 'Are you still worried about those pants?'

'No, go on—'

'You are rather stuffy sometimes, Pink. And you look awfully silly when you are. You really must fight it. Besides there's nothing wrong at all in girls hauling off and on their pants. It's only our terrible education that makes us so worried about that. Those schools and a touch of poor Macdonald.'

'I'm not worried—'

'Nor am I. I think it's a very good thing, really. I mean that girls should. It's part of what pants are for. So long as they're young – the girls, I mean. Then it's really quite a nice idea.'

'Go *on*,' Pink said impatiently. 'You left him standing at the g-g-garden gate.'

'Yes, well then things did go rather badly.'

'Obviously,' he said, and she knew exactly what he meant. He never missed a trick; recognised at once the meaning of her more hectic diversions. She talked much more slowly as she took the last hurdle.

'I grew rather sulky, mainly, I think, because he looked the way he did. So then I just said, "You'd better not come in now. You'd better go back and then come and collect me. I'll pack a case." '

'Oh yes,' said Pink. 'Nice going. And he said, "I never want to see you in my life again, you forward little puss." '

'No. Not exactly.'

'Spit it out.'

'Important timing,' she said. 'Very.' And she sniffed. 'A split-second first. A kind of light in his eye that might have been shock, but I'm pretty sure it was just the blue sky. I mean, this was only a few minutes ago. It was quite light. I think the look was only in my mind. But it scared me, I confess. Like you, with Daddy, sometimes. Kind of absolutely certain that now you're down you're going to get a kick in the teeth. All that rushing through my old nut and I stand there with my toes together, looking a little demure, I believe. That was something to do with the thought about flowers. What's going on in his head I've really no idea. Probably the travelling expenses. He's not very generous, you know. Well, he is, but he grumbles about it, always. In London, he insisted on taking me to lunch at a very swank restaurant then complained about the bill: sort of jokingly. But all this in a split-second and then he's all smiles. Charming and rather formal, and in tails of course, at the garden gate: he even looked rather nice. You know he's got that awful skin that makes him look as if he's spent twenty years down a mine? So useful for a Gaitskellite . . . Big pores, I suppose . . . Anyway, even that wasn't so noticeable. Just big black eyes and short dark hair. The answer to my sort of maiden's prayer. He took me in his arms and kissed me and he was really nice: really hopeful. Saying, "You are a good girl" and nice straightforward things like that. I'm afraid I cried like anything. Then I sent him off and came in here, and now you're up to date.' She said, 'If you have another cup of tea it'll start coming out of your ears. You're getting as bad as Cathie.' Cathie was the maid.

But at the end of all that, she seemed curiously exhausted. Almost panic-stricken. Her face was sad and pale. She looked almost fierce as she took a sip from the flask. She drank another and he made a 'glug-glug' noise. For an instant she did not react.

'Well, don't take it all,' he said. Then he made the 'glug-glug' noise again. He expanded the imitation to a vivid, explosive mock nose trick, and spluttering and coughing she burst out laughing.

'Soaked,' Pink said. 'The fellow's absolutely soaked.'

Mary was holding her sides, coughing and trying to recover herself. The whisky seemed to be coming out of her ears as she cursed him and laughed, at once. She suddenly put her arms round his neck and said very breathlessly:

'Oh, Pink darling, you are the most awful slob, but I do love you and I shall miss you most of all. But you are the most awful slob.'

The last shreds of responsibility were thrown away as Pink now played the slob. A cigarette out of the corner of his mouth, round-shouldered and pot-bellied, he shuffled in a circle, like something out of the sea. 'The smoker' in *Scouting for Boys*.

'Oh, don't, Pink,' she cried. 'It hurts.' Her laughter was very high. 'Don't. It hurts both ways. D'you suppose Stephen's killing himself?'

Pink, very uncertainly, with his hands, wide apart, said, 'It's not wrong. It's better this way, isn't it, than being maudlin and that?'

She nodded.

He went on, at first uncertainly, 'It's always the right time for a little celebration. But it won't be a long parting, old trout. I'll see you in the big city.'

'In London?' she asked, frantically encouraging him. 'Will you, Pink?'

'Absolutely. If your old man will let me in.'

'He will. I promise he's nice.'

Pink said, 'We'll have a party, by God. A big get-together in a low-down cellar. 'We'll trip the light fantastic, Mary and Pink, for auld lang syne and all that cock. Won't we?'

She nodded very hard several times and ran and put her arms round his neck again. She buried her head in his coat and with long pauses in between he slapped her back. It was he who was crying.

A moment later she said rather coolly, as if the thought had just come to her:

'I sometimes think it's rather a pity that Macdonald wasn't our Mum. I mean she'd have had so much more authority, don't you think?'

MARY AND STEPHEN slept in the night nursery, a small room that overlooked the haugh, the ha-ha, the river and the floods, but Stephen had drawn the curtains, perhaps much for the same reason that Pink put on dark glasses. ('I somehow feel,' Pink once said about dark glasses, 'that Lot's wife could have done with a pair of these jobs.') And Stephen's decision to draw the frilly, gay little curtains was curiously prophetic. The worst scene of his life was later to be played in this sweet room with the big white-washed fireplace and the bright yellow paint.

When Mary had begun to pack she had switched on the light. For a while Stephen had lain, like the effigy of a knight, staring straight at the ceiling, but now he was sitting up in bed reading Cozzens: *By Love Possessed*.

Mary's behaviour in the crisis of departure was marvellously female. Although her husband never took his eyes from his book, she continued to talk to him as she packed, almost as if she were preparing to elope with him, not David. It was as if she felt that pleasant chatter would dissolve an insoluble situation. It was Mary at her most typical, not only refusing to believe in her own actions, but denying reality itself.

'Isn't that the end?' she asked, pressing the clothes down in the suitcase. 'These bloody things just won't get in.'

And then a moment later, she said vaguely, 'I know you don't believe me, but I really don't want to go one bit. I mean, I hate London, and that's just the start-off. I've always come back to this room,' and she put the palm of her hand against the wall. 'It's quite absurd,' she said, 'to talk of leaving it.'

At the cupboard which was really Stephen's but which she used as well, because she had always used it, she said, 'You really have got the dullest lot of ties. I shall make a point of buying you one. That I promise. I'll search and search until I get one just right for you. I'll send it for your birthday. Maybe before. One with nice faded colours, not horrid diagonal regimental stripes like these. I . . .' she paused. Then she said cheerfully, 'You can wear it for lunch when we next meet. We obviously will meet. It would be too childish not to. I mean I'm bound to come north sometimes and we'll have a jolly swank lunch on old Dow's money. That'll be fun. I'd hate it if I thought we were parting as enemies, Stiffy. You see, I do love you, kind of – well, maybe it's not the time to say it. But I really do. We must be friends and I'll write to you and you'll get on much better without me anyway.'

He never took his eyes from the book. She went to the curtains and suddenly swept them back. She said, 'They need some extra runners, we must see to that,' as she looked at the ruffled waters of the flood. There were gulls inland, and a pair of swans. She said, 'It's bright too early, it's going to cloud over and the gulls are inland – that means storm.' And then her eyes clouded with tears.

'Oh my darling silly Juniper Bank,' she said, beginning to cry. 'There's nowhere like this in the world. I know there's nowhere like this.'

Almost as suddenly she recovered herself, bit her lip and grabbed a big handkerchief from one of his drawers. 'Very dramatic,' she said. 'Mop up.' Then she walked straight to the telephone to ring David. She sat on the second bed, a foot away from Stephen, and said, 'I hate the phone.'

David's mother answered first. She was slightly deaf and feared the instrument. She took a moment to understand that the call was for her son. She asked who was speaking and Mary wondered if she should tell the truth. It was not easy lying to anyone as charitable as Edith Dow.

'It's Mary Cameron. Ferguson, you know.'

'Oh yes.' She understood at last. She sounded very worried. 'Is something wrong then, Mary?'

'Well, yes, there is.'

'I'm so sorry. Is somebody unwell?'

'Yes.'

'Not your father, I hope?'

'It's not exactly that. If I could speak to David for a moment.'

She looked up and saw that Stephen's eyes were closed again. She turned away from him.

As soon as David came to the phone she explained as quickly as she could that things were more unbearable then she had thought they were going to be. David did not sound helpful or friendly.

'Really,' he said. 'We arranged—'

'I know we did.'

'It's too bad, ringing this number.'

'David, please, I can't talk here.'

'This is exactly the point; no more can I. It's absurdly early.'

There was silence for a moment then she pleaded.

'I can't wait here as I suggested.'

'Why on earth not?'

'It's impossible.'

'Why?'

'Please, David, please. I can't tell you. You must come at once.'

She could hear him sigh.

He said, 'It sounds to me as if you're acting in a very hysterical way.'

'I'm not.'

There was a long pause. At last he spoke again.

He said, 'Very well. But it seems to me a pity.'

'I wouldn't ask unless – David, d'you mind if I bring quite a big case? David?'

'Let's leave it there.'

He ended the call abruptly. Stephen opened his eyes as the telephone 'clicked' in Mary's ear. Then she slowly replaced it. She looked Stephen in the eye, fiercely, for a second and then walked away from the bed. Although there was still much to be packed, she closed the trunk.

She said, 'You heard all that,' and he turned back to his book.

She stayed in the room, with the trunk and case packed, until David arrived an hour later. She looked exhausted again. She sat still and was quite silent. When she heard footsteps on the steep curved stairs she said very slowly, before she stood up:

'I was thinking of a girl sitting in the gun-field blowing clock dandelions, playing "He loves me" and denying "he loves me not."' She shook her head. 'It's not really like that. I mean love and life and Santa Claus and that. But it should be, I promise you.'

'To prove it,' Pink said, at the door, 'he's arrived.'

'I know,' she lied. Then her energy drained back. Much more quickly again she said, 'I know, I know.'

'Good old Mary-bags.'

She put on a big sheepskin coat that hung behind the door. Rather cheerfully now, jokingly, she said:

'Come on, Pink, you've got to help. Here's my overnight bag.'

Pink was more than astonished by the trunk.

'They'll like that at the Dorchester,' he said.

'Go on, haul! I'll take this end.' She pushed the trunk so that Pink never had to come properly into the room and she herself did not look at Stephen again. Immediately outside the bedroom door she dropped her end of the trunk, and closed the bedroom door sharply behind her, saying, 'Bye!'

'Old Sherpa Pink,' Pink said, lifting up the trunk again.

'What's in it then? The family silver? Warm spooneroo-
nies?'

'Pink, do stop staggering so.'

But at the top of the stairs, he made her drop her
end.

'Work study, efficiency, method one,' he said, pointing
one finger in the air. 'To hell with the paintwork.'

He slid the trunk on to the top steps and then pushed.
With enormous crashes and bangs it somehow slid to the
bottom. The banister shuddered. A huge piece of plaster
was removed from the wall. Pink was delighted. 'Bloody
good,' he said. 'I've always wanted to do that.'

But she did not seem to hear him or notice the trunk
crash down the stairs. She walked slowly to her mother's
room which was used as the spare room now. She stood just
inside it for a moment. There were some sweet peas on the
dressing-table but otherwise it looked as blank as any
unoccupied bedroom. Pink came up behind her.

'Nothing to do with Mummy,' she said, and as she did so
they had the same vision of the mild, stupid little woman
who always wore grey to match her eyes.

'Poor pigeon,' she said sadly, and it was as if her mother
was dismissed in death as she had been in life, 'nothing to
do with her.' She swallowed. 'Just the room . . . It smells of
moth balls.'

'Like the Captain's jacket,' Pink said. 'My dotter's
doing.'

Flatly Mary said, 'I suppose he's dead.' Then she went
on in her lowest tones, 'Horrible. Just now I saw this house
quite empty and, Pink, it was all our fault. I don't know
why.'

'Old flesh,' he said.

'Old flesh,' she replied, still sadly and seriously. 'I sometimes wonder if we've any bones. Moral bones.'

They wandered out again, and she looked at the ceiling
and the curved wall round which the staircase ran.

'We mustn't let it empty itself. I saw myself clattering up the stairs, crying "I'll buy it, I'll buy it", just like in a story.'

'Big stuff,' Pink said.

'Yes,' she admitted with a nod. 'I heard myself say, right on this spot, "I love it, I love it, I love it, because I was unhappy here." I don't know why.'

Then they walked downstairs quietly and once again started to manhandle the trunk. Pink was only serious for one moment.

He said, 'Don't go, love,' and she replied, 'I have already gone.'

There is a story told in Edinburgh of an old lawyer who never leaves his house and sleeps for only an hour or so at night, sitting in a chair. And he has lived like this for forty years, during which he has devoted his waking time to preparing a brief for an appeal. He is his own client. When he was only thirty action was taken against him for fraud and it was brought by his colleagues. He has, apparently, inexhaustible energy in the preparation of the case which will exonerate him, but although he never takes more or less sleep, in the winter he grows a little tired and it is said that around the end of February or the beginning of March, he will drink a bottle of bad port and confess with a bitter laugh, to his housekeeper, that he was guilty in the first instance. On the following morning, sober by 4 a.m., he starts work again.

Colonel Sir Henry Ferguson appeared to be a great deal more sane, and slept eight hours every night, but behind the blank stare and the occasional charming smile, there lay hidden a not unsimilar obsession, broken only, from time to time, by the appearance of his daughter, whose spectacular beauty appealed so much to his vanity.

His actions could have hardly been less like the unhappy Edinburgh lawyer's, but in principle the obsession was much the same. Born, however, a baronet and not a lawyer, he took a different line, which he followed equally as selfishly. His life was devoted to playing the unaccusing, injured gentleman. He never once mentioned the card game or anything to do with it again, and it is likely that except when he was with Mary, he never thought about anything else.

Apart from his ignoring a wife who slowly poisoned herself to death (for in the end, Lady Ferguson's diet was solely gin and French), there were, every day, many signs of this astonishing self-absorption.

He spoke very little, he avoided company, he was totally irresponsible where his children were concerned, although he often snapped at Pink whom he intensely disliked; he was close with his money but careful to pay all local tradesmen, he was charming to the odd visitors to the farm, and politically he was immovably Right. People meeting him noticed the far-away look in his eyes and instantly felt sympathy for him. They could never have believed, or had they believed could never have blamed him, for devoting his life entirely to Colonel Sir Henry Ferguson.

His routine, incidentally, in this self-imposed exile, was porridge and an egg for breakfast, *The Times* and the *Scotsman* in the morning, a glass of wine with lunch, a little rough shooting in the afternoon, and then tea with the family and the portable television set, which he carried from room to room. After that there was a bath, a pink gin, some light supper, a little more television, check the doors and up to bed.

But in everything he was a gentleman, almost a King in exile, and one of the ways in which this showed itself happened each morning at breakfast, now usually eaten in the kitchen. The Colonel, demonstrating that obsessional eye for detail, supped his porridge standing up. He usually did so by the Aga cooker, but occasionally he wandered about, and this explained his appearance at the bottom of the stairs beside the little pile of plaster which Mary's trunk had broken off the wall.

Seeing Pink, the Colonel turned savagely on him, telling him it was just the sort of bloody stupidly irresponsible thing he would expect of him. Even if he seldom made any moral judgments or suggestions to his children (because gentlemen in exile don't) he never stopped biting at Pink for his bad manners, his scruffy appearance, his slovenly habits and his stupidity. It was a family joke, which Pink did not enjoy, to say that Pink was in the doghouse if the Colonel ever addressed a civil word to him. The doghouse, beside Flush, the Colonel's Labrador, was a step up. Not that the Colonel ever took the risk of getting involved in a serious talk with his son. He avoided him.

So, while Pink was saying 'Sorry, sir' and 'Won't happen again, sir', and Caliban-like, shuffling forward with the trunk, the Colonel turned away, towards the kitchen. As he did so he murmured, 'I don't know what the hell you want a bloody great trunk like that for anyway,' and then with a short 'huh', he added, 'Montreal, I don't doubt.'

Mary had paused on the stairs. She had a kind of clean, morning 'on stage' brilliance, backed by the light from the big staircase window above and behind her.

'It's mine,' she said.

The Colonel stopped and smiled.

'Hello, my mouse,' he said kindly. 'I didn't see you standing there. You're up and about early.'

She took one step down.

'Daddy, I don't want you to bawl me out,' she said, perfectly confident that there was no possibility of this. 'I know it's rather awful of me and I shall miss you, darling, but I'm eloping, or whatever it's called.'

'Christ almighty,' the Colonel said. 'Well there's a turn-out.' He screwed up his eyes, against the light, as he looked at her. 'You're sure you're right?'

'Not a bit,' she replied, definitely.

'With this Dow fellow?'

'Isn't it awful?'

'It sounds very rash, little one. But I suppose you know what you're doing.'

'I don't really think I do. But actually I've gone. So let's not fuss. It's rather like that awful wedding day. I mean it was too late, wasn't it, by the time we sat in there drinking sherry waiting for the taxi. That was fun.'

'You look even prettier,' the Colonel said.

'You're wonderful how you don't fuss. Daddy, if it all goes wrong I can always come back to you.'

'Always.' He laid down the porridge bowl and she put her arms round his neck. At the end of the hall, by the front door, Pink stood like a frightened butler, moving from foot to foot.

Mary smiled up at her father.

'This time if it's the most frightful muck-up we'll go on that holiday.'

'Fishing?'

She nodded and he squeezed her rather clumsily and tightly. It somehow betrayed his age.

'That is something to look forward to,' she said.

Then she looked over her shoulder and saw Pink and the trunk silhouetted against the bright green lawn beyond.

'Darling, I must go.'

'A little love,' he said and squeezed her again. She batted her eyelids against his cheek. 'A little love' had been a routine for twenty years.

'I'm worried about Stevie,' she said airily. 'You will be kind to him?'

The Colonel nodded as if she had mentioned her budgerigar. 'Tickety-boo' was all he said.

'Daddy, the gulls are inland. D'you think that's a sign of the most awfully bad luck?'

'Oh don't be so silly,' he comforted her. 'You're just a naughty, pretty girl.'

'That's it,' she replied with a delighted smile. 'That's much more in proportion. I knew you'd say the right thing. Come on.' She dragged him to the door by his hand.

He opened the car door for her, but it was Pink who lugged the trunk into the back. David laughed ironically at the size of it, but laughed with Pink, not with Mary, who sat still and upright in the front seat. She said to her father, 'Go away, now please,' and he blew her a kiss and withdrew.

As he walked back to the door, he looked at his watch. He shouted, 'If you get a good run through you should catch the ten o'clock ferry,' and (as Pink later put it) Mary said, quietly, by way of merry reply:

'I feel as if I were going to the gas chamber.'

Cathie, the maid, who had a peculiarly poor grasp of situation, was rather taken by David's looks, and when she gathered what was going on she rushed from the kitchen and threw some rice half-heartedly at the car, wishing them good luck.

'Oh God,' Mary said, dropping her head. 'That is bad luck.' The Colonel sent the girl back to the kitchen saying, 'That's enough of that,' and hearing the command in his voice, Flush, the dog, began to bark.

Mary looked at David as he pressed the self-starter. She said:

'Please don't look angry.'

He took his hand off the steering-wheel and said:

'My sweet, it's your idea.'

She asked very fiercely, 'What's my idea. What is?'

'Steady,' he said, putting both hands back on the wheel, as the car moved off. Pink put his head through the window, held his nose and pulled an imaginary plug.

'Good-bye, old slob,' he said.

Breakfast in the kitchen that morning was a more than usually disturbing meal. Cathie, perhaps because the quiet that had descended rather unnerved her, decided to be cheeky to Pink, who put on his dark glasses again. The

Colonel sat staring out at the floods. When Stephen came down he at once began to set the kitchen table, and Cathie, a little heavily but with the best intentions, said:

'I don't know what we'd do without Mr Stephen, really I don't.'

Shortly after, Macdonald came in, in her cheap fur coat. She and Stephen exchanged glances and seemed tacitly to agree that it was wiser to say nothing. She sat down, away from the table and told Cathie to give her a cup of tea.

Stephen said quietly, 'We'd better hurry, Pink.'

'Oh yes?' Pink asked. 'Why's that? It's the Sabbath, isn't it?'

Stephen pulled in his chair.

'Sabbath or no Sabbath,' he said, 'if you remember, we've got a pack of school children arriving at nine who'll throw spuds at each other and get paid for doing it, unless we're there to shout.'

'By God, yes,' Pink said. 'We'll fix them.'

'You're coming out?'

'Of course I am,' Pink exclaimed.

Stephen nodded and said, 'Good.'

There followed a prolonged silence as they sat eating. It became almost unbearable, but just before Pink felt something had to be said, Macdonald began, in her usual gloomy voice:

'Did you see Mr Thompson at the dance, him with the centre parting?'

Stephen asked, 'The chartered accountant?' But Macdonald did not reply. She looked very tired and dazed.

'There's a story about him,' she went on, as if she were describing a dream. 'When he's on his honeymoon he sends Sheila up to her bed first and after a dram he comes up. He's near fifty when he's married first, and he's got habits. He opens the window just that much – you know, he's fastidious. So he folds his shirt and trousers and all. He puts his shoes, very neat, outside to be cleaned. He lays his dressing-gown, precise, over the chair and he kneels and says his prayers. Then he switches out the light and just before he climbs into bed he says, "And noo Mrs Tampson," he says, "your thingamy if you please."'

She took up her spoon and continued stirring her tea. There was a terrible, embarrassed silence and Stephen very softly laid down his cup. Extremely seriously and quietly Pink said, 'Very good' just before Macdonald dropped her spoon in the saucer again and burst into tears. Covering her face with her hands she said to the Colonel:

'I'm sorry. I'm sorry. I don't know what came over me. I'm sorry—'

And they all rose and reached towards her. It was the first they knew of the Captain's death.

The Colonel said, 'No matter; one of those things,' and then Cathie, who was by the range, began to giggle.

She said, 'You mean Leslie Thompson? I think that's funny.' She laughed out loud. 'I'm sorry, but I do.'

Pink said, 'Shut up,' then softened the blow. 'Nothing personal, old thing—' He got up and walked out of the kitchen, leaving Stephen to cope with Macdonald who was beginning, in a broken sort of way, to talk about the Captain's last moments.

Pink pocketed his dark glasses and smiled gaily at the walled garden, the big lime trees, the yew hedge, the black shed, the dairy and the castellated steadings behind. He looked even happier when he turned his eyes to the white clouds bowling across the sky. He spoke under his breath.

'You old tragedy, you,' he said. 'You rotten thing.' And then, at once, he underwent one of those extraordinarily swift changes of mood. He froze, with his head cocked slightly to one side and his smile was suddenly false and bitter; even cruel. He was thinking of Captain Gordon. At last he raised his eycbrows, sighed, and by way of epitaph applied Rabelais' last words:

Tirez le rideau, la farce est jouée.

THIRTEEN

COUSIN, YOU WITHOUT morals,

When I dropped the receiver back on its rest, my angelic
mother (who had tactfully disappeared into the parlour as I
spoke) returned and she looked upset.

'Nothing amiss, I hope? Is it bad news, David?'

I shook my head. I smiled, even, and said 'No.' I never
lied to my mother except by silence which is only, sadly to
say, that I seldom told her any of the truth. But she
understood. She turned away without complaint. I just
caught sight of the side of her face and I recognised there
exactly the same expression which she had worn ten years
before when I told her of my separation. But she never
uttered judgment; not after I was grown up. She talked that
morning only of tiny creature comforts. Would I like her to
prepare a picnic lunch for the road? 'I shouldn't like to
worry about you,' she said, and added more quickly, 'Not
on that account.'

I think that I must have answered 'no' more abruptly
than I realised.

She bowed her head and said again very quietly, 'I would
prepare it for two.' Angels are not stupid.

I knew, as I drove to you that morning, along deserted roads
through fields of stooked corn, under the huge beeches that
reach across the road, I knew I was about to destroy. All that
can be said for me is that knowing that, I did not feel excited. I
have never felt so depressed. Or is that worse? Here came the
bludgeon, shaped by Calvinist hands.

A dear friend of mine's pet otter was once slaughtered by a Scottish workman who saw it on the road. For apparently no good reason he just picked up his long spade and crushed its head. There in Juniper Bank, were you, as illogical, as selfish and as sweet as any otter. It's a nightmare remembered . . . A big yew hedge, that grows and grows.

You shall not go free. Here comes the spade.

There was a murderer's confession that appeared about that time in one of the Sunday papers. The murderer drove the victim to a deserted marsh near Ely, to do away with her, and as she was perfectly able-bodied it was important, for the smooth success of the crime, that he should give no indication of anything except love as he drove through the last village before the fens. In many other ways he proved to be an extremely subtle and well-controlled operator, but he very nearly failed, in this case, because he found it impossible to be pleasant to the girl during the journey. He bickered and quarrelled with her all the way, so that several times she demanded that he should stop the car. In those last hours he could not, in effect, bring himself to deceive the person he knew he was going to destroy.

He might have been telling the story of the Byronic marriage, the one when the groom turns unbearably hostile between the altar and the first hotel.

It began almost straight away.

'Be glad,' you said, stretching out a cupped hand in which I placed no kiss.

'Darling, don't be huffy. The ferry doesn't matter anyway. Nothing matters now, does it?'

It was my arm you clasped so tightly now.

'Don't look so black. Look out there, it's terribly pretty, it really is. The smoke's not going straight up to the sky –

look,' you said, pointing to a cottage down from the road that led through the first kind, lowland hills. 'It's going downward, the smoke, which isn't a good sign, but that won't matter either. We'll be gone. Will we ever come back here again?'

'You *talk*—'

'You'll have to put up with that,' you said bravely rather than cheerfully, now. 'Everybody does. Darling, I know what you're feeling. I know exactly and I promise I understand. You feel you're trapped. There's a song in Figaro.' You tried a few notes but failed to find a key, then went on, 'You think all the fun's over. That's what it is. I promise I understand.'

'I promise you don't,' I said.

You laughed a little at the trunk in the back seat.

'It is rather excessive,' you said, and then, 'Please, darling, don't frighten me.'

'For heaven's sake—'

'But *tell* me, honestly. Then I'll understand.'

'You sound so bloody cheerful.'

You answered meekly, 'I'm not, if that's a help.'

'Please tell me, darling, try and tell me. I'm sure I'd understand.'

Again and again, your voice: 'Darling, I'm sure I'd understand.'

Oh, but I gave myself a score of reasons. I flattered myself at one moment on the theme of the Byronic marriage. Flattered myself that by reasons of birth, of the long line of Protestants and angels, I alone was complicated and made of many men. That now I was forced (I thought of it as 'forced') to live with you I would give away too much of myself and you, dim one, would not understand. I turned it round so that I was the otter and you the spade. That was merely the first vanity.

The other self-flattery, you will remember. I must have

shouted it at you a hundred, hundred times. I explained to you, talking almost as fast as yourself, in bed, in cars, in the flat, in night-clubs – God knows where – and grew blind with rage at you, cousin, for your dishonesties, saying, 'You do not know the meaning of love.' You came back like a child asking the same questions again. Exactly like a child, because, rightly, my reasons for bullying you, as I then explained them, did not satisfy you.

All I did was to shout the same lies again. At the time, I had convinced myself. After all, the explanation absolved me of blame. It explained too, why I spent so much of the time in Classroom IV and in all the other hundred places, getting to the bottom of your sinless lies. I saw you, I said, so amazed, so confused and frightened of life that you would not accept it at all and therefore were incapable of love. There were a hundred examples all like those odd, frightening stories you told about your mother and Arbuthnot – why choose such an extraordinary name? And so I accused. Your hysteria, your skating on the surface, your very imagination was an insult to my love . . . Do you remember? (And I know the answer to that. You can remember, but you do not.)

I almost beat my chest. My love was something very different. I had lived and come through the turmoils, the girl friends, the harlots, the queers, the wife; my love was real and left unsatisfied. I treated you in bed, when I think of it now, like a clockwork mouse that would not go fast enough.

Oh, cousin, I remember your eyelashes, I don't know why.

And out of bed, I treated you worse. But the explanation, please note, absolved me. I even persuaded some of my more intelligent friends who objected to my treatment of you, that I was the injured party. I did not accuse you precisely of coldness. That would have been too glaringly untrue. Nor precisely of stupidity; for the same reason. I used to say of you, with smiling condescension, 'Poor darling one; she's too frightened to love. It's my mistake. I thought I could help her out of that.'

ON THE FERRY over the Forth, as the sky clouded over, I joined the queue at the ticket office, and picking your way through twenty cars packed closely together, you went aft to the windswept passengers' deck. Half-way across the river, when the ferry passed almost underneath the span of that huge red bridge I rejoined you – remember? You greeted me with such fear in your eyes that it seemed you expected to be murdered, there and then. You held on to the rail and turned to the sea again.

Ignoring the spray that splashed your face, almost enjoying its sting, so it seemed, I remember your nodding towards the Fife coast. Swallowing then speaking even more quickly than you had done in Classroom IV. I can still play it back.

'I never told you, but I went to school down there. I really enjoyed it too. They say those that are happy at school are happy at home, so there you are – that must mean something. Though I don't suppose they approved of me very much. I wasn't actually voted pupil most likely to succeed, I . . .'

I did not help you.

You went on, 'They'd all sorts of silly rules and made an awful fuss when I carved somebody else's name on a desk. Even the other girls thought that was rather off. They all nudged, you know, and looked. I used to lose my temper rather a lot. There wasn't Pink to cool me down. Actually the girl whose name I did carve couldn't have been more pleased. She'd obviously got a crush on me or something. I

suppose that's why I carved her name. Lord, there was such
a fuss – and about other things. But Daddy was marvellous.
He used to come down and look so wonderful that the
houselady or whatever she was called couldn't keep it up at
all. Awful, really, I think it was the title as much as the
looks. Once he quite turned things round. He came down
supposedly to discuss taking me away, which would have
been a pity, really, and ended by taking me and two of my
chums out for a strawberry tea. A great *coup*. Not this other
girl, mind. Two of my healthy hockey-playing friends. I was
good at games. You'd never have guessed that, would you?
That's one of the reasons they kept me, I suppose. Fanny
Blankers Whatsit. I could always run as fast as Pink. I
played on the wing at hockey on all sorts of gloomy days like
this, then all the same girls that had done the nudging and
the looking and the baiting would sidle up after a match and
say I was a good sport. Can you imagine? I think they must
have got the phrase from their mothers, old frumps that
most of them were.'

More slowly you said, 'Oh goodness, I didn't say good-
bye to Macdonald.' Frowned, then went on, 'She used to
come to chapel sometimes. I once wept when she went
away. I was terribly angry about doing that . . .'

Paused, cousin, then managed to say, 'She used to go
and see Pink too, at his ghastly private school. Chuff-chuff,
he was then. He went everywhere like a train.'

Paused again, like a diver hanging in mid-air. Then came
the fall. Head dropped down to your hands on the rail.
Husky and sore-throated:

'Oh God, darling, I hate it, I hate it. Please take me
back. I promise it's a mistake. You don't love me and I
don't even love you. I don't know why I came. I don't
know why I went with you this morning. It's a mistake.
We can still go back.'

Other travellers on the ferry, shunning embarrassment of
any sort, moved away. Sobbing quite hopelessly now, you

leant a little over the rail and let the wind blow your tears into the sea.

'You really do enjoy making an exhibition of yourself.' That is my voice, Oxford cold, that day.

From you, a whispered, 'Go away.'

'Surely,' I replied. 'You'll find me in the car.'

Five minutes later, as the ferry bumped against the quay, I watched you dry your eyes and push your hair off your forehead. You climbed into the car, looked straight ahead, and, bitterly, said something worse than:

'You can bloody well give me a cigarette.'

'Of course. If the cabaret's over.'

We drove on to the border and a T-bone, Scampi-frite type country house hotel. We both got pretty drunk.

Remember the following morning. I always thought of it as one of the happiest times, even if you seemed thoughtful and disturbed. I surprised you when you were still clench-fisted and asleep. I woke without the murderer. For half an hour I forgot the spade.

You woke when I was sitting astride you. You looked so serious. I drew circles round your tummy, playing one of your games, 'Round and round the garden'. You did not trust me, but you were kind.

I remember that as I went and ran the bath I was singing, and I can still see you frown. Disturbed by otter-instinct, you lay with the sheet wound tightly round you, sucking your thumb.

I was pleased with myself. For months, even years, I carried that about as a happy memory. Then one day I saw it in its true light, and it horrified me. The workman was playing at otters. It's, somehow, obscene.

Cousin, forgive.

BOOK THREE

The Big City

BUT THE WORST of it came at the end of it, and David, with the expertise of the professional torturer, worked it obliquely. The really nasty stuff was presented to her from the mouth of the one person she certainly loved.

It happened six months later, at about ten o'clock on a summer's night. Pink, Mary and David sat amongst the dirty glasses and ashtrays in the flat in that tatty, curved and concrete block off the Gray's Inn Road. David had shown the last of the guests out not half an hour before and she had spent most of the intervening period abusing his friends rather wildly, calling them hypocrites, parasites, narcissusites, sodomites and Gaitskellites.

It was Pink's first visit. He had come to the party softly, in suède shoes and his best pin-stripe suit, remembering Mary's birthday and bearing a gift of Edinburgh Rock.

David merely prompted. He sat on a cushion by the fireplace and said, all Oxford, 'No, do tell her, Pink. Do. It was really very interesting. I thought you coped admirably.'

It was the third time David had encouraged him and it was obvious that Pink wanted to get it off his chest.

'Actually, they seemed rather interested in the guv'nor.' Pink was considerably fatter.

'How?' Mary asked, and she was correspondingly thinner.

'Well, about the cards and that. This politician chap, David's chum, knew a bit about it. I don't know. Perhaps his old man was involved too.'

'What did he say?'

'Oh, nothing much. Just another card-scandal theory.'

Mary was sharp; a great deal sharper than when she had left home.

'Don't avoid it, Pink. I know they said something foul.'

'Actually, old thing, they seemed very sympathetic towards the guv'nor. Truly. I was impressed.'

'Tell her,' David said. 'If only for a lesson.' Then he turned to her. He always smiled at her now. 'God knows it would help if you had some of Pink's forbearance.'

She said, swiftly, 'I had. And what did you call me then? An unthinking, self-pitying little yes-girl . . . I believe it was better than that.'

'I hope it was,' David said, again with a false smile, playing the patient, injured party.

She turned back to Pink. David watched.

'What was this theory?'

'Perfectly straightforward, really. I don't suppose there's anything in it, really.' Swiftly again, almost with a swoop, she replied loudly:

'I'm certain there isn't. I'll bet they never even heard about the guv'nor until I came along. Someone'll have made up some nasty story. Probably David planted it.'

'It might be right,' Pink warned.

'Then tell me.'

Suddenly Pink threw the story off as if it were of little importance.

'Suggestion was that there were probably quite a lot of card games in that club, late at night, you know.'

'And Daddy always cheated?'

'No. That's not actually what was suggested. But, you know, those same chaps, more or less the same – one, particularly the same, but I can't remember the fellow's name—'

The more Pink tried to dismiss the story, the more obvious did it become that it had shattered him, only because it had struck him so clearly as true. Mary began to look a little scared. Pink resumed.

'Anyway the same chaps met, most nights. All very influential and rich and so on except for the guv'nor, who they'd kind of taken up, you know – the way these things happen—' he said vaguely and David got up and refilled his glass. 'Well actually, the suggestion is that perhaps they took the guv'nor up for something other than a fourth hand at bridge or whatever it was they played.'

Mary said 'Huh!' almost brassily, a noise she had never made before. Pink looked at her slantwise, wondering if she had already understood the homosexual implication. But she had not quite.

She went on, 'As a kind of innocent. To lend respectability – the fool, I suppose, while the others really gambled illegally?'

'Not actually that,' Pink said, leading her gently, with a kind of low, inadmissible thrill.

'Well, what?'

'Suggestion was that the guv'nor was really rather nice-looking in those days.'

'Go *on*, Pink.' She was refusing to think.

'One of these chaps had taken a bit of a fancy to him. Not exactly for his card-playing, if you see what I mean.'

Mary grew pale as he went on:

'Well, anyway, after a bit of this the guv'nor either fell to it what was happening, maybe even got a little involved, then got pretty worried. Bit of a flutter. Panicky, as one might say. So he turns round and marries the girl from Dundee. She's pretty. Plenty of jute money—. He's a handsome young soldier. Very pleasant. A softness in the voice. That accent, you know. Perfectly right sort of match both sides.'

Mary's voice was much more controlled when she interrupted again. It was as if she spoke along a ruled line.

'That's obviously nonsense. We know perfectly well that they were married when it happened – whatever did happen. You were nearly born. I should think that's the real truth of it even if it would disappoint them. Lots of girls behave in a mad sort of way when they're pregnant. You can imagine Mummy.'

'I should think you're right,' Pink said, unconvinced.

'Of course I am.'

'Mark you, it doesn't mean there weren't those card parties before. Perhaps he got a little involved again. Actually this politician fellow, David's chum, very bright he seemed, discussing this – he had a little theory.'

'I'll bet he did.'

'It could be true,' Pink said. 'Could be. His suggestion was that the guv'nor went back into the lion's den, you see, just to kind of prove something. Either that or to say there were no hard feelings. But if that's true it wasn't the wisest move. I shouldn't think Mumbo understood – she would never have twigged that sort of thing, poor pigeon. Those Dundee blindnesses, and that. Suggestion was that somebody might have said something in her ear. Probably very vague – "Bad influence" or something like that. But they evidently said something that upset her pretty badly. She was tearful for quite a while . . . And these other chaps couldn't help smiling, you know. You can see they would. So this night they do play cards and the guv'nor goes a bit far just to win.'

'They wouldn't dare sue him,' Mary said.

'Not quite the point, old love.'

But before he could go on, as if she, too, scented truth, she asked suddenly, coldly, as she got up for a cigarette:

'D'you mean to say you just stood and listened while they said these horrid things?'

'It was a friendly sort of talk. They weren't just being vicious, you know,' Pink said. 'Cocktail party stuff.'

'Of course they were,' she snapped. 'Can't you see that?

They can't stand the idea that somebody else might be normal. Didn't you even tell them to shut up?'

Pink looked, for a second, as if he were talking to his father, not Mary. His impediment reappeared. After a little circle of the head he said:

'N-no, old bean. Not much point.'

'Oh God,' she said, dropping her head – a head which she was beginning to learn to use. 'I see. And now David makes you tell me this so's I'll start hating you too . . . You don't know, Pink darling. You don't begin to understand the way their minds work. . . . Never mind, never mind.'

Pink checked his fly buttons, shifted in his seat, and sighed. 'Frankly,' he said, 'hitting about didn't really occur to me. I was a bit – what shall we say – a bit put out? You see, old cocky, I couldn't help feeling that maybe they'd got a point. I mean the thing's never been quite explained.'

'Oh, don't be silly,' she replied. 'How could they possibly know? They weren't there.'

'One of their uncles evidently—'

'I don't believe that,' she said at once.

'No, no, he wasn't there, but he was in the club. Not in this particular room, you follow. He was sitting upstairs a bit later on. Also a soldier, so I'm told.' Pink suddenly seemed to want to leave the story there. He drained his glass. 'Well, anyway, that was it.'

'What about this man upstairs?' David asked, breaking the silence that fell.

'Well, evidently he was sitting upstairs. Your chumbo told me this, you follow, saying what a terrible thing it was—'

'You bet—' Mary said disbelievingly.

'While he sat there, this old gent,' Pink went on guiltily with pleasure, again, '– he became aware of a rather unnerving noise and at last he traced it to the writing-room. It was late, I gather. He was the last in the club, or thought he was. Well, to cut out the painful details, it was the guv'nor in there, poor old chap. Crying his heart out.'

Mary sat very still, but tears rolled down her cheeks. It was as if the full meaning of the story had only just begun to dawn on her.

'How dare they say that,' she said in a very low whisper.

Pink now seemed strangely disconnected from the story. He did not look at Mary although David watched her tears. He went on, 'There was another odd little point.' David smiled.

Louder, this time, Mary said with pride, 'How dare they say that.'

Pink said, with definition now; with effective, destroying proof positive: 'This chappie in the club. He's the same man who sold us our farm. Oliphant. So there it is.'

And then she broke. She broke in a way that made Pink stand up and then stand back, and very shakily light a cigarette, not looking at what she did, and for a moment afterwards not daring to glance at her face. As a child, both at school and in Pink's presence, she had several times completely lost control of her temper, perhaps as badly as this, but somehow in a child, it is never so frightening. Her voice rose beyond 'How dare!', beyond all words to a single scream as she attacked David, kicking and scratching. When Pink, at last, very gingerly tried to interfere she also kicked at him and called him a coward.

'Darling, darling,' David said softly. He could not have behaved more kindly, trying to soothe her, trying to press her arms to her side but very gently, and also trying to kiss her tears. At last her voice dropped and she began to weep with long low sobs, and then all of a sudden she was quite still as if she were rigid and dead on her feet. Pink was again in the corner, smoking his cigarette furiously when David helped her out of the room to the bathroom where he held her forehead while she was sick. She washed and he came back first.

Pink, with his usual technique of facing a homicidal lunatic with 'a spot of the butcher's itch, old man?' said:

'Everything sorted out all right?'

David replied:

'She'd drunk far too much, anyway.'

But the manner of her return seemed to suggest that she had in the past months quite often been shaken as deeply as this. Her forehead looked higher because her hair was a little wet from the sponge. She still looked pale. But she made it clear at once that she wanted the incident to be forgotten. She did not apologise. She said:

'Where are we going to eat?'

Pink's teeth were chattering.

SIXTEEN

'COME HOME, Jim Edwards,' Pink said, but she sniffed and shook her head.

'No.' Then she put out a hand to him. 'I'm glad that party was even bloodier. It makes us friends again.'

'Again?' he asked. 'No question of that.'

'No,' she said uncertainly. 'No, of course not.'

'Mark you, you did kick out a bit.'

She brought her fingers together and nodded, firmly. 'That's all it was.' Then she swept back her hair, and asked:

'How's Stephen?'

'Stiffy? Much the same. My jalopy awaits at the door.'

'No.'

'Daddy?' Pink seemed to have to try and remember to whom she referred.

'Jogging along, I think, old thing,' he said, with a frown, at last. 'Square eyeballs. He takes the TV out shooting with him. D'you think that little tale had any truth in it?'

'Don't,' she said sharply.

'Sorry. I thought it might be better to air it. For old Pink, too.'

'It was a stupid story.'

'Lovey, why don't you come home? I'd row you in, I really would.'

'No.'

'Your life, Lilian.'

She nodded. They were sitting on the stairs that led up to the flat door. It was about half past one in the morning. They had left David at the party where they had met all the same guests, one degree drunker. Mary sat a step higher than Pink, who for some potty reason, now lolled back, pretending that he was basking in the sun. He sifted imaginary sand through his fingers as he talked. Light from the hall shone up the lift shaft beside them but otherwise it was dark. A few minutes later, Pink said:

'Give us a statement, guv.'

But she still sat silent. Pink looked up at a small pilot light at the top of the lift shaft.

'That sun', he said, is bloody hot. Very dangerous indeed, I'd say. Pass me the Ambre Solaire.'

'God, I love you, Pink. I do. I promise I do.'

'Thank you.' Pink sat up. 'Chumbo, is it always like this?'

'What exactly?'

'I mean all the big guns, you slamming him and that, and then him just ditching you like this.'

She nodded quickly. 'That sort of thing. It may be a bit worse because you're here. That's what he'll tell me, anyway.'

'But why do you stay?'

She shrugged her shoulders.

'Love?' he suggested.

She shook her head. 'I don't think so.'

'Hate?'

'Not always.'

'Sex?'

'Not altogether.'

'Fear?'

'I'm sometimes scared. You're awfully good at asking questions.'

'You're awfully bad at answering them,' Pink said.

She apologised and he suddenly grabbed her hand. He had never had to do so before. They both noticed that.

'No sorries to me,' he said. 'That's not on at all. Why doesn't he sack you?'

'He says,' she said, 'that he loves me.'

'Funny way to show it.'

'No,' she said thoughtfully. 'It's just that he shows it in too many ways. I really ought to be happy. I get everything. He's practically hitting me one minute and the next he's on his knees begging me. He's insulting or kissing my feet.'

'And bed?'

'She frowned.

'It's probably my fault,' she said.

'Oh, Goderooni,' Pink said. 'Not another Stiffy?'

'Oh no,' she shook her head. 'Not that a bit.'

'But you don't like it?'

She, too, had begun to play with Pink's sand. She passed it from hand to hand.

'Very clean sand.'

'Trust St Andrews,' Pink replied.

'I do at the time,' she said. 'I like it very much indeed at the time.'

'Afterwards, big guilt?'

'She nodded. Then, at last, went on:

'What's awful is that I sometimes think I stay just for it.' She stopped and shook her head. 'That really can't be true. It's not guilt because of Stephen, mind. It's something else.'

'A little bit of sin.'

'Well, it can't be, can it, Pink? I mean we've never had anything to do with all that, you and me. If you say "Stuff Moo", Moo really can't worry you, can he? I mean that's not fair at all.'

'Deepers,' Pink announced. 'We've got an awful lot of Moo tucked away. Could be a throw-back to Moo. What's the feeling? Just, shouldn't be doing it at all?'

'No,' she said steadily. 'It's just a bit of a sham. D'you want to know?'

'You want to tell?'

'Yes. Give me some more sand. I'm going to need it.'

'Come home, Jim,' Pink said, but she ignored that. She frowned as if she were collecting herself to take a big hurdle.

'I'm pretty dim, but I think it works like this. We do everything in the book you see and yet in an odd, awful sort of way he's never slept with me, nor me with him. I told you about that country girl of mine on the bridge – well, like that, only different. And I'm sure it's worse for him than me. He's always somebody else in bed. I don't think he sees how different he is. And I either lie there a bit bewildered, you know, because that's really how I feel, or else I kind of whip up an act as well. When we're both bluffing we're capable of big thrills and we can say "nobody's like us" and all the things everybody says, I'm sure. But you see it's a sham, Pink. I know it's a sham. I don't know who he is, and I don't really think he knows who he is. Look at him even tonight, charming at his own party, wily and all kind of cruel when you were talking about Daddy, then arrogant and womanising at this last do. Yet sometimes, in fact quite often, he's the child. I don't know how he's the energy to keep it up.'

She stopped and looked up.

She said, 'Do you understand any of that lot?'

'You bet,' Pink said. 'Why d'you have to pick the weird ones?'

'There's a question,' she said. 'Why do they hunt me?'

'Because, my love,' Pink said, 'You're the most vulnerable thing on two legs.'

She shook her head, then swept back her hair, again. She wore it longer, now.

'Watch that sand,' Pink said.

'Not now,' she said. 'Not vulnerable now. You should try being a girl.'

'It could be arranged,' he replied. 'This Modern Age.'

'I'll tell you. Now life's getting sorted out. I know now I'm either very soft and breasts and that, or else I'm just a hard little triangle of hair. It's about as simple as that. Only I think I wanted to be soft more than anything . . .'

'What's to stop you?'

'Me. Once you've started being the other sort of girl, it doesn't seem to be so easy to go back. All girls are rakes, so some Pope said, and that's the truth of it. I used to think I'd get fat. But I'll probably end up like a piece of chewed string.'

She paused again, then said:

'Very chewed. Tarts do . . . There's not much of me left.'

'Oh yes there is,' Pink said very quietly, and she seized and squeezed his hands. 'Chumbo, you'd better come home.'

'No.' She looked disturbed as if she wondered why she was so sure. Then very suddenly she said:

'Lovely, we could talk forever, but I'm tired now. You go home. I'm going to bed.'

She stirred and her clothes rustled. Pink sat upright and when she switched on the light, at the top, by the flat door, he rubbed his eyes.

'Are you going to stick to him?' Pink asked.

Again she frowned, deeply this time, and looked down at her shoes. She had one hand on the flat door.

'I don't know till I find him, really,' she said. Then she told Pink to go away. He went, waving up from each landing, all the way down to the hall.

At the last moment, he decided to leave his jalopy where it was, and take a taxi as far as Piccadilly. Then he decided to walk about a bit. Paddling through Belgrave Square, only a couple of hundred yards away from base, he was accosted by a tart on wheels. He did not know that a modern habit was for prostitutes to ride in well-appointed cars and her arrival at the kerb beside him left him speechless. He looked at her dejectedly, and thought what a plain little woman she was. Any colour she might have had by day was washed away by the street light. She managed a very uncertain smile for a professional as she said:

'Hullo, saucy.'

Pink replied only with a faint aspirant as he climbed into the car. 'Winded,' he said to himself, 'I'm winded, not windy.' For the first mile no words passed between them until at last she asked:

'Where do you come from then?'

Pink replied very loudly, 'France!'

When they arrived at the house, which was large and condemned somewhere in the no-man's-land west of the Edgware Road, Pink looked round the room. He had to go through all the business with the homely maid (two and six will do very nicely) and the welcome-home poodle (he's from France, too), and then the girl closed the door behind her.

'I say,' Pink said, sociably, spotting the electrical stimulator nearby. 'The old Vibro on the couch, what?' and she gave him a look that made him unbutton his trousers, at once.

SEVENTEEN

'THE LAST DAYS of Pompey . . .' Your girlish quote. From one of your long letters, which then I dismissed and now wish I'd kept. I can't remember all you said in it, but I remember it was full of apologies, saying you didn't know what came over you to make you bolt at that of all times. You devoted a paragraph to 'good friends' and I was reminded of that tie you were always going to buy for Stephen. You never mentioned my bloodinesses – from the letter one would have guessed that it had been a sunny affair. I can see your upright writing and I remember thinking that it looked as if you had drawn pencil lines across the page, then rubbed them out afterwards. It often struck me as odd that your hands, which usually moved so quickly and competently, produced such childlike writing. But everything was neat and correct. I think you had even checked the spelling, and I'm almost certain you wrote the letter twice. There wasn't a single blot, or scoring out.

I knew much better than you why you left, and at that time I remember telling myself, even if I didn't believe it, that I'd won. Nor was it a surprise when you went. I saw it coming days before. And I knew you wouldn't go home with Pink, cousin. To my eternal shame, I'd fixed that. You frowned whenever I mentioned his name. You may have let him take you back from a party, but you weren't going to go home with him. Not until you'd sorted things out in your mind. I was quite sure of that.

There seem to be only two ways in which the immature –

and I am talking of myself, not you – can display a little of their true identity: first in loving someone so much that they forget their own masks and defences, but if they do this successfully they pass out of the category; they are not of the permanently immature. The other way is to fail. And that's really what happened, on a small scale. And apart from that, in the end, after the thrill of the most damnable act of all, namely upsetting you and Pink, the workman was too tired and sad and sorry for himself to lift the spade. The otter approached with safety.

I remember in the kitchen we managed the sort of conversation that only goes with very grown-up people. I didn't quite believe in it, afterwards, but at the time it was genuine enough. I told you all about the experiment that had gone wrong in this lab, on or about the very bench on which I write this now. You never quite understood, but you frowned (which is to say you tried), and I for my part took lots of trouble trying to explain it all to you. One day I'll write it down carefully for you, because I never quite got it across. I gave you a parallel in communication engineering but you didn't understand what communication engineering was so I suppose that only muddled you more. (I can still see the frown as you tried so hard.) In complicated signal and response systems engineers have proved it's more efficient to duplicate some of the signals; to send the telephone message along two lines, because in this way inefficiencies through outside interference are usually eliminated. Still with me? Read it twice. All I was trying to do was show that this happened in animals as well. I got myself a cat most days from the animal house downstairs and carved out bits of its mid-brain through which I knew certain signals were passed. Things called 'righting reflexes', in fact, which means sticking out a leg to stop yourself falling over, or in the case of a cat, if you put it on its back, trying to get on all fours again. If it did get on all fours, or at least tried to do so, after I'd sliced the one telephone line which everybody knows about, then I'd prove that there was duplication in the system.

Isn't it odd, how I go into all that again? I desperately want to get it across to you now because you were right, in a way, about the schoolmaster. In those moments I found patience. I showed, for a few seconds, anything that's nice about me.

You know I always used to tell you that everybody and especially those mixed-up characters, the children of the angelic, are six people at once? Haunted perhaps, by a lot of ghosts of their fathers who have committed no sins except sins of omission, all saying 'Go on, take everything, we never did!'? I don't really think the haunted idea bears examination, but I know I feel now, at a moment of peace (although not through the storm like you), most like a rather nice uncle of mine who was once Chief Constable in Forfar. He was patient and steady, he ate too many cookies and buns, and maybe he was on the dull side, but he was a much better teacher than his brother, my father, who was headmaster for twenty years. It's not that I'm cast more in his mould than anybody else in the family. It's just that somehow he arrived, and arriving showed effortlessly, I suppose, all that's best about a Dow, and therefore all that's true about a Dow.

That was what you saw, my darling, in the kitchen. I was weary of bullying you, and I was weary of making simple practical experimental mistakes with those cats. (Isn't it significant that I've never been a good experi-mentalist in the practical sense? That needs a steady physical touch.) You found Dow. Just for a few moments. And I can see your eyes now, not at all steady and loving but suddenly, very wary indeed, this way and that, as you fidgeted around. Two days later, amazed at yourself, because these were the best two days we had together, even if we never went to bed, you slipped away, not even leaving a note.

Even then, though I see it so clearly now, I deceived myself. It astonishes me that someone (forty was I? Forty-one?) could have been so blind to himself when he was given such clear clues. I saw you funked love, I saw it the minute, the very second you did. (It's the actual bat of an eyelid that I remember, as if it were yesterday and, at once, I fabricated a whole load of lies.) I swore I felt triumphant. When you had gone, and I wandered through the flat alone, from room to room, I whistled. I kept saying, 'You won, David, you won, she loved you in the end. She proved it so. She ran away, otter that she is, but the victory, Davie boy, is yours alone.'

For a day or two I was hopelessly restless, beginning things, as one does, but I made no effort whatever to find you. I was really glad that you had gone – that was the one true thing. And then I rang Phyllis, the wife that was, who I often see, and saw while you were with me, but was damned careful to make sure that she never met you. The ex-wife's life, selling hats in Regent Street, has put pounds of flesh on her. She's Scottish, too, as you know. I'm as cagey as that. Sleeping with her is a little like having a hot bath, and even to me she tends to quote Shelley before she puts on her clothes again.

I remember saying on the phone:

'The most awful thing's happened.'

'Yes?' Very coyly, from her.

'I'm inconsolable,' I said and explained.

She asked, 'Did she say something nasty?'

And I laughed.

'Worse,' I said. 'If she said anything, I'm sure it was nice.'

She promised to try to look in. She always makes it sound difficult. Everything in her life, she's sure, goes wrong and isn't easy.

'At once,' I hear another man's voice that is my own persuade her. 'That's very sweet of you.' She was there within the hour. We even had an expensive meal afterwards with myself at my most gay.

There's the picture, distant cousin, of a man in defeat.

EIGHTEEN

PINK WAS BACK in Edinburgh by now, at the bar down-stairs in the Café Royal doing his best to sum things up. He did so to a young man who had been with him at private school and who was now one of the grey-suited young men in a brewery which was a subsidiary of the Distillers Companies. He was doing very well. Pink confessed to feeling very shaky. Not really expecting to be understood he said, finishing one pink gin and ordering the next:

'*Reductio ad coitum*, chum. The jolly old R.A.C.'

He went to the basement, to the lavatory, on his own. Perhaps initials reminded him of the jolly old F.F.I. His guilt then and always, in spite of any medical reassurances, or advances in chemotherapy, took a physical form. By lunch-time he was perfectly convinced he had a bad go of the pox. He had to stop himself from telling everybody in the restaurant that he had. Weeping tomorrow, he assured himself, with a belch, and frying tonight. When he went up to the bar again he noticed in one of those awful, unmistakable flashes that the young men he had been talking to, no longer thought of him as a funny chap. They exchanged a glance which, in the years to come, he was to know very well. They were not so rude as to go off to their table without returning hospitality, but they seemed to move an extra inch away, and they were now in a hurry. They thought they were avoiding encouraging a friend who was clearly a potential drunk. They were actually avoiding failure, like the plague.

Pink told them, affably, to carry on and eat, and he

pretended to be waiting for Mary, whom he knew to be in
London. He mentioned her by name. Another gin persuaded him to go along Princes Street and buy a pair of
pearl ear-rings. He would present them to Macdonald on
his return to the farmhouse. Drink up, Pink old man, he
said to himself, looking glassily round the small high room,
with the old, marble oyster bar, and the stained-glass
windows above. Going through the swing doors, when
nobody could hear him he bawled out loud, 'I am afraid.
Yippee!'

At home, only a few days later, he got a letter from Mary
with her friend Jennifer's address in big capitals written
across the top, with a childish joke beside it about next of
kin. The letter itself was very short.

> Dear Pink,
>   It was terribly nice seeing you and it did help.
> Thank you for the Rock which was a comfort when
> packing and unpacking at Jennifer's. Please note new
> address.
>   Am happier: often think of you.
>   Luv from,
>   Martita Hunt.
> Luv to Daddy too. Tell him she's perfectly O.K.

It wasn't her usual style to drop the first person singular
and it was Pink's habit, not hers, to sign with a different
name.

Very suddenly, Pink tore the letter into small pieces, then
he went up to the woods by the gun-field and dropped the
pieces in a clearing, where, as children, Mary and he had
once buried a dead cock robin.

Mary now trod a well-worn path.

The atmosphere in the new flat was unrestful, even
jumpy. Jennifer was one of those girls who do better in

war-time. She was thin and quite smart, but with a strong dash of Edinburgh that showed in the shoes and accessories which were bought to last. She had celebrated her twenty-third birthday with an abortion, the father of the child being her husband, and the experience had marked her more obviously than she imagined. She had a rather brittle, gay manner and she walked always as if she were being pulled along by two huge dogs on a leash. She insisted that life was short, and though she always said of her husband, 'Darling he was really very sweet to me,' she had also found another phrase to obliterate the memory of a very unhappy two years, unhappy particularly for her, as she had behaved badly, and he had behaved well. She said:

'The milk of human kindness just wasn't strong enough for Scott-Dempster.'

Together, they lived an unreal life made up of realities; of house-keeping, rent, washing things in the basin, of seeing cinemas and offering drinks to young men with cars. Before she brought anybody who did not know Mary to meet her, Jennifer would explain quickly that she had just finished a *grande affaire* with David Dow, and if the guest did not recognise David's name she would follow it with Mary's maiden name, saying, 'You know – the scapegoat man – before the war. The baronet.' Mary, in her way, had name enough. That mattered to Jennifer.

And it was with Jennifer, some months later, that Mary went to a party in St John's Wood. She only went because Jennifer could not stand the thought of going there, to a nameless party, on her own. It was held in a house that needed repairing and redecorating and a garden that was little more than a weedy rubbish dump. The party was thrown away, rather than given, by an acquaintance of Jennifer's husband, who wrote copy in an advertising agency. He too was something of a name-man, but amongst fifty, hard (gin-cup) drinking guests, there were only three with names. The first was an I.T.V. interviewer,

an authority on all subjects, the second a young barrister
who had defended a homicidal lunatic and the third a lady
from Berlin who made the unlikely claim that she had slept
with Brecht. To this group Jennifer was immediately led
and Mary landed on the floor next to a man who worked for
a serious film magazine, and sang Burl Ives songs like Burl
Ives. The party needs no description except to say that it
went on and on, until it was enlivened by the arrival of a jazz
band who were on their way back from playing in Wisbech.
Amidst the noise that followed, the bellow of the songs, the
blast of the latest disc and the splash of the unrepeatable
anecdotes, Mary watched herself reflected in the huge
uncurtained, uncleaned window. Her hair seemed more
brown than red. And it was while she was doing this that a
very stupid young man said, not with malice, but because it
was a smart line, 'Honey, take care. You've got that un-
lived-in look.' So she drank more seriously.

At half past three in the morning she was standing, for
some reason which she could not remember, by a half-
opened door to a bedroom, two floors up. She was with an
extremely good-looking subaltern who was perhaps less out
of water than he liked to suggest. He was considerably the
smartest figure there, and there seemed to be no explanation for his attendance. It is doubtful whether he would
have found himself with Mary, had he not heard her
maiden name. The party was neither elegant enough nor
slummy enough for a subaltern of the Brigade. The truth,
which in the correct military fashion, he refrained from
volunteering, was that he had been to school with the
copywriter. They had shared a study together at Haileybury
and their rejection of the solid middle-class background,
although equally violent in both cases, had taken totally
different forms. As he stood in the doorway, staring blandly
at Mary who did not meet his eye, the last few people on the
landing decided to return downstairs. One of the jazz men
wished them luck and with a friend shoved them roughly

into the dark bedroom and slammed the door. The subaltern was old enough not to withdraw, but young enough,
when he was putting on his felt braces again, to make the
mistake of assuming that it all meant as little to Mary as to
himself. He suggested within a couple of minutes of completion that they go and find a drink. It was dark in the
room but there was light enough for him to see her cover
her forehead with her wrist. Like an old and inept husband
he said, cheerfully:

'Come on, old ducks.'

She said, 'Please go away,' and that was that.

The job in publishing was as dull as Mary had been led to
suppose it would be, so she could not complain. All the
other girls she met outside the office were very envious of
her and nothing she could say would persuade them that a
large publishing office was duller than a merchant bank.
Publishers themselves spend their lives telling girls like
Mary this, and she had been further warned that having
no shorthand would exclude her from the few more rewarding jobs in the office. So while her friends envied her
she hammered away on a typewriter, filed things and kept a
little notebook in which all permission payments were
entered. Permissions, in and out; that is to say permission
granted to other publishers to quote extracts from copyright works and vice versa, took most of her time, but even
in this field she was not given full responsibility. By long
usage, and with about half a dozen general exceptions,
publishers ask the same copyright fee of two guineas a
thousand words, but this calculation was not entrusted to a
girl. Instead she took all the letters to a conscientious young
man who marked each one with the appropriate fee.

What she thought about during all those hours, she could
not herself explain. Even her imagination seemed to suffer.
For the last hour each day, however, her thoughts were
always the same. They were focused on her wristwatch and

just as she had done at school, at the end of lessons, she would dash for her coat and escape before the rush. Hating the buses and the tube trains at half past five, she very often walked most of the way home, which was nearly two and a half miles. As she did so, with long steps, her eyes straight in front of her, only very occasionally straying to a shop window which she passed, nobody turned to look at her. Her coat was not very clean, her hair, now certainly more brown than red, was pulled back to a pony tail that was too young for her; her shoes were practical, with low heels. London had swallowed her.

Moreover with the loss of her imagination, facts began to take their toll. Losing part of her own personality she assumed some of the fears and habits of the girls around her, although their lives and natures were quite different from her own. She worried about money. She began to think about age for the first time, and not because her appetite had been whetted by the subaltern at the party, but because the last taboo had been broken, she started going out with other young men. Men know. She met their eye honestly and brightly. She saw several of David's friends. Her name was passed from one to another as worth looking up. She even went out with a married man from her office, in his car.

The extraordinary thing was that the numbness, the feeling of living only in a dream, was not broken when she suspected that she was pregnant. On the contrary, the feeling grew stronger. She was hardly responsible for her own actions.

Then, suddenly, life became real again. It took on a direct urgency which within a few hours threw the time she had spent in the copyright department into correct proportion. She knew then that what was little more than a long-drawn-out restless night's sleep must come to a sharp end. She was sitting half-way through one of the letters biting her nails and thinking that the formula was only one away from 'Grant we beseech thee, O Lord, permission to use two thousand five hundred words—' when she was called next door, to a room full of women, to answer a private telephone call on the outside line. As such calls were not encouraged she was already blushing when she lifted the receiver.

Jenny's 'Dah-ling' rang through the room. All the other women in it seemed to have reached a pause in their work. One rubbed out a word she had just typed, another sorted out some papers.

Mary said, 'What is it?'

'Something awful, darling.'

This could have meant that the gas had been switched off, or that Jennifer's current boy friend was quoted by the evening papers as out last night with Penelope Somebody-else. She knew, by Pink's telegraph, that is to say, not by some undiscovered sense, but by some undiscovered accuracy of the ear, that the news was dramatic and affected only her. Just as physical pain can be tolerated by the mind leaping a split-second ahead of the blow, she was balanced ready when it came.

Jennifer went on: 'D'you want this over the thing or shall I meet you for lunch?'

'Tell me.'

'Pink rang. He said I'd better tell you.'

'Daddy.'

'Yes. Look, he said he could cope and you must do what you want. Darling I'm so sorry.'

'I'll ring you back,' Mary said. She replaced the receiver softly and looked up at the four faces round her. All the women had assumed tragic expressions but they could not quite hide their delight that the morning's routine had been exploded.

She went without hesitation to a call-box to ring David, who sounded perfectly delighted to hear her.

'Look,' she said, 'Daddy's dead.'

'Lunch,' he replied.

'Yes, please.'

When she returned, the manager's permission for leave of absence had been granted. The conscientious young man stood by his desk like a very superior travel agent.

'He would like you to ring tomorrow or the next day telling him when you expect to return. I imagine you will be travelling north. I have looked up the trains for you.'

'That's very kind, Eric,' she said. 'But I think I'll go by plane.'

He blushed at the mention of his Christian name and when he shook her very firmly by the hand he could think of nothing better to say than 'Good luck.'

Other secretaries, hanging about the stairs of the ladies' cloakroom, resembled guests at the end of a wedding reception. They wished her good luck with their smiles and a few on more intimate terms said, 'It's more the shock than anything.' She nodded, and she could not say, 'To tell the truth I haven't given him a thought so please don't push me into a false position.' She was horrified by her own tears as she left the place and took a taxi to Bianchi's, where she went upstairs. David, for once, was not late.

'Excellent,' he said. 'We'll eat a great deal of pasta and send you north drunk.'

'I think that's a good idea.'

'Shall we pitch into the wine or have a strong one first?'

'Just wine.'

'You're an excellent girl. I've always said so.' He looked at her carefully and said without smiling:

'It's a shame we can't live together. No, it is.'

Soon after they got the carafe of wine, he said, 'Money,' and she nodded.

'I really don't see why I should underwrite you when you've got a husband and family quite wealthy enough to do so.'

'I do see why,' she replied.

'Air fare?'

'Yes. And three weeks for the flat.'

'You can borrow that from your firm. They'll advance it. Old established firms are famous for it. That's why they can pay their employees less than everybody else does.'

She said, 'I'm not coming back.'

'You're going back to Stephen?'

'I'm going back home, anyway. Whether he has me back or not.'

'Oh dear,' David said. 'I suppose that means twenty-five pounds.'

'You can easily afford it.'

'I know. I'm afraid I can. If you're very nice and cheerful all through lunch we'll go to a bank and get it in new notes.'

'Before three o'clock,' she said.

'You look fiercer,' he replied.

'Do I?'

'It's not unattractive, but I confess it frightens me a little. I believe you've become a tremendous career woman,' he said kindly. 'I'm told this at every corner. You must advise me on my publisher's contract. I must have an account of modern publishing methods.'

She said, 'Are you writing a book?'

'What's called a series of articles. I've done a great deal of work since we've parted.'

He noticed that she smiled a good deal less.

She said, 'Central Nervous System? Communication and Cats?' and he pushed the points of his fork into the table-cloth.

'Not exactly,' he said, and it was a confession. To slip into 'allied fields' is perhaps more suspect than not to work at all. He began to explain himself at length. He was writing the articles for an American journal called *Moral Philosophy*. 'No doubt,' he said, 'they will also be published in the serious German newspapers and the popular Dutch Press.'

'What about?'

'The obligatory scene.'

She ate patiently as he expanded on the subject.

He seemed to be glad to talk about it. Apart from the milkman (with whom he argued on the most intricate subjects) she thought he might have found few people with whom he could discuss the project. His fellow scientists and his intellectual friends would only have given him a wry look if he had admitted to working in a field so far away from neuro-physiology in which he had done all his important work. She seemed to be listening carefully as she smoked and finished her coffee.

He said, 'Can you imagine the playwright's chagrin, if he watched the curtain rise on the first night only to find that one of his principal characters had decided to skip the whole thing? But in real life, nothing could be more natural. That's the difference between life and drama, surely.'

That he might be talking sense was irrelevant. Mary watched him carefully and thought there is a change here, or else, up to now I have been blind. Even if it is correct, this is talk, only talk. It affects nothing.

David continued with enthusiasm. He talked as if he were dictating the paper to her.

'In ninety-nine cases out of a hundred the obligatory scene is never played. The people concerned so dislike the idea of a heavy emotional struggle that they walk off in different directions, one perhaps, rather faster than the other. They leave their problem, whatever it may be, in mid-air. In a year or two, or even a month or two, because it has been succeeded by so many others, equally acute, the situation disintegrates. The traces of it, by a tacit agreement between the parties, both of whom are now convinced that they are older and wiser, are felt, but socially ignored.'

Finishing her wine, she wondered if he were flirting with her: if this were a new beginning. But it was clearly nothing of the sort. He was not tasting the food, or noting the surroundings; not even very interested in her. He seemed to have escaped into words. She suddenly felt anxious for him, wondering what his friends and colleagues would make of him and say of him, if he continued to stick his head so firmly in the sand.

She said, 'If you believe this, what are you going to do about it?'

He looked mystified.

'Write it.'

'But in your own life?'

'Ah.' He smiled. 'I suppose logically, one should stop skipping things. This would be courageous, but I shouldn't think very rewarding. It would be a trial to one's friends and extremely distressing for one's elderly relations. One would be rather like those explosives which do the silly thing: they try and blast the wall where it resists them most. One would spend one's whole time bouncing from one ghastly scene to the next, in search of the obligatory.'

'Yes,' she said. 'David, it's half past two. D'you think we could go and cash that cheque?'

He frowned and wondered why he thought the request was a rebuke. Then he cheered up, pulled himself together and said:

'Excellent. Pay-up. What a nice lunch we've had.'

Standing rather vaguely, moving pound notes in and out of his wallet, he added, casually:

'I suppose we'll probably never see each other again. That's rather how life works.'

BOOK FOUR

The Wake

WHEN MORALS ARE no more, it's time for efficiency at any price, and women, beyond all things, are practical. Mary's own pregnancy, which she divulged to no one, made her more, not less, determined.

They buried the Colonel on a sunny winter's afternoon, in a new grave in a cemetery on a hill. All the men were there except Pink, who felt he could not leave the car, so Stephen took his cord. Pink's collapse, and the wintry sunlight streaming through bare trees, made the burial a more unnerving ceremony than usual. The moment of silence, afterwards, when all the men looked round like actors starved of words, was at last broken by the landlord of the Queen's, an expert at funerals who had slipped in to take Stephen's cord when Stephen had moved to the head. He said simply, 'I'd forgotten there was so much gravel in the sub-soil up this end,' and all the minds were diverted from the unseen figure in the box to the ground itself and to safety again.

After the wake, which in this part of Scotland is no more than tea and a whisky for the road, Mary got straight to work. Cathie, the maid or ex-maid, had been called down from her new house in the estate in the village but she was dressed as if for a queen's funeral, in indirect respect. Her condolences were brushed aside – and 'condolences' was Cathie's word. Mary, who was dressed neatly and smartly in a green suit, sat in the Colonel's place at the end of the long refectory table and Cathie took one of the chairs at the side. The table was still covered with dirty cups and glasses and spread with the sandwiches and cakes that were left over from the funeral tea.

With the hat and the pram and the house, for she had married John, the policeman, the thickening of the neck and the hardening of the hand, Cathie's very language had changed. She spoke now, aggressively, with little nods of the head. Her eyes were much fiercer. She said:

'It's many things that changed me, Mary. It's no joke being married, either way. But a Bobby's the Law and that affects everything. I get the side-long looks. And I'll tell you for why. Just because he's a good Bobby. That's it.'

Mary frowned. She asked, 'Do people object to him being strict?'

'I don't know, I'm sure,' Cathie said truculently. 'I'm not listening to what they're saying. They'll aye gossip about something, some of those. I'm not caring what they're saying.'

'You've got a child?'

Cathie looked at her sulkily.

'A-huh. Alan. Just a year old.'

Mary carefully avoided making the calculation.

'Have you brought him with you today?'

'No, John's looking after him. John's good with him.'

'I'd like to see him.'

Cathie stared at her for a moment, then she seemed to judge that Mary was sincere. She cocked her head to one side and said:

'He's wee, but he's tough. He's going to be a real tough guy, Alan.' Her pride and anger rose together. 'And he'll not be a policeman, I'm telling you that. It's no easy and I know fine. I'm a Bobby's girl and I married one, and you can take it and do what you like with it. They blame John for doing his job and he's no friends that way. They used to blame my father for not doing his job. The watch committee and that was always on to something.'

'Isn't John happy, then?'

'Would you be?' she asked. 'With no friends just to drink with; always that bit out of it, and parked in a wee place like this while there's others better at sucking up and nothing else, climbing up the scale in front of you? Would you? I can't see any man would.'

The difference in Cathie was extraordinary. She talked with one shoulder in front, her eyes filled with resentment.

She said, '*And* there's no money in it.'

'I thought the police were paid well.'

'Tchah!' she said. 'Maybe on paper it's all right and we get a Council house and all the rest of it. But there's boys over there with nothing in their heads at all makes twice and three times the money on the contracts, at the gravel, or up in the hydro-electric. There's others sitting by a petrol pump making more, and that's no' right. I know what they're saying about us, just because we got a television. It's the smallest screen and the longest payment and they all look at us. They watch with big eyes as the man puts the aerial up – Bob Mackintosh it was, and he makes a pile with his van on expenses and that. I came out the back of the house and I said it outright. I says "Why shouldn't we have one like the rest of them?" Why not?'

'Of course you should,' Mary said, like a much older woman, 'if you can afford it.'

'Exactly,' Cathie said, rising to her feet.

'How's John, in himself?'

'Aw,' said Cathie. 'It's ups and downs. I can't blame him. He gets awful moods of it. That's why I was anxious to get the television. He just sits sometimes hours on end, drinking his tea.'

There was the picture of life in the new house, with Cathie, now a bundle of practical energy and the big young man, with his elbows on his knees. Mary asked Cathie to sit down again and, with a glance at the clock, she obeyed. Mary said she would run her back in the car. When she offered her the job back Cathie said:

'It's no good me coming here if the others don't like it.'

'Don't worry about that.' Then, changing her voice with the subject, she asked, 'Are you not going to have another baby?'

Cathie smiled for the first time.

'Heavens alive,' she said. 'Give a lassie time. Alan's no' eighteen months yet.'

'Did you have a bad time with him?'

'No,' Cathie said. Her mind slipped back to the room in the house in Aberdeen which had been used as a still-room, before it was a hospital. 'It was a long time, but not bad.'

'Who was with you?'

'There were two at the end. A nice wee nurse was with me most of the time, but I think she knew less about it than me.' Cathie smiled.

'What did you talk about?'

'You're asking!'

'You can't remember?'

'I can fine,' Cathie said. 'Just as if it were yesterday. We talked about dogs. I said about Miss Ferguson, you know, your auntie that keeps all the poodles. "A hundred and nine?" she says; she was amazed. I remember that fine. In a kind of a way I remember it better than what comes after.'

Cathie had relaxed now, and at last she said:

'If you want to know I'm glad you're back, Mary. Never mind the job like, we've missed you. I have really; I've said often I've wished you were here.'

As Mary nodded and said. 'Thank you,' she realised that her eyes were filled with tears. She said:

'You're the first one to say it,' and the tears fell down her cheeks.

Cathie, putting the tears down to the Colonel's death, said:

'You've had an awful day of it.'

They both got up and after a moment or two Cathie insisted that she could make her own way back. She said again that Mary had had a day of it. Anyway, she went on, she wanted to get some bread on the way, for their tea. When Mary said she should take some from the kitchen Cathie cut her short. She said, with a frown, 'No thank you. We're not as poor as that.'

Mary showed her out of the house and coming out of the room they passed Macdonald. It was obvious to Mary that she had been listening at the door. She said rather grandly:

'Macdonald, Cathie will be starting again on Monday. She'll be working in the mornings and those afternoons which she can manage.'

'I'm glad, I'm sure,' said Macdonald flatly, and nodded to Cathie, who returned her look with one that was not far short of impudence.

They passed on, but when Mary returned to the dining-room, she closed the door behind her. Macdonald was putting the plates on a tray.

Mary said, 'I know you were listening.'

'I wasn't eavesdropping. As I passed by the door I couldn't help hearing something you said.'

'What?'

'I don't know what your intentions are, but if you want to keep a secret I should have thought you'd be best not to spill it to a young girl like Cathie.'

'I didn't tell her any secrets.'

'No? Well, that's all right then.'

Mary said, sharply, 'Two or three times in the last twenty-four hours you seemed to have been trying to insinuate something, Macdonald.'

'Oh yes? What's that?'

'I wish I knew,' Mary said. 'It's you who's being so mysterious.'

Macdonald said, 'Mary, we used to be very close.'

'I'm not sure what that's got to do with it.'

'I'm not curious. I'm here if you want me.' But she could not help adding, 'I'd have thought looking after you and your mother for near thirty years would make me someone better to turn to than an embittered wee girl like that.'

Mary was rather pink in the cheeks, She gathered up the plates swiftly, as if her hands were saying to Macdonald's, 'You're slow and laborious and boring.'

She used one of Pink's expressions. She said:

'It sounds to me as if you've picked up a fag end. I don't know what you heard.'

'I heard you ask her about Alan being born.'

'Yes, I did. I happen to think Cathie's had rather a rough time.'

'If you don't want to tell me, then I don't want to know—'

Mary said briskly:

'I really can't think what you're talking about, Macdonald. I suppose you're getting all Shetland and mystic. But I do hope you're not going to go ga-ga in your old age. That would be the last straw.'

'A-huh,' Macdonald said, continuing to clear the dishes. 'Lerwick's answer to Cassandra – whatever that may mean.'

The conversation then turned to Pink. Mary gripped the back of the chair at the end of the table as if to anchor herself. She poured herself some tea from the pot which was now cold.

'Did you find out what happened?'

'Yes.'

'Something did go wrong?'

'Yes,' Macdonald nodded. 'I don't know how you knew.'

'I saw him when we left and I saw him afterwards. I saw the boys gather round in here.'

'He didn't have anything to drink.'

'He had a lime juice and soda,' Mary said. 'That's odd enough. But I could have told without that.'

'You can read Pink,' Macdonald said, perhaps with envy. 'You can read him better than I can.' She waited a moment, then she went on, 'Will you not have milk in that tea?'

Mary shook her head.

'You used to have milk in your tea.'

'I don't now.'

'So I see. Mind, I can read you all right. We were always very close.' Macdonald seemed to be taking count of the number of cigarettes Mary smoked.

'Oh, for heaven's sake,' Mary said. 'Is it a crime for me to smoke?'

'No,' Macdonald said. She was standing in her usual place, in front of the fender, at the far side of the table from Mary. She added, 'I don't wonder you smoke.'

'Tell me what happened.'

'It was Wee Alec told me, out there by the cars, when I took him his dram. He told me the episode. Pink didn't manage it.'

Wee Alec was the young man with long hair and suède shoes who ran the Building, Contracting and Undertaker's business.

'Manage what?'

'You know, at the grave. D'you know what happens?'

Almost as if it were a fact of life, not of death, Mary looked down at the ashtray and said, 'I don't suppose I know all the details.'

Macdonald said, 'You've had nothing to eat.'

Quietly Mary replied, 'Go on.'

'They let it down with cords. It's Pink who should hold the main one, but he didn't manage.'

'At the grave-side?'

'Before that, so I gather.'

'Walking through the town?'

'No, he's all right then, walking well, looking straight ahead of him at a point above the flowers on the hearse. I saw him going off. He was fine then. It's when they got to the graveyard, out in the open like. Walking up there on the curve of the hill.'

'What did he do?'

'You know he's got this thing about open spaces now. They've got a name for it. The doctor said—.' She could not remember it. She continued, 'When he came away from the cars at the gate Wee Alec said he sort of panicked. Stephen's by him and he turns back to Peebles and Spud Davidson and some of the boys.'

'Then?'

'They come round him and he's dithering, kind of, Wee Alec said. Anyway, they take him back to the cars.' She paused and then added, 'But Stephen coped.'

Mary said, suddenly, 'You're fond of Stephen.'

Macdonald brought her feet together.

She said, 'Yes, Mary, I am. We all admire Stephen, the way he's kept a straight road. The day you went he was out in the fields until the gang knocked off; on the potatoes then. I think your father would be glad it's him, at the end.'

'He always said he was wet.'

'He's not wet. And your father didn't say things like that, at the end.'

Macdonald moved away and Mary began again.

She asked, 'Did Stephen see much of him?'

'To begin with, but not at the end. You wouldn't have recognised him at the end. The last three months he never saw anybody but myself.'

Mary wanted to ask, 'Why didn't somebody send for me?' but was afraid of 'He didn't ask'. She drank some more. Then Macdonald, seeing how weary she looked, said more softly:

'If you'd been here, you couldn't have done anything. There wasn't any hope. He knew that. But he changed, Mary—'

'You must tell me some day,' Mary said, coolly, and Macdonald looked angry.

'I will, some day.'

'I'm sorry. I didn't mean it like that.'

Macdonald did not reply.

'– I promise I didn't. We really all rely on you. I don't know how you managed.'

But Macdonald was not friendly.

'It was useful I'm big, after all. I had to carry him, in the bedroom, like. He never came downstairs again. I lived the two lives, one here and the other up with him. He moved into your mother's room. He was thin, too, when he went.'

'And not quite white,' Mary said. 'And aged about twenty; I saw.'

Then stubbing out her cigarette she went on:

'It's curious, isn't it, how women know nothing about burials. These cords and things.'

'Only hearsay,' Macdonald replied steadily. 'But we know quite a lot about birth.'

Mary felt the colour rising in her cheeks. Her arm was outstretched, reaching to the ashtray, and she let it rest for a moment, deciding whether she should take up the remark. But the decision was postponed because Pink came in.

He looked shiny. His hair was wet and smoothed down. He advanced rather hesitantly, and then as if he were speaking of a dinner party or a wedding reception he said:

'It seemed to go off all right.' He nodded at the table. 'Jolly good tea.' He congratulated Macdonald with a cock of his head.

Mary looked at him curiously and asked:

'Have you had a bath?'

'Sorry?'

He had taken, lately, to prefacing most of his replies like this, as if he had not quite heard what was said. It gave people the impression that his mind was always occupied elsewhere; that he knew no rest.

'Not a bit of it. Just a wash and brush up.'

'I suppose Stephen's down at the farm,' Macdonald said.

'Trust old Stiffy,' Pink winked. 'He never misses a day.'

Pink did not fail to notice the edge in Mary's voice. She

spoke as if she disliked him. She did not look him in the eye as she asked:

'Why didn't you go with him?'

'Not really an awful lot of point.'

Macdonald came to his rescue.

She said, 'Stephen's the farmer now. They've got it all organised.'

'Then what on earth does Pink do?' Mary asked across his face.

'Sales, promotion of same; market,' Pink replied.

Mary almost snorted.

'Does Stephen do the dairy too, then?'

Macdonald said nothing and Pink, with an old technique of his, instead of saying, 'Well, yes he does,' said with enthusiasm:

'Absolutely, he's a bloody marvel at it.'

'I see.'

'Pink looks after the personnel,' Macdonald said, charitably.

'That's it,' Pink said. 'Sort out their lives for them and that sort of thing.'

Mary said suddenly, 'What have you been doing then?'

'Just now?'

'The others left an hour ago.'

'I say,' Pink said, moving his head sideways and looking at her from another angle, but she did not relax. 'To tell the truth, chaps, I felt a bit lonely, so I wandered in here.'

Quickly sensing that the appeal had failed, he then added, 'But if you want a time and motion study—.' He paused, and moved his mouth as he searched for his next phrase. He, too, had begun to talk as if he disliked Mary.

'Then may I inform you that I have just finished rather a tricky interview with one of our ex-employees?'

'Who's that?' Macdonald asked.

Pink nodded mysteriously, and lit a cigarette. She mentioned the name of an Italian, ex-prisoner of war, whom

Stephen had felt forced to have sacked. But Pink shook his head.

'Dairy and domestic,' he said at last.

'Cathie?'

'Our Cathie,' Pink agreed.

'Mary's given her the job back.'

Pink nodded but he had not listened. 'Tail very much between the legs,' he said unpleasantly. 'I sent her packing.'

It was as if Chuff-chuff had been made a prefect on the death of the old head-master, and turned out to be rather a bully.

Mary said, 'I absolutely demand that you bring back Cathie here.'

'She's gone now, old girl.'

'Look, old girl,' Pink said. 'Economics. We can't afford to pay chaps to come here for a couple of hours – agricultural rates, mind you, oh yes – and then hoof it back to their husbands with a basket full of ham and eggs.'

Macdonald moved. She said:

'He's right enough, Mary. She wasn't doing much good after she was married.'

'If I'm going to stay we'll need somebody else in the house.'

Macdonald contained her surprise.

'Are you thinking of staying?' she asked slowly.

'I may.'

'Sorry,' Pink said. 'The whole thing was thoroughly discussed by the old sub-committee – Macdonald and Stiffy and me.' He smiled. Then said cheerfully, 'Ramsbottom and Enoch and me. Before your time. I suppose.' He put some soda-water in another lime juice and opened his throat. He poured the tumblerful down in one gulp.

Mary said, 'Please go and fetch her back, Macdonald, and tell her my word goes in this.'

'Look, old thing,' Pink said. 'You don't know much about it.'

'I'm not interfering in the farm. Who comes here to help in the house is my business.'

'She's dishonest. She blatantly admitted it.'

'Then she's not dishonest.'

'Oh, come off it, Mary—'

'Please, Macdonald—'

Macdonald hesitated, then moved to the door. Mary's shoulders dropped an inch.

She said, more calmly, 'Do exactly as I say, please.'

'A-huh,' Macdonald said truculently, and when she left the room, Pink said:

'You're playing a bit senior, aren't you?'

'No.'

He said, 'I don't get it at all. Standing there, with all your jacket buttons done up. I don't twig.'

She said quietly, 'Pink, I heard about what happened this afternoon.'

Pink said cheerfully, 'Fair enough. Pink let the party down.'

'I didn't say that.'

'There was a young fellow called Pink,' Pink went on bitterly, with his fattest smile, and she lowered her eyes.

Who did nothing but stutter and blink,
When they lowered his Dad,
He made off with the lads
To the clubs and the pubs, for a drink.

Possibly he had spent the reception thinking that one out; but not necessarily. He was capable of defending himself with astonishing speed. When she said, 'I noticed you weren't drinking,' he replied, with a big nod:

'All right then. "There was a poor fellow called Pink, Who took buckets of Gordons to drink".'

He thought for a second, but before he continued, Mary said, 'Shut up.'

Pink stretched his neck.

'Pity,' he said, speaking of their whole relationship. 'These things happen.'

'Pink, I promise I'm trying to help.'

'Then give us a limerick,' he said.

She replied, 'Maybe you'd like to go and see how Stephen is. He looks awfully tired. I'm sure he overworks. Maybe you could help him.'

Pink's face swelled up and then seemed to break into a thousand pieces. There was a loud wheezing sound, and for a moment Mary thought he was going to cry. But he changed from the music-hall comedian, laughing at his own last joke, into a prisoner with a phlegmy cough. Then he straightened up.

'Poor old Mary,' he said. 'Quite right!' in a sing-song voice. 'Quite right. Busy hands. Think of the other fellow.'

'Pink—'

He raised his hand. 'All right, Sister. I'll go quietly.'

As he left the room he sang gaily, 'For I'm Popeye the sailor man.' Then suddenly and savagely he slammed the door behind him. The pictures on the wall of shipwrecks and Fergusons shuddered, for a moment, then all was quiet. Ten minutes later, Mary made up her mind.

TWENTY

OCTOBER HAD BEEN fine, but the first week in November had brought rain, and the steadings were muddy. She therefore wore her gumboots which were lying by the sink in the back scullery, exactly where she had left them, over a year before. It was dark already, and cold enough for her to put on her sheepskin coat.

Four or five minutes later she appeared in the band of bright light outside the dairy. She exchanged a few words with one of the men who were loading the van. He pointed inside, and she nodded her thanks. With her fingers but not her hands in her pockets, she disappeared into the dairy.

Changes had come fast. There were many signs of heavy new capital investment. There was a new bottling machine. Before there had been a circular affair holding about eight bottles which had to be put in place by hand. They were shifted automatically now, in a continuous process, and the cows, too, poor things, had been 'time and motion' studied. They were not milked in their own stalls any more. They came in at one end of a special milking byre, which held three or four at a time, and went out the other. They had been milked by machine before, but now the milk was weighed and tested straight away. It ran directly to a larger tank which fed the bottling machine. Stephen had not wasted his year.

But the noise in the dairy, and then the smell in the byres, never changed. The clatter of bottles and the throb of the machines made talk impossible but Mary waved back to one of the girls who recognised her and shouted a greeting.

The other girls looked at her oddly, as if she were some sort of actress dressed for a Technicolor serial, that had strayed on to the wrong set.

Stephen, at work, looked much more the factory manager than the farmer. He was still in his grey suit and black tie, but in gumboots too, and he was showing some visiting farmers round the byre. They turned out to be New Zealanders, staying for a week or two in Scotland. They were narrow men, one with thick smooth grey hair. But for their accents and odd manners, as if they had pins and needles in their feet and backs, they looked like a couple of Cavalry officers. Stephen, very calmly, broke off his lecture to introduce them to his wife. As soon as they had said 'How-do-you-do' (although they both avoided the actual expression of 'How-do-you-do' as if it stank of 'actually' and all the other gong words) Stephen continued his talk on the process. Even the feeding was rationalised, if not mechanised, now. In the byre, a little further away from the din of the dairy machines, Stephen still had to raise his voice. The visitors stood nodding and pouting, demonstrating that they were impressed. One of them often looked at Mary who was watching a hose, held by a dark young boy, as it played between the stalls at the other end of the byre that held a hundred cows. A couple of bulls were in their places in the last row, safely chained, separate from the cows who were ambling, in threes and fours, to their stalls. Above each place, marked in white chalk on a little blackboard, was the name of the cow. They had the same fascination as racehorses' names, historical, topical and private. 'Soraya, Mary IV, Greta, Hilary, Margaret Rose, Lolita, Kirsty . . .' Most of the cows were in their places at this time; they had been washed and milked and now they found some turnips in their troughs. The shed looked busy and colourful. But in the early hours of the morning when they were turned out to the fields the byre looked like an illogical penitentiary, all concrete and metal, bathed in thirty arcs of direct white light.

At last Stephen parted from his visitors and he came back to find Mary in the corner where he had left her. She watched him as he came. He passed some cows as if they were people in whom he had no interest, dawdling about in an Underground. He shoo'ed out a dog that had strayed into the byre. But then Stephen, who was shaping up to be one of the best dairy farmers in the country, disliked all animals and was not particularly fond of the outside life.

He approached her with the same smile and in the same bright, slightly official manner that he would have, had she dropped into the byre a year before. He approached her as he had the New Zealand farmers. It was a sort of works manner, developed by a manager who was not absolutely confident of himself, but was certain that he knew more of what was going on around here than anybody else. His manner somehow betrayed that he had no capital interest in the place and his first words to Mary were, 'Have you come to take a look how I'm mis-spending the family's money?' said, may it be added, with the confidence of a man who knew he had spent every penny of it well. As he explained to her, without her asking, some of the improvements he still wanted to make, asking, in an oblique sort of way, for her support where he needed no support, because Pink could sign the cheques, she said, suddenly:

'I don't suppose I ever would have married you, had I never seen you at work, and had I only seen you at work, I don't suppose I ever would have left.'

He quite ignored the remark. But she was right. It was not only a question of his decision and authority here. There was a social factor too. Such things as the fastidiousness of his dress, the over-perfection of his Highland dancing, even the care with which he mixed a cocktail for Pink and her, had an uneasiness. Only here, of all places, in the cowshed, and perhaps in the office too, did he have any social confidence because it was here, alone, that he lost his self-consciousness. It was impossible for her to talk to him here, but by a dart of the eyes it was obvious that she knew she would get more out of him on his own ground. She therefore guided him carefully and as they strolled through the comparative quiet and complete privacy of the calf house, a wooden building just a few yards outside one of the side doors of the byre, she led the conversation away from those words which only farmers recognise as agricultural: cost, margin, return on your money, subsidy, loan, rate of interest, plough back, overhead, turnover and acres enough.

There were eight calves, in open boxes, the youngest ones trembling where they stood, and Mary leant over the first gate and let the calf suck her four fingers. The shed was lit by two unshaded bulbs which threw double shadows on the walls, on the straw and the roof. Although Stephen had plans for a new shed, Mary, who was usually quite unsentimental about the farm and the animals in it, was glad that it had not changed. It smelt the same; more powerfully and much more sharply than the main byre.

She said, when at last he paused, 'You're going to be furious with me.'

'Oh yes?' He was a little nervous.

She smiled and said, 'It's nothing too awful.'

'You'd better own up.'

She did not see how much pain she had already inflicted. By her friendliness, more than by her breathtaking beauty, for in her own country, it was nothing short of that; by her smile alone, she had brought back the months when Stephen had the promise of her love, and the hope, not the task of its satisfaction. Not by a flicker of an eyelid did he give this away.

She said, 'I've re-employed one of your ex-employees without reference to the sub-committee.'

'Oh God,' he said. 'I know. Cathie?'

'I couldn't help it, Stephen.'

'You know she got into the habit of lifting half the housekeeping home?'

'Yes. But I think she feels she deserved it. Anyway it wasn't for herself. It was for her John and her Alan.'

'He's a dreadful little child.' Stephen had grown to the habit of thinking of the employees' children much as he thought of the animals: necessary evils.

'Why?'

'He slobbers,' Stephen said. The curious thing was that when Stephen was truly negative, in the sense of being totally cynical rather than simply without hope, he had a certain rather humorous charm.

She said meekly, 'Anyway I've done it. I think Pink was rather cruel to her.'

He too leant over the stall but only to give the calf a long, uncompromising stare.

Then he said, 'I'm not in the least surprised to hear that. Why anybody ever calls Pink unreliable I cannot fathom. He's the most predictable man that I know.'

He moved to look at the next calf, and went on:

'Pink's got too much conscience to look someone in the face after he's done them a bad turn—'

'Don't say that,' she replied.

Stephen misunderstood. He raised his eyebrows, he said:

'True enough. He refused her. So she went away and married the Bobby.'

'I mean about looking people in the face.'

Stephen had obviously feared the moment when they would leave other people's problems to talk about themselves. It was not a step he would willingly ever have taken. Eight months of work from dawn to dusk had almost seen him sane again. In the last five months he had been, he believed, as happy as he would ever be again. She was now looking him full in the face.

'You seem to manage,' he said.

She replied, 'It doesn't mean I haven't got a conscience.'

He said, in a sensible sort of tone:

'I told you at the time, or tried to, not to blame yourself. It was less your fault than you imagine.'

'In which case you can't have much of a conscience. You manage to look me in the face.'

He smiled slowly and said:

'That's my Boy Scout's training. Patrol Leader of the Bull's Patrol; hardly appropriate,' he added. 'I've got the firmest handshake north of the border. It's a question of interview technique. Those New Zealand gentlemen are still sorting out their knuckles.'

She laughed and he went on, excited by her laughter. 'I could stare out John Knox, and wouldn't mind having a try.' Then suddenly, he did not say, so much as hear himself say, 'It is also because it's a long time since I've seen your face.'

If it had not been plotted before, it was now that the intention formed hard in Mary's mind. It was so clear to her and seemed to be so necessary to her that she feared her anxiety might show in her face. She turned away and moved down to the smallest calf at the end of the row, perhaps with what she hoped would look like modesty. Then she turned her face back towards him and asked, quite loudly, 'Has my face changed?'

When he said, 'Yes, I think it has,' and followed it quickly, in a low, dry voice with, 'It's more beautiful, not less,' she frowned and turned back to the calf. She shook her head.

He said, 'I don't imagine you want or need compliments from me.'

'Stephen, I'm rather frightened. Would you mind if I stayed on for a little? At home.'

'Of course not,' he said. 'Anyway, it's your home, not mine.'

'Why am I frightened?'

Stephen replied sensibly, in a low matter-of-fact sort of voice:

'I don't think you are frightened. You're nervous. Death's unnerving, anyway.' He did not look at her.

Calmly, not really thinking what he was saying, he went on:

'You just don't know whether to take the plunge or stay at home.' Then he said quietly, 'I know you've left David,' and it startled her, because somehow she was certain that he knew nothing of her year away. One of the calves began to moan and she went across to it, as she asked:

'How did you know?'

Stephen said, 'I told you. Pink's a completely reliable character. I think I know everything you've done, while you've been away.'

She paused and calculated, then her shoulders dropped. Calmly she said:

'I left of my own accord. It didn't last very long, you know.'

'I thought you said he'd seen you to the air terminal.'

'Yes, he did. We're quite friendly. But I've been on my own for a while.'

He stood up straight and banged the little gate on the stall.

'I know this job now. It wouldn't be very difficult for me to get a place elsewhere: maybe a better job. I've been asked more than once. If you want to come home for ever, say the word and I'll make the arrangements.'

'No, don't be so silly, I wouldn't think of it. I didn't mean that, I promise. I meant something else, Stephen. I meant would it matter if I stayed here with you?'

'Darling,' Stephen rested his head on his hand. 'You're not using your brain, or your eyes.' He looked straight at the calf's back as he went on. 'I love you. Even if I've never been able to show it very much, that happens to be true. It wouldn't be possible for you to live your own life with my sheep's eyes following—'

Then she said it in one breath. 'I didn't mean to live my own life. I meant to come back to you.'

'No. After David,' Stephen said, 'after all that you couldn't be happy for long—'

'Yes, I could. I would be, I swear. I know it. If you didn't want me in bed, it wouldn't matter.'

Stephen wagged his head from side to side.

'It wouldn't, darling,' she insisted. 'I haven't come back for that. I don't expect a miracle. I've no right to come back, but I want to very much.'

He would not turn to her.

She said, 'Believe me, I'm tired of all the whipped-up passion. I promise I am. Please, Steve. It wouldn't be like last time. Really it wouldn't. Don't worry about that. I expect nothing.'

He kept his hands covering his face.

She said, 'Everybody's told me how wonderful you've been. You say you're not particularly clever and look what you've done here. You said you were a coward and that's not true either. I did my best to ruin your life and you didn't let it be ruined.'

Stephen was pressing his eyes very hard, as if they were painful. He was like a school hero, appearing from the headmaster's study, determined not to cry.

He said, 'Let's get out of here,' and moved out of the shed into the dark. Just outside, there was a pile of coke for the boiler that heated the shed, and it crunched under their feet. The noise of the dairy machines sounded far away.

Outside, Mary stopped and leant back on the door. She suddenly said, guided by infallible instinct:

'I'm here, in the dark, by the door. My eyes are closed.'

He was trembling very badly when his hands first touched her face. His fingers passed all over it, for he too had closed his eyes. Soon he brought his hands down to her arms and, leaning forward, he lowered his head until it rested on the wool in the lapel of her coat. She brought one hand up and held the nape of his neck, and as he wept she said: 'Don't, whatever you do, be ashamed.'

She stroked his hair softly and as she said again, 'Don't be ashamed. Don't be sad, I'm back,' she opened her eyes. To one side was the dark shoulder of the byre, to the other the huge skeleton of the open hay loft. Behind, the cars' lights followed each other up the main road, past the bothie. Above that, the woods, and higher still the Pole star. It was Stephen who at last broke the silence. He squeezed her arms and looked at her. He kissed her firmly and quickly on the lips, saying:

'It will be all right?'

Mary nodded.

'Of course it will,' he said.

'Yes,' she replied, almost absently, and she let him slip back a little. She looked at him curiously as if she had never seen his face before. He was smiling and he took out a huge clean handkerchief to dry his cheeks. She looked very perfect, pale and cold.

He said, 'I've done some batty things.'

'Such as?'

He whispered, 'I got them to chop down our damned silly monkey puzzle tree.' He had carved their initials on it, before he had even proposed to her.

'You didn't,' she exclaimed, in a sudden lively voice, and she began to move away. Their feet crunched over the dross and coke until they came back to the muddy track: a track which Stephen was going to improve.

Still talking of the monkey puzzle, he said:

'I didn't know you'd come back.'

She gave him her hand and rather cheerfully, she said: 'Poor Steve, what else, batty?'

'I read Gibbon's *Decline and Fall* from cover to cover.'

The thought of it made him say 'God help me!' and laugh at himself, and an instant later she laughed too.

She said quickly, 'Oh dear, you must have been upset.'

'And you?'

'Batty things.'

'Weren't you happy?'

'No. Then I didn't really expect to be. I wasn't in love for very long.'

White lying has a curious, curving effect on how things are said. The words run smoothly together and the voice rises or falls at a different place.

'. . . I think for a little longer than he was. That's never very nice.'

It occurred to her that even if she were making up this story, there was no language to explain what happened with David.

'After David?'

'After David? Well, I shared a girlish flat. I got a job too.'

'Publishing.'

'That's what I liked to tell people. It was filing and copy-typing. Not much else.'

'And men?'

'After David?' Coolly, 'None, darling.' She paused, then excitedly she said, 'Oh yes, one. My boss in the office. My very own big white chief,' and she gave a description of Eric, her boss. Stephen said:

'He sounds very nice.'

Stephen did not know much about lying. He did not know that when a Customs man hears a girl say with a laugh, 'Well, I've got a horrible jar for me Mum,' in just the same sort of facetious voice, he knows there is also something else.

'No one really,' she said. 'Except the odd friend of David's being kind and standing me lunch.'

He clasped her hand very tightly and said:

'Darling, it will be all right, it will be all right.'

Again with a coldness, almost a brittleness, she laughed and said, 'Scout's grip.'

But he was talking very seriously. He said:

'It'll probably be as miserable as before, but you won't have to copy-type.'

She stopped and shook her head. They were at the edge of the pool of light that came from the dairy. She said:

'I don't expect miracles. You mustn't either.'

'I never have done,' he replied honestly.

'Dig my down-beat man,' she said, and was surprised this time by her own voice. Trying to find herself again, she said more steadily:

'There's a sort of hopeful pessimism, isn't there, that's you? It's better, I think, than poor Pink's hopeless optimism.'

'Saner,' he said, and she nodded as though she were learning things.

Then, suddenly, she reached for his hand again and she was glad to hold it. It was cold. In this fashion they picked their way back through the puddles which reflected the dairy lights, until they came to the house.

Stephen was quite childishly excited about the reunion and he went through the sitting-room to tell Macdonald and Pink the news. Mary, who was altogether more apprehensive, remained in the kitchen where she was joined, a few moments later, by Pink, who was struggling into his duffle coat. He wore a pork-pie hat, poised on the top of his small head.

Mary was by the Aga. She was preparing, or at least pretending to prepare, some supper. She said, 'You've heard?'

'Sorry, old girl?'

'Stephen's told you.'

'Not my business, old girl.' He shook his head and said with an infuriating smile and little bow:

'Some of us mind our own business, Miss Popham.'

'Aren't you glad?'

Pink said, 'I wish you every happiness in your life

together. But as a matter of fact, old thing, it won't have much to do with Pink. Oh no. I'm expecting a most important letter. Canada, as a matter of fact. Oyez, oyez. You can ring those bells.'

He checked his fly buttons then pushed his feet into an enormous pair of flying boots. 'There's a nip in the air,' he said happily. And then he laughed a noiseless laugh which shook him, and pointed one finger in the air. He raised his eyebrows and cocked his head to one side as he said, 'And high above, a long piercing note . . .'

'Pink, darling,' she said, much more softly. 'You're not going out, tonight?'

Pink pushed back his head and again raised an eyebrow. He spoke with undisguised hostility.

'Does a chap have to sign out, now, eh?'

She shook her head. She said, 'I mean, I want you to stay.'

'Sorry, old thing. Just a bit late.'

'You're huffing.' It was the first thing she said which penetrated, because it was about the only thing she had said since she had returned which was couched in their own language.

'Me, old girl? Not a bit.'

'You were, earlier. Sitting staring into nothing. All that.'

'No.' He shook his head. He would not acknowledge the corners of her mouth which were ready, whenever he was, to break into a smile. 'Not a bit,' he said again.

He nodded and leaned towards her, using his most confidential tone.

'I don't know if I should say it, but I'll tell you the truth, old love. I don't feel bad at all. Pink feels a lot better.'

She looked at him oddly and he nodded again.

He said, 'I don't want to be hard. Of course he was a tragic character and that, our mutual friend, but I'd be fibbing if I didn't say it was a load off my mind.'

'Of course it's a relief,' Mary replied warily. 'If it had to happen—' and Pink waved that aside with his hand.

'It's a relief,' he said. 'Better this way: all that stuff. Baa!' He bleated like a lamb. 'It's the truth. You can like it or lump it. Now he's gone I feel a sight better. Better already. Stevie and I've got the old place ticking over – mainly Stevie, I grant you, oh yes – Well—' He splayed out his hands. 'Things aren't at all bad, you know. Matter of fact we never had it so good, like the gentleman said. Things are looking up.'

'Go out tomorrow,' she said. 'Stay at home and cheer us up tonight.'

'Not actually poss.'

'You're not going down to the steadings, are you?'

'No. Not actually the plan.'

'Well then, where?'

'Questions! Power!' Pink suddenly exclaimed, violently. 'Macdonald's asked me all this. Women! Power!' he said again. ' "Num" questions. You're not going out, *are* you? When will you be back? Who with?' Pink smiled. 'Dear little things,' he said, very quietly. 'Gorgeous sweet charms.'

When Mary began, 'Are you going into . . . ?' he interrupted at once.

'As a matter of fact I am. Anything I can do for you there?'

'No.' She shook her head. She said, 'Peter Forbes, and Peebles and Blue Boy and that crowd?'

'It's Saturday night,' Pink replied.

'The Queen's? Pink, you can't. No, honestly you can't. Not the very same night.'

'Why not? Eh? Private party. Private room.'

'Even then—'

'Now,' Pink warned, 'don't play the heavy with old Pink. What's the alternative, Pink asks? Sitting through there watching TV, or sloping off to my own fart-sack half an hour after the scoff?'

'Just tonight,' she said. 'We could talk.'

'Windy?' he said, looking at her.

'It would be nice.'

'Maudlin,' he replied with a shake of his head. 'Well rowed, maudlin. It would be maudlin talk. But don't get me wrong, old duck, there's no question of a fellow getting high. Peter said it. Wee Forbes. He said, "Now, Pinkie, we've been there every Saturday night for years, now, and Sir Henry'd be the last to stop us, I'm sure. He'd want us to carry on, and that's just what I votes we do." No drunkenness, no singing. No sobbing.'

'It sounds a bit boring,' Mary said.

'Just chums getting together in the quietest possible way.'

Mary knew nothing would shift him. She nodded and said, 'Don't be too late,' and he turned by the scullery door.

'Don't you worry your pretty little head. Not about anything. We've got it all tee'd up, Stiffy and I. I tell you, this is something really different. Sad and that, but I feel a new man. It's going to be a great ranch, little girl, a great ranch. You ask Steve.'

She nodded.

'Oh, yes it is,' he cried, slapping the pork-pie further on to his head. Just before he left he said, as much to himself as to her:

'And great ranches need great men, eh? Chin up. See you, angel-bum.'

Mary was still standing watching the spot from where he had vanished when the kitchen door opened again.

Macdonald came in. Seeing Mary, she stopped for a second, then walked across the room, keeping to the far side of the big kitchen table. She said:

'I think it's wicked. I'm not saying more or less than that.'

THE SAME FALSE quality which had been in Mary's voice when she had said to Stephen outside the dairy, 'Dig my down-beat man', and 'My very own big white chief', often came into play in the days that followed. Pink must have noticed it, because it was the sort of thing he recognised before anybody else, but if he did hear it, he made no comment because he, on the other hand, was far too involved with the Pink problems. He seemed to want to make it quite clear that he was suffering great mental anguish and presented them each meal and each evening with all the physical clues. He assumed an air of ferret-like rather than poetic distraction, rushing at his food then staring blankly out of the window for ten minutes at a time. He counted the cigarettes in his packet most times when he took one and when he was not drinking lime juice and soda he often rushed to the kitchen and grabbed a lemon. This he would eat like a monkey, biting at it savagely and sucking out the juice. Whenever he went to the village or as far as Forfar or Perth, Coupar or Aberdeen, he brought back another couple of bottles of lime juice, a dozen lemons, fifty or sixty cigarettes, the odd cigarette holder, and on one occasion, a clay pipe. He was both secretive and careless. He never mentioned these buying sprees but never failed to leave the objects where they might be found by one of the others. He seemed to enjoy his food very much, but after the heartiest meal he always stuffed in a few vitamins in pill form. He was growing rather paler in the face as he now never ventured out of the house, except in the car. He was also growing fatter. Most of the time he wore too many clothes, and his brow was usually covered with a gleaming surface of sweat, which he mopped from time to time with one of several handkerchiefs he carried, 'just in case, old chum'. Because he was also consuming a large number of Amplex pills and making profligate use of every deodorant on the market, Mary said that she was sure he was drinking. But this was not true, at the time. He was just wildly worried that he stank like a polecat. Once or twice a week a huge parcel would arrive from Trumper's packed with lotions, spirits and eau-de-Cologne. Where all the bottles went was a mystery which none could solve. But the annoying thing for them all was that when they tried to help him he denied stoutly that anything was the matter.

'Old bird, I don't know what you're talking about. Never felt better. Don't I look too good, then?'

He said this to Mary one afternoon when she returned from a walk round the farm with Stephen. She had found Pink at four o'clock in the afternoon, fast asleep in the nursing chair.

She replied, 'Pink, I can't be expected to help you unless you tell me.'

Just then the telephone rang and Pink rolled across the room to it. He landed with a thump in the desk chair and, picking up the receiver, said in the quiet, slightly sapsy voice of a gentleman publican:

'Farm house here, Sir Charles speaking.'

As usual, it was somebody complaining about an error in the local milk delivery. Pink called her Madam, and patiently noted down her requirements.

Still prissily he said:

'In point of fact, delivery isn't my particular pigeon but I quite understand your distress. It shall be seen to immediately. Your cream, Madam, will be at your door by 17.50 hours this evening. There's a van goes to the station at that time. Thank-you!'

He replaced the receiver and made a note. His hand-writing was wilder than usual.

Mary said, 'I never knew a van went to the station at six.'

Pink said, 'You don't know everything, chumbo, oh no!'

She asked who was driving it. The usual milk van would be at the dairy at that time.

'Service,' said Pink. 'I shall drive it myself.'

'But, Pink, that's terribly inefficient. You can't drive ten miles just to deliver a quarter of a pint of cream.'

'Service,' said Pink again. 'It counts.'

He rang the dairy and, mock military now, instructed one of the girls, at that time due for one of the few breaks she had during the long day, to deliver to the house, without a moment's delay, one quarter-pint carton of single cream. When he put down the receiver he sighed, took up the pencil and ticked the note he had made.

Then suddenly, in his sulkiest tones, he said:

'You two are all right, so it would seem. I'm surprised you even notice me about the place.'

But Mary had lived too long with him to accept jealousy as the cause of his uneasiness. That he was pretending to himself, just as his mother might have done, long before, that people did not show him the love due to him, was perfectly likely, but Mary was not deceived. The change had come over him not when she made it up with Stephen, but when the Colonel died. His father's death had had the opposite effect of what he himself had anticipated. He thought his disappearance would leave him free to live and he had found, in a curious way, that it had left him free to stop trying altogether. But he did not confess this to Mary.

She said, 'If you're not going to help yourself, there's not much I can do. If I were you I'd ring up and say that cream won't go until tomorrow.'

When the door closed behind her Pink sat for a while, doodling on the note-pad. In truth he did not know what he wanted, and in this he was much like that poor pigeon, his mother. He just expected more of life; that one day, something would happen that would make it all better. He was reduced, he knew, to believing in a miracle, and vitamin pills, foreign travel, deep sleep, even shock therapy, about which he knew an unhealthy amount, occurred to him as the possible forms which that miracle might take. He sometimes put his hand to his ear, and as it was now his habit to avoid the word God, he would say, with a horrible laugh:

'Moo, I hear thee not!'

And when, at last, it happened, Macdonald was there, on the landing, in the middle of the night. Instinct had kept her awake, and the sound of voices, rising, brought her from her bed.

She stood, breathing very quietly, just outside Stephen and Mary's bedroom door. The lights were on within and a shadow flitted across the bar of light at the bottom of their door. A moment later there was the noise of somebody crying, and expecting it to be Stephen, Macdonald was at first unnerved by the noise, which was pitched high. Only as it continued, and as it was broken now and then by the repetition of a single phrase, did she realise that it was Mary's voice. The noise of the anguish of frustration, as any gaoler, as any nurse or nannie knows, when it reaches the extreme, loses identity. It becomes a note on its own, disembodied, and profoundly alarming. It is a note that passion never reaches, even if, for obvious reasons, it is close to the note of that dream of passion that sometimes rings in the ears. Hearing its wail, Macdonald stood very still, listening for the sound of movement or of another voice, below it. The final exchange between Mary and Stephen, as Macdonald might have guessed, was merely childish reiteration. At first with frenzy and then hollowly Stephen said many times, 'I can't.' The words that Mary was still repeating from time to time, as Macdonald heard only indistinctly, were simply, 'You must.'

Macdonald stood back as Stephen came out: things were quieter by then. She did not try to hide and Stephen said nothing to her, in explanation. He neither ignored her presence nor acknowledged it. It was as if he had passed her on the landing, at any time, as she walked from the bathroom back to her room. For some reason, rather absent-mindedly, he unhooked and closed the nursery gate at the top of the stairs, as if to complete his dissociation from an unbearable, carnal mess. Then he disappeared into the darkness of the hall and corridor below.

Macdonald, without hesitation, as soon as he had gone, pushed open the bedroom door and went in. The picture that was presented to her more than confirmed the situation. It showed, in agonising detail, the story of the preceding hour.

Mary had stopped crying. She was on the single bed farthest from the door and the near bed had not been disturbed. She lay on the flat of her back watching the shadows on the ceiling which were cast by her elbows, arms and interlocked fingers, held above her head. The sheet was lemon, not white, and it matched the paintwork in the room. This, and the darker tone of the wallpaper, affected the quality of the light. It was both yellow and bright although it came from only a single bedside lamp, which had been placed on the floor between the beds and partly covered by Stephen's woollen shirt. The bed clothes of the bed on which she lay had been stripped off and hung over the bottom of it. There were usually two pillows. One lay on the counterpane on the other bed. The other did not rest under Mary's head, but under her hips. Her red hair looked extremely untidy and long and her body looked thin and white. She was not quite naked, as she had chosen to wear a pair of very dark stockings which Macdonald had not seen before. She did not seem to object very strongly to Macdonald's entrance, which showed that, in her mind at least, Macdonald was still considerably more the servant than the mother; but as Macdonald approached she lowered her arms slowly and covered her eyes with the backs of her hands, her fingers still interlocked. It was all there, but for the Vibro.

From the look of distaste on Macdonald's face Mary might have thought that she was going to forget her usual infuriatingly steady manner, but this did not happen. After one short glance at the slight, anonymous body, Macdonald moved to the cupboard in the corner and unhooked Mary's winter dressing-grown. She picked up her bedroom slippers and moved across the room. By then, Mary had slipped her legs round, and was sitting at the edge of the bed pushing her hair from her face. Macdonald bent down and put the slippers on her feet, then helped her into her dressing-gown.

As Macdonald tied the cord tightly round her waist Mary expected her to say, at the very best:

'Either you're going down these stairs, or I am.'

She turned round and looked up at the huge white face. The cheekbones looked as big as ribs. She felt a little afraid, and it showed in her eyes.

'Away you go, now,' Macdonald said very softly. 'Away downstairs, and tell him the truth. It's a game of consequences, so it is.'

Mary nodded gratefully. Before she had even left the room Macdonald had put the lamp back in its place and started to make the bed.

Mary and Stephen did not talk about what was going to happen and when they parted things seemed to be left more in the air, not less.

With the unswerving instinct of a Colonel's daughter, she made for the dining-room, expecting to find him sitting there, consoling himself with a man-sized whisky and soda.

But Stephen was too modest and too honest to settle for this pose. She found him at last in the kitchen where he had poured himself some coffee from the pot which always sat in one of the ovens of the Aga. He was adding milk from a bottle when Mary came in. He was cold, and as he sat down at the little kitchen table by the window, in his trousers and pyjama top, with no dressing-gown, he began to shiver. She sat down at the other end of the same table and said nothing for a while. Meantime he drank his coffee.

At last, in quite a steady low voice, which she addressed to the toes of her bedroom slippers, Mary said:

'If you haven't guessed already, I'm pregnant. I know I should have told you before, but I just couldn't.'

She glanced across to him, boldly, but he did not attempt to say anything or even to turn his head. He continued drinking coffee from the huge, deep cup.

She said, 'If it had worked I don't suppose I'd ever have told you, so I can't really make any excuses. Only you haven't been a girl. It seemed the only thing to do. The only practical thing. If it had worked you'd never have been the wiser and it would probably be a happy family. That's what I'd hoped. But it didn't work, so that's that.'

He said, 'That's why you came to the dairy that night?'

They were both glad that she managed the truth.

'Yes, Stephen, it is.'

'I must say, it makes sense of quite a lot of things I didn't understand.'

'It doesn't mean that I'm not very fond of you—'

She stopped there.

He said, very coldly:

'I don't think that's a line we should follow now.'

For a moment they were silent again, then Mary said:

'I think it is. I can't persuade you it's true. I can only tell you. I'm sorry it's all such a muck-up. Most of the things I've said to you since I've been back have been perfectly true.'

He started stirring the last of his coffee and he sipped the sugar at the bottom with the spoon. He turned suddenly and looked her straight in the eye.

He said, 'Are you hoping that I'll strike you?'

'No.'

'Or at least shout and slap your face?'

'No.'

He said, 'If it's a comfort to you, the performance was spectacular.'

She put her fingers over her eyes and shook her head, saying another sort of 'no' this time.

He went on, clearly:

'It never occurred to me for a moment that you weren't telling me the truth. Then, as you know, conception, gestation and birth only crop up in my brain if they're connected with the farm. Even if you had made a mistake or two, I probably wouldn't have noticed.'

She sat quietly.

He said, 'I suppose the real reason why I am so calm is that I just can't believe it now. I know it's true, but I can't swallow it.'

He got to his feet, and went on:

'If you like to stay down here for a few moments I'll get my clothes out of the room.'

'No, I'll go.'

'I'd rather lie down on the sofa. I'll be going out early, anyway.'

She nodded and said meekly:

'All right, Stephen,' and that finished the conversation.

For want of something better to do, Mary, too, drank a cup of coffee.

When Stephen went upstairs there was no sign of Macdonald but both beds were made with the corner of the bedclothes turned back. The chairs had been tidied and Stephen found his clothes neatly folded. He took them down to the nursery, where he would be less comfortable than in the sitting-room. He did not even notice himself take this monk's choice. He pulled a footstool up to the nursing chair and switched out the light on the desk. He lay there, wide awake, until at last he heard the steps on the stairs as Mary went back to bed. That the strain had been passed from one to the other was now clearly shown. Mary fell asleep within a few minutes, and Stephen sat tensely, alarmed by every board that creaked and startled by the hoots of owls.

Wherever Mary found her story of Uncle Arbuthnot's death, it certainly was unlikely to have been complete invention. It held the essential truth about suicide, as opposed to attempted suicide. The method a person chooses for killing himself is strictly in character, if he truly means to go through with it. And Arbuthnot, the tidy boy, equipped himself with a bucket as well as a knife. There is a reason why a student chooses to hang himself in a college lavatory, why a girl drowns herself in a pretty stream, why a distracted housewife picks the gas oven and the retired Colonel shoots himself in his den. Stephen must have known that he was bluffing.

His approach to suicide demonstrated the astonishing difference between David and himself. They had not after all come from very different homes and they had both taken scholarships to small public schools. Thereafter Stephen had accepted the environment of the idea: patriotism, enterprise, integrity, leadership and all the rest, although he was very conscious of falling short of the ideal. David, on the other hand, perhaps because he came from a home which was very, very slightly lower in the social scale, or perhaps because he was more mature at that age, refused the new environment. His school days were a running intellectual battle against a system which he refused to accept as desirable. Duly extended, it can be seen very easily that even if David ever reached the point of contemplating suicide the possibility of his doing so in Stephen's gentleman's way did not exist.

As soon as Stephen took the Colonel's shot-gun from the cloakroom which, in itself, was a tricky operation, as he was certain that Macdonald was awake, he found himself in difficulties. The Colonel had locked up his cartridges but, after searching his pockets, Stephen found one, in an old hacking jacket, behind the door. It was dawn when he arrived outside the house and he was at once embarrassed by the enthusiasm of the Colonel's Labrador, who appeared from nowhere, barking madly, certain, on seeing Stephen with a gun, that it must be the morning of the Christmas shoot. As quickly as he could, and savagely, Stephen shoved him into the first place he could think of, which was the black shed where all the apples were kept. He then proceeded on his way, more than ever determined to do the right thing, quickly, before he had time to think.

He went up to the woods above the bothie, but in the end, for reasons which were later very obvious to him, he walked right through the wood, where the trees creaked a little in the wind, to a rough patch of moorland at the edge, which long before this incident and for some forgotten historical reason, had been called the Hospital. Perhaps some keeper, years ago, protected wounded birds there. When the moment came, and the woods were behind him, Stephen behaved less like a gentleman and more like a schoolboy. His movements had the formality of a Fascist officer who had come to pay himself a debt of honour, by the grey light of dawn, under the cloud-swept sky. One detail in the following swift physical action which closely resembled the first movement of 'shoulder arms' was highly important. When the gun was cradled in his arm, and his head tilted slightly to one side, he was careful at the last instant to save his eye. This pushing forward of the head would probably in itself have saved his life, but the important fact was that the cartridge was in the first barrel, and it was the choke barrel that dug into his skin. The result was more or less serious than the spirit of farce invited. The best thing that could have happened would surely have been that he missed altogether, or alternatively blew off his head. What did happen was that he shot a considerable hole in his head and collapsed unconscious, with the softness of failure, on a large clump of sphagnum moss. The keeper who found him, not very long afterwards, used this as a first emergency dressing. By mid-day he was conscious, comfortable and silent, in the room in the cottage hospital which Captain Gordon had been so determined to avoid.

The news was brought to Mary by someone who was almost a stranger, and fortunately she heard it when she was alone. How that happened was fairly simple. The gamekeeper, who was employed in the neighbouring estate, came down to the bothie to ring for the ambulance and, before returning to Stephen, told the woman who ran the bothie to go across to the house and tell them what had happened. This woman, however, was of an extremely nervous temperament. She found herself catering for only half a dozen girls, in the heart of the country, because the task of running a small boarding-house at an east coast seaside resort had reduced her to a winter of poverty and tears. She could not possibly have faced the prospect of telling a young wife that her husband had shot himself, and she used as a double excuse, the imminent arrival of the baker's vans and a nose-bleed which she had been trying to control since breakfast-time. One of the girls, therefore, who cannot have been more than sixteen, volunteered to run across to the farm. Like anybody of that age, she enormously enjoyed bearing ill-tidings, even if she denied this to herself.

All this was relatively natural and honest. It was the interview between Mary and this long-faced, bright-eyed girl, that had its bad moment.

Mary was over by the garage, outside the back of the house, when the girl arrived and called breathlessly:

'Mrs Cameron, oh, Mrs Cameron. I've terrible news for you.'

At that, before her mind had time to calculate what the news might be, Mary looked duly alarmed. She looked at the girl severely.

'It's Mr Stephen – Mr Stephen's shot himself.'

Again, nothing went wrong. Mary grew paler and placed on the ground the bucket which she had been taking to the hens.

The girl went on to say:

'They're taking him in the ambulance, Fyvie the keeper's there. They're taking him to the cottage hospital. You're not to worry, Fyvie says. He's going to be all right.'

The girl smiled, but even she was a little mystified by the expression which in that instant passed across Mary's face. Had Pink been there he would have defined it. In a second it was gone, never to be seen again, but Pink would not have missed it. It was an expression of bitter disappointment and it was a moment or two before Mary could find words. The girl thought her confusion was understandable, but she would have backed away had she understood it.

In the next few moments, Mary extracted all the details and immediately afterwards made the necessary telephone calls, but it was that moment of self-revelation, not Stephen's condition, nor, as Macdonald thought, the events of the previous days, that winded her so badly. She never came near to weeping, but for an hour or two after the first frenzy of activity she seemed to be literally struck dumb. Even Macdonald was alarmed by her condition and went into the dining-room where she sat and coaxed her to take some coffee. Macdonald's expression as she did this was cagey. She seemed to be saying, 'Even if I do give you a warm drink, do not imagine that I have changed my opinion of you. It is only by the grace of God that you are not a murderess.' With that last sentiment Mary, for quite different reasons, would have had to agree.

Pink also tried to cover up his first reaction when Macdonald went into the nursery to tell him what had happened. She was by this time generally impatient of his behaviour so she did not stay to examine his reaction. She simply put her head round the door, announced the news, then went back to the kitchen where Cathie stood, petrified with excitement. In fact, Pink, at first, looked deeply offended, rather as if his understudy had been given all the notices. Then after a moment or two he shouted angrily to the closed door:

'Well, there's damn all I can do about it, is there?'

Stephen was kept in hospital for several weeks, and Mary visited him practically every day. Their meetings each afternoon at half past three would have been of interest to David, in his preparation of 'The Obligatory Scene' for *Moral Philosophy* and the Dutch popular Press. They never approached the obligatory in all the weeks Stephen was there and yet, on his return to the house the change had been made, the decision had been taken, the future was as settled as ever it can be. Mary's attitude towards him during these weeks might also have reminded David of his own angelic mother. She never referred to the attempted suicide, or to the days that preceded it, nor did she ever substitute for them some convenient euphemism. It was Macdonald, when she visited, in hat and fur cape, cluttered up with parcels of sweets, shortbread and grapes, who referred to the 'accident'. Mary did not mention it. It was as if she disapproved entirely of his action, never forgot it, but quite forgave it, and was determined to show, as his closest relation, that it did not in any way affect her liking for him. The visits were never cheerful and the two of them often sat in silence, but over the weeks they found the bond between them. Stephen saw very clearly that Mary's attitude to him was identical with her attitude to herself. It was as if she were saying to him, as a request so urgent that it was nearly a command, 'Make no mention of what has gone before and it is possible we will find a way. Mention it once and we are done for.' There was a severe see-no-evil conservatism in her attitude more common in older people, that is often mistaken as mental laziness. It is in essence, a refuge, a tight-rope of compromise, a narrow plank on which it is necessary to walk without saying a single word about the gulf that lies below.

The most cheerful visit, curiously enough, was Pink's. He only came once, at the wrong time, without being announced, but during one of his enlightened days. These grew fewer and fewer now, but when they came they had an extra warm quality. Coming in, as he did, in dark glasses, a week after the New Year, he looked to Stephen as if he were at the bottom of the trough. He brought as a present a 'make it yourself' transistor radio.

'By God,' he said. 'This'll make you wild. Guaranteed to whizz you round the bend.'

And seeing Stephen's dismay, he burst into a long wheeze of a laugh and tucked his dark glasses into his breast pocket, in which, that day, he was sporting five propelling pencils and pens, and a tyre pressure gauge. He looked round the room, which was like any small private room in a hospital, except that it boasted new, plastic, Venetian blinds, and he said:

'Everything, old man. I could take everything except the bed pans.' It was as if he were talking of wild animals. 'They'd get me in the end.' Pink dared subjects which everybody avoided. He approached them with a directness that would have horrified the nurses. He started to laugh again, leaning back, and holding one knee between his hands.

At last he managed to say:

'Old Flush,' which was the name of the Colonel's Labrador, 'Old Flush in the apple shed, eh? That's what got me.'

For a moment he could not manage to say anything more, because he was laughing so much. He pushed his nose to one side, then the other, like a performing seal. He said:

'He was in there seven hours before we found him, tossing Cox's high and low.'

Stephen too began to laugh. He said:

'Don't. I'm not meant to shake about.'

'That's excellent,' Pink exclaimed, and Stephen recognised that he was referring to one of his favourite subjects, laughter in church, when he said:

'Old Stiffy in the front row of the choir, eh?'

Stephen, in his most miserable tones, which delighted Pink, said, 'Well, I couldn't help it. The bloody dog must have thought it was Boxing Day. Started howling around.'

'You should have taken a bang at him.'

'Too British,' Stephen replied, and Pink said:

'Mind, you'd have probably missed him, or taken a lug off. That wouldn't have been at all nice. You'd never have got back in the house that way.'

Then Pink's mood changed. He grew intensely serious and pulled his chair along the polished red linoleum, closer to the bed.

'Mind,' he said again, 'I don't see how that happened. Didn't it put you off, I mean, bloody dog bounding round and licking you? Enough to ruin murder, far less suicide, isn't it?'

Stephen shook his head, very gently.

'Well, come on,' Pink said. 'This is Your Life.'

Stephen said, 'Once you've made up your mind that sort of thing doesn't matter. Lots of tactical difficulties you have to overcome, but you've made up your mind, you've told yourself you're going through with it, INTENTION to annihilate private enemy number one. Things get in the way but they don't stop you. If Flush had wandered into the nursery a couple of hours before things might have been different.'

'Now isn't that fascinating?' Pink said. He shook his head, grasped his knee again, and went on:

'By God, that's good. I get it, though, I get it. D'you suppose murder's that way?'

'Premeditated. More or less.'

'Good old Steve. Ever thought of doing somebody in?'

'Yes, often.'

'Really? I find that most interesting. Thought of murdering me?'

'No.'

'Oh,' Pink said, disappointedly. 'Steady on. There's no need to be rude.'

'How's Flush, by the way?' Stephen asked.

'Joggin' along,' Pink replied. Then he assumed that curious, secretive smile which usually heralded some devastatingly intimate confession. In this context it alarmed Stephen, and he was greatly relieved when Pink merely said, 'Apples', and put one finger in the air. He opened his mouth several times as Stephen, guessing what was coming next, began to smile.

'No, no,' Pink said. 'Serious animal study. Real Pavlov stuff. Interest to Mary's boy friend: old smelly Dow. I've been trying Old Flush. Oyez. The other day he chewed up one of Cathie's ghastly hats, and I went right up to him.' He demonstrated excitedly, 'Like this, hands behind my back. Then I faced him with it. The biggest Cox's I could find. I held it right there in front of his nose. I did.'

He nodded, triumphantly, and leant back again. He seemed inclined to leave the story there.

'What happened? Was he frightened? Tail between his legs?' Stephen asked.

'Well, as a matter of fact, old man,' Pink replied, rather stuffily, 'he ate the thing.'

Soon after, a nurse came in and it was the end of the visit.

Stephen never saw him again until he was let out of hospital, though he got a Valentine card from him with a shot-gun through a bed pan, as device.

But if there was a moment during Stephen's long con-valescence which could be counted as a turning-point it must have occurred one afternoon in February when Macdonald came, instead of Mary. It was thawing. Through the window, as gloomy afternoon turned swiftly to night, the patches of snow on the banks of the lawn outside still showed long after the features of the miserable little garden had faded away. The light was already switched on, in the room, when Macdonald arrived, and by this time Stephen was tired of lying still. At her first glance Macdonald could see he had arrived at a state of what she called 'natural depression' which, in its way, was a subtle definition. She meant by it the sort of straightforward schoolboy depression which comes to everybody who is bored and lonely, as opposed to the type which Pink favoured. Stephen's barometer was at low, but with ordin-ary cheer and new subjects of interest the needle would gradually creep round again. No outside influence on the other hand, had any effect whatsoever on Pink's storms. It was only possible to wait until the needle hit the buffer at 'low' and bounced back to 'Oyez, oyez, ring those bloody bells'.

Within the first five minutes of her visit Macdonald was afraid she had put her foot in it. As he was lying so quietly she searched for subjects and picked on the roads being better, as they had been icy for nearly three weeks. She mentioned that Mary would find it easier driving back from the specialist in Dundee, assuming that Stephen knew where she was that day. Neither she nor anyone else quite realised the narrowness of the plank which the two of them walked together. The attempted suicide was never men-tioned, nor the return from London, nor the bedroom, nor

the bed, and although Mary was now obviously pregnant
they never mentioned that. Macdonald now realised this,
too late, when Stephen asked her questions. Macdonald
said:

'I shouldn't have mentioned it, maybe.' Neatly she found
a reason. 'She wouldn't want to worry you with it, Stephen,
you know what men are when they hear about specialists.
But there's nothing wrong at all. He's the best gynaecol-
ogist round about, that's all there is to it. If she goes to him
he can get her one of the private rooms at the hospital and
that's not nearly such big money as the nursing homes.
Most of it's on the National Health.'

'When's it due?' Stephen was lying back on the pillows.
He was playing with his watch, which rested on the sheets
over his tummy. He buckled and unbuckled the strap.

'Not till May. There's time yet.'

'Does David know about it?'

'I don't think so,' she replied, and she watched him
carefully. Macdonald took some big risks sometimes,
which she never felt to be risks, herself, because her instinct
was so strong. She used to say, 'I just tell the truth, that's all
it is,' but this in itself could not have been less true. She
often told lies. But she had an unerring sense of timing. She
knew when the truth would be most effective. She tried it
now.

'I don't see why he should, either. It's got nothing to do
with him.'

Stephen thought she was being kind, not truthful. He
shook his head and said:

'Nothing to do with me.'

Macdonald, unwrapping a box of Meltis fruits said,
almost casually:

'That doesn't mean to say it's got anything to do with
David, either. Mary wasn't too happy in London, you
know.'

Out of the corner of her eye she saw she had said the right

thing. Jealousy does not work like fear. One cannot measure oneself against the unknown. The sharpest pain comes when one sees the person who has been preferred. Stephen pushed himself up with his elbows.

'Do you know that for a fact?'

'I know nothing as a fact, Steve. But you've only got to look at David Dow, and where he came from. Even when they're tearaways like that, there's some things is always saved. She'd have gone to him if it was his – I'm certain of that.'

Then she put a parcel on one side and said more cheerfully:

'Come on now, Steve, I've no right to be talking to you like this. The walls have ears. D'you want more books yet? The man at the library here says you've read all he's got. We'll have to send up to Foulis Lending, to keep you in stocks.'

That was all there was to it, but when she left him he looked much happier.

Macdonald did not confess to Mary that she had had this conversation, but then Mary no longer confessed things to Macdonald. Yet the hostility that had existed between them when Mary first returned, gradually disappeared. Macdonald, herself, seemed to grow much older that winter, as if only now, after the Colonel's death, could she relax and admit to herself that she was nearly sixty. She would occasionally sit and talk to Mary, and they even began to laugh together, about old times. Mary learnt of her father's last months, indirectly, in this way. Macdonald joked about the terrible things Pink had said to the local minister who had come very often to visit him, because the Colonel turned to God at the end.

'What is it he calls God?' Macdonald asked one evening as they sat on the leather fender, drinking sherry. 'Is it "Moose"?'

'Moo,' Mary said. She always wore a fur hat that winter

and she played with it as they talked. Then she stopped
herself fidgeting, with a conscious effort and put the hat
over with the parcels she had brought back from the shops
in Dundee. She bought all the things for the baby, by
herself. She knitted none. She brought things back each
Tuesday and Thursday when she went to the clinic in
Dundee. She never showed them to Macdonald, but put
them straight into the new white chest of drawers in her
bedroom. That Macdonald and Cathie looked in the
drawers when she was not there did not upset her. Indeed,
she might have been disappointed if they had not done so.
But Mary said very little, these days, that was not absolutely
necessary.

'Moo,' Macdonald repeated. 'Pink was terrible with the
poor man, waving him good-bye, shouting "love to Moo!"
or something like this; you know what he is. He got really
aggressive once or twice, mind; I was worried he'd attack
him at the bottom of the stairs, shouting at him, "If a man
does not love his brother whom he has seen how can he love
Moo whom he hath not seen? Eh? Answer me that!" Pink
looked really angry, you know. The minister's very patient,
mark you. He never complains about this Moo thing, and
he just says where the verse comes from, one of the Epistles,
I think, and says he agrees with the apostle who wrote it.'

Mary nodded. 'What did Pink say to that?'

Macdonald raised her eyebrows.

'That infuriating laugh of his. You know, the one he
always gives when he claims he's won an argument. It used
to drive you crazy as a kid.'

Mary filled Macdonald's glass again.

'You said you'd tell me some day,' Mary said, and
Macdonald nodded. She knew what Mary meant. At last
she replied:

'You'll have guessed the most . . . with the preacher
calling and that. He wasn't the same man, your father, at
the end. He was brought down with grief and no' just fear

either. Mind there was no jokes with him. I think that's why
Stevie and I had to have a laugh at Pink. Your father didn't
know it but he had a kind of dignity at the end. He didn't
come downstairs much and he'd just stare at the television
but he saw nothing and heard nothing. You could turn the
sound down and he'd never notice. The preacher'll tell
you, Mary, he went very bravely, and very humbly too. He
was kinder to me in the last weeks than he'd ever been in
the years before.' She said, 'It was kind of worth it for that.

'We didn't know when he was going. It was sudden at the
end. Your mother, you know, she drove herself to it: she
made herself go. Your father just let himself go. Very
suddenly. I think cancer's like that. It can linger or not.
There's no telling.'

She seemed to leave a gap. She looked at Mary, then
away again, and at last she continued:

'As soon as he moved into your mother's room, and he
was insistent on doing that, mind, he didn't think of anyone
in this world any more. He was on his way, then. But he
went over two incidents in his life. Over and over them, to
the minister and me. Over and over again, his hand
pumping up and down on the arm of his chair and his
eyes quite watery. He'd say, "God forgive my soul."'

Macdonald took a sip of her sherry. Mary looked at her
own toes. She sat alongside, on the leather fender. When
she leant forward she could clasp the back of one of the oak
chairs at the side of the refectory table. The lights were low.
Two brackets on the wall were lit and the faces of the
Fergusons in the portraits were lost against the sheen of
the heavy Victorian gold-painted frames. The silver on the
sideboard caught the light.

Mary said, 'When I was in London I heard a horrible
story about the card cheating. I mean what led up to Daddy
doing it. I should think it was rot.' She swept back her hair
and looked at Macdonald who was staring at the wine-glass
that looked very small in her huge, bony hand.

Quietly, Macdonald said, 'I shouldn't think it was. But it wasn't that that worried the Colonel. Not in the end. He was like all the best men, so the minister said. He was worried only about the negative sins, that's what you call them, the things you leave undone.

'Evidently when he came back from that club and it was old General Oliphant brought him back, kind old soul he was, your father had a talk with his wife. I know he did, as a matter of fact. I heard their voices and wondered what was going on. It was only an hour past dawn. As you know, your mother was a wild kind of frightened wee thing, and she'd never have gone to that club unless she'd got herself into a terrible state. I'm only sorry I didn't know her better then. I'd have stopped her. I wasn't long enough with the family . . . But, let's not deny it, she could be real infuriating, your mother. She couldn't lift a finger to help herself. That was the drawing-room training – Dundee style. She couldn't boil an egg and I don't really think she'd grasped the difference between a cock and a hen. She certainly can't have understood what was going on, but someone must have put the wind up her good and proper. She got the feeling that it was something really sinful and she wasn't far wrong. I fancy, too, her own life wasn't going so well. It was a mystery to me how either of you two came about. A gesture to convention, I'm sure it wasn't much more than that.

'I shouldn't speak ill of the dead, and mind, I don't really. She was a harmless enough body, your mother, but let's just say she wasn't top of the class. Not the brainiest. Your father therefore thought it best not to tell her any-thing, even in the state he was. So she kept asking him questions mainly whether he'd cheated at the cards, be-cause she wouldn't have known how to frame the real questions, at all. I sometimes think she thought the gam-bling was the sin and it ended there. Anyway, she went on and on at your father, who as you can imagine was feeling pretty dithery and she kept saying, "All I want to know, is did you cheat?" And evidently, so he said to the minister and me, he said "No." Isn't it odd? You've got all these awful things happening and when it comes to him dying he's worried about that lie more than any. He says that's what cut her out. If he'd admitted that, he might have got round to admitting everything, getting her to understand and making a marriage out of it. But he failed to tell her – he went on a lot about this, Mary. He failed to tell her and that was maybe the beginning of what happened to her. She needed a hand in life and he just didn't give her it. Even before she started on the booze he'd never say a word to her, you know, except "Good morning" and "Good night." You wouldn't remember that.'

Mary said, 'I understand, I think.'

'It was his own arrogance,' Macdonald said, 'that he was so worried about.'

'What was the other thing?'

'Och, it was the same thing. Just another scene. Evidently one night when I was out, I'd a night a month off in those days, she went as far as his dressing-room. She asked to be forgiven. She said a funny sort of thing. She said, "Let's just pretend we love each other." I can see fine what happened. He just called her a stupid woman and shoved her out the door. She went along to you two that night and woke you up, and later on I found her on the rug in the bedroom, fallen asleep beside the dog.'

Macdonald put her glass down on the table in front of her, then sat back on the fender.

'That was the first Flush of them all,' she said. 'He was a nice enough dog.'

'Oh God,' Mary said, suddenly, and then she put the question she had held back for three months. 'But didn't he ask for me?'

'Of course he did.'

'Kindly?'

'Of course. He was kind about everyone at the end. But before he went into your mother's room he asked for you every day. I was mad, trying to trace you, Mary.'

Mary frowned.

'What d'you mean, "trace me"?'

'Well, I knew you'd left David but none of us—'

She interrupted.

'Pink—' she said. 'He had my address. He . . .'

And then she stopped herself and in a curiously awkward way she put the heel of her hand over her mouth and pressed it very hard. Slowly, Macdonald began to understand. And she knew, too, at that moment that Mary was going to cry.

'It'll not matter, Mary, it'll not matter . . . But he was funny about it, your father, I mean. He wouldn't take any steps to find you, the police or that. He wouldn't let me do that. He said it was a kind of judgment on him—'

'No.' Mary spoke almost under her breath.

Macdonald said, 'He talked a lot about you. And then he made his mind up and moved into your mother's room.'

'Was he there long?'

'Just a week.'

There was a short pause and Mary clenched her fists very tightly. At last, Macdonald said, 'Did Pink not even tell you he was sick?'

Mary looked very frightened and pale.

'I didn't see him.'

'Of course you did. In London, with David at your birthday time. That's why Pink went down.'

At first it was a moan, a dry sort of moan, and then at last she began to weep. When Macdonald held out her huge arms she fell against her and pressed.

'Old Rock,' she kept saying. 'Bloody Cassandra. Oh, darling Macdonald. Old Moo-Morality!'

SHE CAME DOWN later that night and found him sitting in the nursery, staring straight in front of him, playing the *Marche Funèbre* on the radiogram, behind which he at once hid his glass.

She approached him and knelt in front of him but he did not turn down the sound. She put her hands on his knees and said:

'Pink, love, if it's about not giving Daddy my address; if that's what's really eating you, it doesn't matter, I promise.'

He stared at her stupidly.

'I beg your pardon, old flesh?'

'I wouldn't harbour it. I love you. I do.'

His expression never changed. He reached out, but not to turn down the volume. Instead he retrieved his glass.

'In point of fact, old thing,' he said, 'I'm a triffle predestinately pissed.'

A moment later she turned round and left.

'California,' Pink said, as the door closed, 'here I come.'

BOOK FIVE

From the Lab

ALMOST THE LAST picture is of her standing in front of a swagger golfing hotel looking quite exhausted, her eyes washed out with tears. She is oblivious both of the porters by the swing-doors who stare at her and of the broad-beamed business men who look over their shoulders at her as they pass by, pushing trolleys of expensive matching sets of golf clubs in enormous bags. There has already been a shower of rain, and the porters' two big striped umbrellas lie open, on their sides, by the front step. Mary herself looks a little heavier. She is in a cotton frock and a suède coat with a dark green silk square tied loosely round her neck. She is not looking at me, but staring blankly at the mauve clouds, at the formal borders of flowers by the perfect lawns, at the fountains, and beyond, at the first green Lowland hills, and she is saying flatly:

'I've sinned. This time, I've torn it. This time I've sinned, I know.'

And I reach out and seize both her hands and shake them but I have no argument. I close my eyes and say again and again:

'No, no, no! We have. Not you.' And I think I meant both Stephen and Pink in that 'we'.

Let me take it from the telephone call. I suppose it was about eighteen months after the Colonel died: a little more, because they were hay-making at the edges of the fairways on the course, that morning, before it rained. It must have been June. I rang from a box in the internal Post Office. It was that sort of hotel.

Her voice, then, was flat enough.

'Who is it?'

'David.'

She sounded weary and asked only for facts. I told her where I was and why. I was staying at the hotel by invitation, with all expenses paid, to read a paper at a Conference on Management in Industry. I talked brightly and made it sound as if I were enjoying myself. The title of my paper, believe it or not, was 'Work and Play', and the invitation to prepare it had followed the successful publication of *Obligatory Scenes*. In the allied fields, in and around social science, I promise you, one can get away with murder.

'Oh, yes,' she said to all that.

'Hundreds of brisk business men,' I said cheerfully. 'Pretty Wildian pages and happy Dickensian boot-boys constantly at one's service. All with Glasgow accents. The Secretary of the Conference calls me D.D. You must come at once and rescue me from unqualified success.'

'It's not very easy,' she said at last. 'Stevie's got the Jaguar.' I remember particularly that she did not just say 'car'.

'Oh come.' My accent, I suppose, as usual, grew more affected and 'Oxford', as I sensed the possibility of failure. 'Let's be pals. You can't leave me to the sharks. I'll give you the hell of a lot to drink.'

She replied, after a pause, 'Macdonald's out in the fields just now. They're hay-making.'

'I'll come and fetch you, I've got a car.'

'No.' She was very definite about that. 'I might catch a bus about twelve.'

'Excellent. It only takes an hour.'

'Why are you inviting me to lunch, David?'

'That's not allowed. No. That's a wrong question. Because I want to ask you to lunch. You must come.'

'All right. Things need organising, that's all. There's Pink trouble. I won't be able to stay very long. And there's a

baby-feed at two, but Cathie might manage that. All right.
I'll come. How are you?'

'Bloody,' David said with a loud laugh.

'I thought you must be.'

'One o'clock then.'

'About then.'

It is easy, and oddly enough, comforting, after the disaster,
to write it all down in the dark hours and passionately
blame and abuse oneself. It gives one the same kick that
drives young people at those horrifying Retreat week-ends
to confess publicly to sins which they never committed.
This I have already done in a pile of unposted letters to her,
now burnt along with the dead cats. But this I am determined not to do, for a simple reason. I blame my breed
almost as much as myself. Some of the responsibility, after
two years of exhausting self-examination, I place bitterly
and sadly on the angels.

Before I rang her from the hotel, I was very certain of my
position. I rang her because I wanted to put things right. I
wanted to see her so that I could explain; which is to say,
apologise; which is to say take the blame; which would have
meant abusing myself. I had had nearly two years in which
to try to find out why I had been so unbearably cruel to her,
because when I was with her, I had better make it quite
plain, not a day passed without its cruelty. I never lost an
opportunity to damage her self-confidence. I actually
struck her on several occasions and in the end, of course,
I went to great lengths to break her faith in the two people
who loved her. But last of all (a point which I failed to
notice on my first examination), I somehow got it across to
her, at the same time, that I was myself shocked by my
treatment of her. By a look a day or a word a week I
managed to tug at her sympathy, and this, because it made
her stay on, was perhaps the most cruel of all.

I now wanted to tell her the curious conclusion I had

come to. On all previous occasions, when she had asked
me, like a child (she would simply ask 'why' again) what
made me treat her so, I had talked a little mysteriously of *odi
et amo*, and all that. I accused her, quoting all her fabulous
fibs in evidence, of skating on life's surface, or refusing to
be real, and therefore of being unable to love. As my love, I
explained and flattered myself, was real and fundamental,
I reacted violently against all her falseness. I honestly think
I convinced myself. And of course love is complicated for
the complicated just as it is simple for Romeo or Juliet. But
so conditioned was I by the arguments and discussions of
my mind-bending friends that the utter absurdity of the
suggestion that we hate those we love, as it were, by
definition (and if you don't hate her, then, my goodness,
you had better whip up your passion) did not occur to me.
That we are capable of this hatred is undeniable: but that is
to say something quite different.

Gradually I came round to the workman, the spade and
the otter and very gingerly, because it was far from comforting, I began to face the fact that the most passionate
affair of my life, with Mary, had very little to do with love
and much to do with envy. Mine was the bite of the dog in
the manger. 'You shall not be free.' With a nasty cold
feeling in the very middle of me, I began to see that I was
acting out a very old play.

For many years, usually when drunkish, I have bored my
friends with the suggestion that the Scots, of all people, are
misunderstood. A glance at their history or literature (and
especially if you count Byron as a Scot, which after dinner,
at least, is permissible) reveals what lies underneath the
slow accent, the respectability and the solid flesh. Under
the cake lies Bonny Dundee. But even as I put forward
these theories with enthusiasm I was doing everything in
my power to suppress the one contemporary sign of that
splendid vitality which I had ever come across. They
christened her Mary. I cast myself, perversely, as Knox.

This much I realised when I went north to read 'Work and Play' for big business in the swell hotel, and the reasons for my envy seemed clear enough. Anybody who has shared the heavily moral, non-conformist unbringing knows how the hoodoos stick even into middle life. Mary, although she was due for just such an education, had, primarily by the accident of her father's indiscretion and her mother's subsequent death, avoided these troubles, even if she and poor Pink had run into a load of others. Nor do I withdraw any of these conclusions, now. But they were not enough, because knowing this much, and already loving Mary in the way which is truly best described by her own 'cousin-style' I then waded in again and probably, in that one afternoon, did more damage than in the six months that had gone before.

What is perfectly horrifying is that I now believe I knew I was going to do this as I waited for her in that plush cocktail bar which looks like the waiting-room in a Warsaw brothel. There is always a clue. When I had said, on the phone, 'I've got a car. Shall I come and collect you?' she had said, at once, quite definitely 'No,' meaning 'Don't show yourself here, at the farm.' I can at this moment, still feel my heart leap.

That we are the perverts and the peeping-toms, the sex maniacs and even the murderers, we, the sons of the righteous, everybody knows. But we are something else, whose childhood was stolen from us, who never, without correction (not necessarily punishment) told Mary's splendid stories; who never went with Alice through the looking-glass. It is the curbing of our imaginations, the firm guidance back to the grammar and the prose, that make us so hungry now for experience. But for a special sort of experience; a kind of imagination of the flesh. We are the tinkers, who move on; who invite experience but flee from consequence. At the last moment our eyes turn furtively away. This is to say that we are the most dangerous of all: the permanently immature. And for that I blame the angels.

Physically there was quite an alarming difference. She was already sunburnt and her hair was at its lightest red. Her eyes, therefore, looked their most brilliant green, and none of the other men in the American bar failed to take a second look at her. Rather blandly, she stared them out. Her movements seemed to be slower. Her shoulders, barely covered by the loose cotton frock, looked heavier, and she was wearing a pair of brown sandals with no heels. There was something more than careless in her dress. It was a slovenly quality, which in the ordinary way I might have associated with a Lesbian. She had developed the same off-hand manner as if she felt it no longer necessary to please. And yet, by the looks on the faces of both the men and women round about, it was clear that she now caused considerably more stir, wherever she went. We played the name-game.

'Not Mary,' I said, after a long pause.

'Brenda,' she replied. It was not the only time that she seemed to take pleasure in disparaging herself, but I shook my head.

'No,' I said. 'What about Georgina or Margaret?'

'You tell me.' She ate another olive.

'I think it's Georgina.'

'Heather,' she suggested.

'You really mustn't be so rude to yourself,' I pleaded, 'it's embarrassing. Tell me, in one word, if we can't get it in a name.'

She looked at me for a moment, then said, 'David, if I'm to get back before tea-time we had better go in to lunch.'

From a huge menu, she chose a straightforward meal, without delay or hesitation. The last time I'd lunched her, even on that day at Bianchi's, she had been unable to decide on a meal. It used to infuriate me when she made me decide first, then chose exactly the same menu. There was none of that, and I thought I had found the clue.

'Ah,' I said, 'you lunch here often?'

'No.'

'This sort of place?'

'We often go out on a Saturday,' she said.

'To a country club?'

'That sort of thing,' she replied. 'Or one of the hotels.'

'Fair enough,' I nodded. 'For a dinner dance?'

'That sort of thing,' again, she replied.

'Money,' I said. 'You've come into money.'

'I hate to think what I look like,' she said slowly. 'You're staring at me as if I'm something out of a museum.'

'You look very beautiful.'

'But not so vulnerable,' she said.

'Not so obviously,' I remember replying (and how wrongly), adding the academic 'I confess.'

VULNERABLE ONE, cousin. If all these things were revealed to me, if I wasn't in love with you and knew it, if I could not give before I ever came upstairs that afternoon, how, you ask, did I continue to make physical love? But there is no problem here. Those of us who have failed to break the bonds that tie our hearts, still manage, by a trip to the big city, by a journey back to *boue* to cure the rest. We may have no passion, but we are wanton enough. Give us a girl, a boy, a prostitute, give us even a scone for a wife, we can perform and do. Stephen is no Scotsman there. His fastidiousness is foreign to the line that leads back to the wynds of old Edinburgh and to your friends Ina and Elspeth and all the others in that inaccurate, timeless, fanciful but true tenement in the back streets by the Tay. His troubles are surely the responsibility of the more civilised successors of Dr Arnold; the makers of agnostic monasteries.

I go through the scenes in the swell hotel, often, often, usually late at night in the lab when I wait for the cigarette to burn down, the Pentothal to wear off, or the cat to right itself. My lab's on the top floor now. I look down on Mill Hill and Hendon and the lights of London beyond and am transported back, wondering what trick it is that brings all the ghosts of passion that make a soul so fluently to the surfaces of the skin and into those special tears that are never shed. For a moment, or an hour, they brought a sweet and unfathomable depth into your eyes. There was an ocean sounded by a deep bell. I heard it from the shore.

I sat for a quarter of an hour as you surfaced. The white sheet tucked round your waist made your skin browner than I had seen it before and I remember that my thoughts for moments on end could not leap beyond the sensation of colour. Your hair looked darker red against the big pink coral shells on your breast. You slipped noiselessly into shore.

Cousin, to watch you and look after you was almost enough. Then, at least, I felt a strength, a protection, which I had never known was there. If not a lover, I was a man, and am thankful.

But to be loved like that, deep bell, is frightening. And as soon as you awoke, I was afraid. The ponk-ponk of the tennis balls came back, the jazz pattern on the curtains, the horrid wardrobe, the glass that still said L.M.S. I remember the little white chair which I'd taken from the bathroom squeaked as I moved back, ashamed that my eyes had woken you. Oh, this time it was David who spoke.

I can't go through all that again. The meaningless piles of words, none as imaginative as yours used to be, but even greater fibs. I used every Dundee cake of an argument. Even facts. Money, my own divorce, the child, Stephen, even the differences in our age. Forget me walking up and down; forget me standing, dry-mouthed, by the window, quickly trying to think of a new argument, a new card to lay on top of the house that I had built. I was shaking, not in the hand but right in the middle of me.

At the end of it, when somehow I had returned to your side, you drew an arm out of the crushed summer sheet and touched my cheeks with your finger-tips.

Do you remember saying, 'Your guttersnipe face'?

Once in Classroom IV, I spoke for you when you asked me to . . . But in the swell hotel you had the courage and the faith to give me my lines.

'I'll tell you what to say, Davie. Say "I want you to marry me. I don't think I ever want to let you out of my sight again. I want to look after you always. I don't want anything or anybody else. Say that." '

I think you already knew. You said it with the same conviction with which you used to speak of your father and mother in those splendid fibs. You were saying it against yourself and I knew, I knew that we were sailing headlong for the rocks. I could hear the noises of the wreck. So could you.

There was no possibility of a reply. There was no hope of explanation. I stuck. Just stuck. How long after? You'd begun playing with your fingers, stretching a long red hair, scowling up at it, with your head still on the pillows.

Very calmly, you said, 'We condemn ourselves out of our own mouths, David.' It was not Davie, then. You were quite matter of fact. You looked at me, and you went on, 'It was I who was the teaser, that's what you said. It was I who was the tamperer with life. So you said.'

I remember biting my finger: sticking again. For ten minutes, was it? It might even have been more. I jumped up cheerfully in the end.

'Let's go down and get some tea.'

A pause. 'Fine.'

IT ONLY REMAINS for me to write down what I said and did for the rest of the day. I do so with a coolness, an attempt at objectivity which is false. The worst was to come.

When she was dressed, we wandered downstairs to the huge lounge where the palm court orchestra was reducing itself to tears. I sat, sweating slightly, ordering tea, and she went and telephoned home. She used no guile with Stephen.

She said, 'I was having lunch with David Dow, darling, and it's gone on. We'll be coming back soon. How's things?'

Stephen trusted her implicitly. He was very cheerful, he had had a good day in Perth. At home, so she said, the combine had not broken down once. The gun-field was finished.

Back in the lounge, the orchestra and the central heating had reduced the guests to such depths of apathy and depression, with a kind of nostalgia for nothing, that they took no interest in us. I drank several cups of tea but I gave my cake ration to her and she ate, in all, five chocolate éclairs.

I said, 'I must have lost my balance altogether; I want to give you five more.'

About five minutes after, she swore it was only the music and the cakes, and apologised for becoming a schoolgirl again. But she began to cry so badly that I had to take her out. Everything in the hotel was miserably depressing as we moved down long corridors, trying to find something to cheer her up. She would not let me buy anything for her in the little shops by the main entrance. We went and looked at the empty ballroom and the billiards room filled with industrialists who had done their eighteen holes that morning. Both were equally depressing. We watched two boys who could not really play, banging about in a squash court, and somewhere else we heard the hydropathic click of ping-pong balls. In the swimming-pool, four children were yelling their heads off and the attendant was nowhere to be seen. Mary was still crying hopelessly so I ushered her into the spray room where we stood on the wet cork matting, along from the marble stalls. Steam swirled about the ceiling and I held her firmly by the arms. She looked younger then than I had ever seen her.

I tried to comfort her.

'You've done more good for me in one afternoon than the twenty-five years that went before. That's not bullying to say that.'

'No, darling.'

'Come on then,' gently.

'I promise it's only that awful music. I know it was only that . . .' Then she broke down again. She put it back to front in mirror writing. She spoke as if she had refused. 'Oh, Davie darling, I can't, I can't. There's Stephen, and – I promised. I swore. I can't.' She sobbed very loudly as I held her. She tried to stop crying until she said it made her throat sore, and then she cried again. 'I'd give anything to be able to, don't you see, but I promise I can't.'

For a second poor Lucy Ashton came to mind. I wondered if it were possible, after all, to drive somebody mad. She had no idea what was going on round about her. She asked me what the spray was for.

I sat her down on an old, gilt cane chair that had found its way from the ballroom to the sprays, and I unfolded a huge white handkerchief and said, 'Blow it to bits.'

Then I said, 'I refuse to do more damage, darling.' This

time it was not mirror writing. With a great wail she replied, 'God damn you, Davie, or damn whoever made you, or spoiled you, so you can say a bloody silly thing like that. Don't you understand what you're doing?'

'Darling, calm.'

'No,' she cried, 'I shan't be. I shan't be calm. It's a horrible dream, one of the ones when your feet stick to the ground. What else do I have to do for you? Don't you see I've really found you? I've reached through all your faces and edges. We're there!' And then with a laugh, 'No, we're not!'

Then, for a moment, she tried to control herself again. She pressed her head down and wiped her eyes and forehead with the back of her hand. But she was losing grip again.

'It'll break – Davie, I promise it'll break. My heart will break.'

She flung back her head suddenly and her whole face was wet. Her eyes looked curiously light. She said, 'I shall have to go to Moo.'

I replied, hopelessly, 'It's just – you must have been working up to this.'

'Oh Christ,' she said, rolling her head again in a curious, almost bear-like motion. 'Oh Christ, I shall have to go back to Moo. Don't let me go there – we could live, darling. I don't care where. I'd have your babies, with keely faces too . . . It's hopeless!' She said quietly, like an older woman now, 'I wouldn't lie any more. I wouldn't have to. I'd keep you sane. You'd keep me sane. Just that?'

And as I still could find no reply, she said, looking hard at the floor, 'I'm not sorry I spoke – I shan't be ashamed.'

'Of course you mustn't be,' I insisted, very quietly, but there I stuck again. I held her shoulders. I believe I was afraid lest she might literally break into pieces.

Then all the children came running, from the baths, to the sprays.

But by the time we got back to the main entrance, where I had left my car, she was much recovered. She still was frowning. We stopped for a moment to look at the conference's Notice of Events and she asked me, then, if I had anything to do that night. 'Work and Play' had completed my obligations that morning, and I said if I did not simply eat and sleep I would probably drive south. But I added:

'Don't ask me to supper.'

She said, 'No. I was going to ask you a favour.'

'On you go.' The Oxford accent had vanished.

'I'm meant to be doing something terribly depressing tonight, and I really feel too weak.'

She was red about the eyes. The porters watched us with undisguised curiosity.

'What?'

'I said I'd run Pink over to Arbroath. He's to go into a place there.'

'A place?'

'It's not as bad as all that. Looking round,' she said, 'I should think it's much like this. Anyway it's about the same price. It's voluntary and so forth. He's all right about it. But they might be able to do something for him. Make baskets, I suppose. Would you do that?'

She was quite calm. A hostess asking a favour.

'Go with you, you mean?'

Firmly she replied, 'No. Alone, please.'

'What about Stephen?'

She brought her finger down her face, pressing the bone of her nose. 'He's working so hard. I don't really want him to drive late at night.' Then she added, 'Anyway, I want to be with Stephen tonight. Would you?'

'For you.'

'And for old Pink,' she said carelessly. 'I think he'll be pleased it's not me. Together we might get terribly gloomy . . . A little dodgy, I think.'

*   *   *

It was soon after that, just outside, that she stopped and spoke of sin while I cried, 'No.' I could not find the words to say 'Now that you are there, that you feel love, that you have given, don't already start making rules and feeling sin; just be glad.' And not finding the right words I made a pompous sort of statement.

I think I said, 'It's better to start just with life and find out about right and wrong than to be burdened with so many hoodoos that you spend all your time in revolt, and miss out on love and life altogether.'

She cut straight through that.

'Do you love me?' Then, under her breath, 'Can you love me?'

Why couldn't I have lied? I do, in a way. Cousin, I do. But then came the furtive look. I moved a step forward. Something was sticking in my throat.

In a horrible stony silence, we climbed into the car.

A big mauve thunder cloud came up from the west as I drove her home, still in silence, and when we arrived the house had a bright, clear, well-washed look. From the gravel, it was like a child's painting. Directly in front, one could not see how far back it stretched, and in the odd bright light, it looked oddly two-dimensional, with the door in the middle, a square window either side, and three windows above. The roof did not look quite straight. To the right were the chestnut trees and the yew hedge, to the left the small lawn and the walled garden. Flush came up to be patted on the head. The windows, too, were full of faces, just like a child's drawing. They were all waiting for Mary. Pink waved supremely gaily from an upstairs window. Cathie came to another with the baby in her arms, and tried to make it wave to its mother.

'My goodness.' The tinker was beginning to regret the visit. 'I'd nearly forgotten about that one. He or she?'

'It's a "he". A boy called Harry,' she said. 'Don't

worry, you won't have to meet him. If he's up there, he's been fed.'

Just before she reached the door she said, 'Do I look a wreck?'

'You could have been crying.'

'It doesn't matter.'

The last private thing that she said to me was, 'Do I look a bit more Mary?' but I was still too cold and stuck to do more than nod. She was much more relaxed than me: curiously, calmly resigned.

She said, 'I'm glad about that. The only girl I knew called Georgina was a kleptomaniac.'

In the sitting-room Cathie recognised me, but it took me a moment to remember her. She had developed a more aggressive, impudent manner which barely covered a sense of happiness. Cathie was gradually replacing Macdonald, and although she was meant to leave at four she evidently always stayed until six or seven at night. Macdonald herself seemed to have slipped gradually but certainly into the background. Telling all seemed to have left her without wind in her sails, as if those evenings with Mary had completed a life which, more obviously, might have been expected to finish with the Colonel's burial. Age seemed to be catching up with her, all of a sudden. She had even lost confidence with the baby and Cathie, unthinkingly, had stepped in.

Cathie asked me fiercely, 'Have you not been offered a drink?'

Before I had time to reply she said, 'A fine house you'll be thinking this is, and you're given no hospitality.' She looked up at me and went on, aggressively but not unpleasantly, unsmilingly but not without humour, 'And a fine sort of guest it is, too, who doesn't even go up and see the son and heir. Mary says you've to go in the dining-room and pour yourself a whisky.'

'Thank you. I'll manage that.' But I could not then remember her name. At the door, she said:

'Pink'll be down in a moment. We're trying to persuade him to take a reasonable amount of stuff. You know what he is with all his things. He's everything there but the kitchen stove. You'd never get your car up the hill.'

Soon after, both Mary and Stephen arrived and we all had a drink together. She had made up her face again. She looked me perfectly warmly and friendlily in the eye, as if I'd become, in an hour, an old family friend. Stephen looked brown and well. He greeted me with great enthusiasm and even asked me to stay the night. The cut on his forehead rather improved his looks, I thought. What might be called informally formal, he was correct, but did not stand on ceremony. His manner was energetic and verging on the hearty. He was in shirt sleeves, and he was meaning to go out again after supper, because the hay harvest had prevented him doing a thousand and one things round the garden. But he still had the old habit of throwing all his worst cards on the table. I can't remember how he came to it but one self-disparaging phrase sticks in my mind. 'Well, well,' he said. 'I've got a 3.4 Jaguar and oil heating throughout. I can always tell St Peter that.'

Pink, when he appeared, was dressed for the city. He was in his best suit and Old School tie. He had a case in each hand and an umbrella under his arm.

'V-very good of you, old man,' he said to me, making the best of his stutter. Then he stood looking into thin air. He would not even accept a lime juice and soda and silence fell, as we stood round the door of the dining-room. As Stephen began to ask me about the conference, Mary hurried us along.

She said, 'David doesn't want to be late. Let's put these cases in the car.' We took them outside and it was then that Macdonald appeared for a few seconds. She stood at the back of the hall, and stared. We bundled Pink into the car

and Mary nodded quickly to me so that I should not wait
any longer. Pink was looking white and strained. The gay
wave from the upper window was already forgotten.

Then, at the last moment, as if Pink were going off to
school, Mary suddenly dashed into the house, and when
she returned she slipped him a five-pound note. His last
remark to her before we left had a curious, triumphant lift
to it, but I did not see how she reacted. I could no longer
look her in the face. As the wheels turned on the gravel he
smiled and wound down the car window.

'*T-tirez la* whatsit, Belle,' he said. '*La farce est jouée.*'

'It's most awfully good of you,' Pink said to me as we
approached the huge baronial mansion, on the outskirts of
Arbroath. 'In point of fact it's nothing much more than a
five-thousand-mile check-up. Thirty-fifth year, I am.
Oyez.'

The Superintendent of the baronial nut-house (as Pink
would have it) was uncertain of himself, it seemed to me,
only in the sense that he could not quite make up his mind
which part to play. There were several alternatives that
went with an actor's hoody face and a thick shock of white
hair. To the patients, I fancy, he liked to present himself as,
frankly, an angel. He had a way with him, everybody
agreed, and if one of the male nurses was having difficulty
with a patient he would not fail to go and help, and usually
he did good. Sometimes he used a slug of Pentothal or
Soneryl, or one of those with more or less Biblical names,
but occasionally he just talked. That was what he called, 'a
little touch of Hector in the night'. To the patients' relations he was the brilliant scientist – 'We're mapping out the
mind, Mrs Robertson, we're charting it.' He talked of deep
sleep and physical methods, of analysis and occupational
therapy. To the visiting scientists, officials, students or
professors he was the prophet and the poet. He played

all these parts with great energy, and his real genius lay in the fact that he persuaded himself he was being entirely honest in each.

The interview with Pink and me gave him full scope for his powers, and it was not until the end that he discovered that I was a scientist. Even then, he bluffed it out. Most of the conversation was directed to Pink who was more than prepared to discuss, in painful detail, the methods that they used. Hector then insisted on showing us round the place although I was anxious to go as quickly as possible.

'I say,' Pink asked him. 'Have you tried any surgery?'

'Oh, no, no, lad. We don't have the bad boys here. No bad boys.'

The Superintendent cleaned his glasses. He did not appear to enjoy the suggestion.

Pink said he was glad about that and then, alarmingly suddenly, both he and Hector started roaring with laughter.

Hector said, 'Were you thinking we might be chopping out hunks of your grey matter?'

Pink giggled and Hector slapped him on the back.

'I'm glad you've come, lad,' he said. 'I can see you'll be an asset to the place. You've got to have a sense of humour, you know. It's exactly like on board ship.'

But it was a curious, unnerving, sort of ship. Mary had been nearer right in the hall, that afternoon, when she had suggested it would be like the alco-pathic golfing hotel. I trailed from room to room, and did not smile. It was agonisingly depressing. Some of the rooms were bright and filled with people, playing bridge, listening to records, making rugs or dancing the cha-cha. There were several Buns and Belles playing clock golf and they looked at us as if we were men from Mars. In no case could the Superintendent define the nature of the patient's complaint.

'Nervous,' he said, certainly. He made a very dramatic speech, in one corridor. The rhetorical questions bowled along the vaulted roof like buckled wheels.

'What is a drunk? Or a dipso? Or an alcoholic? Or an unhappy fellow, eh? I defy you to define it, eh? Doctor, I defy you.'

One or two men and women, in spite of being jollied along by Hector as he passed, still sat alone, firmly determined to remain within themselves. But whether the faces, as they passed, were miserable or ludicrously happy, they filled me with the same terror. I saw one red-headed woman there, and wondered whose cousin she was.

Pink behaved as if he were being delivered to his private school. He seemed to find the whole idea of the place so awful that he made himself live entirely in the present. When I left him, with a sudden, strange, personal sadness, he was happily accepting a cup of cocoa from a trolley wheeled by a man with a handlebar moustache.

'Smoking,' Hector said to me, as we passed back to the main entrance of the huge converted Victorian house, 'is allowed everywhere. Send him cigarettes, eh?' Hector put an arm round my shoulder. 'Of course you're depressed,' he said. 'But your brother'll do well here. I'm sure he will. We don't guarantee things. You know that, as a scientist.' I fear I only wanted to get away. Hector had a curiously cynical phrase for it all.

'God, bottle and bed,' he said. 'That's what brings them here— But Bedlam? No. Not if I can help it. It's a question of organising them. Just giving them things to do.' He went on about Pink, at last. 'But we'll do no harm. And I bet we do good with your brother. I bet we do. You never can tell, but I bet we do good. It's not all science, you know. There's a bit of water-divining too. A lot of it's instinctive. We look into the dark, we do that. "We look into the dark and there's always someone there." That's Yeats, you know,' he said.

I felt very tired. I shook hands rather hurriedly and walked back to my car. I did not stay at the hotel that night. I picked up my things there and drove through the night, south to London again. The road passed Juniper Bank, and as if to mock me, the clouds drifted away from the moon as I came down past the bothie. The farm lay below, neat, toy-like, by the old hooped bridge and the bend of the river. As I swung round the corner and crossed over the new bridge I saw the house at its own level, and it looked solid, safe, permanent and un-neurotic. For a moment, it seemed to me unbearably beautiful.

We look into the dark and there's always someone there. We look into the dark and see the faces of those we have already destroyed, by our own ignorance of ourselves; our immaturity.

We look into the dark, sweet cousin, and no wonder we are afraid.

Silence

THE DOCTOR THOUGHT: I wish I could believe her. I wish I could take the story at its face value. I wish I could accept what the Sister had to say. I wish I could say I were a simple man, but none of us can say that any more.

He was sitting in an almost empty movie-house watching a bad western about a cowboy and an Indian girl. He thought, If I had told the hospital authorities that I too was a doctor they would have let me in, they'd have let me see Lilian, they wouldn't then have said how she was under sedation and not to be visited.

The movie wasn't very good. It had some kind of pioneering evangelist in it who didn't ring true; not, anyway, to the doctor who was himself, surprisingly, a believer. Surprisingly, because he was at the age of disbelief: over forty. But he happened to believe. He accepted the Christian rules. Which was odd, in 1968. His name was Larry Ewing, and he was one of the world's listeners.

The movie wasn't just bad; it made no sense at all. The doctor wished it would divert him. He thought, If it were half bad it would stop me thinking about their forbidding me to see my daughter. Thought, If it were a really good movie, if it were maybe *High Noon* or *Sweet Smell of Success* or even *Shane* it would also stop me thinking about the interview that lies ahead. It's years since I saw a movie. I used to go with Lilian. But now they have to put a message in. The doctor had an appointment at his son-in-law's club. His son-in-law was a fifth-generation Merchant Banker. He was very successful. He was called Mike Angel and he was a power in this club.

The doctor was funking the meeting. Otherwise he wouldn't have been sitting in an empty movie-house at 3.45 p.m. on a Sunday; he knew that. Now Lilian was the doctor's only daughter. For eighteen years out of her total twenty she had lived with him, at home, lovingly.

There is no mystery. People think of mental illness as something beyond their comprehension, to do with words like id and complex; to do with longer words than that. They listen to the drugstore analysts and feel incapable of arguing. They throw away the usual disciplines of thought. If you put someone under sedation, which only means that you help them more or less insistently to sleep, they do not then go berserk. The doctor thought, If I pass someone in the street and pretend not to recognise him it means that I do not want to speak to him. If I pass a good friend to avoid him, or even unwittingly cut him, it means, nearly always, that I am feeling guilty about him.

The doctor thought, therefore, that Lilian must herself have done something very bad; so shameful that she couldn't even confess it to him. How strange and tidy she looked, through the glass panelling: how already like a wife.

The doctor had paused beside the Sister's office, which was only a glass booth set in a carpeted corridor. It was a very expensive nursing home.

The doctor said, 'She didn't recognise me.'

He was in his tweed overcoat. He half turned away, then looked back over his shoulders. He wasn't a big man but he had a good sharp face and remarkable eyes.

The Sister said, 'It only happened last night, she's been under sedation ever since.'

The doctor never interrupted other people. He watched and waited until they had finished speaking, then either did or did not reply. In this case he did not. It takes intelligence to listen the way the doctor did.

The Sister said, 'She spoke with her husband this morn-

ing. She told him most of what had happened. You've just
come at a bad moment. You're sure you won't have a little
coffee? You do look rather pale.'

The doctor still watched the Sister's mouth. Then he
noticed that the Sister was really quite pretty, which is the
way good nurses should be. She wasn't as pretty as Lilian,
but she was pretty enough for her trade. The doctor
thanked her and refused the coffee. He didn't make any
excuses. He just said, 'No thanks', and took the elevator.

He wished the movie amused him more. He wished he
could have seen *Gunfight* or *Shane*. The movie-house stank.
The doctor buttoned up his coat and left. Outside it was
terribly cold. He thought: Maybe Lilian is really asleep
lying flat on her back with her yellow hair trailing over the
side of her bed; my daughter Lilian; her face a little freckled
and now very pale.

'Really, Mr Angel,' the Sister had told Mike. 'If you give me
your home number, I'll call you as soon as she wakes.' She
referred to his wife, Lilian.

He wasn't listening to her too closely. He looked pre-
occupied; not quite distracted. His collar was unbuttoned
and at four in the morning his chin was a shadowy blue. He
was half leaning against the Sister's glass booth in the
corridor and standing there, cross-legged, drinking his fifth
cup of coffee, he somehow still looked rich. He wasn't a big
man but he was springy and fit; almost suspiciously so, as if
he felt he had a long, long way to go.

'The doses have been exceptionally strong,' the Sister
said. She was quite a nice-looking, solid sort of girl.

Mike nodded. He was staring blankly at the carpet which
had an infuriatingly asymmetrical pattern in yellow and
orange and brown and blue.

The Sister wore the face of her watch on the inside of her
wrist. As she raised it, something clicked; her cuffs were
starched.

She said, 'Under such heavy sedation I'd say it would be eleven o'clock or twelve noon before we hear a peep from her.'

Then Lilian screamed. Mike moved like lightning.

'Darling, Lilian, Lilian, it's me.'

She was screaming and yelling indistinctly, 'Get away, get away.' She was more or less on her feet on the bed and stumbling back towards the wall. But the bed was on castors and it slipped a foot or two. She half fell, then, between wall and bed.

As the Sister reached across towards her she upset the low bedside light which had an expensive shade. Lilian's voice rose a pitch. Her nightie was short and white. She kept pulling it away from her body. Her blonde hair looked paradoxically tidy and orderly. Somebody must have brushed it as she went off to sleep; Mike had brushed it. Her eyes were smoky and pale blue.

'It's Mike.'

'No.'

'It's *Mike*, Lilian, darling.'

She stopped screaming. 'Oh, Michael,' she said suddenly, without emphasis or feeling. He reached out.

She took his hand, and sat down in the bed. Mike dismissed the Sister; said he'd deal with it, thank you; thank you, Sister. She went.

Lilian sat quite rigidly. She said, 'I know exactly where I am.'

'You've had a bad dream.'

'I remember everything.' Her lower lip began to tremble. Then she took in a gulp of air and steadied. She talked swiftly, almost like an English girl. There was money in her voice. She said, 'You promise not to do anything about it. Not *anything*.'

'Forget it, darling,' he reassured her. 'It never happened.'

She still sat quite rigidly. He persuaded her to lie back on the pillows. He didn't touch her shoulders or face, but kept a firm grip on her small white hand.

After a moment, she said, 'There's a difference between a girl being spoilt and not knowing it and a girl knowing she's spoilt.' Then very suddenly she sat up again and threw her arms round his neck. She said, 'Don't go away, Michael.'

'I'm right here.'

'Michael, I thought it was all over—'

'Forget it.'

'I don't mean I thought, I'll die, he'll kill me, I thought, It'll be all over with Michael, Michael won't touch me now.'

'Steady, darling, steady, don't go back.' But she had already retired too far, recalled too much. The edge of the cliff began to crumble. She didn't scream, this time, but let out a low, very frightening drone; almost a buzz.

'It's all over, my darling Lilian, don't think about it, it's over—'

But the buzz grew harder; the drone, louder. She started pulling her nightie away from her body; started to yell that she wanted a bath. 'Run a bath.' Next she was coughing, trying to make herself vomit. She withdrew from Mike again. She tore off her nightie, screaming, and lashed out with her arms and legs. She was twenty, Lilian, and her figure was perfection.

The Sister returned. She had a hypodermic syringe. Mike held his wife down and she screamed until the veins stood out in her neck.

The drug, whatever it was, worked almost instantaneously. Lilian was laid out naked, almost with that frightening, ageless calm of the dead. The nurse tucked up the bedclothes, Mike stepped out of the room. He went as far as the staircase; walked down to the landing below. He didn't want the Sister to see his red eyes or to witness his trembling like this.

He didn't smoke. He breathed deeply then he ran upstairs lightly and walked straight past the Sister's booth. He re-entered the little, single private ward. He looked at his wife's angelic face. He believed her to be the most beautiful girl on earth. He thought, Maybe she'll never be right again. Never. He didn't dare kiss her cheek lest that disturbed her. With his finger-tip he touched her hair, just where it shone, in the dim light.

Stepping back into the corridor, he gave the Sister two numbers. He wrote a note to be given to Lilian in the event of her coming round again. It was a comfortable, relaxed kind of note; composed carefully that way. He had already arranged to meet her old man for drinks at the club. In the note he casually added, '. . . and I'm not going to tell him a word about what we're both going to forget; have forgotten. Love, my darling, my forever one – Mike.'

He asked for an envelope, then he found his coat which had a smart velvet collar. He looked, now, completely composed. As he handed over the note, he warned the Sister not to give information to anybody about Lilian. She was sure about that.

'You're very kind,' he said briefly and took the stairs, not the elevator. He ran lightly down four flights and stepped into the street. The temperature was sixteen below zero and the wind was blowing hard across the frozen lake. He set his teeth against it and half bowed his head. He had some calls to make.

On Sunday afternoons, in the wintertime, the club organised concerts. They had good people, even great people, who came and played or sang. They played Bach or sang Schubert or sent things up, like Victor Borge. The concerts were a signal, not a confirmation, of the contention that members and their wives weren't altogether philistine. And now the concert was over, the huge premises were filled with well-dressed men and women taking cocktails and telling less or more than all. Some of the past presidents – senators, bankers and railroad millionaires, portrayed within massive gilt frames themselves – looked pained by the chatter. The rooms were very high and lit only with wall lights and standard lamps with red shades. It was as if the dark area above were filled with humming-birds and rooks and the occasional wild parakeet.

The doctor had green, penetrating eyes. Even in the crowded lobby, the porter recognised him again. As he stepped across to the bar, which was what he thought of as Angel's club, he had to take a couple of deep breaths in order to try and be calm. He told himself, don't be a fool, know yourself better, you were bound to disapprove of anyone Lilian married; but he knew too, that he didn't believe that. Thought, maybe I hate the rich. Why? Because they see nothing, that's why; because they're blind. Money protects, which is to say blunts truth.

The doctor had been there before but this afternoon he found the atmosphere unusual. It was far less noisy than the anterooms, but that was not what struck him. The difference lay in the light. The room, which was the best part of seventy feet long, had no windows. Daylight was afforded by a flat glass roof with red margins. Today the bar seemed darker because the glass was covered with two or three inches of newly fallen snow.

Michael Angel was the youngest director in the firm for which Lawrence Junior now worked. The doctor couldn't remember the name of the boy in the nursery rhyme who sold his sister for a pair of shoes, but he thought Lawrence Junior maybe sold his sister for the promise of a place on the board. But Angel, the son-in-law, was not so bad as he seemed. He looked very beautiful, brown, athletic, with bright dark eyes and very, very expensive clothes. He looked like the candidate, so to speak; the candidate for anything. But he really wasn't so bad. For instance he hadn't yet given Lawrence Junior a place on the board; which was smart of him, the doctor thought.

Now Lawrence Junior kept saying 'Literally'. He said, 'Dad, I am not talking metaphorically. No wonder Lilian's where she is. He pissed on her. Dad. Literally. Dad. Literally pissed on Lilian. Doesn't that do something to you? He pissed on her. He failed to seduce her. Failed to rape her. He drove her to this place. He drove her right there down the darkest street, just by the lake. Dad, he literally pissed on her. Or doesn't that penetrate your head?'

The doctor's son Lawrence Junior was talking with more than usual intensity, and he was often forceful and intense. He had sweat on his brow. His eyes were a little pink, maybe from the cold wind that blew outside. Junior was already fatter than the doctor. Both men needed spectacles to read the list of special Sunday cocktails in the windowless club bar. The doctor wore gold wire-rimmed spectacles: his son's were heavy, in tortoiseshell.

'She's under sedation,' the doctor said.

'You've seen her?'

'They wouldn't allow me to see her.'

'Of course they'd allow you to see her. Jesus, who's paying? You're a doctor, aren't you? Oh Dad. Why didn't you go in? Sometimes I think you like being pushed around.'

'No. I don't like being pushed around,' the doctor said, and Angel rescued him, then:

'Maybe Doc was right, Lawrence. It's good Lilian gets sleep.'

They brought the second round of Bloody Marys. Or was it the third? The boys had been there for a while, discussing things, deciding what to say to the doc.

The bar and panelling were of oak, also the few tables at the end of the room. All the fittings including the dozen or so chairs were solid and Ivy League and big. The floor was polished and red.

Because the doctor had said he did not like being pushed around Lawrence Junior waited a little before coming back into the attack. The doctor could see his game. We read our children indifferently, we do not know their hearts, but we perceive their methods, just as we recognise their lies. The doctor thought, the Bloody Marys only seem stronger because it is so cold, so very cold outside, with that wind blowing across the icy lake. The warmth of the club bar itself made him feel a little light-headed, at half past four that Sunday afternoon.

Angel said, 'Well, the long and the short of it, Doc, is that Lawrence has a plan of action and while I am not a retributive kind of man . . .'

The doctor thought, Why does he use words like 're-tributive'? Really, he should be a politician.

'. . . far from it, I hate the idea of vendetta – but in this case I think Lawrence is right. This is an extreme case. And sooner or later a man must stand up and be called.'

Some of these phrases, the doctor thought, roll off his tongue too easily. Maybe John F. Kennedy said that about standing up and being called. Angel saw himself as a Kennedy type. His suits demonstrated that to the doctor.

Angel went on, 'In the end, we're the children of the pioneers, and even if we've gotten a little soft, we can't be that soft. We can't let somebody do that to Lilian, then just walk away.' He took a sip of the club's blood, which is what they called their Bloody Marys in Angel's club, and added, 'Or I can't. Nor can Lawrence.'

The doctor hesitated.

'Would you like some cheese, Doc? The crackers are highly recommended.'

The doctor said, 'Sister told me you were down there this morning.'

'Certainly I was.'

'She seemed a competent kind of girl. The Sister.'

'Fuck her,' Angel said, eating a couple of crackers. 'How was it with Lilian?'

'She seemed badly disturbed.'

'Right.'

'Did she make any sense to you?'

'A little,' Angel said.

'Did you find out how it happened to her?' the doctor asked.

Angel tipped back in his chair. He looked round at his friends' faces. The very blond one, Bob Dunn, said, 'Angel has a pretty good idea.'

Angel said, 'Bill, would you ask these gentlemen to stop hogging the cheese? We have a guest in the club.'

'Not for me,' the doctor said.

Angel brushed some crumbs off his lapel. The doctor screwed up his eyes.

'She was on her way back from a dance.'

'With you?'

Mike shook his head. So Hansen asked, 'What kind of dance?'

'Down at the Lakeside Youth Centre,' which was a downtown club run by uptown people.

Mike said, 'He hitched a lift with her from the club after their Saturday dance. He failed to seduce her. He hit her. He failed to rape her.' He had grown very pale. He seemed incapable of going on.

'Do you know who he is?'

'Yes I do.'

Bob Dunn said, 'Then there is something we can do, for Christ's sake. You two are not going down there on your own.' He looked round at the others, and they were with him, everyone except Walter and Tom Shaw.

Mike said, 'I'm not going anywhere. I promised Lilian that.'

'Did he hit her bad?' Dunn asked.

Mike shook his head. Then he said quickly, 'He literally

pissed on her. Shoved her out of the car. Dumped her. And blew. It was about ten below zero last night, but she got to a phone. I picked her up.'

'Oh for Christ's sake,' someone else said.

The doctor said, 'Aren't the police involved?' The doctor wasn't a big man. When he asked a good question he looked a little short-sighted, looked very much like a professor who would be pushed around. Which drove his son mad.

'No, thank God. And they're not going to be. This is one of these cases when it is necessary for the husband to act privately. If you involve the police you involve the press. We don't want that.' Angel finished his Bloody Mary. One of the others persuaded the doctor to finish his drink. He was thinking, My son is very much like a guilty German; he is handsome and forceful and something hurt him, early on. Maybe he didn't like it that I never went to the army. He's right. That was one of the real reasons I studied medicine. My old man decided that. He frog-marched me to the medical school, in 1940. I felt bad because I knew it was a dodge for me, not a vocation at all. Maybe some of my guilt is visited upon this aggressive young man who is so certain that he is always right. But I haven't made too bad a doctor; my patients know that.

One of the men by the cheeseboard, in the adjoining group, said, 'Angel, it's ten of five.'

Angel nodded. He said, 'Bob, could you get them to fill a couple of flasks of this stuff?' and the doctor began to see that the plans were already laid.

He found it hard to say what was on his mind; what had been on his mind since he left the little private ward. Then he began, 'It doesn't seem that a man would go to those lengths without provocation,' and Angel cut in. He did not raise his voice but replied in the same swift smooth even tone, 'Why, isn't that a nice thing to say about your daughter? But it doesn't apply to my wife.'

There was a pause. The doctor thought, I hate him, of course.

'I don't know,' Tom Shaw joined in. 'It's never too good a thing to take the law in your own hands.'

'This isn't the law. This is private,' Dunn said. 'This is Mike's wife.'

'Right,' Mike replied. And now his suppressed anger seemed to collect itself. Bob, over by the bar, broke the awkward silence.

'Two flasks?'

'Right,' Angel said. Angel didn't carry his own cigarettes. He affected not to smoke. He grinned when he reached to a pack belonging to one of his friends. He turned back.

'So don't worry,' he told the doctor. 'I'm fortunate in my friends.'

The doctor was thinking, No wonder I went into that cinema, I must have known it was going to work out like this. The ice was clinking against the side of his glass.

He said, '*Is* it the best idea to take the law into your own hands?'

Angel said, 'He'll have his say.'

Tom Shaw added, 'That's the whole point.'

'And if he's found guilty?' the doctor asked. 'If you find him guilty?'

Nobody answered.

Somebody said, 'We don't need three cars, do we?' He was answered 'No, God no, two's enough.'

The doctor thought how strange it was that a certain type of rich man often believed that fathers had been castrated. He wondered if it was his profession, his income or merely his age that led them so brightly to this insulting assumption. He finished his vodka and very gently asked the question, 'Do I take it that we are leaving at five?'

In putting it that way, he was being less than true to himself. He was answering Angel and his friends in their own terms. He knew that. Almost as he said it he asked himself, Why on earth should I have done that? How inconsistent we are.

'Good for the Doc,' one of them said generously, thereby applauding him for having made the worst decision of his life.

Angel now mentioned a downtown address. He said, 'That is the apartment where this perverted gentleman lives.'

They were all watching the doctor as the news sank in.

'That's in the Negro quarter,' he said, at last.

'Does that alter the principle?' Angel asked. The doctor kept staring at his own shoes. 'Does it?' Angel said.

It didn't. Perfectly true. It *changed* things but it didn't alter the principle. Say nothing, doctor, if you have nothing relevant to say.

Shaw tried to help again. 'It's simply a matter of going down there and extracting the man. He'll have his say. We can hear what he says.' Somebody else agreed, 'It's as simple as that.'

Angel stood up and finished his drink. It was one minute to five. The porter came in to tell him that the boy had brought his car to the door.

'Thank you, John,' Angel said. He led the way.

The doctor thought, I ought to go at once and call the police.

Angel's car was a Rolls, of course: the newest in navy blue. The advertisement used to say that when a Rolls was travelling a mile each minute the only sound to be heard was the ticking of the clock – and the makers were seeing to that. Heavy clods of snow thudded against the mud-guards because the city snow ploughs hadn't yet cleared the downtown lakeside highway. The temperature wasn't far below zero, but it had been cold for a week. The lake itself was frozen and the wind was still blowing across it from east of north. It threw the snow up in gusts which covered the windscreen. The lights on the dashboard shone brightly now. It was growing dark. The doctor felt cold and lonely, crouched in the back of that fast car.

Why had he said, 'Do I take it that we are leaving at five?' He liked to think it was the sight of Lilian in that little private ward which had led him into this but he knew that to be a lie. He supposed three vodkas had helped. Angel's quip had stung him, too. But in the end, he wondered, wasn't it just a vanity, a daring-do resulting from his own sense of inadequacy in that damnable atmosphere with the red linoleum, the signet rings and gold watches, the dark suits and the polished London brogues? He sat thinking these things in the car. Sat thinking, If we are true to ourselves are we ever satisfied that we are men? And if I were a simple man, I should be proud. I always used to see movies about the little men fighting back. Here I am with a son and a son-in-law both brave boys and they're not going to let anybody hurt my daughter. I should be happy. Junior must love his sister very much to do this for her.

But the doctor wasn't a simple man. He didn't behave like the plucky Jewish immigrant. He didn't really have to; not where he practised. Besides, he couldn't quite believe that the boys were reacting from love of Lilian.

Angel said, 'You know he worked at the Mission? This mission to which Lilian came twice a week? It's a friendship mission. A human rights organisation. The war on poverty, right down here, somewhere. This bastard worked alongside her for quite a few weeks. Then, pow.'

'That's nothing to do with colour, Mike, not a thing like that. And you can't let it be, not whatever Lilian said, you know that.' The blond boy, Dunn, seemed to be some kind of personal assistant to Angel: he drove. Angel sat in the front beside him. In the back were Shaw, the doctor in the middle, and another younger man called Cross who was the top athlete in the group. The others followed in a big steely Buick sedan.

Apart from the clock and the thud of the snow there was soon another intermittent noise. Shaw kept talking. Shortly, the doctor began to work out why. Shaw was either more cowardly or more imaginative than the rest. He was talking compulsively. To begin with, he spoke about the weather. He went on to talk of the misery of the district into which they now penetrated. They passed from the wide freeway into a kind of temporary shanty town, then into the slums themselves.

'Right,' Dunn said, at the end of Shaw's long dissertation on the sad history of the place, and when the commentary was about to continue Angel told Cross, 'Give him a swig.' Cross had the thermos flask filled with the icy club's blood.

The doctor still kept absolutely quiet. When Shaw had swigged, he passed the flask forward to Angel who did not then forget his manners. He turned back.

'Doc?' he invited. 'It's the best Bloody Mary in the world.'

The doctor accepted the flask. He, too, took a swig then passed it forward again to his son-in-law.

Once more, Shaw began to talk. This time he seemed determined to persuade the doctor that their actions were justified. Meantime Dunn, the driver, took a drink. Angel was not a drinking man. He had sunk three or four at the club which was more than he had done for the past month. His face was a little paler than usual, his eyes brighter. He was breathing deeply as if he were trying to restrain himself.

The district maybe looked better in the snow which covered the garbage and jetsam on the sidewalks, and the bricks and bottles and old iron on the road. I'm scared of these streets, I mustn't open my mouth, the doctor thought.

Shaw began again.

'Oh, for Christ's sake,' Cross said.

Shaw said, 'I'm telling the doctor, he doesn't know it all.

This bastard must have been plotting the assault the whole time . . . And he'd seemed a nice young man.'

'Okay,' Angel said, trying gently to shut him up. But it isn't possible to silence a man gently when his nerve begins to go.

In the front, Dunn gave a groan. He yelled at Shaw to shut up. Angel chuckled.

About then, they slowed down. Angel and Dunn peered ahead through the snow which was blown in strange patterns by the wind. They found it hard to read the street signs. Then, passing a crossing, Dunn swore at himself. They had overshot the turning. Dunn swung the Rolls round into the middle of the avenue and turned about. Somebody hooted and swerved by in an old Mustang. He was yelling. He was black. Angel was very calm. He read out the number of the street.

Angel seemed to be changing one part of the plan, because he no longer trusted Tom Shaw. He told the driver, 'You come up with me, Bill. Tom, you stay with the car.'

Shaw at once understood the implication and began to protest. But Angel, stepping out on to the sidewalk and buttoning his black coat with the velvet collar, had authority. He did not raise his voice as he said again, 'Tom, you stay with the car.' Angel moved off towards the Buick.

Cross and the doctor had now scrambled out. They stood in the roadway, waiting for Angel. How very ugly it all is, the doctor thought. Dunn climbed out, but before he could close the door Angel turned back and restrained him, reached in and took the ignition key. Poor Shaw was too busy scrambling from the back to the front to observe this cut-off to possible flight: it isn't easy to start a Rolls without a key.

The snow helped. If it hadn't been for the snow the streets would have been crowded, but now there was no-body, except just inside the tenement door. There were some children there, staring out. Their legs looked very thin and black. One had on a navy blue anorak.

As Angel said, 'This way, gentlemen,' and led on with his gloved fingers tucked lightly into his coat pockets, the doctor wondered if he were armed. He hoped not: then glancing back and seeing coloured men emerging on to the sidewalk, he thought, I'm damned if I'll hope so.

The apartment was on the second floor, Number 217. The building was only six stories high. The snow didn't seem so thick. Perhaps the high building opposite protected the house from the wind. But some snow had drifted on to the balconies and lay against the windows and doors.

The doctor didn't know the plan of action, but it was obvious to him that everything had been worked out, beforehand. The Buick was strictly in reserve. No one had climbed out of it. The doctor thought, I shouldn't be here.

There was no need to ring or knock. The occupants of Number 217 were already on the balcony. There was an old man, a middle-aged woman, a girl about sixteen and a younger boy. Angel said, 'Good evening, Mr Clarke,' and walked straight into the apartment, with Cross on his heels. Protesting only mildly, the old man and his family followed him in. The doctor and Dunn brought up the rear.

Angel and Cross and the family moved straight into the living-room. Dunn locked the front door and then stepped into the kitchen which overlooked the balcony and also the road and the Rolls below. He switched off the lights and took up a position in which he could see outwards and downwards at an acute angle. He sat on a cheap, maybe home-made cupboard to do this.

The doctor walked through to the living-room where Angel and Cross had already started work. Like all plans, this one had already gone awry: there was no sign of the villain. Meantime Cross upturned the beds and opened every cupboard door. Pulling back a curtain he tore it off the rail.

The doctor was almost sure that there was about to be violence. It is the sins of omission, he thought, which we always live to regret. Of course I should have rung the police. Simultaneously, he observed the situation. It was fairly obvious that these were the parents and brother and sister of the boy who had assaulted Lilian. The next step would seem to be for Cross to twist the old man's arm and ask for the son's whereabouts. The Negro family stood almost in an exact line. They seemed to lack spirit. Their expressions were sorrowful rather than indignant. They did not look so frightened. It was as if they had expected the visit and in a sad sort of way were glad their time had come.

The doctor was therefore warning his son-in-law when he said, 'We can't bear the responsibility for our children all their lives. It isn't Mr Clarke's fault any more.'

But the doctor again underestimated Angel, who had style.

'What is your girl's name?' Angel asked the father.

The girl herself answered 'Christina.'

Angel didn't turn to her. He never took his eyes off the old man who was lean and creased and not very big; with a mouth that hung open.

Angel said, 'My wife, whose father, Dr Ewing, is standing there by the door, is not very much older than Christina. If I had promised to run her home, attempted and failed to seduce her, attempted and failed to rape her, then driven her to a dark place, removed her from the automobile and urinated on her, I do not imagine that you would have left the matter there.'

The mother said, 'Rex'd never done that.'

'Rex did,' Angel answered briefly.

'Not without reason, he wouldn't of,' the old man said, and Angel turned sharply away, in anger.

'Where is he?' Cross asked, woodenly.

'He's gone.'

'Gone where?' Cross asked.

'Don't say where he's going.'

Angel had recovered himself. He said, 'Why should he have disappeared if he weren't guilty?'

''Cos he know he won't get a fair shake-out, that's exactly why,' the old man said. At that point, just when the doctor was beginning to feel that things maybe weren't going to work out quite so badly as he had anticipated, there was a surge of noise outside and from the kitchen Dunn shouted, 'Angel. Here.'

Angel didn't run. The doctor followed. They looked out.

In the space of less than half a minute there was to be total bloody confusion in which men would die. Possibly, if it hadn't started in the street, Angel and Cross would have soon used violence against the family and fused an explosion, anyway; but that's not how it happened.

Ironically, the trouble stemmed from the traffic misdemeanour: the prohibited U-turn. The men in the car that had skidded to a stop were belligerent and not quite sober. Maybe their club too had blood. Whatever, they had enough liquor in them to persevere. They followed in the Buick's track: then parked behind it.

Now, joined by a dozen other Negroes who had appeared on the sidewalk, they were shouting and rocking the Buick. The noise they made brought everybody on to the street. As Angel and the doctor watched, the car was overturned, with its occupants trapped inside.

There were screams and shouts. Then a shot was fired. Shaw had found the gun that Angel always kept in the pocket of the Rolls. He fired back towards the group round the Buick: fired wildly, but winged one man. He leapt back into the car only to find that the key wasn't there. His fingers fumbled up and down the dashboard. With a little yelp of fear, he jumped out into the road again and backed away. Frightened by the growing crowd he fired several more shots, but above their heads. He then took to his heels and ran.

Dunn, Cross, Angel and the doctor were by this time out of apartment 217 and running along the balcony, but they were far, far too late. There wasn't one man, not even one dozen: every man for miles around seemed to be converging from above and below. And there were more and more running up the street. They went to the Buick, to help kick in Whitey's head, or else they joined the mob by the stone stairs.

It was to take many days before the doctor worked out just what happened next. Only one got clean away. Angel, in the Rolls. Lawrence Junior fled in the other direction. The doctor managed to throw himself across the car, over the trunk at the back but he got flung clear at the first corner. About fifty black people were pouring out of the tenement. The doctor ran blindly until he thought his legs and heart would break. He kept stumbling and falling and each place where he fell he left red marks in the snow. The blood was coming from a knife wound in his side.

The wound was in his side just above the trouser belt and he suspected that his liver was punctured, which would give him an hour or two, not more. But still he ran and staggered and fell and picked himself up again. He was, at this point, no braver than Tom Shaw or any other frightened man.

In fact he was saved by the wind and the snow. Had it been better weather there would have been people in the street. Had it been calm the drifting snow would not have covered his trail of redness.

Turning at the first crossing, in what he imagined to be an uptown direction, he saw what he had hoped for: a telephone kiosk. He kept striking the building with the side of his fist as if that helped to push him along. He thought, Steady. I dial Emergency, that's all I have to do. But then he remembered that he had no idea where he was. He ran back to the crossing to get the numbers of street and avenue, which were still a long, long way downtown. The street sign was covered with snow and the light wasn't clear. He banged the signpost so that the snow would fall away and reveal the writing. The snow fell in his face and he wiped it away with his sleeve. He was still staring up at it when a car suddenly swung into the street. Its headlights dazzled him for a moment. He turned and started to run back to the kiosk.

But he never reached it. The car too, turned at the crossing. It skidded in the loose snow. It was coming very fast. As it revved and followed the kerb behind him, he crazily hurtled straight across the street then started to run back to the crossing. The car drew up by the phone opposite. The doctor cowered into a dark doorstep beside a shop that was boarded up – Premises To Let. A couple climbed out of the car. They both went into the kiosk. For a moment the doctor couldn't believe his luck. He stood pressing his shoulder against the lintel.

The door behind him opened up. It wasn't locked.

The doctor's wound did not hurt him too badly, but he was beginning to shake. It wasn't only the pain that made him tremble. It was what he had seen back there: in the fighting one of their children, a boy about twelve, was shoved over the edge of the balcony and he must have been hurt very badly. The doctor thought, They will kill me, lynch me, tear me apart.

The couple left the kiosk and jumped into their big car. The young man started it foolishly again and his wheels spun round in the snow. Then he skidded off into the distance. The doctor moved up the street in the shadows but before he had even stepped into the light, he heard the pursuers. This time there was no mistake. There were three or four cars. One stopped at the crossing and five or six men got out. They were debating which side of the street they should take. They were searching for him. He thought,

Somebody must have seen me fall off the back of the Rolls. Hark, hark the dogs do bark.

Keeping in the shadow he stepped swiftly back towards the shop with the shutters and the broken front door. Quickly he stepped inside. For some extraordinary reason, no kid had bothered to break the frosted glass in the door. The doctor thought he could hear the hunters trying the doors farther down the street. He knew he was panicking. He could see himself from above. He thought he'd better lie down on the floor with his back against the door. He did so, dropping down just as a couple more cars swung by. He could hear the men in the cars shouting, 'We'll find him. Keep a look out for the footsteps in the snow.' Then the car was gone.

The doctor crouched and held his breath. He couldn't hear anybody now. Like anyone who has let fear take its grip he was unable to act consistently any more. He almost wanted to give himself up. How like me, he thought. At the worst possible moment, at the instant of maximum risk, as he heard the men just coming up alongside, he moved and ran across the hall, up the first flight of stairs. There was a bulb burning on the landing above. The walls of the place were painted marine blue. He *must* have thrown a shadow on the frosted glass.

He heard their voices again. They seemed to have paused. They were talking about the phone kiosk. Another two cars came by and one stopped. It seemed that more men were getting out, though the doctor couldn't see. He imagined hundreds, with sticks and oily cloths round their hair. And with that he heard dogs. He thought he heard the bark of a dog. That made him stagger up the second flight of stairs. He thought, I'll hide. I'll find some cover, then get back to the phone when they've gone. In the distance there was the sound of sirens: of police cars and ambulances; of a fire engine, maybe, to wash away the red snow.

At the top of the first flight of stairs, on the mean landing facing him, there was a door which would lead into a room overlooking the street and it seemed to be open. They must have seen that the building is deserted, he thought, they must have guessed that he'd come in here. The snow and the sweat had made his face wet and when he tried to wipe his eyes clear he left blood on his cheeks. Hark, hark, he thought, the dogs do bark; he used to tell Lilian all those rhymes. God, how the mind flits and yet sticks when we finally panic. What a white skin I have, the doctor thought. How irrelevant is the mind, in fear.

The door in front of the doctor must have had some story. Again the doctor's mind switched in that haphazard, tripping, incredibly swift way: this time, to the imagined story of the door.

The voices were calling outside: and calling back.

There wasn't a lock on the door; there was, so to speak, a no-lock. The lock that had been there was battered away; amputated. Axed, axed out and replaced by plywood and boxwood all nailed together; and some kind of hook and chain. Chain to the lintel.

Another car had drawn up outside in the snowy street. Men with black voices were asking each other, 'Left, Right, this way, that?'

So somebody sometime must have broken into this room, maybe yelling to get at a woman or to set free a child or a dog, or to mend some broken pipe.

The doctor moved in, suddenly, and the chain rattled against his hand as he stepped into the dark. Inside, the doctor fumbled with the chain. He could still hear those voices out there.

If he hooked up the chain, then nobody could open the door from outside. Not if he hooked it properly and twisted and knotted it. The doctor did that, frantically; tied it, looped it, pulled it. Fear. There was no kind of padlock, but the hook seemed strong. So tie it again, the doctor told himself, you will be safe for a second or two, even for half a minute, safe from every damn black-power running dog downstairs and outside in the bleak street. Safe maybe for a minute.

As he tried it again, and the chain zipped and rattled in his nervous hands, the doctor kept saying to himself, 'Safe, safe', only 'safe'. The doctor thought, Three club drinks, that stage just before group drunkenness where you see your own complexion reflected in the ruddiness of the others' faces. He felt ashamed. Tabasco on the old liver wound. He shivered and breathed out his held breath. He thought, The window must be covered up. I must go to the window and watch the street from there: watch the kiosk; wait my time.

He breathed again, feeling his knees sag.

Then, all of a sudden his body reacted. His body reacted before his mind. His spine, his legs, his fingers even stiffened. His mouth went dry. His hair stood up at the back of his neck. Then he froze. Absolutely froze. He closed his eyes shut and hung on to the chain behind his back.

The doctor knew that he was not alone in the room.

The doctor came round again as he hit the floor. He groaned. His sense of fear awoke before his power of reason and before his pain. He suppressed his groan. He did not dare close his eyes. He stared at the darkness which must have been the floor, stared at it as if he was no longer capable of closing his eyes.

The doctor knew that he was behaving like a coward. He thought, Worse than talkative Tom Shaw. Then, at once, he tried to reason with himself. Said, 'Don't too easily condemn yourself. That never helps. There's a difference between unnecessary cowardice and justifiable fear.'

He could hear It breathing. He knew It was awake. The door was chained, tied up in knots. The room was almost totally dark. Almost. Perhaps a dog, he thought, a wild dog.

The voices were dying away. Perhaps snow was falling

more heavily. They'd lost the track . . . Now he was sorry they'd lost the track.

The doctor stayed absolutely still, as rigid as a stone, listening to the faint, faint sound of breathing. He was quite sure he heard the breathing. He was almost certain that he was in the presence of an animal. Then he thought, No, there are many people in here. He strained to listen as he had never listened. The breathing was regular. He must look up.

He did so, and yelped, and lay back.

He had seen absolutely nothing. But the sound of his own emasculated voice brought him a little to his senses. He was now in a different position, his back more or less against the door. He was behaving like a schoolgirl in a haunted house. He could see that. The pain – sudden, hot, wet pain – from his side helped his control. The touch of the blood greatly encouraged him. He dared lift his eyes.

The room was no longer totally dark. He could make out the rectangle of the window, which seemed to be covered with some kind of sacking or cloth. Then below that rectangle, in what seemed to be the corner of the room, there were two holes, two sources of light. For a moment the doctor thought that they must be peepholes into an adjoining room in which there was light. But something about the angles made that hard to accept. The light must therefore be reflected. Perhaps there was something metal or glass on a shelf.

The two sources moved. Again the doctor let out a little yelp of terror, then at once suppressed it. They were eyes. They were eyes and he was on the floor, his back to a door that would take a minute to open. Maybe they were dog's eyes, after all. They seemed to be yellow, but the colour was hard to tell in the street light.

Because the eyes were at a low level in the room the doctor kept asking himself what kind of animal they might belong to. But the mind, always complex, is more than ever so, in fear. It appears to be frozen but, in truth, it is in ten places at once. Even as he went through the list from police-dog to chimpanzee, the doctor didn't believe himself. He knew he was locked in the room with another human being; and not a white one. He hardly dared recognise the odds he was really reckoning; the animal choice was only a cover to the important, more frightening calculation.

It was the door that made him think of a lunatic. It was a fugitive's door. And it had recently been broken down, axed down, maybe more than once. The room was barely heated, and apparently unfurnished. It followed that it was the resting place of some hermit, some untouchable.

Again almost imperceptively, the eyes moved. Now there was no shouting in the street any more. The doctor's shoes and trousers were soaking wet from the snow. His shirt was wet from the blood and the sweat. He felt both cold and warm at once. He thought, What a poor kind of soldier I would have made. I have acted to preserve myself. I have run. Have escaped. Have closed the door. But he could not bring himself to try more. He was aware of his self-pity as he closed his eyes again and fell half back to sleep. Faintly aware, too, that this whole mood of surrender, this opiate feeling was in truth a ruse. It was a message to the monster in the corner of the room: pity me.

At last, the eyes turned away. A long arm reached out towards the corner of the cloth by the window and opened up a bright triangular patch of light. A long black arm, with bangles on it. The light shone like an arc on to a bed without sheets. And then this thing, this person shifted across the bed, into the light which now seemed curiously green. She unwrapped the blanket in which she had been lying.

She was very big, she was most certainly 'she', wearing diamanté buttons over her nipples, and she was decked up, more or less, like a vaudeville bride. Her hair was dyed not golden but light brown. She wore some kind of tiara in it which held up a strange veil. Perhaps she was a mad, abandoned bride, the doctor thought. She had long finger-nails covered in silver polish, except for the index finger which was a dark brown kind of colour in this light: but which the doctor rightly reckoned to be red. Round her waist she wore a velvet strap decorated, again, with diamanté. She had white, apparently luminous panties on. They were the size of the briefest bikini. After that came her enormous, powerful long thighs and calves. She had the body of an Olympic sportswoman. She wore satin slippers on her feet.

The doctor sat absolutely still. The female said nothing. She lay on the bed looking his way, dangling her slipper on her toe. There was a sound, again, from the street. The doctor knew that in the light his face must look very white. She only had to reach behind her and knock one of her bracelets or big rings against the window pane. The boys would hear it and come up and do the rest.

She reached up her arm. The doctor heard himself say, 'Please don't.'

She kept her hand up at the window.

The doctor said, 'I'm bleeding to death.'

She still kept her hand up at the window. The voices died away again. Then she lowered it. She pulled the veil off her hair. The doctor sighed and closing his eyes, this time only pretended to black out. He could hear another siren approaching. He thought it was a police car, but it could have been an ambulance. It didn't really matter which. If he could get out and throw himself on to the road, they'd stop and pick him up. By the time he had worked this out the vehicle with the siren was already passing down the street. The female opened a chink in the sacking curtain again. She looked down, but said nothing. She turned back and stared at him, disbelieving his closed eyes.

At last he heard another siren on the uptown side, coming downtown. It might take this avenue or others on each side. He had to hope that this vehicle was routed in the same way as the previous one. If he were going to make it he'd better start now. He began to unravel the doorchain. He worked fast and nervously as if saying, 'Sorry I called. You don't want to get into this, I'll go, I'm sorry,' and he almost had the chain untied when she moved.

She had observed him well. She kicked him in the side and he let out a terrible cry of pain. She swatted him, then, across the face. She didn't slap him, but struck him with the flat of her wrist and hand. He was knocked right over. The siren came and went.

He laughed, and that surprised her. Very weakly he laughed because he couldn't tell the lie that he had only been trying to get up to go to the other end of the room. His hair wasn't so thick or long, and it was speckled with grey. She suddenly grabbed it and pulled up his head to look either at him or at the phenomenon of white laughter. He had the feeling that she had never left this district, that she would keep him as a curiosity, as a white little freak. The doctor felt thirsty. He had often seen this thirst in terminal cases and thought it came from the drugs, the morphine and heroin. But he'd had no drugs.

'Water,' he croaked. Gently, she let go of his hair and his head fell back on to his chest. She took some time to decide. Then he felt the water against his face. She was pushing his brow to lift up his head. She was looking for his cracked mouth.

She didn't seem to have a cup. So maybe she didn't usually live here. She too perhaps was on the run. She went to and from the closet, bringing water in the cup of her big hand. She must have done the journey thirty times. Then she put water over his face and head. She kept going over to the closet, then coming back and throwing the cold water at him. She tied up the chain again. Then she moved to the end of the room where the door led into the water closet. It was difficult to see what else, from the doctor's angle, but she seemed to keep her clothes in there. He could see a white plastic raincoat.

She returned with a padlock and fixed it on the big chain. As she did so the doctor looked up. His head was still on the floorboards. She was aware of his curiosity. She still didn't say a word. She didn't give him a blanket, or a cigarette. She wrapped herself up again and lay in bed smoking. After a moment or two the doctor recognised the acrid smell. She wasn't smoking tobacco; it was pot. The doctor was glad that she smoked, glad that she didn't smell like a girl.

In the distance he could still hear the sirens. They must have been police cars, maybe making inquiries, searching for weapons, making arrests. Their sounds went farther and farther away; came back, but never too near. The night went by and after a long, long while she closed her eyes. The bed was very low and he moved over towards it as imperceptibly as the grey white light of dawn stole in through the window.

He didn't know which part of her was so close; it could have been a thigh or a calf or an arm, or maybe part of her amazing trunk. He reckoned that it was hairless, that it was curiously imperfect. In a strange, waking dream the doctor reflected: Black skin isn't black at all, none of it is black. There are pores, pink pigment, shades of brown. She had a great many flaws and blemishes and creases. She smelt but she was warm.

An age after that – all time was losing its meaning – she snored and the doctor thought irritably – which is to say fearlessly – God damn it, doesn't she realise I'm dying? I'm dying of thirst.

The boards were very rough. Trying to pull himself across towards the closet he caught some splinters in his bottom and his hand. They seemed very sore. That struck him as odd. He was dying with a knife wound in his liver, and a splinter of wood felt sore. He only wanted to get to the basin. The easy way seemed to be to slide against this shiny painted wall. But he had to get up to do this, so he tried to use the chain on the door.

He tried to pull himself to his feet. The wound felt like a lump, like the swelling after a hornet's sting; incredibly sensitive and also throbbing. But the bleeding seemed to have stopped. When he pulled his cuff away from his shirt and trousers there was a little crackling noise. The blood had dried up.

He was bent in the shape of a U. He couldn't straighten up at all, not without the pain becoming intolerable. Standing like this, bent double, he still felt giddy, but he managed to push himself off with the bed, across the room to the wall, and pressing his shoulder against its painted surface he slid and shoved himself along. At the end, he saw the basin. He stepped across to it. He stumbled. He saw the china edge coming up and knew it was going to strike him on the face.

He accepted the pain. He didn't yelp any more. The water seemed too far away. He felt warmer as he passed out.

The doctor had no idea how long he was unconscious. He thought it might have been for hours, even twenty-four hours. The female was still in bed.

In fact he'd only been out for a moment or two. He'd woken to a sound – to a new and dangerous sound. Somebody had opened the front door downstairs. The doctor pulled his knees up and sheltered, pointlessly, under the basin as he heard the footsteps on the stairs. Whoever it was ran up, with a light young step. He or she might have been wearing sneakers. In a split second the doctor made several wild deductions which brought him to the conclusion that the caller was this female's boyfriend; that he was some kind of athlete, probably a boxer.

There was a knock on the door. The doctor's eyes were

very bright. The female didn't move. There was another knock and a voice, a small voice said, 'It's me, Delivery.' It was a child's voice. But even a child can raise an alarm. The doctor looked at the female who was awake. Her eyes were open. She did not move.

The door hinges were the doctor's end of the room. Therefore, when the delivery boy pushed the door open until the chain and lock restrained it he could see the windows and maybe the female, through the crack, but still could not see the doctor. He pushed through a big bottle of Coke and a carton of milk.

The boy said, 'Why don't you come out today? There's been a riot. You heard? They burnt a car with all the men in it. Harry got hurt bad. He's in the hospital. His back's bust up. You got to come out tonight. Big cabaret when they come in. You don't just want to lie there and smoke pot, do you? Big drinking in Charlie's.'

She did not move. It was hard to tell the relationship between the female and the boy but it seemed the boy liked her. Yet respected her, was a little too much in awe of her to be her brother. The doctor couldn't see the boy but he thought he must be twelve at most. The arm and hand that poked through the crack delivering the bottle and the carton was thin and small and very black.

Her eyes were on the doctor, not the boy. The doctor thought, She's enjoying this. She wants to see my fear. It's a tension she enjoys.'

The boy still didn't leave. The doctor thought he was probably kneeling, or maybe sitting on his heels out there.

The boy said, 'I just come from the Rib Room. Charlie says you got to come out. Says like you need the money anyhow. Why don't you come out? Though you got a chain and lock they'll just axe it down like the cops done last time. Charlie says to tell you he got a hatchet, too. But it's good for you to come out, not just lie smoking the old pot. Please, eh?'

Still she watched the doctor and the doctor watched her. 'What you looking at?' the boy asked her. 'You wink at me, I go back to the Rib Room, tell Charlie alright. Eh?'

And she didn't move. After what seemed like an hour the boy said, 'Sometime you gotta come out,' and she closed her eyes. Then, long moments afterwards, the doctor heard the boy move. He didn't say anything more. Curiously he knocked and then his hand appeared on the door not much higher than the chain. He waggled it to and fro for a moment, not as if he were trying to break the chain, but as if he were sad: even despairing. He stood doing that for a long time, just as if there wasn't anything else for him to do all day. Then, maybe quarter of an hour later he wandered away. He went downstairs like a very young child sent out to play on a cold, cold day: dawdling all the way.

Only when he heard the street door slam did the doctor relax a little. His shoulders dropped an inch. Even that amount of movement could be heard in the room. She opened her eyes.

The doctor closed his. Waited as long as he could bear it, then opened them. Her eyes were still on him. Again he closed his and pretended to sleep. When he next opened his eyes hers were closed. Wrongly he took her to be asleep.

The wound was very tender and there was a board that creaked. But the basin after all was just above his head. He only had to shift a foot sideways, then reached up to the faucet. He began to make the move, then froze when the board creaked. Her eyes were still closed. He shifted again, then began to push himself up. He reached a twisted kind of kneeling position and then for some reason glanced back. Her eyes were wide open. But his thirst was terrible, now that he was so very close. Turning away from her he raised his arm, turned on the faucet and let out a 'Yes. Water. Yes.' He turned it and turned it. There was no water. The tap didn't work. It seemed to take him a long time to appreciate this. Then with a groan he dropped on to the floor again. He lay, too weak to cry. After a while he rolled over so that he could see her.

She was sitting up in the bed drinking the milk. One of the diamanté buttons had come away in her sleep. She had a nipple like a huge dark disc.

When she'd finished the milk she seemed to feel better. She took a mentholated cigarette. She kept the pack on the window sill and she put the milk carton and the Coke bottle there too.

The dust on the floor choked up the doctor's nostrils and mouth, making his thirst more insistent. He kept fading in and out of consciousness now. But he came round as soon as she stepped out of the bed.

Grabbing his collar and shoulders with both hands she hauled him up the room, and as he was on his belly the pain was appalling and hot as if he were being disembowelled with white-hot instruments. She left him between the door and the bed. She went around the corner of the cubicle to the water-closet.

The Coke and the milk were not far out of his reach. But it was necessary for him to haul himself up as far as the bed. He didn't really have the use of his right arm. He felt compelled to keep his hand and wrist over his wound, as if that held him together. But he grabbed the chain on the door with his left hand and pulled and struggled, and in a quick second, found himself on the bed. He had no time to pause, but even as he struggled over to the sill he thought how futile, how pathetic it was that he should go through all this for a drink when so obviously he was going to die anyway.

He didn't reach the carton or the bottle of Coke. She took him by the ankles and pulled him back so he was now half on and half off the lousy bed. He was gripping with his elbows because he thought he couldn't bear the pain of another fall. She had a tremendous strength. She seized him under the armpits and in one movement she hauled him on to the bed where he remained in a sitting position. She brought him water in the milk carton. The water came from the cistern above the water closet. Then she patiently, methodically dressed herself while the doctor, shivering with pain, began a story. He didn't know why he was telling it. And it took him a long time in the telling.

He said, 'I was in hospital. I was a patient in the same hospital where I was taught. I lay there quite ill, in bed.'

She didn't seem at all interested.

'A boy, just a child, can't have been more than nine or ten which is a kind of heartbreaking age, this boy was in the next bed to mine.'

'He'd been burnt quite badly. A week or two before. So one night he starts to cry. One Sunday evening. I asked him why he should cry. He said, "Things are crawling out of my bandage." '

She went out, not long after that. She never showed that the story had affected her. Really, the doctor couldn't believe that she spoke any language, except that she looked at him sometimes, very slowly, almost, almost smiled. She went out in her jeans and shiny boots and plastic coat. And the doctor lay back with his eyes shut and still didn't dare to look down at his wound. That little boy's whimpering and his sweetness and life's appalling cruelty would never leave him, he thought.

He woke to find her immediately in front of him, kneeling on the floor. When he opened his eyes her huge yellow orbs were about two inches away. She woke him that way, by just staring him awake. Maybe she wondered if he were dead.

Her expression gave him no clue towards her feelings. But she had been and bought various things from the drugstore. She had a basin and some disinfectant and a sponge and a bandage and lint. She'd laid them all out on the filthy floor and seemed to have no idea whatsoever what to do with them, now. It did not occur to the doctor, until very much later, what a risk she must have taken by going into a shop in this district where a white man was known to be hiding and wounded; by daring to buy these things.

Together, so to speak, they stretched out the body of the doctor; which meant pain.

She hadn't bought any scissors. He asked her, snipping his fingers in gesture because he was never confident that she understood him. She looked at his fingers and thought. She grabbed his hand in her big hand and looked at it as if it were new to her. The doctor's was a good, sensitive hand. Then she put it to one side again as if it bored her and she wandered over to the other side of the room.

The doctor who was now laid out, knew that the straightening process had once again opened the wound. He couldn't move. He just managed to tip his neck. He saw that she was idling about, smoking a cigarette. Evidently she'd brought some provisions, too. And a paraffin stove, which was good news. It was already lit.

The doctor said, 'I'm bleeding, I think.'

She was opening a tin of peanut butter. She paused. Then she screwed it up tight again. She moved to the basin and picked up a rusty razor-blade there. She took a long drag at her cigarette, then stubbed it out. She removed her satin slippers. She gave one to the doctor and opened and closed her mouth indicating that he should bite hard.

He did not at once obey and as she began to slice away the cloth of shirt and trousers which was congealed with blood he let out a cry. She slapped his face. The slipper fell inside the bed against the wall. She burrowed underneath, knocked some of the dust off it and gave it back to him. The doctor stared at it. He stared absently at the toe of the satin slipper. He saw it was marked. Looking closer he rightly recognised blood. He supposed it to be his own. She picked up the rusty razor-blade again. It was as if, until this moment, she had decided to leave everything in the hands of God. Now something had made her decide to cope: maybe the maggots on the boy's burn.

But she didn't find it easy. The doctor could tell that from the sweat on her brow. He hardly trusted his judgments about her, she was always unpredictable, but he thought she perhaps was squeamish about the sight of blood.

He still thought that as she cut and tugged and tore, and pulled the cloth away. He had to chew the slipper all the time now as she took the sponge. He thought about the blood: how quickly it congealed. For a moment he dared to look down. There were no maggots. She shoved his face back, with her big hand.

She seemed very puzzled about the bandaging once she had laid the lint. But eventually she decided that the only possible way was round and round his waist. He arched his back a little. It took a long time but in the end the pain was easier. She had remembered to buy a safety pin.

When she had finished, she smiled; the first time he had ever seen that huge, generous golden grin: literally golden, thanks to the gold-capped teeth. She seemed most pleased with the final pin. She seemed pleased with herself. She didn't smile at him, but at the bandage and the pin. She walked away and lit another cigarette. She smoked mentholated cigarettes.

The doctor thought that that knife, that little knife, couldn't have touched his liver or he wouldn't be alive still. It must have missed it by a fraction of an inch. Now maybe he was bleeding internally, but there was a chance of life.

She pulled a blanket over him, then put on her plastic coat and walked out.

He heard a Sinatra tune, played on some scratchy disc. When it stopped there was a short pause, then it began again: 'Come Fly With Me'. And began again and again.

She was smoking pot. He was on the end of the bed. Her toes were under his thighs; he was her hot-water bottle. Even if she saw him stir and recognised that he was awake, it seemed she wasn't interested. It was dark. She looked so contented that he dared not disturb her. He could see out of her window. The sky was quite clear. There was a moon with a frosty ring around it. He stretched to look down at the telephone kiosk. The disc ended. Then started again. They might be nearing dawn. It was very cold.

He drifted. Then the record stopped without starting again. It was a little bakelite machine that worked on batteries. She'd finished her smoke.

Quite suddenly he said, 'I used to give my daughter Lilian candies.' He had no idea what prompted him to say that out loud just like that. Some complicated defensive system; some instinct about salvation.

Then he shut up again. His mind flitted from childhood to the early days with Lilian. He didn't seem to have the concentration to stick to any memory or problem for more than a few seconds at a stretch.

She was moving her toes; moving them persistently, pressing and knocking but not quite kicking him. She didn't put them anywhere near his wound. She began to move her feet more impatiently, insistently, disturbing him.

He said, 'You've got to have a blonde daughter.'

The toes stopped. He took one. She buffeted his leg with her feet again. He nodded. He said, 'I'll tell you about Lilian.' The buffeting stopped. He couldn't remember anything about Lilian, suddenly. But he tried.

He said, 'A man who loses a wife and gains a daughter has got to hate his daughter or else love her too much. To spoil her. That's what you'd think.'

He took a long pause. Then he said, 'But that leaves out the daughter. It isn't just up to the man. I got a good one. I got one that didn't want to be spoilt. Maybe that's because she has yellow hair and a very fine straightforward kind of face. With my eyes, exactly my eyes. Lilian never needed me, she just liked me, loved me. Lilian isn't selfish, never was. She's self-whatever it is. She's composed. She's self-sufficient. She never got in my way. Some folk say we lived in parallel, that's not true. We love each other. We're a good-mannered father and daughter. She knew how her mother made me the loser, so she didn't have to ask about that. Once I started to tell her how maybe it wasn't all her mother's fault, she just put her hand over my mouth. We're the best-mannered father and daughter. We didn't go in for big scenes. She's never seen me cry and I hardly ever saw her. We lived in the doctor's house. She was very good with the patients if they rang. What a blessing Lilian was. Is.'

The doctor had run out. She waited for a while. Then she suddenly lifted up her knees and, with one big shove, pushed him right off the end of the bed. Two minutes later she was snoring, asleep.

He thought, If I could find that padlock key. It's late now. Must be the middle of the night. Only the sounds of the war in the distance. The kiosk was almost exactly opposite, not more than fifty yards. He could make that. While she snored he sat up. He looked around the place. Where would she keep the key? Maybe in the pocket of her jeans or the pocket of her coat? Maybe under her pillow? Maybe on the sill?

He started to creep around. He didn't find it in any of these places. He found something else on the sill. He found a newspaper and something about the headline caught his attention. The paper was three months old. Looking down the front page he saw how she'd marked a photograph with this big jumbo biro pen, a kind of joke pen she had. The picture was of some kind of disturbance or riot and it was in front of MISTER CHARLES'S RIB ROOM written up in lights. She'd ringed a girl fighting with the cops. The face was unrecognisable, half hidden by the police truncheons raining down on the victim: but the girl was wearing a white plastic raincoat.

Searching again for the key, even daring to put his hand under the bolster, the truth didn't occur to the doctor. Was the padlock self-locking? There was no key. Neither, now, was there a lock.

She never said a word. Occasionally she'd hum that Sinatra tune in a weird way of her own. But she had a tongue. She could laugh, too. She had the strangest sense of humour.

Waking one morning – and the doctor never knew whether it was two days or three days after – he felt altogether different. He felt stronger and it took him a moment to understand why. The sun had broken through the clouds outside. There was a noise of people and cars in the street. She must have opened the window. And as he lay watching the dust in the sunbeam that fell on to the bed and floor he felt a persistent pressure against the back of his neck. He moved a little then again felt the tickle. He didn't think what it might be. He was warm in the sun. To begin with, he had thought she was more like an animal than a woman, she slept so much, night and day, but now he had quite taken to her ways. He too slept most of the time. Then again there was a pressing against the nape of his neck.

It was her toe. Her great big toe. He looked beyond it, over the mountains and forests of the great feline body, some hilltops in the sunshine, some valleys in the dark; he saw she was leaning on one elbow, grinning at him. He remembered now. They had eaten well the night before. She had gone out and bought hot dogs and some Mexican muck and bread and milk and beer. Now she was playful. But she was always dangerous. Sometimes, as they slept, he would move towards her, because he was cold, in his sleep. She more than once shoved him right out of the bed.

Again the toe wriggled and invited games. She pushed his nose and began to chuckle when he turned away and rubbed it with his hand. The toe pushed at his shoulder. It was a powerful great toe. So he caught hold of it and tickled the sole of her foot until she began to laugh. He twisted her other foot and she rolled over, laughing. She was more or less naked in the sun. She tried to get away from being tickled now. But the doctor knew the pressure points and the nerve centres. They moved round the bed in a childish, slumbrous, ridiculous kind of way, and the doctor was calling her names, in the way that a lion-tamer called a lioness all sorts of names. The message lay in his tone which went with the lazy morning sunbeam.

At last he put his thumb in that junction of the nerve that lies between shoulder and neck. The doctor's hands were delicate, but they had strength. That was when she really began to laugh and without her saying a word the doctor understood why, completely. She really could not believe that this old invalid could hold her down. She tried to move out of his hold and he laughed at her. He was applying pressure only with one hand but he still had her face pinned to the awful filthy striped bolster on that buggy bed. She moved her hips and legs and arms, without ever striking near his wound, but still she couldn't fight free. Eventually she became so weak with laughter that he was holding her only with his thumb.

At last he let her go. She was determined that he should teach her where exactly to apply the pressure for this old, old hold. So the doctor became the victim, and she laughed as much again when she found she could pin him down with one finger. When she let go she took hold of his hair affectionately and shook his head about. For an instant he wondered if she had broken his neck. Then they had another big meal. The doctor developed a great taste for beer. He found some dollars in his pocket and told her to buy more, but she didn't take his money. And the doctor asked her, 'Why the hell are you doing this?' At that she'd turned away.

It was the pressure point, strangely, that led to the only bad quarrel. Lord knows how many days later. They had eaten many more sausages and in the corner there were piles of beer cans. This time, it was later at night, maybe after too many beers, when she started fooling around. She pinned his head not on to the blanket but on to the floor, and it hurt. He tried to break free, but she applied the pressure much more strongly, and the pain increased. Like a boy, the doctor suddenly grew angry, and tried very hard to get free. Possibly she knew that he was in earnest and for some contrary reason continued to apply pressure.

He managed to catch her forefinger and sharply, very sharply bent it back. Not only did she release the pressure, she let out a cry and fell back in the corner by all the cans. Still angry, and swearing at her, vindictively, he slapped her face, to warn and punish her. Bitch.

She held her head to one side, as if waiting for him to strike again. She remained absolutely still. He felt afraid. He withdrew a step but did not apologise. He stood up and stared down at her. He was stronger, now, but not that strong. Besides, she still only had to call out the window and he would be dead. He knew that.

But the politics of the room had suddenly changed.

Very slowly she turned her face and stared at him, unblinkingly. He held her stare only for a moment, then, with a shrug, he turned away. He went over to the shelf where they kept the food. He said, 'Come on, there's more cheese and bread.' He said, 'Anyway you haven't finished your beer.' His voice was far from confident.

After a little while, she picked herself up and came across and drank a little. She spread some peanut butter on her bread.

The doctor was anxious to express what had happened. Also to apologise for it. He said, 'You don't know your own strength, that's the trouble. You had me half dead on the floor. Why did you want to do a thing like that?' Somehow everything he said rang false. Secretly he knew why. She might have made a mistake. But with that last blow of his – that 'Down, slave', that 'Take that and mind your manners' – he had made no mistake. He had called something up from the unforgotten past. It was therefore for him to say sorry. Yet as soon as he opened his mouth to do so, he knew he had made a mistake. He had confessed to something of which she had not previously been absolutely sure.

'Look, Cat, I'm sorry if—'

With a single swipe of her hand she removed plates, cans, knife, bread, peanut butter – the whole damned shooting match on to the floor. Everything was smashed and scattered about.

He was shaken and enraged. He stood quite still, white and trembling with anger. She watched him again. With great effort he managed to recover himself. He then said very quickly, 'You are inviting me to strike you again. I will not do so.'

She stared at him for moments on end. Then she turned away, pulled on her jeans and her big pullover; put on her plastic coat. She lit a cigarette, hummed 'Strangers in the Night', and stepping over the debris she unrolled the chain and walked out of the dump.

The doctor was still shaking. He did not attempt to tidy up. He suddenly felt desperately depressed. He climbed on to the bed, rolled a blanket round him and, white man, prayed for sleep.

The next morning broke gloomily with the sky low and overcast. Bad dreams weren't scattered away. The doctor moved her arm without waking her and stepped over her. He put on his shoes and his coat, still without waking her. He finished an open can of beer and lit one of her cigarettes. Very gently he took the chain off the door. He laid it on the floor, soundlessly. He opened the door swiftly so that it would not creak and closed it similarly, once he had stepped out into the landing.

Downstairs, in the deserted hall, he knew that he had been bluffing; had been praying that she should wake up. So it was only now that he seriously considered his escape.

He had no idea how many days had passed since the night that Angel got away, but he reckoned it must have been the best part of two weeks. The real world outside was still at this moment no more than black shadows seen through the frosted glass on the closed front door, but it frightened him. Patients, like released prisoners, first feel alarmed by reality. He'd forgotten just how much.

He thought the best plan would simply be to bluff it out. Just walk out there, clap his hands, yell 'Taxi'.

He felt quite unreal as he stepped outside. The door banged behind him. He was scared that it had locked but did not dare hesitate now. He had forgotten the coldness of the wind. It was still coming across the frozen lake. It hit him very hard and took his breath away. Buttoning up, he looked left and right and thought he saw some kind of junction two or three blocks up to the right. He would find a taxi there.

At the first crossing, just as he was about to step off the island towards the sidewalk on the far side he looked up and caught a man's eye. That man knew him. Whether he was posted there the doctor never knew. He emerged from a doorway and looked. The doctor panicked, at once. There was only one white man in the world.

The doctor was almost run over by a truck as he ran back. He darted and dodged through the coloured men and women struggling up the street against the wind. They must have heard a shout, but most of them were too cold to appreciate its meaning, fast enough.

The doctor found the door. It wasn't locked. He banged it shut behind him. He rushed upstairs, like a frightened schoolboy: Mummy, Mummy. When he came to the landing he flung open the door. In the space of five seconds, without any words, the pair of them exchanged two chapters.

She was up. She was dressed. She was tidying up. She was half smiling as if to say, 'I knew you were only bluffing going downstairs and banging the door like that, old man, but I too am sorry about last night. I've thought, and you're right. I was provoking you to behave like a white man, but now we can forget it. I want to forget it, that's why I'm doing this thing for you. That's why I'm tidying up the joint.'

And he was saying, 'Cat, no. No. I've gone and torn it. I must have been crazy. You made me feel so safe I got proud. I went out. I didn't bluff. I went out and they've seen me.' He said out loud, 'They're coming.' And there was the sound of voices, of several men coming together in the street down below.

The black panther is a remarkable animal.

The doctor knew that: knew about panthers and cheetahs and leopards. He'd had quite an obsession about them all his life. He'd always loved animals and the cats, the cat family intrigued him most of all.

These feline animals never run in the way people imagine them to do. They leap and bound forward a little faster than the eye can accurately follow. But they can't run for long. Not like a dog or a deer. For an instant their power seems to be limitless, its speed infinite. But they can't run at all.

She took the stairs to the second floor in two bounds. She grabbed the doctor's hand and pulled him up the next flight as together they heard the front door bang, below. When he stumbled, she yanked him to his feet. She leapt up into an attic area, and pulled him up behind her with both hands. She crashed through a door on to the flat roof. She didn't give the doctor time to grow giddy. She leapt from one roof to the next over chasms that dropped five storeys to the street. It was icy and slippery.

But in all, they didn't cover more than half the block. She opened a skylight. The roofs seemed to be a world she knew. She dropped through the skylight and the doctor tumbled after. At once, again, she pulled him to his feet. She closed the skylight. She took the first six or seven down steps in a bound. The doctor rattled behind. Then the next. They passed like this through a house filled with astonished mothers and children, most of whom seemed to be oriental. They simply saw the flash of white plastic coat and the doctor, banana legged, falling behind.

Then they were in a street of dilapidated redstone houses with steps up to each front door. There were still piles of frozen snow, but it was brown and doggy now. At this stage the doctor could have taken over the lead. The cat can't run. When she stopped at the seventh house he thought she was pausing for breath. He urged her on.

But she had some plan. She looked all the way round. The whole environment, every detail of it from the roof to the ash-can blown in the wind was contained, for an instant, in those unblinking, yellow eyes.

Suddenly she took the doctor's hand and strode across the street to a house that was labelled DENTAL SURGEON.

The house had a double door. The first was unlocked. Inside were the bells for the different apartments. She pressed 'Consulting Room' and hummed uneasily as she waited. The doctor had his hand over his side. He was bent forward, trying to regain his breath. The inner door was glazed. The glass plate rattled as the nurse opened it. It rattled again as the nurse was flung aside. She protested too late. The fugitives had arrived. Even the doctor was learning to react fast, like that.

The dentist's waiting-room was dingy and yet also tawdry with touches of red and gold on curtains and carpet. It was not very clean.

The nurse went to fetch the dentist, who wasn't next door in the surgery, but upstairs, in his apartment, drinking hot soup. It must have been about 11.00 a.m. and he hadn't seen any patients yet. Meantime, the doctor half sat and half lay on a greasy upholstered sofa while his saviour paced up and down and round the room, much like an athlete infuriated by an unjust decision at the finish of a race.

In crisis, some men, especially frightened men, seem to speak in code. Or maybe some know no other language. They have to approximate their actual reaction to arche- typal form. The coloured dentist was thin with horn- rimmed glasses. His clothes didn't seem to fit him too well. His wrists stuck out of his white coat. His trousers were too short.

He called her by the name the doctor had never heard. It was such an obvious name. He said, 'Silence, honey, you can't do this to me, Silence. You got to go. You can't stay here. You know it. That's not fair to me or mine, baby. Silence, you got to be on your way.'

She looked down at him and waited until he stopped. Then she led the way into the surgery. They closed the door behind them, leaving the doctor out.

The doctor could not then hear what the dentist said. He could pick up the perturbed, insistent, not too persuasive tone but he was missing the words, even when he crossed to the door to try to learn more. The doctor was not at all sure where the dentist stood. He had noticed only one thing: the dentist had behaved as if Silence were on her own. He had not acknowledged the doctor's presence at all, not by the bat of an eyelid. It was as if he were already preparing his testimony to some Moslem inquisition: 'Sure, Silence came round, but I never saw anybody with her. I saw nobody else, at all.'

The doctor thought he heard Silence moan in a strange way, but the sound was not repeated, so soon he came away from the door. The waiting-room had some kind of central heating which did not make him feel more confident. It worried him after the cold: even made him feel a little sick. And he was troubled with the wound. He had stuffed his dirty handkerchief into place over the ruckled bandage underneath his belt. He dreaded that the wound had opened again. But he stuck his finger down the bandage and there was no redness. Just sweat.

He sat back.

It took him half a minute to recognise the picture which was not a photograph but a painting on the cover of a weekly news magazine. It was lying on the table in front of his eyes. His daughter Lilian was where all the pretty girls hope one day to be; in glorious colour, on the cover. And underneath there was a caption: 'The girl it's all about.'

It frightened the doctor. He hardly dared open the magazine. He suddenly didn't want to know. He felt that there were only bad things to be learnt. It wasn't that he wanted simply not to read the magazine: he wanted the magazine and the story never to have been. Suddenly he didn't want to see Lilian again. He didn't want to go home, ever. He wanted to be back in the room that smelt of paraffin, the room that was newly tidied up. And he knew how much he had been fighting to bury the truth. Just as he had avoided all inquiry about his son, his son also was there in front of him, staring at him. He thought, I cannot read it, even as his eye started down the page. The story occupied three, nearly four pages. It was the national lead.

Angel had got back to tell his version, which wasn't too untrue. But the doctor couldn't read it. He turned over the page and there were pictures of himself and Angel and Junior, and of the coloured boy who was dead. The doctor took that in. He still kept skipping the lines about Junior.

Junior wasn't his only son, he was just the one most likely to succeed. Throughout his school career other men and women used to stop the doctor in the street and say, 'Boy but you've got a winner there.' Junior played football, came top of the class. A fine boy, doctor. A fine, unsmiling young God who always made the grade.

There was another photograph which suddenly took the doctor's attention. It was a horrible blown-up snapshot of

Silence. She had dark hair cut quite short and it gave no
impression of her size nor her dignity. Her eyes looked
brown. The caption underneath the picture said, 'Silence is
black,' in the funny, punning way that magazines favour.
The doctor read the paragraph about her. She had a
previous record of crime; also of crime with violence.
She was one of five coloured men and women whom the
police were anxious to interview concerning the murder by
lynching in the street, two days after 'the battle', of Lawrence Ewing Junior.

The doctor began to shake. He closed the magazine,
again. He had somehow already, magically, picked up the
truth. He had read the whole article while he pretended not
to, and he was left with one blazing impression on his mind.
It was of a satin slipper with his son's blood.

He tried to make himself open the paper again and read
all the things not only that the newsmen had reported but
what important politicians and international commentators
had said. He closed the pages yet again. He began to feel
very shivery and weird, then knew suddenly that he was
going to be sick. He needed somewhere to vomit. The
surgery would have a basin. He rushed through, caught
sight of the basin, ran to it and retched; then retched again.

When he recovered he saw that there was nobody in the
room. This frightened him more, because his fear was
running ahead of his reasoning again. It seemed to be
the exposure, the sheer exposure of the story, the simple
horror of being involved in all this that most frightened
him. His mind would not settle on any particular aspect: on
the death of the child; on Silence's actions; on Junior's
death; on the dentist's panic; on the sudden disappearance
of both the dentist and Silence. Somehow the magazine
itself became the object of terror for him. He felt the whole
world to be against him; black and white. The doctor knew
his physical condition had something to do with it. He
recognised in himself some kind of shock but he could not

separate the true reason behind it yet. He just didn't have the energy to be brave. He didn't even want to cry. There simply wasn't anywhere in the world to go, he felt, where there would be safety. Nowhere, except to Silence.

As he picked up the magazine again, there was a noise at the front door. He threw the paper away. He wanted to hide. Then he guessed that somebody was leaving, not arriving.

Very frightened, he tiptoed to the window, and peeping through the side of the curtain, looked down at the street a few feet away, below.

The dentist and his wife and children were getting into their Chevrolet. They seemed to have come downstairs and left the building unnaturally quietly, but now in the street, the dentist seemed anxious to convey the impression that he was starting on a normal family outing, maybe going to the movies, or the ball game, or even a prayer meeting. The dentist was wearing a strangely formal hat with a broad brim, almost like a Dutch Protestant's. He had to hold on to it, in the wind. It is extraordinary which detail the mind retains.

The doctor should have been able to deduce certain things from his departure. He could not bring his mind to bear on the problems logically any more. The doctor wasn't coping very well.

Not well at all. The doctor had often seen patients in the strange state of mind which he had now reached. Usually they were widows who had lost, or felt that they had lost all incentive to live. They operated with extreme inefficiency, constantly busy, but achieving nothing. It was a phenomenon the doctor always watched very carefully, because unless checked it developed into total breakdown or withdrawal. The widow's mind became fixed upon her husband's last sickness or the moment of death. The doctor could not take his mind off the satin slipper and the pencilled ring on the photograph he had seen in her paper which had seemed to be of a lynching.

He wandered back into the surgery. He took up the magazine again and read it now, dully, as if it concerned some other family. Yes, the coloured boy had broken his spine. He had died the next day. Yes, Lawrence Ewing Junior had been discovered two days after the battle and had been killed by the mob before the police arrived on the spot. Yes, Angel had given a full and honest account of the whole affair. Doctor Ewing himself was reported to be badly wounded, and few people believed him still alive.

In the dentist's drawer, there were some surgical instruments, including a very small sharp knife with a blade even thinner than the one which the doctor had seen for an instant as it passed into his side. The handle of the dentist's knife was steel. Because it didn't fold, the doctor wrapped the blade round with some cotton wool, then he placed it in his breast pocket, diagonally, so that it didn't show.

The doctor wasn't coping very well. He knew he was incapable of killing anybody else with that knife. He knew he had no intentions of killing himself. It was a pointless acquisition which still he seemed to need.

Then, from the waiting-room he picked up another magazine. This one also had a full report on the 'Lilian' affair. But this was a coloured weekly for coloured people. More accurately, a semi-coloured weekly for those coloured people who wanted to enjoy the privileges of the white. The advertisements showed girls with straight smooth hair and firm, straight noses. The doctor looked at the articles in it with vague dismay. They were nauseating. They had nothing to do with Silence and nothing to do with him. Yet he read on, for a while, sitting in the dentist's chair.

The chair itself was modern. Perhaps dentists can hire them. The rest of the equipment looked old and not even clean.

He began to think that perhaps the dentist had persuaded Silence to leave him. There was logic in that he could see. She had every reason to fear the police but no reason to fear her own people, so long as she remained alone. To them she was no traitor. But seen with him, father of the man she had helped to murder, she was an enemy of the coloured people. The doctor thought, I never before wanted to fall into the hands of the police. I do now. Badly.

The doctor was still sitting, frozen, when he heard the front door open and close. He stood up, like an old man and stared through the open door into the other room, waiting for he did not know what.

When she walked in, he thought, I shan't mention to her that she murdered my son. He thought that quite undramatically much as if he were at home when his mother called round unexpectedly: I shan't tell her I have a toothache, it will only involve us in an unnecessary scene.

It wasn't easy to bluff Silence. Because she had dismissed words altogether her visual sense was astonishingly acute. She could see the shadow of a shade. She could read the tiniest movement of the lines round the doctor's eyes and mouth. She could see his hands tremble inside his coat pockets. The doctor therefore could not recover the subsequent situation. The more he protested, in order to save her feelings, the less he persuaded her.

She had been out. She had been to the shops. She had bought herself an exotic new dress and some fantastic costume jewelry, not in order to impress the doctor, but to please him; he knew that. And she looked just awful: so bad that she came to resemble some of the hybrids in that vulgar magazine which the doctor had left on the floor by the dentist's chair.

The doctor had come to admire her looks when she was naked or in her jeans and pullover. He didn't know if he desired her. Possibly he did. Does a child desire the

mother? Not that she was purely mother. The circumstances were not such that he then had to answer that.
Perhaps he didn't have the courage to desire her. The
doctor was a modest man and over forty years old.

She quite broke down; collapsed like the wife in a bad
domestic comedy, the one who has spent the housekeeping
money on an ugly mink hat. The doctor reassured her in
vain. She tugged off her earrings, hurting herself; she threw
them into the corner of the mangy waiting-room.

The doctor took off his overcoat, as if he were prepared
to spend some hours convincing her that she had spent her
money well.

What a strange farce, the doctor thought; how odd is
reality; does she also know that she murdered Lawrence my
son?

She moved into the surgery, carrying her parcels with
her. The doctor followed. While she was a goddess she was
also always a child. She tore open one paper shopping bag,
tore it and threw her jeans and pullover across the linoleum
floor. She had decided to change. The doctor kept saying,
'No, don't please,' but nothing would stop her. She was
unzipping the new dress.

'Silence, don't. Really I like it,' the doctor said, then
both, for an instant, froze. He had never used her name
before. Both minds moved swiftly, in exact parallel. Both
had the alibi. Both knew that the dentist had called her
Silence. Both also knew that he had learnt 'Silence' from
the press. But both had the alibi.

The zip stuck. She wouldn't let him help. She tore the
dress. Ripped it and stepped out of it. Really, no grown-up
white girl could have changed her clothes like this, not even
if she were with her lover. Still angry, she paced round like a
huffy ten-year-old, in pants, but for some reason without a
bra. Then she hauled on her jeans and got lost in her
sweater which should have been unbuttoned before she
tried to pull it over her big head.

The performance quite humanised the doctor. He laughed and at last she let him help. But she didn't laugh herself. She was still too deeply disappointed and offended. When he tried to hold on to her, once the sweater was buttoned at the neck, she moved away. What a body it was. She could bend and pick something off the floor without even dipping her knees. It was one of the magazines she picked up. The white one, so to speak. She strutted next door. She closed the curtains against the dull day and the world that was full of their enemies. She switched on the overhead light which had a cheap shade to make it look like a Japanese lantern.

Silence never sat in an orderly way. Now she sprawled on the floor on her stomach, and began to turn over the pages. She was looking at the lead article; of course she was. She read it as if it bored her slightly, as if it had nothing whatsoever to do with the two of them. The doctor sat on the greasy sofa, watching her. He took one of her cigarettes which she put on the floor close to his feet. Only when she turned over the page, did he say, 'It's not a very good photograph of you. I wouldn't have recognised you.'

She tipped up her head. For some reason he expected her to grin. Perhaps the very way that she lifted her head made him sure that she was glad he thought it was a lousy photograph too. But her expression was utterly different. It was blank and hostile, and yet tears were running down her cheeks. That was her confession. He could see that. It caught him unawares. He began to sway backwards and forwards, like a lean little bear; a very unhappy, cornered animal of some sort. She'd forced the moment on him. It was no longer possible to avoid the issue. He felt stuck; completely stuck. She never took her yellow eyes off him, waiting for his judgment. Even morally, the doctor thought, I am a coward and she is brave.

'Shock,' he said out loud, at last. 'Shock. Just a state of shock.'

He smoked half the cigarette, but she still stared. Still she wouldn't let him off the hook. She was frowning now, deeply, as if she were afraid that he would disappoint her. How little we need words, the doctor thought.

'Shocked by the terrible truth,' he said very quietly. 'Shocked by how little I care that my own son is dead.'

He looked up as if to ask her reassurance and help. Her reaction was neutral. It was as if she could not quite accept what he said. She was staring at him, her eyes less wide open than usual.

'He seemed very separate once he was grown up,' the doctor said flatly. 'But I didn't know how separate.' Still she looked dissatisfied. The doctor was beginning to tremble badly. To tremble unexpectedly and very violently. To tremble as it were, at the foundations, which is to say in those ditches of life where we find the meetings of mothers and daughters, of fathers and sons.

She sat. She laid her big hand on his knee. He continued to smoke and shake like a leaf. He looked only at her hand and touched a finger of it, saying, 'God knows why you paint one nail red.' Then almost without a break he continued, 'Why did you take such a vow, who tortured you, or am I wrong? Can't you speak? Is it your throat? I know you have a tongue. What terrible event moved you to take such a desperate protest? If you can talk, talk now.'

He looked up and saw only the top of her head. The black hair grew beneath the dry brown. She was lighting herself a cigarette. He said, 'I didn't feel at all. When I knew about the boy I didn't feel anything. That was the shock. Maybe I guessed ten days ago. I can't see why you've saved me. You've only seen the worst in me. The coward in me. You've seen nothing in me. I wish we'd never left that ghastly hovel. I didn't feel anything for him. I couldn't find Absalom. That is why I shake.'

He heard her say, 'Shsh.' Say, 'Shsh,' again. But she

wouldn't speak. They waited like that for a moment or two, both smoking again.

He asked, 'Did you say out loud to somebody – did you say to some Court? Did you say "I'll never speak again"?' He turned her face up and she smiled quite mildly and he saw her beauty as he had never recognised it before. It was sculptured and strong and not aggressive at all. He asked, 'Or did you say it two hundred years ago?'

She turned away, but he insisted, as if it helped him to stop trembling. He said, 'We can't get away from slavery,' and bent and kissed her hand which she then withdrew. She was beginning to grow very restless. He used her name in a strange way. He said, 'In Silence's company, slavery was yesterday. If I get through, I'll tell them only that. But I can't show you how strongly I feel it. I see you often on some African coast, herded on board a crowded ship amongst the shouting and wailing and noise of despair. There is a staggering strength in your silence. Believe me, the most magnificent pathetic protest of them all.'

She began to sway as if caged. To pull away. But he held on to her wrist very hard. He spoke in a most unusually animated way as if it had to be said. 'You decided on this silence, complete, utter, unbroken. Alone, standing alone on board this terrible ship as it pulled away from the quay. Give me one word. Say "yes". Say, "Yes, you're right, that's when I decided not to speak."'

She broke away. Began to hum some unrecognisable tune. She moved like an animal, swiftly and smoothly. She had taken off her boots. She went to the surgery and brought back one of her parcels. She grinned and spun round as if to say 'Party, party!' She had bought Coca Cola and rum.

And the doctor thought, How strange it is, but if you know that you're not going to get any answer you begin to stop asking about the future. There was no point in his asking, 'What happened to the dentist?' No point in saying,

'You were in there while he talked to you for half an hour, so what did he say? I heard you moan.' No point in inquiring, 'Where do we go from here?' For she lived in the present, she lived for now as if she alone understood the immediacy and magnitude of the war.

The spirit steadied the doctor considerably. How quickly moods change in crisis. Not hers, but his. The liquor went straight to his head. The doctor soon could envisage a moment in which his behaviour could be called something like heroic. The doctor thought, Half the battle is won if you see yourself being brave.

She got drunk, too. Drunk enough to show him suddenly a big gap in her front teeth. Then only did he begin to understand their present circumstances. All the gold had gone, and that was a lot of gold. Several teeth had been capped that way. The gold must have paid for more than rum and Coke.

The doctor was beginning to cope again, beginning to be able to connect ideas, to build the chains which alone keep us sane; to link cause and effect. The dentist had extracted the gold, then she had gone out shopping. Maybe she had also paid the dentist for the apartment. He could have needed cash. He certainly didn't have many customers. Then, Maybe it's Sunday, the doctor thought. For a second his mind flitted home to Sunday and church and boredom and belief: to telling the children the right things, how to behave . . .

Lawrence Junior dead.

She grew hopelessly, helplessly drunk. She laughed and hummed and danced about. She slipped, fell, knocked things over and invited the doctor to jive or twist or whatever it was. She had no head for liquor at all. She must have known that.

She also was sick in the surgery basin, but that didn't hold her back for too long. It simply revealed what he knew, namely that she wasn't happy at all. Revealed what they both knew, namely that neither of them felt any joy. He helped her back into the waiting-room and put a cushion under her head. It wasn't exactly a cushion, but the back pad of the only easy-chair. One of the springs was piercing through. She indicated that the world was going round and round, then began to look very green.

When she closed her eyes the doctor returned to the surgery and put an inch of water in a tumbler full of rum. He vowed he'd never again go to Angel's club without first drinking a full tumbler of rum.

The telephone rang. Thinking she was still incapably drunk, the doctor tried to prevent her from removing the receiver from the rest. She gave him one of those blows with the inside of the wrist. She caught him very hard, just over the right eye, and, rum-logged, he still felt the pain.

It was the dentist on the line. It wasn't the voice but the phoney smooth phrases, the 'honeys' and 'babies' that made the doctor sure.

The instrument was attached to the surgery wall. Silence stood cross-legged as if she were listening to some idle gossip and she never opened her mouth. At the end she simply hung up. The doctor wondered how the dentist could have been confident that he was speaking to her in the first place. Yet if I'd rung Silence, the doctor thought, I'd have known. Which sounds ridiculous but still was true: he'd have felt Silence at the end of the phone.

The message was perfectly simple. A price had been accepted. The dentist had handed over a pack of dollars to some intermediary character and it was up to the doctor to complete payment when he arrived safely in Whitesville; uptown. The dentist referred to the doctor as 'the passenger', which had style. The driver was to come to the house after dark, at exactly ten.

She'd bought some food; some awful Chinese food, this time, in foil-lined cartons. The doctor obligingly ate in the surgery, but he never could bluff her. Seeing that he was not enjoying the food she soon moved away and lay down in the waiting-room again.

He didn't ask her to come close this last hour. He sat on the sofa and soon she went back to him. She laid her head on his lap not just because she felt tired and a little sick. The only thing he said in that long, long hour of no war was, 'Even lose your front teeth, for God's sake. You silly big bitch.' She smiled at the tone, not the words.

She was still asleep when the taxi drew up outside and the man came up the steps. But as he pressed the bell, a split instant before it rang, there were eyes – yellow eyes, blazing, unblinking, awake, aware, taking in the shadowy red room.

The bell rang.

She moved swiftly into the surgery. She grabbed a white coat, a dirty white cotton coat which was hanging behind the door. She insisted that he wear it and carry his own. She shoved notes, a hundred dollar notes into his hand.

'Aren't you coming?'

Yellow eyes.

'Not even to the door?'

There was no war at that given moment, no colour at all; just the mutual danger and alarm as the bell rang once more.

She dropped her head. He put his hand out and touched her face. Her cheeks were quite dry. She didn't raise her head again. She was standing by the dentist's chair: that's where he saw her, standing immediately beside the hydraulic chair.

The doctor said, 'Take care.'

He left the surgery, the waiting-room, the hall. There was nobody on the doorstep but the taxi double-parked in the street below. Some other car had filled the dentist's place. The taxi-driver leant back and opened the back door. It wasn't too light which helped and the doctor kept his head bent low. His courage had been at a lower ebb. Perhaps the dollars in his pocket helped: they often do.

As soon as he was in the car the driver started away. He just seemed like a rude, impatient boy.

They'd gone about three blocks. Then this boy, the driver said, 'Move over to the left.'

The doctor didn't catch it. In truth his mind had remained beside the dentist's chair. He was as calm or as silly as that. So many moods in peril.

'Move over the seat.'

The boy's voice was hostile but most city cabmen's voices seemed to the doctor unfriendly like that. He still did not grasp the danger he was in. He thought that the boy wanted him to move over because he was obstructing the view from the driver's mirror. He therefore said, 'Sorry', as he shifted across.

The boy then reached in the pocket of the car and the doctor's blood froze. Again his instinct seemed to leap ahead of reason. His spine knew that the boy had reached for a gun.

He met the boy's eye in the driving mirror. The boy had big whites to his eyes. As the car drew up at a crossing the boy said, 'You're no fucking dentist.'

The doctor was still coping. He was scared but he was still making those necessary links. He thought, If I show him the dollar notes at this point, he'll only take them. He thought, Say nothing, doctor, if there's nothing to say.

The lights changed. The boy drove forward again.

They were on the lakeside, the doctor was sure of that, on the lakeside driving north, which was the direction in which he wanted to travel, but there was still a long long way to go. The roads were icy but the sky seemed to be clear.

The boy was driving very fast, as if he wanted to confuse his passenger. Left. Right and right again. Yet they never reached the lakeside highway. They didn't get as far as that. The boy evidently knew that the doctor was due to pay him a hundred, uptown. And maybe he had worked out what the doctor was thinking about. Suddenly he spoke.

'I don't want your money,' he said.

He never added, 'Whitey' or 'scum' or whatever. He had put on driving glasses now, which were tinted blue. They acted as a mask. But he kept watching the doctor in the mirror.

'Don't piss yourself in my cab,' he said, and so gave the doctor an important link.

The doctor's wound, for some reason, had begun to throb. Maybe the rush of adrenalin had some strange indirect influence on the pulses there. Not that the doctor cared about that. He found the throbbing reassuring. He'd been hurt before and was still living to tell the tale. Boy, he thought, if you think I look frightened, you should have seen me earlier on. The doctor was coping better. He was observing well. The streets were much emptier now. The boy despised him. 'At the next crossing, you start running,' he said.

The doctor thought to himself, What a sporting boy. Not going to shoot a sitting white bird?

The car came very suddenly to a halt. But the doctor was getting a lot, lot better. He did not crumple forward as the boy had hoped. He already had his hand on the door handle. As the car stopped he therefore catapulted straight on to the road. He somersaulted more or less, and began running almost before he found his feet. Fortunately there was no traffic coming the other way. He reached the opposite sidewalk before a truck came by.

He didn't look back. He didn't want to know if the boy was cruising after him. He ran, turned right, and ran. At the next corner he was pretty sure that he was not being followed. He had turned up a one-way lane and the boy would have had to speed round another block or else leave his car and chase on foot. There was so sign of him.

The doctor was doing better. He ran back up the block and at the next corner took the decision of his life. He turned right again. His body had seemed to take the decision for him. In moments of courage as in moments of fear, we're no longer controlled by our heads. The doctor slackened his pace. He walked. He wasn't running away.

He reckoned he should now be approaching the crossing at which the boy had dumped him. The white coat, by the way, was a stroke of genius. It was possible to walk and run in it without arousing suspicion. At the worst, the doctor thought, I can say, 'Baby', or 'Accident', or, 'I'm a doctor pretending to be a doctor, get out of my road!'

He wondered if maybe he should always drink rum. But then he had to stop for a second. He had something more than a stitch. As he bent to regain his breath he saw a little mark on the coat. The wound must have burst open somehow. It was wet and red again. Still he didn't lose his nerve. He kept thinking of these strange, almost witty things. He said to himself as he started to run again, 'Why doctor, you're a doctor running to your own emergency.'

And he wasn't running north. He had re-orientated himself and was running back into the ghetto, the idiot. He laughed at himself as he ran and walked and ran again: a left at the second crossing, then there was a warehouse, then a right.

There was no sign of the taxi, but as he ran the doctor thought about the boy. The boy was a genuine cabman, the doctor felt sure of that. The way the boy had said 'my cab' – 'Don't piss in my cab' – convinced him so. And the boy wasn't an ordinary crook, else he would have seen to it that he grabbed the hundred bucks before he lost his passenger. The boy wasn't corruptible, the doctor knew. Instinctively he hadn't tried any bribes, knowing from the boy's face that they wouldn't work. The boy had a gun. It seemed to follow that the boy was a boy with a cause and the doctor knew very well what kind of cause that might be.

So he turned his thoughts to Silence and her situation. Doing so he was beginning to discover why he was heading back that way. Silence, in the boy's eyes, must be a traitor to the cause. She had harboured the man he knew to be 'no fucking dentist'. She had harboured a man wanted by the members of this cause. Moreover, what was doubly dangerous, she had been involved with the members of this cause. She was herself wanted by the police and presumably therefore protected by the members of the cause. In their eyes she had therefore double-crossed the cause. No wonder the dentist had fled.

It would take the doctor about twenty minutes to reach the dentist's house, he thought, so long as he took no wrong turn. At least he had the dentist's knife.

When he reached the street he paused. His legs were feeling very weak. Then looking along the dim row of houses he couldn't find the dentist's surgery sign. It had been painted on a globe light shade. Indeed the more he looked at the street, the less confident did he feel. The situation was nightmarish. He was at the end of the right street. He knew he had taken no wrong turning. Yet it wasn't the same street. Hardly any cars were parked in it. There weren't any lights in the windows any more. There was nobody to be seen. Not a car. It was a ghost street. He felt as bewildered as scared. Slowly he walked along.

There wasn't a dentist's sign because it had been stoned. There weren't any dentist's windows because they had been smashed. The lace curtains swung about in the gaping space like ignominious white flags. The doctor felt the crunch of broken glass under his feet. He was being watched. He was sure of that. He turned round sharply, but nobody was there. Yet he was being watched. Not watched by one pair of eyes, the doctor thought, but by a hundred or more. The lights might be out but the people were still in their houses. Maybe the sight of a couple of shadows made the doctor sure of that: something did.

At the limit, courage closely resembles cowardice. It has its own motor: Go-man-go or Run-man-run. The doctor looked tense but composed as he stepped up then walked straight into the house.

She was naked. They may have gang-banged her first, but probably not. Nobody will ever know. She was standing, or almost standing, stark naked. Her back was like an uncooked steak that had been thrashed by a tennis racket strung with wire.

And the doctor thought, Maybe it *is* Sunday, but there is no longer any belief. So help me, they didn't do as much to Christ.

Yes, it could be called standing. She was bowed, but she was on her feet, not her knees, exactly between the waiting-room and the surgery, in the doorway. She was making absolutely no sound. Not a moan. No sound at all.

'It's me,' the doctor said. 'I've come for you. You knew I would. Show me your face. I don't care what they've done to it, show me your eyes.'

She must have been at the limit of consciousness, because when she turned round he thought for an appalling second that they had taken her eyes. The whites only were showing. But that wasn't true. She came back. The yellow eyes returned, but they were empty of all expression.

Her face could have been worse. It was bruised, smudged and scratched but it wasn't so bad.

Then the doctor saw that she wasn't tied to the door as at first he'd thought. Her hands weren't tied there, just a few inches above her big head. They were nailed. Nailed to the lintel with one big square nail.

'God,' the doctor murmured, 'they won't have left me any tools.' But somehow he got it out. With his bare hands. As he put it in his pocket, he thought, I want it in my grave, I do. He was holding her up now, dragging her into the surgery. The doctor could never have used the little knife, but when she lost consciousness he thought, If I had a gun I would shoot her in the temple now, because there is a god; there is a careless god. So bloody careless he makes us in his own hopelessly split image and Silence here pays in pain.

The doctor was aware that his courage was no longer coming from the money or the rum. It was coming from an historic horror: man's enslavement of man. It was an indomitable courage, a bitter courage now. He had the energy of guilt. For a second she woke. But she did not recognise him. Even his face was changed.

The dentist had been right to leave. His chair was torn from its moorings, his instruments and files scattered all over the floor. Not an hour had gone by since the boy told the doctor, 'You're no fucking dentist.' Communications have grown to be very fast in the slowest, surest war of all: the one that some merchants started when they pulled the boats away from the African and Island coasts.

Water for her. 'Christ,' he said, 'it's in our hands, not yours, not God's.' He told Silence. 'You kept *me* parched, you big black. Tip your head back now.' And in his hand, because all the vessels were smashed, he brought water from the tap in the corner to the place by the door where she lay. He must have made the journey twenty or thirty times. 'Don't you want to sit up. Not even now? Don't want to sit, don't want to talk? Don't you want to say one word to me now?'

Not that his own words mattered any more. The tone did. The tone was not so arrogant as to give confidence. It promised no relief. But he said with every breath, I'm not going to go, I'm not going to leave you, not ever, not until the end. 'So kneel, okay, kneel if that's better for the pain, kneel, or get on all fours you big cow, why the hell did you do this for me?' And he thought, Maybe it is only in our impossible love for each other that we can defeat the carelessness of God.

'We have to put something over your shoulders,' he said and she watched him as he took off his shirt. He said, 'It's damned cold outside but I'll wear your sweater, I'd like to do that.'

She shied away from him only for a second, but he caught her by the arm. She was sitting on her heels now. He said, 'We have to put something over your back because of that boy in hospital, the one with the burns. We got to cover the wound because we don't want things crawling out of the bandage.' She stayed absolutely still and he opened up the shirt. Just before he put it round her he thought, Woman, we need a sculptor to catch you sitting on your heels, waiting for more pain. For here is the result of the power and the glory of God and the indelible cruelty of man.

She hardly flinched. Out loud he said, 'Oh dear, why did I find myself such a big moose, why did I ever take that particular door? Look, you know who I am. Idiot, I came back. Now big animal, get up on your feet. Please get up on your feet. Oh my darling Silence, help me to help you to stand.'

They found her jeans. They found no boots. That bit wasn't so hard. They even found a beautiful, ironic mouthful of rum. She put the white coat on, this time. He took the sweater. She was standing now with her bleeding hands held straight in front of her. The doctor saw that something had to be done about them. He could see no bandage, though there was plenty of cotton wool. There was also some mild disinfectant, normally used for mouthwash. The doctor filled a basin and diluted the disinfectant. She obeyed him absolutely now. He pulled her over to the basin by her wrists and dipped her hands in the water. It evidently wasn't so painful as she had expected.

By the basin the doctor found a big pair of rubber gloves. He wished Silence's hands were smaller, because he could have packed the gloves with cotton wool. But he managed some sort of covering to the wounds with lint and wool dipped in the same disinfectant, then as gently as he could, stretching the gloves open with his own slim strong fingers, he pulled them over her hands.

So now she was in jeans, shirt, a white surgery coat and red rubber gloves. He put her plastic coat over all that, buttoning it like a cloak. He found a scarf belonging either to the dentist or some patient who had left it behind. He tied that round her neck. He had her sweater, his torn trousers and his coat turned up at the collar. But she looked round for something and he saw she was barefoot. 'I suppose you want your Cinderella slippers? Christ, that's really you. A moment like this when I'm calling forth the saints and you've got to have your horrible spangled slippers!' He found them for her and she even looked a little content. He smiled and said, 'We're a couple of swells.' She just looked at him: and looked. He pressed her arm very gently. He said, 'And we'll walk up the avenue, yes, we'll walk up the avenue.'

He took her out by the elbow. It was as if she couldn't believe a return of the love which she had never been able to explain in herself: that's how she stared at him.

Enemies, meaning people, frightened people could have been waiting outside with stones or guns. The wind had come up. The doctor and Silence both felt it hard and cold as they took the first few steps. Shakily they stepped down to the sidewalk and paused for a second in the iciness, their feet on frosted snow and broken glass.

The wind seemed to freeze the doctor's tired face. He'd put on his spectacles for some reason as they came out of the door. Perhaps he thought the lenses would give him some protection. The lines on his face looked very deep in the street light. Beside his, her face looked rounded and smooth in pain. The doctor looked all the way round the houses. Perhaps that's why he put his glasses on. But he didn't need them. He could feel that the night was filled with eyes.

His own family wouldn't have recognised the doctor now. They never knew he had a temper as terrible as this.

He yelled at the windows which only appeared to be empty. 'Thank God. Oh yes. Thank God there are thousands of eyes upon us now!'

And as they walked down the street, heads appeared at the windows behind them, the onlookers gradually becoming less cautious. None of them tried to stop the couple and none of them offered to help.

Lord knows how she managed to walk. She rose to the occasion. She was too confused probably to think exactly what their walk might mean to those who saw it. She was amazed still that the doctor had come back to her, pulled her back from death. Maybe surprised that nobody shot at them. Nobody threw a single stone. They walked with more and more confidence until they were both almost straight-backed, like an ancient couple determined not to reveal their infirmities. Look what's become of Adam and Eve; that's what the doctor thought.

So the eyes dwindled away. And the wind blew across this strange couple. It blew hard and cold across the lake, until there were no longer any eyes. Even the stars and moon were covered with clouds coming in from the north-east. It was then necessary for them to walk only for the benefit of each other. We are walking under the vigilance of no eyes at all, the doctor told himself, looking from her extraordinary face up to the dark and empty sky.

By a miracle, or through the strength of this rum love of theirs, they covered the four miles and reached the park which is no-man's-land in this present undeclared war. At night it is avoided by everyone except the junkies and jackals from both camps: but that night the wind was too cold even for them.

They were only a quarter of a mile into it when the doctor saw the irony of things. Not even the taxi-drivers came into the park at nights, because they were afraid, so nobody would find them until morning. And even under one of the scrubby bushes they would not stand a chance of survival through the night. Not at this temperature. Silence was already very shaky, with her eyes tightly closed; she was swaying on the point of collapse. The doctor no longer considered his own state of health. He talked to her, but even talking was pain in that wind. And as the clouds came over thicker it grew very very dark. Nobody could frighten them now.

Twice she collapsed. The second time he had to kick and swear at her and call her coward. He said terrible things to her, made obscene threats, then tugged and pulled until she was on her feet again. The park was as wide as a desert, it seemed, as cold as the Pole.

Then the doctor began to hear banging noises. He headed them towards the sounds until they heard machinery running and he knew they were near the railway. A long building loomed in front of them and as they got closer they were met by an undeniable odour and the desolate, restless lowing and kicking of cattle. The doctor thought of hoboes and thought of them, the two of them, riding the freight train with all the cattle. But then he remembered the cattle weren't going any further than this either.

They got in out of the wind and Silence collapsed and lay on her side in the straw. Engines juddered in the marshalling yards and shunted trucks clanged in unmelodic scales. The smell of disinfectant did battle with the animal smell and neither was winning. A door flapped on its hinges, trying to destroy itself in the wind. The doctor went off in search of it, the cattle didn't frighten him in the least, he felt he loved them. He felt he wanted to open all the doors and let them out into the park. He wanted to laugh. The wind tears were laughter tears starting before the laugh. Then there was a blood-curdling scream. For a second he thought it to be one of the animals. But when it came again he knew it was Silence's scream. He dashed back along the cattle pens.

Nothing terrible had happened. The big door had

slammed shut at the other end and she'd woken up in the pitch dark. She must have thought she was in hell. He talked through her awful shouting and found her wrist and face and throat and told her funny silly truths and lies about how they were safe. 'For heaven's sake,' he said, 'we're in the best place. Give me animals any day. If we judge from the people we know. The cattle are lowing, a crib for a bed.' Again it was the tone, not the words. She steadied and he managed to coax her into the warmth of the house itself. The doctor arranged some clean straw as best he could, and she sank back in it. She lay on her tummy half beside and half across him with her head in his neck. Almost at once and together, they slept.

At 7 a.m. they began to move the cattle to the slaughter-houses. By 8 a.m. the doctor had betrayed her.

A slaughterhouse is very like a hospital. At an unearthly hour the doors were slid back and the lights switched on. The slaughtermen and porters came in noisily, shouting to each other and waking the dozy cattle. Silence was still alive and still asleep trustingly in his arms. He simply thought, I'm damned if I'll wake her to pain. Moreover, he wasn't feeling like exercise himself. Half cramped by the weight of her body, but also weakened by his wound and the exertions of escape he felt almost incapable of movement.

Of course, it wasn't long until someone spotted them. In fact it was a uniformed porter who seemed at that time of the morning to find it hard to believe his eyes. He was at first startled, then amused because he thought they were junkies or lovers. Then he looked defensive and concerned. He called to his buddy who was already wheeling great carcasses of meat through from the other side. The doctor thought, This is a place where delicacy is not observed. There was a great deal of noise by now in this echoing place and the cattle waited patiently.

Two more came over and a fat one who had been at work

with a shovel and sounded Irish recognised the two of them.

'That's her,' he said at a glance, 'that's the one they call Silence. That's the one they want.'

Then looking at the doctor he snapped his fingers.

'Jesus!'

'Ewing,' the doctor said.

'That's it,' he said.

Their subsequent actions were enough to kill any kind feelings the doctor might still have entertained for the citizens of this city. The fat porter knew he was on to something of value. Even in his profession he must have seen something of the state of the pair, but he could have had no finer feelings, no compassion. None. 'You two stay exactly where you are. Just you two stay there. D'you hear me? You stay absolutely still.' He sounded threatening.

The cattle bellowed, frightened, smelling hot blood. The young man had a hurried conference with the other after which he called out, 'Down the middle, fifty-fifty,' as he hurried away stumbling. Silence still slept.

A moment later the doors at both ends were shut. Their bolts clanged home. In another couple of minutes the uniformed one and the fat Irishman appeared back. He had a little camera. It had a flashbulb, and that woke up Silence.

Something about her yellow eyes, or the sudden movement of her head, must have surprised or even alarmed the onlookers – and now there were ten or twelve of them – at the other side of the iron bars. In embarrassed reaction there was a little titter of laughter.

The doctor said, 'Close your eyes.'

A moment later some big policemen shouldered their way through. There was one quite senior man. He was extremely nice and polite. He said, 'Thank God you're alive, doctor,' and told his assistant to clear everybody else out. The porter had taken another two snapshots. He had what he needed.

Then the inner door was unlocked and two officers crawled through. The doctor told them to be very careful of Silence. They said, 'Don't you worry, doc, we will be,' and for a second the doctor could not or would not understand the way they said that. They helped her through the door of the pen civilly enough while the doctor explained about her hands and her back. They assimilated the information without any show of emotion. They're trained that way, the doctor thought.

The one thing the doctor had told her was that he would not leave her. The manner of his betrayal was spectacular. By the time he emerged into the open where two or three police cars were now gathered, he knew there was danger. He was thinking, You have to see both sides to recognise how hostile your own side can look. They were implacable. They had already handcuffed her and somebody had cautioned her. As soon as the doctor came out they helped him. Two men even shook his hand. They seemed to think that he had brought Silence back to Justice. Why not? She had murdered his son.

The doctor's head felt very sore in the cold wind. He asked that he could go in the same car with Silence. They just said, 'No, no.' He tried to insist for a moment and again they reassured him that she'd be treated fine. 'Wrapped in cotton wool,' one said. 'Don't . . .' the doctor began. And he'd wanted to say, Don't make her talk.

When he looked across at Silence, who was about to be put in one of the cars, she did not seem upset. There was no yell, no terrible plea in her eyes. She seemed to expect the separation and to be resigned, quite resigned to it.

The doctor spread out his arms, looked down at his wound, saw the mess, the bloody, pussy mess, and felt his knees begin to collapse.

'Catch him,' an officer yelled. But too late. He was out, in the snow.

*   *   *

About a week later, all the newspapers had it that Ewing was recovering well, after three very dangerous days. His mother had been to visit him but had only stayed a few moments. The doctor still seemed too painful to speak. The police had no further information about the girl called 'Silence': she was being held.

'Is it true,' one journalist asked, 'that she can't speak?'

'I don't know about that,' the spokesman replied. 'But she'll talk.'

The report of that reply was what made the doctor determined to get up. The police doctors had been very good to him. In fact both he and Silence were in the same wing though neither knew it. She was only two floors above, in a more heavily guarded section. The hospital itself was fundamentally for policemen and attached to the Central Police Station.

They allowed him up and gave him back his clothes. He had, be it remembered, been involved in a fight which led to the death of a twelve-year-old coloured boy. When they returned his clothes to him now, he found that they hadn't even searched them. In his breast pocket he could still feel the dentist's slim, steel surgical knife.

Before formal questioning, they wanted him to have a few hours' relaxation. The officers in charge of him (who couldn't have been more warm and friendly to him) gave each other a wink and said they might take a little time off between the Hospital and the Station.

The doctor did not see the force of the joke until he was taken across the street into a bar which he soon discovered was also just outside the Station. It was strictly a policemen's bar with a few good looking policemen's molls – keep your hands off that one, fella, that's the sergeant's girl.

Here again the doctor found himself to be something of a hero. The barman wanted to shake him by the hand. Only one of the girls seemed to think that he had brought Silence back for some other reason than vengeance. She'd seen the stockyard photo. 'She really seemed to be trusting you.'

Answer: 'Yes, she did.'

Because something had been said that might spoil the party, the boys poured out more drinks. The doctor was a difficult guest of honour. They took him aside to tell him to stop worrying. Through this creature Silence they were going to get every man and woman that touched Junior. Every bastard in that lynching. And they said it again, 'Don't you worry, we'll make her talk.' When they said that the ice in the doctor's whisky began to tinkle against the glass.

He played along with them as best he could, because he wanted a favour. There were several charges against her. She already had this police record. They told him that. She was conscious. She was being looked after mainly by women, but with a coloured doctor. 'Now you can't be fairer than that.' Eventually they divulged that she was in the same building.

The doctor asked to see her as soon as they were back in the building. The policemen couldn't understand why. The doctor didn't want to explain except to say that together they had been through some tough experiences. The policemen seemed to appreciate that. They thought of it, perhaps, as a man who wanted to look at his retrograde dog. They detailed an officer to go up with him. Someone said that they'd been looking for him all over, that Lilian and Angel had come to visit him. Lilian was fine, fine.

He was introduced to the young coloured surgeon on the wing who was not too impressive, the doctor thought. Police-trained. The strange thing is that the doctor telegraphed the whole thing to him, but he was far too dumb to see it. The doctor said – about nothing – 'It's bad when they cut the jugular, doctor.' The younger man did not look at the doctor as if he thought he was cracked; he said, 'It's also pretty quick.'

'What's pretty, doctor?'

'It isn't too pretty, I guess.'

He must have thought the doctor was referring to Lawrence Junior or one of the others.

'But they wouldn't sense too much. There's some kind of misting up,' the doctor added. The doctor had been prepared to sit outside the ward in which the girl was kept, but another policeman on guard there unbolted the door, saying, 'She's pretty sleepy, don't think you'll get much sense.'

The doctor went into the little blazingly white room. The door wasn't locked behind him, but pushed almost closed. The knife was in his pocket still.

He asked her. Of course, he asked her. The second he went into the room, he said, 'They're going to make you talk.'

And she shook her head. He let his eyes fall from hers to the column, the strong column of her neck. She turned painfully on to her side. She always liked it if he pushed her head against him. He pressed it against his own wound so it hurt very badly. The voice behind him said, 'Please don't do that.'

But he dropped his head on to her sweet, strong still surviving heart and thanked God. Thanked God that dentists keep sweet, sharp knives.

Then there was blood over everybody and a hell of a lot of people seemed to be there. He stood. He kept his eyes on her until he knew suddenly and gloriously that she was dead. He wiped the tears from his face with his sleeve, then he spoke. He said levelly, 'Notice the blood. It is also red.'

He now seemed to be beyond sadness. Then he turned and looked at all the others who were still standing round in an appalling silence. He said, 'Now, please will somebody take me away?'

There followed a bloody accusing confusion and crying noise.